John Huggins was born
Sheffield since the earl
is his fifth book and ac
Returns Home which v

Previous works by the Author:

'**Mothballed**' (2010)
'**Angel Smith Returns Home**' (2015)
'**A Dip in the Gene Pool**' (2016)
'**Consequences**' (2017)

The author is a member of the Sheffield Authors Forum:
http://www.sheffieldauthors.co.uk/john-huggins.

WRONG PERSON SINGULAR

JOHN HUGGINS

My profuse thanks to Nick Garrett for his technical wizardry and cover design and to my wife Anne for her editorial skills and unfailing support.

MAIN CHARACTERS

Dick Brinsworth: Original owner of the Black Bear Pub House; Charlie's father.

Charlie Brinsworth: Career criminal; son of Dick.

Mickey Smith: Manager of Black Bear in partnership with Charlie Brinsworth.

Big Trevor: Bouncer at the Black Bear.

Sharon: Barmaid at the Black Bear.

Rachael Broadbent: Mickey Smith's fiancé.

'Old' Henry: Rachael Broadbent's neighbour.

Lee: Son of the owner of the local fish & chip shop.

Stephanie 'Stevie' Armitage: Ex-model; Mickey Smith's oldest friend.

Ziggy: International businessman: Stephanie Armitage's husband.

Jilly 'Fishface' Gurnard: Ziggy's personal assistant.

Martin Shaffer: Owner of the Wellington Casino.

Anthony Noone: Mystery man with a job offer for Charlie Brinsworth.

Albert Dunn: Odd job man in the field of driving and thuggery.

Sebastian Cragg & Arnold Watson: Asset Strippers.

Wally: Supplier to the criminal classes of electrical & electronic equipment.

Oliver Dearlove: Artist.

Detective Sergeant Geoff Strickland: D.S. with Organised

Crime Unit.

Detective Inspector Daniel Loache: D.I. running Organised Crime Unit.

Miriam Loache: Wife of Daniel Loache.

Detective Inspector Alan Bateman: D.I. in local constabulary.

Detective Sergeant Kevin Gull: D.S. in local constabulary.

Gary Ishland: Leader of gang known as Bridgeland Crew.

'Big' Nat Dawson: Past leader of Eastgate gang.

Terry Brean: Leader of Eastgate gang.

Spanner Hopkins: Eastgate gang heavy with a big reputation.

Jimmy Jones: Driver and long term member of Eastgate gang

The Tyson Gang: Gang with controlling interest in the poorer part of the city.

Leroy Brown: Leader of West Indian Rasta gang who control their own enclave.

Brendan O'Sullivan: Ex member of Eastgate gang now running a funeral parlour. Spanner Hopkins' best friend.

Ike Green: Terry Brean's solicitor.

Simon Bartol: Ex-colleague of Charlie Brinsworth in gangland life who now runs a taxi business and distributes dope.

Big Bird: Driver and bodyguard employed by Simon Bartol.

Seamus MacGregor: Freelance Burglar and housebreaker.

CHAPTER ONE

PROLOGUE: December 2016

None of the regulars seemed aware of any connection between the seemly Charlotte Langthorpe and the Black Bear public house but her portrait had hung on the side wall of the saloon bar for as long as anyone could remember. And very fine she looked too, even if the colour of her dress had mellowed from bright blue to midnight black with the passing of the years, and her clear eyed expression now appeared a trifle bleary after decades absorbing the fumes of cheap whiskey and stale beer that floated like dandelion clocks in the torpid air.

Not that the room in which Miss Charlotte took pride of place was in any way referenced as the *saloon bar* any longer. The days were long gone when it cost an extra penny to have a decent piece of carpet under your feet while you were quaffing your half pint of best bitter or having your port and lemon served in the right type of glass, so any delineation between one part of a pub and another was something of a waste of time. What was the point? There was even the distinct possibility it might give offence to the overly righteous by inferring the management had been a mite dilatory in embracing the utopian classless society that our betters had chosen to visit upon us.

It could even imply that it was the sort of hangout where the dark skinned bloke with the shaven head, dressed in the black bomber jacket and steel capped shoes, would possibly be loitering just inside the main entrance only for the purpose of leaping forward to hold open the door if he saw a suitably attractive piece of skirt approaching, distracted by a text message on her mobile phone. Taking his life in his very large but surprisingly uncalloused hands if the flash of a well turned ankle had caused his practised eye to misjudge a dyed in the wool feminist looking for any opportunity to espouse her cause. Though, fair to say, in this particular instance any concern in that direction would have been wholly unwarranted. Big Trevor cast most of his attentions on people coming in, not people going out of the bar-room; and even the most ardent women's libber would have considered it contrary to her best interests to throw a punch at the twenty stone Nigerian doorman even if she could have kicked off her brightly coloured Doc Martens shoes and leapt high enough into the air so she could take aim at something that would make her pugilistic efforts worthy of the exertion.

It could of course be argued, and with some justification, that if you were choosing to meet someone in a sprawling licenced premises like the Black Bear, then a smidgen of demarcation could have proved of assistance when it came to stipulating a specific point at which you could be located. But as an awful lot of people were now choosing to huddle in front of their boxed-sets clutching supermarket purchased cans of cheap, pissy lager in preference to venturing up the road for a swift half of something a tad more gratifying, perhaps that premise served to overstate the case.

In any event, none of the above appeared to be having any affect the spirits of Charlie Brinsworth. Charlie was back walking the streets after having been out of circulation for a very long time; and he chose to freely advertise his return to the great wide world by telling anyone who displayed an interest that he could be found at the feet of Charlotte Langthorpe in the Saloon bar of the Black Bear public house between the hours of 1pm and 2pm should they have any wish to seek him out. And there might be some small suspicion Charlie did this in the hope of easing himself gently back into a community he had once been very eager to abandon; one which might not necessarily reference him foremost in a list of their most favourite sons.

It was no secret in the district that Charlie Brinsworth

was the owner of the Black Bear public house, even if he had rarely set foot across the threshold in the last twenty five years; and people who lived locally were in little doubt precisely when he had returned to the pub to take up residence. As to where he could be located at lunchtime? That would come as no surprise to anybody who was in anyway acquainted with the man. The Black Bear offered the best food in the district, so where else would Charlie be likely to be found? Mr Brinsworth's dedication to satisfying the demands of an overly healthy appetite had been legendary long before he re-established his rights to a resident's permit in this part of town. And people round here would be the last to hold that against him after what the poor mite had been obliged to suffer in his formative years.

In truth, the locals' interest in where Charlie chose to eat his meals was not pronounced; neither for that matter, was their concern with what he had been doing with himself in the intervening years. Answers to both of those questions were readily available if you knew who to ask; and if you didn't then you probably didn't get out as often as was advisable.

The real interest from the local community centred on why Charlie Brinsworth had ever decided to return home in the first place, because it was no secret that he had never displayed the slightest ambition to run a pub; and if he wasn't returning for that reason then where the hell would he fit in? After all, this was a respectable part of town; well, if not exactly reputable, then certainly a big step up from where he had previously been hanging his hat.

That notwithstanding, it was fair to say nobody had chosen to tackle Charlie directly on the subject. And that would be because Charlie Brinsworth wasn't the type of person to which you could ask that sort of question straight out. And, you didn't want to get on the wrong side of somebody who had been making a living the way Charlie had for a quarter of a century if there was no real need. Besides, it would all come out sooner or later; that sort of thing always did.

So if you were in possession of a naturally inquisitive disposition it was probably best not to rush in with all guns blazing as it was probable you would be told in no uncertain terms to keep your nose out his affairs. The best bet would be to adopt a more relaxed approach; keep your ears open, sit back and wait.

CHAPTER TWO

RETROSPECTIVE: 2004

A dozen years earlier Charlie Brinsworth had stood alone at his father's graveside, unable to summon up any feeling of genuine sorrow. The church service had been short and poorly attended. He had expected no different. Dick had never been a well-loved man. He hadn't even appeared to like himself for much of the time. Charlie would have liked to feel some degree of gratitude for having been remembered in the will of his unloved parent but had rapidly realised he had no use for his unexpected inheritance. After the horrors he had experienced in his childhood years he wanted nothing to do with the Black Bear public house.

His father, Dick, (never Richard, and Dicky only on pain of a lifetime ban and a close encounter with a size ten) had bequeathed the pub to Charlie solely on the basis that there was nobody else to take charge. Dick's wife had long since passed on to better things, and what precisely they might have been nobody had ever summoned up sufficient courage to enquire. In subsequent years Brinsworth senior had never again ventured in the direction of the registry office and existing relatives had little time for the man. Added to which, Dick Brinsworth had no real friends; and certainly which he would have considered sufficiently close to merit such a substantial inheritance. In consequence, it had come down to Charlie or nothing; and even then it had been a pretty tight call because Dick didn't think much of the fruit of his loins and in the end had only been swayed by the fact he despised the Inland Revenue Service marginally more than his headstrong son.

When Dick had received his summons from the almighty Charlie had taken possession of his legacy in the same way he had accepted the urn containing his father's ashes. Something coming his way that he had no use for and little idea what to do with. He later came to wonder why he hadn't just sold the place outright. It was the logical move and would undoubtedly have proved the simplest solution to his dilemma; and Charlie was a man who liked easy options better than long priced runners to which a stable lad had given a surreptitious nod. When he thought back and pondered the matter he could honestly say the idea of a sale had never entered his head; and whether that was because of divine intervention or the fact his thoughts had been focussed in an entirely different direction is a question that Charlie never felt equipped to answer.

Charlie's reluctance to position himself behind the brass knurled hand pumps and adopt the friendly, welcoming smile that would add silver to the till and direction to his chaotic life were multifarious; but high on the list was the fact that he had been raised in an environment which had centred around cigarette clouded rooms fragranced by the odour of stale beer and urine; and like the butcher's daughter who at the first opportunity distances herself from meat products and turns militantly vegan, he had grown up to react strongly against this form of nurturing. Not so say, if his childhood playground had failed to be decorated with discarded pint pots and over full ashtrays things would necessarily have turned out very differently; but in that eventuality, some might consider, there would at least have been a somewhat better chance.

Certainly, having existed almost exclusively on a diet of pork pies, pickled eggs and crisps with a variety of exotic flavourings for the majority of his formative years served to sow such a marked aversion to this form of sustenance that Charlie found it difficult to shake off his distaste for this range of sustenance long into his adult years. In fact, it was whispered among friends and close associates that you would get more reaction from Charlie Brinsworth by waving a packet of pork scratchings under his nose than if you directed his attention to the existence of a freshly battered corpse.

There was also a far more pressing reason why Charlie Brinsworth had not been greatly tempted to place his substantial frame behind the ale pumps of the Black Bear public house; be it one that he would quite understandably have preferred to keep to himself. Charlie had for a number of years been steadily working his way up the pecking order in Gary Ishland's Bridgeland Crew, and had finally reached a position of sufficient seniority that he was beginning to rake in some serious cash.

This notwithstanding, Charlie recognised a gift horse when it presented itself. A pub was a pub even if it amounted to little more than a shitty backstreet drinking den like this one and it was all too clear he needed to take positive action.

So Charlie tore himself away from what he firmly believed to be more pressing business commitments and sought out a person who would be less likely to display homicidal tendencies towards any objectionable stranger who trampled mud onto an already bedraggled carpet before proceeding to bore the arse off anyone in the immediate vicinity by talking twenty four caret bollocks in an overloud voice. Someone who had it within their power to be over brimming with tolerance towards any son of a bitch who was willing to keep the cash register in gainful employment while they were paying for the privilege of wrecking their livers. And, with the aid of an ad in the local paper and a few words whispered into sympathetic ears, just such a person was located and invited to exhibit his credentials on the less than shiny top of one of the back bar's beer stained tables.

On first sight Mickey Smith didn't look to have a lot going for him. He appeared far too young to handle the responsibility and was able to offer little evidence of qualifications other than those bestowed by the University of Life. As it happened, none of this had served to count heavily against him. Charlie was engaged in the type of

7

work where you were obliged to work primarily on gut instinct and there was something about this fresh faced kid that took his fancy. He put Mickey Smith on trial for a week and once safely ensconced behind a bar a transformation was quickly seen to occur.

Mickey took little time to demonstrate that he knew how many beans made three without the assistance of an abacus. He displayed no conscience about supping with the devil providing the customer with the horns was drinking doubles, paying in cash and not cussing too loudly or spitting on the varnished floorboards. He showed an ability to join in any argument undertaken by the locals, fiercely defend his personal beliefs, and still leave both parties convinced he had been right behind their ill-conceived viewpoint. He was a natural. He had a twinkle in his eye that the older ladies found dashing and a knowledge of football that their hairy arsed escorts looked upon as a mandatory requirement for any custodian of the pumps. Mickey was a man for all seasons; a diamond in the rough; someone who had answered his calling and was now quite happy to suffer the consequences.

As it later transpired, Mickey was also no slouch at keeping matters in order. He could spot trouble before it got three steps over the threshold. He knew who to serve quickly, who waited their turn and who got a cold, hard stare and a solitary finger pointing towards the bleak outdoors. It was a skill you couldn't teach which was just as well because Mickey's mind didn't hover in any place for very long; it was always on the move and usually flitting in the direction that anybody who had entered the premises with a poor attitude towards conformity was least likely to appreciate.

Charlie and Mickey struck a deal with Charlie dictating the terms. A six month extended trial. A hand in the till and the fingers got amputated with bolt cutters and returned by second class post. No drugs unless mutually agreed by both parties. Ladies of the night only if there were likely to be no come backs; that choice to be at

Mickey's discretion. Mickey's name went up over the door and he ran the pub the way he wanted. Charlie kept his nose out and they split the profits, if indeed any profits were ever seen to be forthcoming from this backstreet rat-trap, straight down the middle.

Mickey got to fix the place up as he saw fit; nothing heavy duty; a change of feel; a grand and a half tops with payment in the hand and a boot up the arse of anyone who got disrespectful and started referencing contingency payments VAT.

Mickey immediately set to work. People with paint splattered overalls and a natural ability to drink vast quantities of tea materialised overnight. Any carpeting quickly found its way to a skip, as did anything that resembled a vase, a pot or was decorated with a flower motif, a frill or a tassel. The floorboards were sandblasted and everything else stripped back to the grain. Any wood that wasn't already oak by inclination was very quickly oak stained. Stark didn't come into it; neither did any vestige of colour. The rooms of the pub ended up looking very like the inside of a brewery barrel.

New toilets, which weren't actually new in the strictest sense of the word, were quickly installed, the plumbing was renovated to something approaching an acceptable standard, and any light bulb giving out less than 100 watts was given to the cleaning lady to take home along with her two bottles of ruby stout on Friday night.

All rooms were then scrubbed from floor to ceiling. Whilst that didn't exactly cause them to gleam, it gave the distinct impression that whatever dust now remained was considerably less confident about its future.

Voila!! The makeover worked like a treat. New won punters were quickly across the threshold and liked what they saw; and trade could clearly be seen to be on the up even before the month was out.

So Mickey got entrusted to do what Mickey did best and Charlie Brinsworth slunk out of the door and quickly headed back to the other side of town where he re-joined the meatheads that had chosen to gather under Gary Ishland's banner, in an unloved territory bordered by a disused abattoir, the canal and a main motorway turnoff.

CHAPTER THREE

EARLY JANUARY 2017

Twelve years down the line the world was a very different place. Charlie Brinsworth returned to the Black Bear after having completed a five stretch in Armley which had seen him banged up for slightly less than half the time the judge had chosen to allocate. He claimed from Mickey Smith an upstairs room, overlooking the street, which had previously been used to store the sort of stuff that didn't have an obvious home anywhere else in the building and in the blink of an eye had moved in his meagre possessions. Charlie made it clear he didn't intend to get in the way. Maybe, just use the Bear as a staging post while he planned his next move. Even if he chose to settle in for a more extended period he would be sure to keep himself well out of the way.

Mickey seemed alright with this though it's fair to say he didn't have a lot of choice in the matter. In Charlie's extended absence he had set on a chef with a bit of imagination to cater to the lunchtime trade and pretty soon Charlie took to eating his lunch in the bar and smiling warmly at anyone who happened to catch his eye.

Charlie's current situation had pluses and minuses. Money was no problem. He had a sizeable wad stashed from his elicit activities; and during the period of his incarceration the Bear had been turning a half decent profit, which he had been in no position to spend.

However, other matters were not nearly as simple. The Bridgeland Crew were no more. In the intervening years Gary Ishland had trodden on too many of the wrong toes and was now rumoured to be taking an extended holiday in foreign parts. After a brief period of infighting his territory had been taken over by a family concern from the east coast called Tyson who had recruited a number of the old order to supplement their ever swelling ranks. They had also advised anyone who didn't like the way things were going to bugger off while that still remained a viable option. When he was first released Charlie had received an invitation to appear before an interview panel at Tyson headquarters but had decided to give it a miss. He hadn't been asked twice; he had been surprised to get the first invitation if the truth were known.

The next thing he needed to consider was the fact the Black Bear didn't fall within the Tyson's sphere of influence. He was now residing in the Eastgate gang's domain and his arrival could hardly have gone unnoticed. Eastgate were a big outfit and a tricky proposition. They had the best parts of the south side of the city stitched up and were unlikely to take kindly to his arrival unless he explained that he was now out of the business.

Charlie decided the best course of action would be to tackle the problem head on. He brushed down his work suit, which fitted in most of the places it still touched, and stomped a half a mile towards town to confront the Eastgate leader, Nat Dawson, in his own backyard.

The Golden Pheasant was Eastgate gang headquarters and had been for any number of years. Like The Black Bear it was large in size but there the similarities came to an abrupt halt. Some idiot had decided to theme-decorate the Pheasant in mock Elizabethan splendour but had skimped in all the wrong places so the pub looked as comfortable with its new image as a fifty quid hooker at a Buckingham Palace garden party.

That having been said the Pheasant wasn't short of trade; though a lot of the punters didn't look like they would be holidaying in the Bahamas any time soon. It was plain to see the little barmaid knew her way round the pumps though; and she was a decent looker which never did turnover a great degree of harm. Charlie was still staring across and wondering if Mickey would think he was interfering if he enquired whether she was interested in a change of scenery when a hand the size of a bin lid rested gently on his shoulder before squeezing very tight.

'Keep your eyes in their sockets, Charlie Boy; she ain't open to offers from naughty boys like you. You here by invitation or just looking to get your head kicked in?' This ventured as a genuine enquiry, seeking to establish a specific preference.

'Good to see they haven't pensioned you off yet, Spanner. Just wanted a quick word with Big Nat if he can spare the time. Is he at home to visitors or sunning himself on the Costa Brava?' A big smile to show there was no malice; it was best not to do malice with Spanner Hopkins if there was any possibility of it being avoided.

Ten minutes later Charlie was on his way out of the door. Spanner, with his regulation pint pot in his left hand and a liquorice papered rollup in his right, accompanied him onto the pavement.

'You really hanging up your boots, Charlie? Never thought I'd live to see the day. The way things are going there'll be nobody to aggravate me left in this trade by the end of the year. Look, sorry Nat was a bit arsey; he's usually got better manners but just now he's got a lot on his plate.....and let's be honest, you did roll up here without an invite. Listen, I'll come down to your place for a pint as soon as things settle down a bit and we can talk about old times. Like when I kicked your arse two hundred yards up the high street that night you fancied your chances. Enjoy your retirement, Charlie Boy, and remember to keep your nose clean. There's a few I would rather put in hospital than you so watch your step now you've pitched up in civilised society.'

That was fine by Charlie. A grudging acceptance from Nat Dawson was all he could have expected. Now he could devote his energies to pulling his cash together; and then maybe starting up a couple of legitimate enterprises. Well, half way legitimate, otherwise where was the fun to be had?

CHAPTER FOUR

TUESDAY 31st JANUARY 2017

The best part of a month had rolled by since his meeting at the Pheasant and Charlie now felt settled into his new way of life. Spanner Hopkins had come over the week before for a night of reminiscences and done his level best to drink the pub dry as they retold old stories and struggled to remember what had happened to faces that had years before disappeared from the scene. Spanner provided an eloquent update on what was happening in the City. Eastgate were still going along nicely but had started to cast nervous glances to the other side of town where the Tyson Gang had made themselves very much at home. Geoff Strickland, a mutual nemesis from years gone by, was still a Detective Sergeant and was now with an Organised Crime unit run by a D.I. called Daniel Loache whom Charlie had never come across. According to Spanner, Organised Crime didn't have enough bodies to be a serious inconvenience to Eastgate's illegal activities but nonetheless needed keeping an eye on. Strickland, however, remained a class A bastard and acted like the criminal he probably should have become.

Brendon O'Sullivan, ex-Eastgate and Hopkins' bosom buddy since they were both in short trousers, was running a successful Funeral Parlour. Charlie knew this; O'Sullivan had been set up in his business for years; but Spanner obviously enjoyed retelling the story so Charlie listened politely and looked dutifully horrified at what could become of a man with O'Sullivan's obvious criminal potential once he took the decision to go straight.

They hadn't called it a day on their long trip down memory lane until Charlie was pissed as a fart and Mickey Smith's glares from behind the bar were starting to burn holes in the woodwork. Spanner walked out like he had been sipping tea at a Vicar's tea party. The big bastard always did have hollow legs and time showed no sign of having affected his enviable metabolism.

In the last month, Charlie hadn't allowed the grass to grow under his feet. He had secured an old terraced house a couple of hundred yards up the road from the pub and close to a big roundabout on the main drag into town. He was in the process of getting it converted into a wood burning pizza bar. Nothing flash; eat in or take out initially; maybe moped deliveries or even one of those mobile ovens they were sticking up outside the larger pub outlets to catch the yummy mummies who fancied a glass of cold white wine while they watched their children roll around in the dirt on a warm summer's night. According to his research the market was worth £3.5 billion and the mark-up was colossal. As far as he could see there were more than enough bone idle students slouching around the streets looking for an easy meal to make it anything other than a no-brainer. There probably wouldn't even be the need to hire a team to put in the windows of the local competition as it looked like there was plenty of business to go round; and his planning application would go through in double quick time on the strength of the five hundred notes he had used to lubricate an old contact who had somehow managed to hang on to his job down at the Town Hall.

In order to temper legitimacy with something a little closer to his heart he had made contact with a couple of Vietnamese refugees who were now busy setting up a cannabis farm for him in a scummy suburb about six miles out of town. The outlay hadn't been ridiculous and if his figures were right his expenditure would be absorbed by the business inside six months. Initially, he didn't intend going anywhere near the distribution end of things for fear of upsetting Eastgate; but given time that might need to change. Simon Bartol, an old friend who was also ex-Bridgeland and was now running a taxi company as a cover for a door to door dope delivery service, would handle that side of the business. As soon as the gear was harvested and packaged he would have it delivered to Simon, get paid in cash and wash his hands. Where Simon peddled the dope was none of his business; though it was impossible not to notice the flash git must be making good money out of the enterprise if you cast an eye over the tasty set of wheels he was now piloting up and down the high street in his leisure hours.

Charlie tidied up a bit of paperwork and shuffled down the stairs with a relatively clear conscience. It was nearly lunchtime and he was heading for his favourite seat having placed an advance order for faggots, peas and chips with the kitchen. The Chef Mickey has set on was currently obsessed with traditional dishes and bubble and squeak was on a rota, along with lamb kidneys, bangers and mash, saveloy with pease pudding and anything else he could glean from a mildewed cook book he had picked up from a second hand book shop in town. Thank God he hadn't yet reached the section on tripe and onions, blood pudding or sheep's head, but you could bet your boots that sooner or later they would put in an appearance.

As he reached his seat Mickey Smith appeared from nowhere and slid elegantly onto the bench opposite. He engaged his three hundred watt smile, leaned conspiratorially forward and Charlie knew immediately that whatever Mickey was about to suggest it was going to cost him money. He became even more convinced on that score after he heard the opening salvo.

'Charlie my friend, satisfied with the way things are going?'

'Yes Mickey, no problems as far as I can see; everything seems fine.'

That was obviously the right answer because Mickey looked pleased. Mickey always looked happy if there was a compliment paid to the pub; the bloke was bloody obsessed. Mickey took a quick peek back over his shoulder. The next bit of news was obviously far too important to be shared with the outside world.

'Well, I think this place would do even better if we tidied it up a bit. I think the time has come for us to introduce a bit of style.'

'I've got used to the wood Mickey but it's your place, in a manner of speaking, so as long as you don't paint the ceiling purple then decisions like that fall your side of the fence. Just tell me what you want to do and if it's just a lick of paint I'll stump up the cash.'

'Half each Charlie; it's only fair. I want to colour wash a couple of walls and whack up a few expressionist works that will lift the whole ambience of the bars. I can pick up the sort of thing I've got in mind from an old friend who owns a gallery up the road and it will come out at next to nothing; you'll remember Stevie Armitage the ex-model? We would probably only be talking seven or eight hundred each to cover the whole upgrade, give or take a few quid.'

Charlie certainly remembered Stephanie Armitage. She was hard to forget. The woman looked a million dollars but there was something about her that had always made Charlie feel vaguely uneasy. He had seen eyes like hers before and they had usually been looking out of someone working their way through a life sentence for chopping up members of their immediate family.

'Mickey, I wouldn't know an ambience if it bit me in the arse. Just do what you reckon and let me know the damage. Only leave the old paintings up on the walls. They're about all I've got to remind me of the way things used to look when I was a nipper.'

'It might be difficult to blend the old stuff in with the new, Charlie. I think it's time to move forward and chuck the whole lot out of the door. Trust me on this; I know what I'm doing. Listen, if you let me have my way I'll put up all the finance myself.'

'Very generous, Mickey but really no need. How about a compromise? You can yank out everything but that old girl perched over my head. We've got history, me and her. The place wouldn't be the same without her glaring down at me every time I lift my pint.'

Mickey didn't seem overly delighted with the way things had turned out. He was one of those all or nothing merchants and it obviously rankled with him when things didn't go entirely his way. But after another couple of tries at using different words to say exactly the same thing he accepted defeat and allowed Charlie to set about addressing his faggots with the gusto they deserved. On first sight the Chef might come over as a big girl's blouse, but Jesus, the man could cook up a storm when he set his mind to it.

As he was eating it occurred to Charlie he should have seen Mickey's approach coming. There had been some fat pillock in a suit staring at the wall like he was trying to see through it when he had arrived back the previous day; and Mickey had scuttled him out of the door without so much as an introduction. God knows why. A few hundred on a change of decoration was never going to bust the bank. What was the problem?

CHAPTER FIVE

WEDNESDAY 8th FEBRUARY 2017

Charlie had woken that morning with the firm impression Wednesday was going to be a quiet day; but for some reason life forces beyond his control had taken a different view. The morning was fine, but after that things went steadily downhill.

Early the previous Friday the decorators had made their initial visit and taken it upon themselves to yank a load of pine boarding off the back wall. The cheap timber had been fixed there masquerading as oak panelling for a dozen or more years and Charlie was sorry to see it go. The workmen then set about filling in numerous large holes in the crumbling plasterwork that a less ham-fisted crew of itinerant bodgers wouldn't have caused in the first place. Charlie didn't get it. If the wood had been left up doing nobody any harm none of this would have been necessary.

By Monday, the same wall in what Charlie still liked to unfashionably term the 'saloon bar' had turned a hideous hue referenced in some poncy retailer's colour chart as crimson sunset. The remaining woodwork was then lightly sanded and over-painted a slimy shade of bilious green. Charlie had taken the opportunity to question if this was not going to put the paying customers off their beer, but had been informed by Mickey it was all the rage in the better parts of town that it was likely Charlie had never had cause to visit.

Verdant turquoise, which sounded an outright contradiction before you even got round to wedging your oldest wood chisel under the lid of the tin, was then skilfully daubed into a number of apertures to complement the flagrant act of creative vandalism.

To Charlie's untutored eye this just gave the impression

that patches of the old distemper were showing through from some previous incarnation of the wall's turbulent past, but what did he know about the nuances of twenty first century sophistication? The walls in his prison cell had been made out of blocks of rough-hewn stone.

By Tuesday, any number of canvasses that looked like they had been produced when a gang of heavily inebriated surgeons had needed somewhere to wipe their bloody scalpel blades, had been placed in prominent positions around the walls. When Charlie enquired what had happened to his picture of the high born lady, Mickey had smiled sweetly and pointed with his index finger upwards towards the heavens.

Well, even if you had been blessed with twenty twenty vision you would have needed a telescope to get a view of the poor cow. She was up there hovering in the stratosphere less than six inches below the rafters. Charlie picked the nearest painter up by the throat and much to Mickey's consternation Ms Langthorpe was speedily repositioned several feet lower. But despite the realigning, due not least to the arrival of an unedifying masterpiece entitled *The Rage of Andromeda,* her placement had now been elevated by at least two and a half feet.

Charlie spoke firmly to Mickey; so firmly mothers walking their children home from school had been obliged to put their hands over their loved ones' ears and encourage them to sing marching songs until they were fifty yards further up the road.

By Wednesday the portrait had been returned to somewhere approaching its normal position but, much though Mickey fiercely denied it, Charlie knew for a fact it was at least a foot and a half higher than it used to be and most definitely nine inches nearer to the front entrance.

Anyway, at least it served as a partial concession and honour was satisfied. Charlie removed a heap of paint splattered dust sheets and assumed his usual seating position feeling he had at least made his voice heard on the subject even if it was totally apparent nobody had taken the slightest notice of what he had to say. Mickey was back behind the bar but pretending to be busy to disguise the fact he was still having a strop over his artistic vision having been undermined. Bugger Mickey's finer feelings, there was lunch in the offing. You had to get your priorities right if you were going to get anywhere in this life.

Cow heel pie? Who the fuck eats cow heel pie in this day and age? Charlie gave it a go anyway and very decent it turned out to be.

Although the 'saloon bar' was officially closed to the public a succession of heads continued to poke through from the street doorway and the adjoining bar areas so they could keep up to speed with how work was progressing on the upgrade. In consequence, it came as no great surprise to Charlie when he heard an all too familiar thump and a shuffling of feet; and as by now he had become hardened to the regular disturbances he didn't immediately take the trouble to look up to find who was creating the noise. Mickey, however, still loitering behind the bar with dishcloth in hand, was immediately on the case.

'Not today thank you.'

The entrance of three large blokes of West Indian descent was momentarily stopped in its tracks as they formed collective scowls to denote a lack of appreciation at the manner of their welcome. Charlie quickly stood up, wishing he was a couple of feet taller or had taken one of those courses they kept encouraging you to get involved in when you were behind bars; the one headlined 'Persuasion and Diplomacy' looked like it might have come in useful right about now.

'You opratin a colour bar in dis pub?' spoken quietly but with confidence; slowly and calmly with each word distinctly enunciated by the big black bloke who appeared to be conducting the orchestra.

Mickey stooped slightly as he replied and Charlie knew he was reaching down for the baseball bat he kept on the top shelf underneath the bar.

'No mate, but we've got an anti-drugs policy and I could smell the dope on you before you opened the door. No offence; fuck off.'

Charlie took a pace forward. This probably wasn't going to work out well. He could feel it in his water. The men were too big to be intimidated and too stoned to care.

'Dis the way you treat a man lookin to catch up wi an old fren?' said the oldest of the three black men as they fanned out across the bar, hands delving into pockets for God alone knew what.

Charlie wasn't sure if Mickey was very good or very stupid but either way he never gave an inch.

'Try making some new ones, mate; it might turn out easier.'

Charlie stuck his oar in. More to gain time than anything else; at least to alter the direction of the conversation which looked like coming to only one conclusion.

'Who you looking for, Bruv?'

The lead man swivelled neatly on his feet. He was the one calling the shots without a doubt. The other two wouldn't consider farting unless he gave them the nod.

'You, Mr Charlie Brinsworth. Din you know? You a fren of a fren.'

Following that, things didn't immediately show a lot of improvement but at least they stopped getting worse. Charlie brokered a peace deal. No drinks would be served but the older man got five minutes to state his case while his two mates waited outside. It was a sensible compromise; such a good trade-off that Charlie wondered why he was the only one who seemed vaguely happy with what had been accomplished.

So now it was Charlie's time to play the diplomat. Start off nice and gentle. Lower the temperature by a few degrees; appear both open and friendly. No bother, he had done it a hundred times before. He was so good at handling this sort of situation that occasionally things had even worked the way he intended.

'What's your name, Brother? How come you know me if I don't know you?'

In reply, a stare that fixed you to the seat like a steel pin through your guts; this accompanied by a big smile with not an ounce of warmth.

'In prison; you frens wi Shank. I got a lil problem. Shank got me word you the man who help it get sorted. You don need my name; not yet.......and just so you know, white boy, I ain't you fucking Bruver.'

Was he bloody joking? Alright, he had known Shank inside. So did everybody. The man carried that sort of reputation. There were three classes of prisoner in Armley Nick, those you exchanged a few words with, those you avoided and those you avoided like the plague. Shank slotted neatly into category three. He was permanently stoned, could take offence at absolutely anything and had a violent streak that ran through him like a seam of coal. To make it worse he had a following. Shitheads like him always did. Charlie had avoided any social interaction with Mr Shank as soon as he could put a face to the bastard and looked on that as one of his top three decisions for that year.

'I was in prison with Shank but I don't think we ever said a word to one another. I certainly wasn't friends with him. If he says different he's winding you up.'

The large black man either wasn't interested or pretended not to hear.

'Listen careful, Mr Charlie Brinsworth. You were running wi dat Gary Ishland from Bridgeland fo years so I guess you be quainted with Mr Tyson who kick his arse out of town. I got a little problem down on my patch with Romani and I wan to meet with Mr Tyson to put together......how you say...... a liance. I want to get together wi de main man and push der gypsy boys back over de river.'

At least Charlie now knew who he was talking to. Leroy Brown bossed a gang called the Rastas who controlled an enclave just north of the inner city. It only covered one postcode district and it was the one where you wound up the windows and pushed down the button locking the car doors when you passed through it. When police cars got a call out to the area the only time they exceeded the speed limit was on the return journey. Charlie had never heard Shank was part of Leroy's team but as they hadn't often met up for coffee and cake that wasn't really surprising. It certainly made as much sense as anything else.

'I have never met with Mr Tyson and I don't want to. I'm retired and I don't intend doing any more bird. If I could help I would but I swear on my mother's life I never met the man. Sorry mate, that's all I've got to say.'

Leroy Brown gave a long hard look then slowly got to his feet and walked towards the door. He stopped briefly on the threshold and looked back.

'I check you out a bit more, Mr Charlie 'doan know nothin'. I used good petrol drivin over here and I doan like wastin my time. Maybe we need to talk again. You too Bartender,' he said, turning to point a finger in Mickey's general direction. 'You got a lot of lip for a man spens is days washin glasses.'

The door closed with a bang and thirty seconds later a house brick smashed through the side window of the pub. Charlie headed for the front door; taking his time without making it appear too obvious. There was nobody to be seen but a five series BMW with a caved in wing was driving slowly up the road with three figures on board. As far as Charlie could make out the faces of the occupants were all black and none of them appeared to be smiling.

CHAPTER SIX

THURSDAY 9th FEBRUARY 2017

The next morning Charlie went out early to check on the progress of the pizza parlour conversion. Then he wandered the streets to reacquaint himself with the snickets and gennels that had provided such good escape routes in his formative years. Seeing his old hang-outs made him feel quite nostalgic. Over there was the place where he had committed his first serious mugging; a hundred yards from the jewellers he and a group of his mates had ram raided, only to end up with a carrier bag full of paste and precious little else. Christ, the stuff they had got up to back in the day. They deserved to be locked up; as indeed most of them now were.

While wandering the street Charlie had decided it might not be a bad idea to talk over Leroy Brown's visit with Spanner Hopkins. However, that was hardly likely to be regarded as complying with company ethics by the Eastgate platoon. They would probably hold him responsible for the fact Leroy Brown had strayed onto their patch in the first place. Best forget approaching Spanner for the time being and see what happened next.

By the time he got back to the pub it was nearly lunchtime. Soused herring on today's menu if his memory served. The glass in the side window had already been replaced. Shatterproof for sure, if he knew anything about Mickey Smith's way of doing things.

He ordered a pint from the barmaid; a lovely girl called Sharon who had worked here on and off for the last eight to ten years. Mickey was noticeable by his absence so he ventured an enquiry. A bit of personal business the barmaid confided, giving him a cheeky wink. Charlie watched her retreat up the bar; was the extra wiggle perhaps for his benefit? If it was he definitely appreciated the effort. He knew Sharon had a nipper but wasn't clear if she was hooked up with anyone at the moment. He made a mental note to make enquiries. He'd spent a lot of years inside dreaming about a wiggle like that.

There was an immediate tapping on the front window. What the fuck now! It was too polite by half to herald the return of Leroy Brown and his crew. The saloon bar was still closed to allow the paint to finish drying and he had made it clear the front entrance was to remain locked and bolted until the grand reopening took place. None the less, with nobody else being about he supposed it was his responsibility to deal with the situation.

'Bugger off; this bar is closed; go round the other side if you want a drink.' Not a classic response in the field of customer diplomacy but at least it got the message across.

'It's Lee from over the road. I've got a message,'

'Lee. Lee from the chip shop?'

'No, the one from outer space. Do you want the fucking message or don't you?'

Kids today. No bloody manners.......and the attitude. This one could do with a belt round the back of the head but he was only about four foot six in his stockinged feet. Anyway, Charlie couldn't take the chance. Lee's mother kept him back a bit of skate when he told her he would be calling in later in the day and that wasn't easy to come across this far from the city centre. He answered the door and retreated to his customary seat.

'Are you going to get me a drink or what?'

'What do you want?' Sniffy little bleeder, Lee; he always had been. Why the fuck weren't kids taught any manners these days.

'A gin and tonic.'

'A gin and tonic, PLEASE. How old are you, anyway?'

'Nearly fourteen'

'Sharon, a coke for my esteemed guest. Leave it in the bottle and don't bother with a straw; he won't be stopping.'

'Tight git.'

'Are you going to give me that message or do I have to beat it out of you, you cheeky little bastard?'

Lee hesitated as if this was something worth considering.

'I'll tell my mum you called me a bastard.'

'Are you going to tell her you pinched Sharon's bum as well?' Quick look up to the barmaid and a knowing wink to make sure she was on the same ticket. Charlie really hoped she wasn't in a relationship. The more he saw of her the better he liked the look.

'I didn't!' Lee reddened with pure indignation.

'Your word against Sharon's and I was a witness.'

A heavy scowl from junior.

'Alright, but I want the coke in a glass with a slice of lemon and some ice.'

'Deal.'

This one had a degree of promise. They ought to teach kids negotiating skills at school. It would do the little buggers a lot more good than learning foreign languages. As far as Charlie could see everybody spoke English these days, anyway. Most of them a bloody sight better than they did on this side of the water.

'He gave me this and told me to bring it over early today.' Lee had now sorted out all the angles and was down to business.

A sealed envelope; very cloak and dagger. A bit dog eared but that would be accounted for by it being carted about in Lee's pocket for half the day. Charlie examined the seal to check if his messenger had taken the opportunity to steam it open and reseal it and was slightly disappointed to find that he hadn't.

'I don't call this early; who was the bloke who gave it to you?'

'I had to go to school, didn't I?'

'And the bloke?'

'Never seen him before.'

Charlie turned the envelope over in his hand without opening it. Sharon shouted over that the herring was ready when he was but he held up a hand to delay the delivery. Lee sat, slurping at his drink and jiggling the ice cubes in his glass putting on a perfect portrayal of impatience.

'How much did he give you to deliver it?'

'A tenner,'

'Show me.'

'I only got a five left.'

'So he gave you a fiver, told you to deliver the envelope and did he maybe say when I asked you what he looked like to give a lousy description?'

'Did Spangles tell you that? I'll bloody kill him!'

'And who is Spangles when he's at home?'

'My mate; he's the only one I told.'

'No, Spangles is clean but I was a bit like you a couple of hundred years ago so I know how this stuff works. What are you going to try to con out of me for a decent description of the bloke who delivered the envelope?'

'A gin and tonic.'

'Sharon, another coke with ice and lemon when you're ready. You; start talking before I bang your head on the table to see if anything jingles.'

'Tall and posh; not from round here. Long hair combed backwards. Nice clothes; suit or a jacket; didn't see his legs. Bit of a dick.'

'Age?'

'Old; well past it. Not quite as ancient as you but not far off; but with a posher voice and better manners.'

'Car?'

'He had one but he must have parked it up the road.'

'How do you know?'

'It was raining last night, wasn't it? You wouldn't go out on foot in just a jacket if it was raining, would you?'

'Here's another fiver. Take it and piss off before I put my boot up your arse.'

Lee scampered to the door, collecting his drink from the bar on the way, and barged out of the door taking the full glass with him. His poor mother, thought Charlie. That child will be a real little git in a couple of years' time. I hope the woman's got strong nerves. Smart enough though; perhaps by then he would be thinking of taking on an apprentice and Lee from the chip shop had all the makings.

The front door of the pub swung open again.

'Whoever you want, he's out,' shouted Charlie still fingering his unopened letter and trying to second guess the contents.

'Actually, he's not. Want to stand me a scotch, Charlie boy, or have I got to buy my own?'

Charlie didn't need to look up. The voice was unmistakable; it was one he had heard numerous times before; the one that still continued to make guest appearances in all his worst nightmares. Geoff Strickland; his least favourite member of Her Majesty's Constabulary and quite possibly the most bent copper in the entire service.

'Was that an underage drinker I saw exiting this pub? It's a matter we are obliged to take very seriously these days, underage drinking. You had better make it a double so I have something to help me get over the shock. Do you know what the fines are currently running at for serving minors who haven't shown you identification to demonstrate they are entitled to enter a den of iniquity like this place? A man could lose his Licence over that sort of thing.'

Charlie nodded at Sharon who had been listening in on the conversation. Strickland collected his drink and settled in the seat Lee had recently vacated.

'What can I do for you, Mr Strickland? I'm sure you have a busy afternoon lined up and I don't want to detain you.'

'Nothing, Charlie, nothing at all. Just passing your door and I thought it would be impolite not to renew an old friendship. I hear you've been a busy little bee since you got out. All those comings and goings. The doors to this place will need new hinges if you keep on like this for much longer. There's been so many worrying faces in and out of this pub in the last couple of weeks it's been difficult to work out which bunch of crooks you have decided to honour with your services.'

'I'm retired, Mr Strickland. Last time was the last time. Driving the golden chariot on the straight road to redemption. Cross my name from the pages of your little black book because you won't be needing to reference it anytime soon. I can assure you, this time I have truly seen the light.'

'I heard a rumour to that effect and assumed my informant was trying to be funny. I was so convinced he was taking the piss that I pushed him down a flight of stairs. I must remember to offer my apologies when he gets discharged from Intensive Care. Charlie, let's get real; if you are going straight why have half the City's villains been slogging their way up the high road in this direction? Were they getting their names down to join your Sunday school choir? It's Detective Sergeant by the way, as you are very well aware; and I'm with organised crime these days, so I think there's every chance we will be renewing our acquaintanceship before very long.'

Strickland threw back his drink and padded to the bar; as he did so, beckoning Sharon over with a wave of his arm. When he had got her full attention he cast his eyes theatrically round in a circle before fixing his face with a look of horror.

'Madam, when the Licensee puts in an appearance can you make him fully aware that these premises are not licensed for paint ball parties. The state of these walls is utterly unacceptable for a place that serves alcohol to the general public.'

Then, without cracking a smile the Detective Sergeant dropped his glass on the nearest table and sauntered out of the door without so much as a backward glance.

CHAPTER SEVEN

THURSDAY 9th FEBRUARY 2017

Mickey Smith wasn't happy. He had needed to get away from the Bear for a couple of hours so he could think straight, because he was burning up inside. As a kid he had attended a Taekwondo club for the best part of four years and had been acknowledged as an exceptional talent. Back at the pub he had a baseball bat lodged underneath the bar but that was only a fall-back option. If it came down to it he was more than happy to have his hands free if anyone wanted to mix it.

He would rather have taken on those three West Indian scum than let them defile his pub; the same went for that huge bloke from Eastgate that Charlie seemed to regard as a long lost brother. He didn't like the current turn of events. It was Charlie who was the root cause of all this bloody trouble but right now there wasn't a lot he could do about the situation. His name might be over the door but it was Charlie's whose was on the deeds and that was what really counted if they ever had a major bust up.

He had sweated blood over that place for the last fifteen years; been barely a kid when he first took over the running and now he was nudging thirty five ....and when you considered, what did he have to show for all the effort he had put in? A few grand in the bank and a reputation as someone who knew his way around behind the pumps, and that pretty much summed it up.

Alright, he could pick up another job tomorrow on the strength of what he had done with the Bear, but that wasn't the point. He had built the pub up from nothing and it was his baby; and you didn't let anybody mess with your family, did you? Not if you wanted to be able to look yourself straight in the eye.

The trouble was there wasn't much profit in beer these

days and he had been a bit slow off the mark getting into food. It hadn't been his fault; well not really. Some cunt had kicked up over the pub not being registered and then the Food Standards Agency had come up with a list of compliances half a mile long that it had taken literally years to sort it all out. Some of the stuff had to be seen to be believed. Even when he had put that lot to bed there had been the question of getting in someone who could cook. Not just any cook; a proper chef who would enhance the reputation of the Black Bear; not some spotty faced teenager who could knock out a hamburger and fries and bugger all else.

It was alright for Charlie. He had another source of income and the Bear only acted as a back-up to his shabby day job; and of course somewhere to launder the odd bit of dodgy money when the need came around. Even when he was banged up inside Charlie had been laughing; zero expenditure with a bit of dope dealing on the side while his share of the profits from the pub earned interest in a dubious offshore account he had fixed up with one of his gangster mates.

It hadn't mattered too much before Rachael; well it had.......but up to then his attention had been focussed in all the wrong places. She had arrived to temp while Sharon was knocking out her sprog two and a half years back and they had just sort of hit it off. Hair far too red, eyes so blue and bright they looked positively unnatural with that freckled pale complexion.

Nothing much had happened while they had worked together for best part of a year; a few laughs together over a drink or two, a cuddle that might have gone further if he hadn't held himself back; that was about it. Besides, at that time Rachael had been in a relationship; and Mickey had always made it a policy not to mix business with pleasure no matter how much he fancied the prospect; not that he hadn't been tempted, mind you, but you had to set yourself standards if you wanted to be respected when you were running a pub.

Then one day, out of the blue, Sharon told him she was ready to come back to work and he knew he would have to let Rachael go. God, he had felt absolutely terrible as he plucked up the courage to tell her. To make matters worse she obviously didn't want to leave and asked if there was any way he could keep her on if she worked fewer hours. It had cut him in half as he stumbled to find the right words to say no, and he could tell by her face she thought he was a hard arsed bastard. He had never found tough decisions like that one all that difficult in the past; you just had to grit your teeth and do what you thought to be right. But this time round everything was different; from the time he first saw her the woman had managed to get inside his head. The truth of the matter was, he found Rachael Broadbent just plain wonderful and he knew she didn't deserve to get her bum toed out of the door by a tosser like him.

He had moped about turning it over in his mind for a complete day before the solution came to him. Martin Shaffer from the posh gaming house half a mile up the hill owed him a favour or two so he had jumped in the car and driven to the Wellington Casino and put on his most charming smile. *'Got a great girl Martin; wasted at the Bear. Really going places this one; bright as a button.'* Whether he had entirely swallowed the story Mickey hadn't been sure but Martin had taken her on anyway; even believed the inflated salary he had told Martin he would need to pay in order to secure her services; a damn sight more than she had been earning down at the Bear, that was for sure. Mickey wasn't dumb; he had known how to sweeten the pot. *'Tell you what mate; give me a bundle of those hand-outs. I'll put them on the bar and give your place a plug when I've got a party in who fancy making a night of it after we are shutting up shop. Least I can do for a friend.'*

Then he and Martin had enjoyed a few drinks and swapped a couple of stories as they watched the punters throwing their money down the drain on a closed circuit

33

television system that had a monitor in the Manager's office; and because of that it hadn't been far short of eleven when he eventually got free and headed round to Rachael's place to tell her the news.

He remembered, he had paced up and down outside like an expectant father before he got up the courage to ring the bell. Suppose she had a boyfriend staying over? Suppose she told him to take his job and stick it where the sun didn't shine? Then, when he had eventually screwed up the courage to lean on the buzzer, some old bloke with muscles like Popeye had answered the door and eyed him up and down like he might be thinking of buying one for Christmas but wasn't sure if he fancied it in that colour; and only after the thorough appraisal was completed did the old geezer slowly turn his head to one side and shout up the stairs, *'Kit, it's some bloke for you. He ain't much to look at but he seems half way respectable.'*

After a short pause that went on for several hours she came slowly down the stairs, bare pink feet looking strangely delicate against the centuries old wooden floor boards; tousled hair and sleepy blue eyes; a towelling dressing gown tied with something that didn't quite match the colour. It was then he got the chest pain that nearly stopped him from breathing; it was then he knew for sure that this was the one.

'Why did he call you Kit?' was all he could think to whisper as she invited him up for coffee with the old codger leaning on the banister giving him a sceptical glare. *'He's got the downstairs; lovely old man; calls me Kitten. I've got no idea why. Treats me like his daughter.'*

They were inside her flat-let; coffee; both unsure how this was going to work out. She listened intently as he told her about the job opportunity and responded with a smile that made his heart leap. He plucked up the courage to ask her out on a date and she kissed him on the nose as she shooed him out twenty minutes later, with her aged minder keeping a watch from his doorway in case he tried anything the lady didn't like.

So it worked out for Rachael and just as importantly it worked out for Mickey Smith as well. Not straight away but within a few weeks they became what you might call 'an item'. And it was all perfectly wonderful, and for Mickey, falling in love with Rachael had proved amazingly easy; no problem at all.

But it hadn't taken very long for doubts to creep in. He had won the heart of the most wonderful woman on the face of the earth and she deserved more than he could possibly deliver. He wanted Rachael to be wearing a diamond engagement ring with a stone so big and bright everybody would be dazzled as it glistened in the moonlight. He wanted to take her to the best restaurants and on Caribbean holidays. He wanted the best for her because it was the very least she deserved. He wanted the opportunity to spoil her to death because she was worth nothing less.

And while he had been worrying himself to death about something that looked impossible to achieve a window of opportunity had opened up; and after a short period of reflection Mickey had thrown caution to the wind and clambered through to the other side. Then, once he had regained his balance, he had looked around and seen the possibilities that lay before his eyes; and without hesitation he had embraced them; bitten so deep into the apple of temptation his tongue could feel the texture of the pips and the roughness of the core.

So, while Mickey wasn't currently happy he was at least resolute. He could put up with Charlie bringing that big bastard from Eastgate and those West Indian scumbags into his front room because he wouldn't need to tolerate that sort of thing for very much longer. Mickey had a plan and whilst it wouldn't be easy to execute it was a long way from impossible; and any risk was worth taking when you were on the arm of the most wonderful woman in the world.

He pushed it all to the back of his mind. It was a big night tonight and there was a lot to think about. He

manufactured a smile and fixed it in place. No worries my
son; no risk was too great when you considered the prize.

CHAPTER EIGHT

THURSDAY 9th FEBRUARY 2017

It was now late afternoon and Charlie Brinsworth had retired to his room to put his feet up for half an hour. Earlier in the day he had driven over to check on the Vietnamese kids who were setting up the cannabis farm and as far as he could tell everything appeared to be proceeding to plan. They had finished clearing the cellar of the house and were now in the process of setting up the lighting and ventilation units. A pile of grow bags lay slumped in the corner awaiting deployment. The loft area was also going to be utilised once the development of the cellar was completed and the kids had already rigged up a bypass to the meter in case any smartarsed pen pusher from the electricity company noticed the usage going through the roof. They seemed to know what they were doing so Charlie walked around nodding knowledgeably, then made his excuses and got back in his car.

On the way into town he dropped in at Simon Bartol's taxi firm but was told the main man was away on business and wasn't expected back anytime soon. Charlie half recognised the bloke relaying the message but couldn't put a name to him. Probably a foot soldier from the old days Simon had taken with him when he moved away from Bridgeland to set up his own business.

Now all the immediate stuff had been dealt with and the last of the weak winter sunlight was completely gone Charlie found himself sitting on the foot of his bed fingering the unopened letter and wondering for the fiftieth time what was inside. He had purposely made no attempt to read it any earlier because according to the trainee mafia representative from the chip shop over the road the letter should have been delivered early that morning. Charlie wasn't working to anybody's timetable other than his own.

He would read the bloody sheets of paper when he was good and ready to do so.

There was something about the means of communication that spooked him; it had been set up with some care to be certain the letter found its way directly into his hands. People didn't do that sort of thing in this day and age; mainly because it wasn't necessary. Charlie had never made any secret of his mobile number. If the caller wanted to remain anonymous they just needed to get a pay-as-you-go phone and a block of sim cards. The chances were they would get away with ringing direct without being recognised, the way reception was in this part of the country.

The other thing was, he had a gut feeling the letter might be the prelude to something big and right now he was still feeling his way back into circulation after a very long layoff; and like a vintage car he wanted a nice steady run in until he was confident he was back up to speed.

Open it you dumb arse, the unhelpful voice in his head proposed for the umpteenth time; *what the fuck are you frightened of; did you lose your bottle while you were counting off the days until you were released?*

He wasn't sure why but he was tempted to rip the envelope into shreds and flush it down the loo. Instead he rested it on a picture rail, propped his back against the headrest of his bed and stared at it. After thirty seconds he couldn't bear the suspense and retrieved it from its perch and slid the penknife from his trouser pocket through the flap. Might as well get it over with; at least that way the voice inside his head should give him a bit of peace.

Good quality paper; no return address but explicit and concise. Clearly calculated to sound intriguing and whet his appetite.

Mr Brinsworth

Excuse this intrusion. I was put on to you by a friend who has knowledge of your line of work.

I have a business proposition to put to you which I think you might find of interest.

I will be in the Lounge bar of the Egret public house, on the road to Ingersall, at 7.30 this evening if you are interested in discussing the matter further. The contract would be short term and extremely lucrative.

Kind Regards,

A.Noone.

It certainly sounded interesting but there wouldn't have been a lot of point in the author taking the trouble to put pen to paper if it wasn't successful in sucking him in. Ingersall was a chocolate box village about eight miles from the city. Full of farm labourers' cottages that that had been lovingly renovated until they looked suitably cute and then sold at inflated prices to city dwellers who used them in the summer months as second homes. At this time of the year that road would be very quiet and ideal for an ambush. He tried to bring to mind anybody who would like to see him dead and ran out of fingers without needing to stretch his memory back too far. Enemies had always been easy to come by in his line of work.

The Egret was a poncy country pub which was now referenced as a coaching inn without much evidence to support the claim. At this time of the year its clientele would consist of local land owners, Reps touting agricultural equipment and farm supplies and courting couples looking for a bite to eat as a prelude to a quick grope in a lay-by on the return journey. It was too early in the year for the tweed jacketed brigade of townies to put in an appearance. They would currently be huddled round their log burning stoves in their Islington townhouses knocking back a glass of red while they reminisced over the New Year skiing trip that had doubtless been utterly fantastic.

Still uncommitted to the assignation Charlie dismissed

the proposed meeting as a set up for a hit. If they were aware of his line of work they would also know he wasn't naive and had ready access to the required muscle to take care of his personal wellbeing. Besides, too much notice had been given. When you did that sort of thing the object was to tempt the target into a rushed and ill-considered decision. He should know; he had done it enough times over the course of his career.

So it came down to a straight choice; did he fancy it or didn't he? Five minutes later he was taking a shower prior to picking out a sports jacket and a pair of corduroy trousers that he thought would blend him in nicely with the Egret's class of clientele.

CHAPTER NINE

THURSDAY 9th FEBRUARY 2017

As anticipated, the traffic had been fairly light on the drive out of town and Charlie arrived at the Egret public house twenty minutes ahead of the appointed time. This was intentional. He wanted to get a feel of the place and know where the exits were in case there was any need for a hurried departure. He had parked in clear view at the front of the pub, directly under the house lights and pointed the bonnet at the open road.

As he had suspected the main bar was sparsely populated; the only party of any size consisting of a group of locals who were happily overcooking a tea time session without any apparent feeling of guilt. The beer was decent and he was three quarters of the way down his second pint when the door slid open.

Young Lee's description had been pretty good. Late thirties, longish hair combed backwards in no particular style; a waistcoat and jacket that were so ill matched they blended together quite nicely; slightly gangly looking, possibly accentuated by his height and the fact his trousers were a shade too tight in the leg. Brogue shoes, expensive but scuffed and unpolished. Well to do, by the look of it and, as far as Charlie could ascertain from first viewing, constituting absolutely nothing of a threat.

Without hesitation he walked towards Charlie at the bar; loping stride, hand extended in greeting several paces before he was in any position to press the flesh. They shook hands and stood awkwardly weighing each other up.

'Anthony Noone, good to meet you; shall we grab the table near the window? Fancy another? I'll go for a beer as well, I think. Is the one you're drinking any good?'

Noone ordered the drinks striving to give the impression he was completely at ease. Charlie felt it was a bit like one of those situations when work colleagues met on a social occasion outside business hours; goodwill on both sides to try to make things go as smoothly as possible, but tempered by a degree of caution because they were entering uncharted waters.

'Well, as you see I got your letter. Before we start would you mind telling me who gave you my name?' Charlie, straight out of the blocks, eager to grab the initiative before his new found friend could get properly settled.

'Sorry Mr Brinsworth.....alright if I call you Charlie?......I can't do that. I promised my contact I wouldn't divulge his identity under any circumstances.'

'Then I'm very sorry, Anthony, but we had better leave it at that. You'll understand my position; without a reference that I can check back on, I could be talking to anyone.'

'That is of course your right, Charlie; but if I could just make two points before you sever connections. Firstly, if I now told you who gave me your name, you would immediately know you couldn't trust me. If I broke my word once, there's every chance I would do it again. Secondly, I'll be the one who's leaving himself wide open. I'll do all the talking. All you need to do is listen and evaluate. I don't want to check out your C.V.; if I didn't think you were capable of handling what I am about to propose we wouldn't be having this conversation. Might I suggest you look on it as if a drunk stumbles up to your table in a crowded bar and begins to tell you a preposterous story........it's nothing to you one way or the other but you lose nothing by humouring him for a short time and seeing what it is he's got to say; and there's always the outside chance you might learn something to your advantage.'

Well, when he put it that way it was hard to argue. Charlie wasn't overly happy with the situation but what the lanky git said made some degree of sense. What skin was it off his nose if all he had to do was listen? He finished his second pint, shifted the replacement onto the newly vacated beer mat and shrugged his shoulders in a manner that suggested reluctant acquiescence.

Anthony Noone made an effort not to smile. The first hurdle has been overcome with comparative ease. He ignored his drink as he organised his thoughts on the presentation of phase two.

'My father was a captain of industry. He ran a large business the details of which we will need to touch on in greater detail allowing that circumstances permit.'

He gave Charlie a pursed look, intended to indicate that the further detail would of course be forthcoming only if he signed up for the project.

'Father's company employed nearly a thousand workers, a lot of whom were engaged in industrial production and back in those days a lot of them didn't have much truck with bank accounts. In consequence, at certain times during any given month there was a lot of cash held on the premises; sometimes overnight or even for a matter of days.'

He hesitated; possibly noticing the flicker of interest showing in Charlie Brinsworth's eyes.

'The old man was careful in his ways; always had been. He had moved a long way up the social ladder in the course of his lifetime, but had initially come from humble beginnings where it was second nature to treat every penny piece with the respect it deserved. He knew that having money like this laying around would sooner or later prove a temptation to somebody or other and he also knew it was his responsibility to make sure nothing untoward was allowed to happen to it. In consequence, he set about taking the necessary precautions.'

A slight pause. Anthony Noone's beer still remained untouched. Charlie sipped at his pint and maintained a practised look of casual indifference.

'He researched the possibilities and eventually settled on an Italian firm that manufacture and installed safes that were advertised as being both fireproof and virtually impregnable. He then rigorously checked out the various specifications before placing an order for the model that he thought would best serve his purpose. When doing so he specified he would require the base of the box to be bolted into a reinforced concrete floor. Very much my father's way; belt and braces every time. He left little to chance.'

'Why Italian?' Charlie had promised himself he would keep his mouth shut but professional interest had sparked him into life.

'If you were an English safecracker how much would you know about a continental model? Besides, at the time the safe he had selected was regarded as pretty much the best model on the market. It was something of a brute, weighing well over a ton and standing about eight feet tall. So even if thieves were ever successful in breaking into the building, they would have been confronted by something that was virtually impossible to open and far too heavy to remove from the premises. Added to which the exchange rate made it good business to buy from abroad because as usual the Lira was on its knees. But there was also one other relevant factor; my father had fought in Italy during the war and his posting had kept him in the country for many months after the armistice. By the time he returned home he was pretty much fluent in Italian and inordinately proud of the fact.'

Another pause. This time Noone did condescend to take a sip of his drink but it was only a very small one.

'After a couple of months all the kit was delivered and Signor Roberto Baldini graced us with his much anticipated presence. This man, father had been assured, was the company's top installer and an expert on the particular model of safe that had been ordered. As father was renowned as something of a skinflint, Signor Baldini moved in with us at the family home. This was not a gesture of hospitality, you understand; my father was saving on a hotel bill that was to be picked up by the company as a part of the deal.

The long and the short of it was Roberto Baldini and

my father ended up getting on like a house on fire. They sat up to all hours with bottles of red wine gesticulating wildly in the air and babbling about who knows what. I remember my mother being quite put out by the whole episode, though I'm not entirely sure why. Possibly, because for this period in our lives my father became something of a stranger to the rest of the family.'

Another pause; a marginally larger sip of beer; despite which Noone still failed to make any discernible impression on the glass of frothy liquid.

'Once the installation was completed father held a small ceremony to welcome his new acquisition into service and at this time he set a new company policy. To further enhance security the combination to the safe was to be shared by only two people and the Accountant and the Credit Controller were chosen for the job. They were presumably selected on the basis that they were very steady individuals who had been in the company's employ since the first day it opened. So now it would take two people to be present in order to get the safe door open......and you can imagine the unnecessary kerfuffle this caused during a busy working day; not least because the object of the exercise would be totally defeated if either one of the two employees ever gained knowledge of the other person's half of the combination. Quite naturally they complained, and quite rightly so; but father was adamant that security was his principal concern and that jobs would be forfeit if his instructions were not meticulously obeyed. He also made it crystal clear he didn't care a jot how much inconvenience the new system caused to the accounts staff and he would tolerate no more complaints.'

'Sorry, I don't get it. If even your father wasn't aware of the complete combination number, what would happen if........'

Anthony Noone had his arm raised in the air like a traffic policeman indicating a stop command. Charlie's enquiry was cut off in mid flow.

'Hang on for a minute, Charlie, while I tell you the best bit. The combination was to be set by the two appointed figures and changed at least twice a year. As each knew only half the code, father insisted they come up with a fall-back strategy in case one had a heart attack or got hit by a bus. I later found out how it worked and you might find the details vaguely amusing. They both purchased a toy moneybox which could be opened by a small key to which they each had their own copy. In their personal box they both lodged the name of a company employee which they secreted it in a place in their home that they deemed both inaccessible and completely safe. Under the lagging in the roof space; in a cavity that could be accessed by unscrewing a floor board; anywhere the moneybox would be totally invisible to anybody other than the one other person who knew the location. It was security at its paranoiac best. I doubt if the contents of Fort Knox had ever been very much safer.'

'I don't see why knowing the name of a worker at the company would be of any help in opening the safe door.'

'It was the very heart of a complex and fool proof system. If by the remotest chance anyone did come across the moneybox and lever open the top then all they would have in their possession was a name which in itself would tell them absolutely nothing. Only the Accountant and the Credit Controller were aware that if they then checked the payroll print out and obtained the clock number of the designated employee it would provide a three digit number that equated to a half of the safes combination. Crackers, eh? Total lunacy. However, it made my dear father happy, so I suppose in that regard it served a useful purpose.'

'Just as a matter of interest, what was the name of the Italian company that manufactured the safe?'

'Don't even go there, Charlie. Dear old daddy even refused to have the company's logo displayed on the front face in case it would assist somebody in breaking it open. Father should have got a job with Brink's-Mat. He would have saved the company a small fortune.'

Charlie took a pull of his pint. This was a mildly interesting story but he couldn't figure out where it was going. Still, at least he hadn't been bored to death; not yet anyway.

Anthony Noone appeared to have grown into his role as raconteur and now looked totally relaxed and was seemingly enjoying himself.

'Time passed on and the company's fortunes took a turn for the worse. The tooling coming in from the Far-East that we once used to dismiss as a joke was now at least as good as the product we manufactured domestically and often a good deal better. It was also half the price. The overseas competition had invested in new machinery while Companies in this country had been complacent. All the British manufacturing plants now had going for them was a past reputation and a few brand names that still resonated in certain markets but were unlikely to continue to do so for very much longer. In the end the wrong shareholder died at the wrong time and asset strippers managed to secure control of the company and hasten the downward spiral. Needless to say father was the first person out of the door. He was marched out and pretty much dumped on the pavement by security guards who took his keys and even searched his pockets before they abandoned him without even offering the courtesy of a lift home. It was humiliating and he took it extremely badly. The nasty men were intent on dismembering the thing he loved best and there was absolutely nothing he could do about the situation. Father was by now of an age where he should have just shrugged his shoulders and set about enjoying his retirement years but that wasn't in his nature. He let it get on top of him and pretty soon he had worried himself into a wooden box.'

A slight pause; then a small feeling of excitement appeared to infuse the air. The punch line was about to arrive and Charlie considered it was some way overdue.

'On his death bed father called me in for a final goodbye. He told me the state of family finances; there was enough to see mother through in the style to which she had become accustomed providing she didn't take up playing the ponies or develop a crack habit, but that was about it. For me he could only provide a small nugget of information that possibly I might at some stage be able to use to my advantage.'

A long halt. A wet from the glass. A smile playing at the corners of his lips. Come on, spit it out you bastard. I haven't got all night.

'When father had sat long into the night with Roberto Baldini all those year before he hadn't been discussing the special taste of authentic pasta sauce. He had been persuading the good Signor to design a special opening operation for his beloved safe which responded not just to the code put in by the Accountant and the Credit Controller but also one that he alone would possess. In simple terms, an override that only he could make use of; and with virtually his dying breath the old man told me what it was.'

Well we got there in the end. Told it well mind you, the toffee nosed git. Interesting to see what comes along next. Would Noone choose to lay his cards out on the table or hedge around a bit? The story sounded vaguely plausible. Just the sort of thing you would have expected from a control freak like Anthony's old man. The miserable bastard would have enjoyed watching his minions scurry around as they worked to come up with a fall-back plan that was as complicated as it was totally unnecessary. The joy he must have gained from sneaking a peek at the contents of the safe when the building was empty after all his staff had gone home for the night. There were some bloody strange people about and Anthony Noone's father certainly appeared to have been one of them. He wondered how many of his genes had filtered their way through to the next generation.

Perhaps this was now the time to hustle things along a bit or would that be a mistake? What the hell. Now he knew the direction in which they would inevitably be travelling, what harm could it do?

'So, Anthony, are you going to tell me this safe is still in use?'

A long hesitation. Perhaps having got this far Mr Noone now felt it expedient to think for a minute and reassess the situation. So far all he had done was relate a story he had probably gone over in his head a hundred times. Now he was breaking totally new ground and unless he was a complete fool he would realise that he would need to be very careful with his words.

'Yes, that's exactly what I'm saying.'

'And you think the safe might still hold cash or items of value.'

'Quite possibly both, but if you are thinking in that direction you would be entirely missing the point.'

Well bite the bullet, son. Don't sit there pussy footing around for half the night. Make up your mind how much you are going to share before they call last orders. Charlie swilled down the last of his drink and plonked the empty glass heavily on the table in encouragement.

'Well Charlie, are you interested?'

'How can I answer that if I don't know what you want me to do?'

'I thought from what I've just told you that would be completely obvious.'

'Did you? Well pal, you were very wrong on that score. Spell it out, Mr Noone.'

Another period of quiet while friend Anthony summoned up the right words.

'I want you to facilitate breaking into a building, opening the safe I have already described and retrieving some of its contents.'

Now that wasn't all that difficult, was it? I bet Mr Noone felt a lot better now he had actually managed to spit out the words. Probably best to push him a bit while he was still groggy. Maybe he hadn't yet weighed up the implications of saying too much.

'Well, in principle that sounds a possibility; but of

49

course I will need a lot more detail before I can make a commitment. Let's start with the location......'

'Next time, Charlie. I'll provide all the detail you need to know the next time we meet. For now I just wanted to know if this was a project you would consider of interest. Something you would be prepared to handle. I understand you have been out of commission for a while and I wasn't sure if..........look, give me your mobile number and I'll get back to you in a couple of days; then we can sit down quietly and iron out the fine detail.'

CHAPTER TEN

THURSDAY 9th FEBRUARY /
FRIDAY 10th FEBRUARY 2017

It was well gone nine o'clock by the time Charlie
Brinsworth had completed his journey home. He pushed
his way through the main door of the Black Bear and came
to an abrupt halt. Bloody idiot; with the stream of visitors
he had received earlier in the day, followed by the abrupt
summons to the Egret, it had gone completely out of his
head. It was tonight Mickey was launching the official
reopening of the pub.

He hesitated in the doorway and surveyed the scene
before his eyes with complete horror. To say the place was
heaving with bodies was probably the understatement of
the year. He had been to Premier League football matches
with crowds thinner than this. The Bear was now playing
host to a crowd that would have done credit to a New
Year's Eve in Trafalgar Square.

He knew Mickey had intended persuading Sharon to
don a little black cocktail dress and circulate throughout
the premises distributing a selection of those poxy little
biscuits with bits of stuff plastered on the top that looked
like mashed frog. Ever the businessman, Mickey had
intended to follow up with glasses of chilled prosecco for
the regulars; Sharon having already been coached to
whisper in the strictest confidence that it was actually
vintage champagne, the cost of which alone would be
enough to bring in the bailiffs. Charlie could only admire
Mickey's acumen. The plan appeared to have been a
resounding success.

Whether in response to the perceived generosity of
their host or because they just fancied making a night of it,
the Bear's clientele seemed to have got fully into the spirit
of things, with the result the bar now looked as if it was

hosting a drinking contest for relapsed alcoholics.

Charlie stepped over the carnage and fought his way to the front of the crowd. Mickey, shirtsleeves rolled to the elbow, was pulling pints nineteen to the dozen and issuing instructions in the manner of the Captain of the Titanic. The back of the bar looked nearly as crowded as the front. Even Big Trevor the massive Nigerian Bouncer had been withdrawn from his duties on the door to squeeze himself into an oversize niche and help out by washing glasses.

Mickey spotted Charlie loitering uncertainly and took this as a sign that his partner was displaying insufficient evidence of any intent to encourage the cash register into greater use. He was after him in a flash.

'Charlie, it's been crazy here all night. I've had to call two of the part timers in and set Trevor up as a pot washer. Make yourself useful. Go and collect some glasses. Come on; move yourself; there are paying customers out there waiting to be served.'

After the day he had just experienced there were several things Charlie would have rather been doing than engaging in battle with a seething crowd of inebriates. But, ever the man to recognise when he was on a hiding to nothing, he proceeded to spend the next couple of hours retrieving empty drinking vessels from the most unlikely of locations and transporting them back to the twenty stone Nigerian who viewed his efforts as a major cause for hilarity.

By the time the last customer had eventually been persuaded from the premises it was midnight. Mickey was pleased with the night's takings, but at the same time mortified at his customer's lack of taste.

'You won't believe it; not one of that bunch of philistines said a word about the new decorations,' he complained bitterly.

Charlie flopped in a chair surrounded by the exhausted bar staff. Mickey, quick to recover from his customer's perceived slight, enquired if anyone wanted a quick drink before they shut up shop for the night.

'I'll have a whiskey if you're offering. Did you know your back door had been left open?' said a voice that made Charlie quickly look up. Detective Sergeant Geoff Strickland hove into view and moved to Charlie's side.

'A quick word, Mr Brinsworth, if you can spare me a moment of your valuable time,' he requested in an unusually soft voice.

They retreated to the back wall and pulled up chairs. Strickland looked tired and slightly dishevelled; pretty much like he usually did in fact. Whatever he was after, Charlie just wanted to get it over and done with so he could be off to his bed. He had a lot to consider and the day had already gone on a good deal too long for his liking.

'Bit of a strange occurrence up at Eastgate. The word has it their boss man has done a disappearing act. Nothing reported officially you understand but my gaffer asked me to do the rounds and make a few discreet enquiries. Anything you would care to offer on the subject?'

Mickey arrived with two extremely small whiskeys and dispensed scowls in both directions.

'Why are you asking me? I'm retired, remember?'

'Thought you might just be keeping your hand in, Charlie boy. I know how you like to keep busy. I'm just going through the motions as it happens. Nat Dawson has had it coming for a long time and if he's been topped it's one less scumbag on the street as far as I'm concerned. However, my boss likes to keep on top of things and for once I'm working with someone who's earned the right to a bit of respect. Let's face it, if Big Nat's been jumped by anyone the odds are strongly in favour of the Tysons; but if you hear anything to the contrary it never hurts to have a favour in the locker and I never forget a good turn as you are well aware. Keep it to yourself for the present. We could be in for interesting times if he doesn't show up at the Pheasant with a blinding hangover sometime in the next few hours.'

Strickland drained his glass, before focussing his

attention on the newly decorated walls with an expression of utter disgust. He shook his head sadly and muttered to himself as he headed for the exit. The man had a reputation for never sleeping and always appeared happiest when he was working after dark. Charlie remembered being dragged out of bed by the bastard several years back. At least these days he was treated with a little more civility.

There was now even more to mull over. Charlie moved over to re-join the bar staff and leaned his arms on the back of a chair next to Sharon. She smiled up at him and edged along the seat until she was a little closer; still wearing the little black cocktail dress she looked good enough to eat. Suddenly he didn't feel quite so tired anymore; especially when she dropped into the conversation that her babysitter was sleeping over for the night. All of a sudden any intention to pursue a programme of intensive mulling was demoted some way down the agenda.

CHAPTER ELEVEN

FRIDAY 10ᵗʰ FEBRUARY 2017

By midday Charlie had exhausted every computer search he could think to try. As far as he had been able to determine Anthony Noone didn't seem to exist. He had also been dumb enough not to get a Christian name for Noone's father, so running a trace on him had been something of a nonstarter. In exasperation he had even tried Googling 'Italian safe manufacturers' but had given up on that one pretty damn fast.

Undaunted, he had instead decided to try a trawl by phone; calling about a half dozen people he knew who had legitimate connections with the posh boys with money in the bank and casually introduced the Noone name into the conversation. He might as well have not bothered. All this succeeded in doing was to saddle him with a series of drink dates that he could happily have managed without.

Sharon had spent the night, disappearing with a kiss and a giggle at the crack of dawn to scamper off home. Some girl that. The idiot who had put her in the family way and then decided to disappear before the happy event must have wanted his head seeing to. Charlie thought she was a terrific bit of skirt and hoped that a replay of their extracurricular activities might soon be on the cards.

For the time being, it was probably best to keep quiet about it, though. He knew he wasn't currently Mickey's favourite person on the planet and it was a safe bet the workaholic Landlord wouldn't be overly delighted to know of his amorous intentions towards his prize pint puller.

Charlie had only managed to drag himself out of bed at ten o'clock and had already wasted two hours in a vain search for the mysterious Anthony Noone. Now he needed to get his arse in gear and the old grey cells working at double quick time or he would very soon find himself walking into a very dark tunnel carrying a candle with a burned down wick.

He hadn't given much thought to the situation over at Eastgate either. He wasn't even sure who would be most likely to step up to the plate if Nat Dawson didn't put in a hasty appearance. The only consolation was whoever that might be would have too much on their plate to pay him much attention at the present time.

The situation would of course be manna from heaven for the Tyson mob. Regardless of whether or not they had personally organised Nat Dawson's highly successful disappearing act they must now be rubbing their hands together with glee. It was a fairly safe bet that if Dawson didn't launch a speedy resurrection then a turf war would kick off. This would of course be the reason that Geoff Strickland had been forced into doing the pub circuit late last night, even if he would have been the last person to admit to the fact. Strickland would have come across as a strangely reassuring presence to the landlords in the area in these uncertain times. With Strickland, at least you knew what you were getting; and as he carried a reputation for handling trouble in his own indomitable fashion, it would come as no surprise to the proprietors when it ended up costing them, one way or another.

Charlie wasn't sure how the odds would balance out these days; Eastgate would probably still be ahead on numbers but word had it the Tysons had been busily recruiting for the last eighteen months so it was doubtful if these days there was very much in it. There was also a perception the Tysons might be the hungrier outfit. Eastgate had been top dog over this way for a lot of years and maybe they had become a little bit complacent. Only time would tell how this one would pan out and Charlie certainly wouldn't be putting any money on who might come out on top. Mind you, he wouldn't have bet against Eastgate under any circumstances, having seen Spanner Hopkins in action first hand......and that had been before he'd got a few pints down him, if Charlie's memory was working correctly.

'Where's Mickey?' he asked the elderly lady putting the final touches to wiping out the last evidence of the previous night's carnage.

'He'll be round at his lady friend's,' she shouted, turning off the vacuum cleaner for a moment as the opportunity for a chat presented itself.

'The crazy one with the two yards of leg?' said Charlie, instantly interested.

'No, she's just his friend. Rachael's his proper girlfriend. He thinks it's a secret but everybody knows about her though we never let on. Nice girl with freckles and bright red hair. She did a bit of bar work here a year or two back. Everybody liked her. She was a good worker as well.'

So Mickey had a proper girlfriend and it wasn't the head-case with the legs and the scary eyes.......and he was keeping her tucked away well out of sight. Charlie pondered the implications. Mickey could evidently be a sly old dog when it suited him. No wonder he kept disappearing for a couple of hours at a time and looked a bit dreamy when he thought no one was watching. Women could have that effect on a man if you didn't watch out for yourself and Mickey had always been a bit vulnerable in that direction.

Sausage and mash was on the menu today; or it would have been if the Bear boasted a proper menu instead of the Chef just printing a bit of card that told you what to expect if you ordered his food. No point in Charlie going out until he had eaten. He had missed breakfast already and his stomach was getting more convinced by the minute that his throat had been cut. Besides which he had a lunchtime appointment and if he wasn't mistaken the voice drifting in from the roadway outside would match perfectly with his expected arrival. Immediately, the door clanked and Simon Bartol swung into view, clad only in a leather jacket and jeans despite the temperature, which was hovering only a shade above freezing.

'Heard about Eastgate? They'll be shitting themselves if that fat bastard Dawson doesn't turn in a Lazarus impersonation in the next few hours. He steered the ship single handed according to Brendan O'Sullivan. I ran across Brendan, the miserable bastard, down on the High Street wearing his best black suit and practising looking solemn to make sure he didn't miss out on any passing trade. Old Brendan must have made a small fortune out of that bloody Undertakers business over the years, what with his trade connections and Spanner Hopkins putting a good word in for him at Eastgate.'

'How come O'Sullivan's an expert on Eastgate affairs all of a sudden. He went private years back; before I went inside for the first time if memory serves.'

'Mr Hopkins still marks his card though he probably isn't supposed to; thick as thieves those two; always were.'

'Listen Simon, a small favour if you could see your way. I'm looking for a bloke called Anthony Noone, posh git, nice clothes, streak of piss with a look of money about him; about forty, longish combed back hair with a bit of inbreeding lurking somewhere in the background. Can you ask around?'

'Got a photo?'

'Nope.'

'O.K. the name doesn't ring any bells but I'll put out the word. If he's from round here one of my boys will know where he hangs out. I'll shout you back if I come up with anything.'

'Another thing, Simon. I called in at your taxi place yesterday while you were out. Who's the bloke behind the counter, bald, fat, fiftyish; suit, but looked like he sleeps in it.'

'Keith Woods.......Woody, to his friends but he ain't got many.'

'How well do you know him?'

'Well enough; not well. Woody's a foot soldier who does a bit of running around on deliveries when we're busy. Not the sharpest if I'm being truthful but handy with a cosh.'

'It's just I know him from somewhere and can't put my finger on where that might be. I thought maybe we had done time together but it's not that. I got the feeling he recognised me as well but he was quick to cover it up. There's something about him that's floating about at the back of my head but I can't put a nail in it. The only thing I'm sure about; it ain't good. No chance he's a plant I suppose?'

'Not much chance of that. Woody's solid from the neck up. Thanks for the tip anyway. I'll have a feel around just in case he slipped through the net.'

'I'm looking after my own wellbeing as well, Simon. Once we get the Vietnamese boys up and running your interests will be the same as mine.'

CHAPTER TWELVE

FRIDAY 10th FEBRUARY 2017

Mickey Smith made the decision to walk into town. There was no logic to this judgement; it was bloody freezing and already there was the odd flake of snow in the air. He had only opted to walk because it gave him more time to think of the best way to present the bad news he would very soon be obliged to deliver.

By the time he reached the main shopping area the snow had turned to light rain though the temperature didn't seem to have got a lot warmer. Mickey checked his watch, straightened his collar, screwed up his courage and pushed open the door to the Albatross, an up market bistro that specialised in light bites to cater to its clientele of choice.

And there they were in all their glory; the massed battalions of ladies who lunched. Admittedly, lunch might be something of an exaggeration as each plate seemed to display either half a prawn sandwich or a slender slice of quiche. A second glance and it quickly became apparent that as a mandatory accessory either lunch option was invariably accompanied by a chilled glass of white wine. The food and drink, if meagre in proportion, must quite definitely have been of extremely high quality because the place was positively thronged; and being cash strapped didn't seem to account for the derisory quantity of calories on each of the diner's plates, as the occupant of every chair was tastefully dressed, beautifully coiffeured and gave every sign of being extremely affluent.

As you forced open the door, first impressions might have suggested the clientele were engaged in some form of mass hysteria which necessitated everyone talking at the same time; however, if you paid closer attention it soon became apparent that it was in fact a sophisticated game which was being played to extremely rigid rules. No listening was permitted, stopping to draw breath was not encouraged and could easily draw penalty points for unnecessary hesitation; and the permitted subjects of discourse seemed to be limited almost exclusively to the difficulties in planning a visit to the hair salon, the nail bar or the beautician.

Mickey steeled himself and forced his way forward, his ears assailed by the cacophonous volume. He ran his eyes forlornly up and down the busy aisles but every seat appeared occupied. Then his luck seemed to change as he spotted a vacant chair opposite a slender woman in her thirties with strikingly angular features, shoulder length blonde hair and clear grey eyes. Even in this menagerie of the ultimately pampered she still somehow contrived to look strangely aloof; like a vision you might be allowed to dream about on the condition you never tried to touch.

'Is this seat taken,' Mickey enquired politely, turning on his best two hundred watt smile.

The woman raised her eyes from the magazine she had been idly perusing and looked him calmly up and down, before speculatively glancing around the busy bistro in search of an alternative option.

Mickey hovered for several seconds, seemingly uncertain; then pulled the chair free from the table, settling the outcome of the unspoken debate by taking decisive action. As he pulled off his sodden anorak and deposited it on the floor between the legs of his chair, his lips pulled back into a leer.

'I wanted this particular seat because if I lean back a bit I can study the shape of your beautiful legs without making it seem too obvious to anyone who's watching. If I slide my chair a little closer I could even reach out and touch your knee, then slowly slide my hand a little higher and caress your thigh. I've already had a good look around this place and it didn't take me long to notice that you're the tastiest dish on the menu. Everything about you makes me feel warm.......warm and very excited. Just thought I ought to explain why I wanted to sit down close to you. I didn't want to come across as rude but it was the only way to express my interest. I thought it might be a good way for us to get to know each another a little bit better. Hey, listen, perhaps we could fast forward a little. It just occurred to me.......if you've not got much on for the rest of the day how about you skip the coffee and we could maybe book into a hotel. I promise I'll do my very best to keep you entertained.'

The woman looked up from the page she was scrutinising with a shocked expression; she coloured slightly, then smiled and poked out her tongue.

'One of these days, Mickey Smith, I'm going to take you up on that offer; then I'll watch, laughing my head off, as you go scurrying for the nearest door with your tail between your legs. I've met so many like you; all patter and no performance. Now, order a drink to wash out that dirty mouth of yours. I can't imagine what my husband would say if I told him I'd been propositioned by the likes of you. He'd have a fit. You don't even own a decent car let alone something with leather upholstery.'

Stephanie Armitage sat back and practised looking serene as Mickey ordered an Americano; it was the only coffee on the listing he found vaguely comprehensible.

The waiter fussed around smiling lovingly at his chic companion who was obviously an esteemed patron. Ms Armitage sat back in the best seat in the house, paying little heed to the attention; plainly being the entire focus of as server's devotion was nothing unusual.

'Well Mr Smith, what have you got to tell me?'

'Stevie, I'm sorry but we need to go to Plan B.'

She leaned further forward placing her sharp elbows delicately on the table; then cupped her chin in her hands as she fixed Mickey with her steel grey eyes; the grey was that of 9 millimetre bullets not scudding clouds floating in a mildly troubled sky.

'Which presumably means Plan A didn't work.'

'It's ongoing but I don't want to leave this thing drifting in the air. Let's go for something that will be sure to get a result.'

'Well, you've totally changed your tune, Mickey Smith. Last time we spoke you were bristling with confidence about how you would pull it off and now you're suggesting a complete rethink. You realise if we go for the second option we will be talking a minimum of a couple of weeks delay and an outlay of maybe five or six thousand; and that's if I can persuade the little toad with egomania and severe halitosis to consider playing along.'

'I came to see the wisdom of your words, Stevie. When you add up the numbers it's a small outlay when you compare it to the return. Your words if I remember. I just didn't think that a woman as beautiful and sexy as you could be right all the time as well.'

'You cheeky little bastard. You haven't changed one bit in all the years I've known you. Be careful of that smile, Mickey Smith. It could get you into a lot of trouble. I hope you are very careful where you use it when Rachael isn't around. Alright, I'll speak to my man and see if I can sweet talk him into showing a bit of interest. Let's hope he's had a bad run on the ponies and is running short of funds. I'll have to get out the full body armour as well. It's like sharing a water tank with an octopus.'

'Have you got everything you need?'

'Yes, I told Bernie to cover all possibilities when he came to your place just in case something went wrong and you finished up changing your mind. I thought that was meant to be a woman's prerogative, by the way. There isn't anything you've been frightened to tell me, is there Mickey?'

'Thanks Stevie, you know I'll love you 'til the day I die. I still remember the first day I saw you. I was twelve and you were nearly fifteen. As soon as you walked out of the door I rushed to my bedroom and locked the door. It was a moment a man never forgets. You were my first fantasy; and one I could actually have touched if it wasn't for the fact you would never let me.'

'You were a horrible little pervert at twelve and you

63

haven't changed a bit. I don't know why I even bother talking to you. You are clearly a long way beyond redemption.'

'Talking of which, where's the husband?'

'Having a romantic interlude with his secretary in Milan, in the guise of attending an important business meeting. He's a total shit, Mickey, but at least he's an exceedingly rich total shit. I wonder what you'll turn out like once you're a wealthy man of leisure. If history repeats itself you'll probably end up a total shit as well. Men are always so horribly predictable.'

CHAPTER THIRTEEN

FRIDAY 10th FEBRUARY 2017

Charlie was totally replete, if feeling like your trousers were bursting covered the meaning of the word. He had found it a bit surprising that the Chef had stuck the sausages into the mashed potato so they stood up like soldiers on guard duty but at least they were decent sausages with plenty of meat; and the onion gravy had been good enough to die for. It made you proud to be British, that sort of thing; clearly superior to that foreign muck with the tasteless German mustard, buried somewhere under a foot and a half of watery, white cabbage.

Charlie had been planning things out in his head over lunch and decided a good way forward might be to have a quick word with the ex-Eastgate gang member, turned undertaker, Brendan O'Sullivan. He had known O'Sullivan to nod at as a kid because they had grown up in the same area; and whilst their paths had gone in different directions in the intervening years he had plenty of excuses to stop off for a bit of a chat about old times. In O'Sullivan's line of work he must come into contact with a lot of people from different walks of life and maybe he could provide some clue to the mysterious Anthony Noone.

Then he had stopped to analyse the situation more carefully. How likely was it that the subject of this meeting wouldn't later be relayed back to O'Sullivan's best mate, Spanner Hopkins? Not very; and an Eastgate interest in any of his current activities was the last thing he needed at the present time. No, maybe the smarter move was to give that one a miss and come at the problem from a different angle altogether.

He collected his car keys, fired up the motor and

headed across town in a northerly direction. He was heading into Tyson territory so he would need to keep his head down. Even in semi-retirement Charlie Brinsworth putting in an appearance on the Tyson manor would be viewed with outright suspicion and possibly a little bit more than that if his luck was out.

He dumped his aged Toyota out of harm's way on a piece of waste ground that had been nothing different in all the years he could remember; then walked along a stretch of dual carriageway that used to lead past a series of vast steel plants and similar bastions of heavy industry, all of which had long since been put out of commission. The reason he had been prepared to swallow the story Anthony Noone had told him in the Egret was because it rang so horribly true. A high proportion of the city's workforce had ended up on the dole when the market had been flooded with cheap foreign imports after the government had chosen to turn their backs on anything that might have smacked of protectionism. The stupid cunts in Whitehall had even offered grants which helped the slit eyes bastards set up shop in our own back yard. No wonder nobody had any faith in politicians anymore; at best they were an expenses fiddling, self-serving, bunch of tossers and in a lot of cases something a bloody sight worse. The way they went on was enough to tempt a man into a life of crime.......not that he had needed all that much tempting if he remembered correctly.

Charlie arrived at his final destination; a building half way up a hill that resembled something midway between an army pillbox, a post war prefab and a pigeon loft. He tried to look in through the windows but they were caked in grime, the majority of which was on the inside.

'Wally, you wanker; open the fucking door before I kick it in.'

Total silence. Perhaps the old bastard had dropped dead because he sure as hell would never have found anybody dumb enough to buy him out. Charlie decided to brave the mud and the long grass and approach the building from the back. He hadn't banked on the shopping trolley, the car chassis or the neatly bagged dog turds that were in vast abundance but he eventually made it to the rear of the building, working up a sweat on the way.

It was no better. The back entrance had a padlock the size of a tin of furniture polish holding it shut and a section of quarter inch steel sheet riveted into the face of the door to discourage anyone who fancied their chances with a sledge hammer. The tiny horizontal strips that passed for windows contained thick reinforced glass and were covered in a crust of dirt and enclosed by lethal looking pieces of rusted steel grill. How did daylight ever get into the building? It clearly didn't and presumably that suited the occupant admirably, allowing there was one still in existence.

Charlie returned to the front, doing his best to ignore the layer of thick, glutinous mud and dog shit that now coated his shoes and was starting to seep into his socks.

'Wally, it's Charlie Brinsworth from Bridgetown. Open the bloody door. I've not come to kill you; it's business.'

'What's my dog's name?' It was loud enough but came in more of a croak than a shout.

'Badger.'

'Why is it called badger?'

'Because the bloody animals got less fur on its body than you've got hairs on your head, you silly old sod. Now stop poncing about and open this bloody door, before I put my boot through it.'

A shuffling could be heard from within, followed by the sound of about three dozen locks and bolts being released. Then a very white face that would have given school children nightmares squeezed into the crack between door and frame.

'Quick, come in. You can't be too careful round here these days. I've got a lot of expensive equipment on these premises. Wipe your boots on the mat. I've been cleaning up all week as it is.'

Charlie entered, trying to breath as little as possible.

The inside of Wally's shop resembled a scrap yard; the kind that wasn't fussy about what it took because sooner or later it would all come in useful for something or other. He tried to spot the parts of the building Wally had spent all week cleaning up but his efforts proved unsuccessful. He decided it would be best to get through this bit of business as quickly as possible, before he died of asphyxiation or caught something not yet recognised by medical science.

'Where's Badger?'

'Died last year. A hundred and thirty in dog years. Brave as a lion, was Badger. Couldn't even get out for a shit towards the end but he never gave up. Hey, I hear you've been inside again. Told you, didn't I, when you hired that pneumatic drill the other year. Always catches up with you sooner or later. Lead a simple God-fearing life like me and you'll not go far wrong.'

Charlie cast his mind back. He had hired the drill at least ten years ago. He hoped it had been returned somewhere along the line or you could bet it would be in Wally's notebook and sooner or later he would end up being charged back rental.

'I want a magnetic tracker. Something with a decent radius that can be easily used from a moving car. What's the best you've got in stock? I need to take it home with me today. No invoice required.'

Suddenly Wally looked a lot happier. When the prospect of overcharging someone for an item he already had in stock presented itself it always lifted his spirits.

'Want a cup of tea while I check my stock? Magnetic trackers don't come cheap you know.'

'Forget the tea, Wally; find the tracker. The last time you made me a cup of tea I was on the bog half the night. You didn't bury Badger under that pile of shit in the corner did you?'

''Cause I didn't; don't be stupid.'

'Get yourself another dog, Wally; and make it a bloody big one. That heap of rubbish by the wall just moved a foot and a half of its own accord.'

When Charlie arrived back at the pub he was delighted to discover Wally had only charged him twice the price he could have purchased the unit for on the internet. He had also received a terse voicemail from Anthony Noone. *Same time, same place, tomorrow night.*

Right Mr Noone, tomorrow it is; and this time I'll arrive a lot better prepared.

CHAPTER FOURTEEN

SATURDAY 11th FEBRUARY 2017

'I think we might be distantly related,' said the middle aged man in the raincoat looking somewhat out of place in the confines of the bar. He was sipping tentatively at a half of bitter as if it might be laced with arsenic and Mickey had a funny feeling he could be some sort of Policeman. Though, in fairness he seemed a bit too mild mannered for that sort of job, so maybe he had got it wrong.

'My wife Miriam has you down as cousins; said she minded you on the odd occasion when you were a growing up.'

It had been a long day already and Mickey Smith really didn't need this. The bar had been reasonably busy early on but had now thinned out as people moved on to Saturday night venues with late night opening. He had briefly turned his mind to going round to Rachael's to await her return from the Casino; but Saturday was always a busy night at the Wellington and there was no real guarantee what time she would put in an appearance. Instead, he had decided to retreat to his room upstairs and watch a bit of football on the telly; though inevitably, he would once again find himself going over the plan in his head and trying to second guess any problems that might choose to present themselves, even if they only existed in his brain.

Now there was this; someone who seemed to be looking for a chat; someone he desperately wished would finish up his drink and go away. He had better say something to this bloke but what exactly did you say in a situation like this? It was true, there had been a cousin called Miriam in the family but he had no recollection of having seen her since he was out of short trousers. It wasn't as if they still exchanged Christmas cards or anything; as far as Mickey was concerned she might as well be dead; and even if that had been the case it was highly unlikely he would have received an invite to the funeral.

'Pleased to meet you Mr........'

'Loache, Daniel Loache. I'm a D.I. up at Eden Place. I think you know my Sergeant, Geoff Strickland. Great guy Geoff; salt of the earth.'

Mickey was immediately back in his stride; warm handshake; big smile. A copper in the family; that was certainly something to think about; even if this one appeared a rather unusual variety of the species. A Detective Inspector, no less; and the very one who was D.S. Strickland's boss. That must be worth something...........or possibly it wasn't. He had heard Strickland referenced as many things over the years but as far as he could remember *salt of the earth* had never been one of them.

'Business or pleasure, then I'll know whether to call you Daniel or Detective Inspector?' Big smile to let him know this was light-hearted banter and nothing to be taken seriously. 'How is Miriam these days? Haven't seen her in God knows how long.'

'She's doing fine, Mickey. We've got two girls of school age so she takes care of the house while I get kicked out of the door to keep the three of them in lipstick and mascara. She sends her regards.'

Well, wasn't this happy families? Miriam Smith, who he could walk past in the street without knowing it, was sending over her regards.

Although the smile had never left his face Mickey had been thinking all the time. Hadn't he heard some years back Miriam had been up to her neck in trouble? Booze or on the gear, he couldn't clearly remember which; someone had insinuated she put it about for England, he remembered; and he had taken it upon himself to make sure they didn't say it twice. They might not have seen each other for donkey's years but Miriam was still family and that had to stand for something. Anyway, this was all a

71

very long time ago, so maybe he had got it all wrong, which was more than possible, with the stuff he currently had whizzing round his head.

'Good to hear it, Mr Loache. You need to get a sitter and drag your old lady over one of these nights. It's been so long I'm not even sure I'd recognise her.'

'She's still a striking looking woman, even if I say so myself, Mickey. It's difficult with the job, as you'll understand, but I'll pass on your kind invitation. This place is looking good; have you had it redecorated?'

'Just a quick tidy up. I like to keep on top of things decoration-wise.'

Mickey sensed it was coming. Loache had started to look thoughtful; like he was trying to find the words. Any minute now the real reason for his visit was going to be made common knowledge. That would be good because he was beginning to get an aching jaw from smiling inanely across the bar at someone who didn't seem to slot comfortably into any of the usual categories.

'Anyway the reason I put my head in tonight was to warn you to be extra vigilant over the next week or two. As I think my D.S. has already informed you there is a possibility of gang activity in the area and whilst we are trying to ensure it comes to nothing we are currently a little short on numbers. There were minor disruptions at The Flag and The Happy Hound last night and Geoff Strickland thinks it quite likely you might get paid a visit sooner or later; he's got a good nose for this sort of thing has my D.S., so it's worth taking precautions. We'll have extra uniformed policemen on the streets of course but......well; you know how it is, what with the cutbacks and stuff.'

'As you can see I've got a bouncer on the door and we actively discourage anyone who we feel might be looking for trouble. I'll keep on my toes though. Thanks for the warning, Daniel.'

'It was actually Miriam who prompted me to call in. I was talking shop and she asked that I made sure you were fully aware of the current situation. She remembers you with great affection. Said you were a very happy child; always smiling.'

'Well thank her for keeping me in mind. Hey, I just thought of something. Whatever became of her brother; bit of a lad if I remember........Gerald, was it?'

Obviously not a welcome subject. Loache's face dropped like stone and he quickly finished his drink and belted his raincoat.

'Gabriel,' he said, already turning on his heels. 'He went abroad a very long time ago and he and Miriam completely lost contact,' and within seconds the Detective Inspector had crossed the floor and disappeared out of the door.

CHAPTER FIFTEEN

SATURDAY 11th FEBRUARY 2017

8.17 PM.

As Anthony Noone left the Egret public house he briefly conferred with a tall, rotund man with short cropped hair, dressed in a dark suit. They straightway proceeded to the pub's car-park with Noone leading the way. Wasting no time Noone clambered into a blue-grey Rover, turned the key in the ignition and gunned the throttle. He quickly turned onto the roadway and was lost from sight, heading in an easterly direction. The man in the dark suit turned on his heels and hurried towards the back of the parking area; he was immediately hidden from sight.

Charlie Brinsworth's face dropped as he watched this outcome from the security of the pub's doorway. The tracker he had gone to such lengths to acquire had been secreted on the Honda 4 x 4 that Noone had been driving when he arrived. His plan was already in shreds and there wasn't a single thing he could do about it.

As Charlie continued to stare in the direction of the road, the Honda Noone had been driving earlier hove into view. It quickly crossed the tarmac and parked in front of the main entrance, thereby prohibiting access in or out of the parking area. Seconds later a white stretch limousine lumbered forward but found it was impossible to make its way onto the outside road due to the Honda driver's blocking manoeuvre.

The driver of the limousine honked a warning but this was duly ignored; a moment later this was followed by a continuous blast from the horn which received a similar lack of attention. When this action failed to fulfil its purpose, the driver, a short, thin woman dressed in a patterned purple jumpsuit that swamped her like a potato sack, moved from behind the wheel to remonstrate with the driver of the Honda, who duly lowered the window of his car in order to better engage in the debate. Charlie was unsurprised to see the man in the offending vehicle was of a bulky build, had short cropped hair and appeared to be wearing a dark coloured suit.

At this point a campervan arrived at the car-park entrance but found it impossible to gain entry into the parking area due to the vehicle blockade being mounted by the stationary Honda. This vehicle's driver also seemed somewhat unimpressed by the situation and duly resorted to tooting his horn.

In the meantime the discussion between the lady dressed in the purple sack and the Honda driver appeared to have reached something of an impasse; so much so, that the man in the suit found it desirable to vacate his motor vehicle in order to further develop the theme of his argument.

By now, both parties had become somewhat agitated and allowed themselves to be drawn into some severe vilification. This Charlie could clearly hear despite being a good twenty five metres from the scene of the action.

'Get back in your oversized pimpmobile you old bat or I'll see that you finish your shift in A & E. I'll move this car when I'm good and fucking ready.'

'Get that heap of scrap metal out of my way you fat, arrogant twat unless you want me to move it for you.'

A short pause ensued while the combatants glared at one another. Then the lady dressed in purple robes, clearly feeling vexed that the announcement of her intentions had failed to solicit the required response, threw her full seven and a half stone bodyweight in the direction of the door of the Honda which swung back sharply, hitting the dark suited man in the area of the knees. As he collapsed forward she forced the car door back open and kicked him in the lower stomach area; before proceeding to render him unconscious with a head butt that redistributed large quantities of his nose to a variety of different locations.

Then, with surprisingly little difficulty she eased the semi recumbent figure back inside the vehicle, leaned across and loosened the hand brake; before, as a parting gesture, giving the steering wheel a sharp yank in an anticlockwise direction. As she vacated the vehicle with a nifty backward hop the car could be seen to quickly gather speed as it careered down the open road; its progress coming to a dramatic halt only when it failed to negotiate a sharp corner, causing it to make loud contact with a dry-stone wall. The purple clad maiden then slowly retraced her steps, re-entered her shiny limousine, touched up her makeup in the driving mirror and wiped her hands and face delicately with some sheets of pink tissue. She then drove off at considerable speed looking as if she wasn't going to lose any sleep over what had just occurred.

The campervan driver sat for some seconds with his mouth open, clearly completely aghast. Once he had taken stock of the situation he quickly cancelled his blinking indicator, engaged first gear and sped up the road in the opposite direction to that taken by the female aggressor. Doubtless in search of a more convivial hostelry at which to purchase the liquid sustenance he now so clearly required.

9.24 AM.

Charlie had wanted to set his plan in motion in plenty of time. He telephoned Simon Bartol and advised him he would need an anonymous looking car and a driver for that night; then filled him in on a list of ancillary requirements. Once Bartol knew it was a paying job he listened carefully and made a number of suggestions.

'Charlie, I'm not telling you how to run this operation but if you are laying on a tail it's better to go for the unexpected. The obvious is what the mark will be looking for so think outside the box. Why don't you just leave it up to me? I do this sort of thing for a living.'

'That's fine by me. Just make sure the driver is smart

76

and shit hot at driving. He will also need to be able to handle himself. I'm still not sure which way this is likely to go. Oh, and forget Keith Woods. I still can't place the bastard but that alone makes me nervous.'

'No problem, Big Bird is sharp enough to understand anything a shithead like you can come up with; anyone who used to work the front door at Mulligan's isn't going to work up a sweat over a little run out in the country. What time do you want to be away from here? I'll need to make a couple of calls. '

7.15 PM.

The drive out to the Egret had again been uneventful. The driver of the second car had kept a steady fifty metres in Charlie's wake for the entire journey. Now he needed to do the briefing and make absolutely certain that what he required to happen was clearly understood. He winced; he really wasn't at all convinced about this but Simon had staked his reputation on a satisfactory outcome so he had reluctantly agreed.

'No need to talk; just listen. In about fifteen minutes a tall skinny bloke of about forty with back combed hair who looks like he should be carrying a shotgun under his arm that hasn't had the barrels sawn off is going to arrive in this car-park. I'm betting that he won't be alone so keep an eye out for a second car. You know how the tracker works so when the coast is clear stick it under the back bumper of the bloke's car. When he reappears you follow him and get back to me by text with an address once he arrives back home. If another car is involved I'll try to hold it back but don't bank on anything going to plan so keep your wits about you. If anything goes wrong then improvise because you can bet your boots I won't have a clue what to do. There's a bonus if this works out and it's between you and me so Simon doesn't need to know anything about it. Now, have you got all that or do you want me to run through it again?'

The pitying look he received in reply cut through Charlie like a knife.

4.48 PM.

'You are fucking joking?'

Apparently he wasn't. Simon Bartol gave a reassuring smile and placed his arm around Charlie's shoulder in the manner of a supportive comrade.

'Charlie, just relax and have a little faith. She's one of the best I have ever worked with.'

'Please tell me this is a wind-up, Simon. Big Bird? I've eaten turkeys bigger than her for Christmas dinner, then gone back for seconds.'

'Don't let her size fool you; she's handy if anything kicks off. You don't get to do the door at Mulligan's if you are nervous about chipping your nail varnish. Those Paddies aren't easy to keep in line after a skinfull.'

'Even if I take your word on that one, what about the wheels? This is meant to be a discreet tailing job. I didn't ask if you could provide transport for driving a Hen Party to Blackpool for a pre-nuptial piss-up. The way I see it, someone is taking the piss.'

'Think about it. If the tracking device doesn't work out then what could be better? Nobody in their right mind uses a stretch limousine for a tailing job so the mark will automatically discount it as a possibility. She's got a tape in the limo' she puts on full blast with twenty odd drunken middle aged women singing *I will survive*. It's one of the most frightening sounds I've heard in my entire life. Trust me; nobody will look at her twice; it's the best cover anybody could ask for.'

'Alright, I suppose there's not much I can do about it now, but I can tell you one thing for sure, I ain't fucking happy. I suppose I had better give her a run through on how the tracker works. You're not holding anything else back, are you? She does speak English, I suppose?'

9.27 PM.

Text received by Charlie Brinsworth.
Address is 14, Mount Drive, Thorton Chumley.
He drives like a tosser, your poncy mate. I was on his back bumper two miles down the road. How do I collect the bonus you promised? Don't make me come over unless you've got readies. I never take cheques.
B.B.

CHAPTER SIXTEEN

SUNDAY 12th FEBRUARY 2017

Charlie woke early, rolled over, remembered the events of the previous evening and immediately sat bolt upright. There were things that needed his attention so he had better get his arse in gear.

First he phoned Simon Bartol and dragged him out of bed. That call would perhaps have been better left until later in the day but Charlie didn't want it playing on his mind. Simon had been right and he had been wrong so he needed to mend a few fences.

The call didn't go anywhere near as well as Charlie might have hoped. Simon Bartol had only got to bed at 4am after being involved in some clandestine after hour activities that he was reluctant to discuss. This had been Mr Bartol's first chance of a decent lay-in in weeks and Charlie had effectively ruined it. Charlie stuttered out an apology and got off the phone as quickly as possible hoping he hadn't put his foot in it still further with the irate Mr Bartol.

Next thing, he needed to check out Thorton Chumley on the map. He knew roughly where it was; little more than three or four miles south east as the crow flies but quite difficult to get to by road. He also needed to get himself over there today because it was the sort of place where people often took walks after their Sunday lunch and if he dressed up in the right sort of gear he would blend in neatly with the crowd.

On a weekday it would be a totally different matter. Unless he could pass himself off as a builder or a painter he would stick out like a sore thumb. Everybody would know everybody else in that sort of village; who belonged on their hallowed turf and who didn't. Charlie had been born with the wrong sort of face to wander round places like that and look anything other than totally out of place.

So that was the afternoon taken care of and what he now needed to do with the rest of this morning was run back over the information he had gleaned from Anthony Noone. Charlie tore a tissue in half, stuffed a piece in each ear, and pressed the play button on the part of his brain that stored recent recollections; hoping it worked better than the section responsible for long term stuff, which gave the impression it was out of order.

Noone had arrived pretty promptly at seven thirty and been followed into the bar a few minutes later by a hefty character without much hair, dressed in a dark suit. The look of this bloke had immediately put Charlie on alert. You could smell hired muscle a mile away. A quick appraisal and Charlie reached the conclusion that whilst he might be big and dressed for the occasion he probably wasn't a hardened professional. The way he took in the rest of the bar while being careful not to look in Charlie's direction smacked of amateur's night out.

He and Noone had retreated to a couple of aged armchairs separated by a small coffee table The window seat they had used last time was occupied by a couple who must have been married as they didn't appear to exchange a single word for the entire duration of their visit.

Noone was drinking whiskey this time, Charlie noted. He hadn't looked like a beer drinker from the off and whatever he chose to order Charlie had no intention of standing him a refill. The man in the suit remained at the bar, sucking on a frosted glass of lager or one of those shitty cider concoctions that were currently enjoying their fifteen minutes of fame before they disappeared down life's ever open plughole.

'Where did I get to?' enquired Anthony Noone theatrically.

Charlie ignored the question. Young Anthony would have prepared for this moment in front of the mirror for several hours if he was any judge.

'Remember my father?'

Charlie took a mouthful from his glass. Mr Noone would get started in his own good time and the bitter he was drinking had a pleasant hoppy sort of taste so he was in no particular hurry. He took the opportunity to steal a quick glance out of the window but as far as he could see there was no sign of activity in the parking area. He hoped the slight figure in the purple jumpsuit was more useful than she looked but he wasn't holding his breath.

'I think I might have slightly misled you on one point at our previous discussion. You remember me telling you that father was a little late returning to these shores following the surrender of the Axis forces at the end of the war? It wasn't due to extended war service as I previously intimated; the old boy was in prison.'

So Noone's old man was a wrong 'un. Charlie probably would have had more in common with Noone senior than his toffee nosed git of a son.

'Germany didn't officially surrender until 1945 but the Italians had waved a white flag when Mussolini made a run for it more than eighteen months before that happened. There followed a period of utter confusion. Some Italians effectively changed sides; a few went on fighting; most just laid down their arms and tried to get back home. There was a state of complete chaos in the country which lasted for years; and when it comes to a state of chaos, the Italians are absolute masters of the requirements. At some stage my father used the prevailing circumstances to set himself up in business.......and the business, it appeared, was highly illegal.'

Noone wasn't bad at this. There would probably have been a career in it if Jackanory had still been running on children's television.

'I don't know any detail of his business activities other than the fact it involved the Black Market. Pharmaceuticals possibly, maybe guns or liquor, even food. Take your pick; there was a shortage of pretty much everything, so I have been informed. I don't even know if his partners were English or Italian. The only detail that's relevant as far as this discussion is concerned, is that the old boy kept his mouth shut when he was nabbed. He remained completely silent from the moment he was charged and throughout the entire court procedure. It seems like a deal had been struck that if he took the rap for the illegal activity then there would be adequate compensation made available once he was released. If that was what he was offered, then it looked like he signed up for the deal, because he never said a word to the authorities; and being an Englishman incarcerated in Italy at that particular time, following a dishonourable discharge, wouldn't have been anyone's idea of a great deal of fun.

Sorry, another thing I might have failed to mention, the old man was judged by many to have got off with an extremely light sentence. Possibly he had the right sort of people pulling strings on his behalf. If he had rich friends on the outside maybe he was similarly looked after once he was behind bars. I'm afraid I don't know the answer to that one either, though it seems quite possible it might have been the case. I think, unquestionably, some pretty important people had been involved in the caper........but again, I have no specific detail so anything further would just be idle speculation. And that is about all I can tell you. In précis form, that is how my father came into possession of the money he used to start his business in this country when he eventually made it home after the war.'

It was the same as the other night. Another interesting story that didn't seem to be leading anywhere. Charlie took another pull on his pint and awaited developments.

'You will have read about the local library?' Now he was into his stride Noone seemed keen to quickly push on.

'No.'

'Rebecca Hinchliffe? The mad woman from the town hall who is a country mile left of Lenin? The Central Library in town that was sold to the Chinese to turn into a hotel?'

'Look, I've been behind bars for the last two and a half years and believe it or not the sale of a Library in a neighbouring city is not the prime topic of conversation when you are sat staring at a bowl of congealed porridge. Just spell it out then I might have a hope of understanding what the hell you are talking about.'

'Rebecca Hinchliffe is the mad cow who currently presides over the fortunes of the local Town Council. She sold the Central Library to a Chinese consortium to bankroll one of her lunatic schemes. I don't know which one; she comes up with fresh ideas with alarming regularity and each one is crazier than the one before.'

It amused Charlie that Noone looked genuinely annoyed. Was he perhaps involved in politics himself? Christ alone knew the answer to that one.

'Marsh Lane Works,' said Noone, as if that explained everything.

'What?'

'That's what was designated as the new location of the old Central Library that had been sold to the Chinese. The daft cow had to have something to offer to her adoring public as a replacement, didn't she? Even the dumb arsed voters from round here wouldn't have let her get away with selling off the family silver without providing something in return. She couldn't just throw the books on a bonfire. She's not Stalin, let alone Hitler; well, not yet anyway.'

'I'm sorry, Anthony, I have no fucking idea what you are talking about.'

'That's where it is; the safe. That was my father's centre of operations before he was kicked out onto the street by the asset strippers.'

'Sorry to come over as a bit thick but just let me see if I've got it straight. Your father ran his business from Marsh Lane and that building went through the hands of asset strippers and is now owned by the Council who are using it as a library?'

'Is there another language you might find easier to understand, Charlie? Isn't that what I've just been telling you? The idiot woman sold the building in town on the basis the Marsh Lane site was ideal as a replacement library because the surrounding area is one of the poorest districts in the city and has one of the lowest literacy rates.'

'So you want me to break into a Municipal building, open a safe and steal........steal what precisely?'

'I can't tell you that Charlie because if I did you would know as much as I do; and if that were the case, what would you need me for?'

'Look at it another way; suppose I just got a team together and went over to Marsh Lane Works and broke in? I would suspect that someone could tell me where the place is and I'm sure somewhere in my address book there will be the name of a person who could crack open a safe that's over fifty years old even if it is Italian. I would also lay a bet that once I got it open I could recognise what was worth stealing and what wasn't. You might as well tell me the rest; you've already come too far to start being coy.'

'You would be wasting your time, Charlie. Even if I drew you a map and gave you the combination to the safe right this very minute it would prove of no help whatever. You could waltz in the front entrance and throw open the doors and you would find nothing that would prove of the slightest interest. Sorry, that's always assuming you don't get your jollies out of pocketing a few pounds that might have been taken in library fines.'

'If I accept that, why the hell have you dragged me all the way out here to have this conversation?'

'Two reasons, Charlie. The person who put me on to you said you were half way straight; and if you shook hands on a deal you wouldn't backtrack once an agreement was made. And secondly he said you wouldn't be able to resist the fee which I'm prepared to pay for your services, which will be one hundred thousand pounds. So, now you know how things stand it's your call; are we going to shake on a deal or not?'

CHAPTER SEVENTEEN

SUNDAY 12th FEBRUARY 2017

Mickey Smith was loitering behind the bar of the Black Bear twiddling his thumbs. It was twelve o'clock midday and the weather outside was as bleak as many would have predicted for this time of year. The lunchtime staff had all arrived but the anticipated Sunday rush to knock back a few pints before getting to grips with a roast beef dinner had failed to materialise. The weather seemed to have had the final word on that one.

The front door to the pub eased open and Henry, Rachael's aged downstairs neighbour, eased himself into the bar area looking like he would be happier if he were heading in the opposite direction. Henry ordered a pint of mild, replied with a couple of monosyllabic grunts to Mickey's best opening lines and stood there looking a picture of pure misery. He then reached into the inside pocket of his well-worn tweed overcoat and presented Mickey with an envelope; before hastily retreating in the direction of the back door; feeling in his jacket pocket for his tobacco pouch before he had completed the first half dozen strides.

Mickey surveyed the envelope, studied the writing and knew immediately what to expect. He took a deep breath, retreated to the far end of the bar and extracted a single sheet of notepaper.

Mickey, I'm out of here.

You are a great bloke and our time together has been wonderful but now I need to do something different.

It's so difficult because I don't want to hurt you but know that I can't avoid it. It has been wonderful to be loved. Great to be with someone who made me feel special but also very safe. Terrific to find a man, who, whatever the circumstances, always put me before anything else.

You were exactly what I needed when we got together but you are not what I need right now. I want to travel and see new things. I want to be on my own so I can make mistakes; if I am honest some will probably be with men who will never be as good or as kind as you are, but that's still what I have to do.

Please don't try to find me. This way it is perfect; for me if not for you....and I don't want anything to ruin the memory of you that I will always cherish.

If I had any sense I would ask you to wait for me for six months or even a year because it will probably all go wrong and then I could come running back and tell you I had been a fool and beg for your forgiveness. I'm not asking for that, my love. In fact I'm telling you just the opposite. I don't want any sort of safety net because that would make it too easy for me to fall off the tightrope and still survive.....and I know in my heart I can never come back because it would be the wrong thing for both of us.

Have a happy life Mickey Smith and please know there will always be a place for you in my heart.

I haven't disgraced you. I paid the rent up to date. I told Martin at the Wellington I was leaving so he could sort out a replacement. (She better not be as good as me or I will be really miffed!) I wrote Henry a note and asked him to act as messenger. Pure cowardice, I'm afraid. If I faced you I know I would end up backing down and crying all over your nice clean shirt. I also know that wouldn't be the best thing for either of us in the long run.

With all my Love,

Rachael

Mickey pushed the optic on the whiskey bottle enough times to fill most of a spirit glass and tracked Henry to the smoking area in the pub's backyard. Their eyes met but neither said a word. Mickey had never understood the description of feeling numb after a break up but he sure as hell felt pretty damn numb at this precise moment. He reached for a plastic chair, knocked off a couple of slivers of ice and pulled it nearer to the damp wooden table.

Henry looked like a dog that had lost its bone. He slipped Mickey an expertly tailored roll up, threw back the dregs of his pint and padded off, mumbling something about getting together at a happier time for a chat over a pot of tea. They both knew that was never going to happen but Mickey dredged up a weak smile from somewhere, which he followed up with a half-hearted wave.

Bloody women! He had put everything into this relationship with Rachael; tried for once to do everything right instead of making it up as he went along. Yet it still looked like he had been successful only in totally misjudging the situation. He hadn't been unfaithful; not once in the whole time they had been together. Even when temptation had presented itself on a plate he had somehow managed to go against character and resist getting involved. He could honestly say with hand on heart that from the day they first got together he had always tried to do the right thing; and a lot of bloody good it had done him.

He had made sure to remember her birthday and the timing of anniversaries and stuff like that. He had always arrived on time for dates with suitably extravagant bunches of flowers and had even taken to wearing a jacket and properly pressed trousers instead of jeans when they were going out somewhere a bit special. Added to which, he had stopped going round to Stephanie Armitage's place so regularly, recognising that whilst Stevie was a lot of fun she could also be something of a bad influence. He had reasoned this would also help to avoid Rachael misinterpreting the relationship he enjoyed with Stevie and maybe end up getting the wrong end of the stick. All in all he couldn't think of a lot more he could possibly have done.

He dragged deeply on Henry's industrial strength cigarette, drinking in the feeling of pure solitude that hurt worse than any physical pain he could ever remember. Where did he go from here? Why hadn't he seen it coming? What could he possibly have done differently?

The thing that really surprised him was that he did not feel the slightest sense of relief. No feeling that somehow a weight of responsibility had just been eased off his shoulders. No sense that he had now regained the freedom to be the old Mickey Smith who was up for a laugh and didn't give a hoot about anybody or anything. He had been in this sort of situation before......of course he had; it was an intrinsic part of life's pattern......but when relationships had previously come to a conclusion his sadness had always been tinged with a sense that he had been slightly fortunate at the way things had ultimately worked out; an escape from the gallows; a reprieve from a life sentence at the eleventh hour. This felt completely different. He had been totally committed to this relationship and now felt genuinely distraught; and for him it was a whole new experience.

No doubt, in time he would get over it; though at the moment he felt too raw to believe that could actually be true. It was his fault for playing the knight in shining armour. Love 'em and leave 'em tactics had always worked just fine for him in the past and he should never have abandoned a winning formula. What did he do now? He didn't like the empty feeling in the pit of his stomach one little bit.

Bugger the lot of them! Mickey Smith would come through it because that is what Mickey Smith bloody well did. He would survive with a broad grin on his face as well, because there was no way he was sharing his feeling of pain with anybody else. It felt too agonising for that.

He needed to find some sort of consolation to give him something positive to hang on to. That was easier said than done. Well, alright, there was at least a small something to get him started. Now Rachael was no longer part of the equation there would be no need to go ahead with the cockeyed plan he and Stevie had devised to make him a wealthy man. There wasn't going to be any sort of future that needed that sort of money; not with Rachael, that was for sure; and probably after this experience not with anybody else. He could at least take that as some sort of plus, be it a very minor one.

Yes, if he wasn't about to play happy families then he could take his bat home and bring the game to a shuddering conclusion. Totally abandon the scheme to stab his old mate Charlie neatly between the shoulder blades. Charlie Brinsworth, the one person who had always looked out for him and never really done him anything but good.

Well, that at least took one hell of a weight off his mind. He hadn't felt right about that little number right from the start and with Rachael now out of the picture he was under no pressure to continue with the idiotic plan for one minute longer.

Despite the feeling of shock still pulsing through his system, Mickey felt slightly comforted by this realisation. What he had been planning made no real sense anyway and it made him feel good inside to think he could now turn his back on the whole ridiculous plot before any real harm had been done.

The only thing he couldn't yet silence was the nagging voice at the back of his head that even at this early stage was doing everything in its power to gain his attention. The urgent whisper that was telling him that just because the situation had changed a little, that was no good reason to abandon the plan. The insistent undertone seeking to persuade him that it didn't very much matter that Rachael had packed her bags; because the way things currently stood a heap of used bank notes would prove very useful in helping to carve out a brand new career; and maybe even open the doors to a totally different future. A future that after this experience he would be prepared to grab with both hands.

CHAPTER EIGHTEEN

SUNDAY 12th FEBRUARY 2017

It was pretty much as Charlie had anticipated. The day was cold with snow flurries in the air; but even as the thin winter light faded behind the nearby hills the village of Thorton Chumley could still quite easily have been mistaken for an out-take from the filming of a Barbour advertisement.

There they were, the British middle classes in all their glory, yomping along without a care in the world. Adults not weighed down by haversacks were being ridden mercilessly by small children carrying sticks with which to encourage their flagging steeds into greater efforts. The next generation seated in majestic splendour in their metal framed baby-carriers with faces aglow; their small mouths protruding from betwixt a conflagration of soft wool and fur that would have been welcomed by an expedition exploring the inner reaches of the Arctic circle; their breath emerging from cherubic little mouths like steam from a boiling kettle, instantly to be whipped away by the strong north easterly that blew with unrelenting force down the cobbled carriageway that gave the village its smack of charm and character. Mothers bringing up the rear, dragging older siblings from hedgerows and puddles of glutinous mud that attracted them like the Sirens that haunted the mythological seas of old; as they attempted valiantly to achieve the impossible and still look vaguely glamorous with a force seven whistling unforgivingly through the same hair that Raymondo or Gervais had toiled over so diligently barely twenty four hours previously.

Charlie leaned on a dry stone wall that might have been constructed hundreds of years ago by rural labourers earning little more than a few pence a day and wondered what they would have made of it all; before burping loudly and coming to the conclusion that whatever that might have been, he didn't give a toss. He reengaged with the task at hand, deftly lobbed the polystyrene box that had only moments before been home to a rancid beef-burger into a nearby hedgerow, and strode off like a man who knew precisely what needed to be done.

Mount Drive was a cul-de-sac situated several hundred yards further down the same roadway. Past the small cafe that had been careful to close its doors several hours before those in the direst need of sustenance would ever be given the opportunity to darken its doors. Further even than the tiny inn that appeared to scowl out at the world through leaded windows, so thick they might have been glazed with the bottoms of milk bottles.

As Charlie walked on more became evident. Now he could see the general layout more plainly it became patently clear the houses and shops had been cleverly constructed in a defensive formation. And that, well dug in with plenty of ammunition and supplies, the residents would now feel they were in a position to stage something of a last stand. Nicely positioned to battle to the last against unwanted intrusion until the last drops of their blood mingled with the soil that their families had tilled for generation upon generation. Recognising that retreat was not an option because in this day and age where else was there to go? And recognising in their hearts the cruellest fact of all; that the most fearsome assault could be expected from their age-old, natural enemy; those who they loathed worst of all but despite all their years of trying had never truly managed to overcome. The unspeakable hordes of townies who, laden with thermos flasks and hampers had travelled out from the nearby city, situated barely three miles distant.

Charlie could picture the local population nervously lodged, behind locked doors and shuttered windows, spurring themselves to remain ever vigilant; because at any moment, those self-same enemies might be gathering their forces and preparing to institute a merciless frontal assault. Starting out from the aged sign post at the unobtrusive turnoff, then marching along the rutted cart-track by the north field and right into the very heart of their beloved hamlet. And being fully aware that come the dreaded hour, whilst the valour of their troops would not be in question, numbers would clearly be against them and courage alone might prove not enough.

Charlie shook his head. His mind was wandering. Taking this much exercise with only a beef-burger for sustenance obviously did not agree with him. Something more substantial was required before he became delirious. No wonder they said armies marched on their stomachs.

Regardless, he steeled himself and marched on with cobbles underfoot and half an eye scanning the windswept, bleak surroundings. Why anybody would voluntarily undertake this sort of privation on a freezing Sunday afternoon was beyond his comprehension.

As he cast his eyes in all directions one thing immediately became evident. The reason why the farthest reaches of this rural idol had been so carefully masked from prying eyes was quickly apparent to even an untrained eye. The mixture of four bedroomed, detached houses and large squat bungalows committed the two cardinal sins that even a newcomer of merely three or four generations might have recognised as totally unforgivable. Firstly all the dwellings were constructed of London brick instead of rough-hewn stone; and secondly, they had clearly been erected for less than three centuries and in consequence could not have been intended by the good Lord to have any place in the architectural heritage of this part of the countryside. To people who had been sharpening their scythes in this locality since before the Norman Conquest the new-builds very existence must have come like a metropolitan slap in the face.

Charlie reached his destination and settled himself astride a cunningly disguised grit bin at the top of a deserted stretch of pristine tarmac. He had never been a great lover of cul-de-sacs and felt the one he was now looking down was unlikely to persuade him to substantially alter his viewpoint on the subject. It was impossible to have a valid excuse to enter a road that didn't lead anywhere on a freezing Sunday afternoon unless you lived on it or were visiting somebody; and as he suspected every mortal in a five mile radius would be able to immediately identify a bona fide resident of Thorton Chumley at fifty paces, and he had no claim to kinship with anyone in this vicinity, the situation was far from ideal.

His dilemma was eventually solved by the emergence of two figures from the hostelry down the road who staggered uncertainly in his direction. Charlie made efforts to waylay them before they took the branch road which lead to open country. The men looked sufficiently inbred to qualify as nearby residents and gave the impression of having drunk enough not to take undue offence if the fact was drawn to their attention; however, quite possibly subtlety would prove a better ploy. The pair looked vaguely like the sort of farm labourer you saw in old photographs at a museum or who popped up on the television advertising whole wheat breakfast cereals that were highly nutritious and good for the bowels. One was old and the other quite young but they were dressed in exactly the same manner and if you had hidden their faces it would have been very difficult to differentiate between the pair on the basis of anything else.

'Oi! I'm trying to trace an Anthony Noone and I was told he lived on this road. Any idea which house that might be?'

A look of deep suspicion. They were tempted closer and Charlie offered round his cigarettes. A look of even deeper suspicion, but they accepted one anyway. The younger man considered then spoke.

'We live up at the farm. We don't have a lot to do with the newcomers.'

'Number fourteen looked a bit familiar but I'm not

94

really sure.'

'No, it won't be fourteen. That's the Garfield house. The son lives there now. The old fella passed away a while back......God rest his soul. He used to take a trailer load of manure every year, the old man, but the son don't seem bothered about the condition of his soil.'

Charlie said a silent prayer. Even though it was Sunday he hadn't been banking on help from above.

'Any idea of his Christian name?'

'Don't think he is a Christian. Leastways, never seen him in church of a Sunday. Can't mistake him though; looks miserable as buggery and thin like he ain't taken a bite since Christmas.'

CHAPTER NINETEEN

MONDAY 13th FEBRUARY 2017

Stephanie Armitage wandered aimlessly around her Gallery looking again at the miscellaneous assortment of object d'art she had cast her eyes over a hundred times before. She was bored; and that was where Mickey Smith had a place in her life because Mickey was a lot of things, but boring had never been one of them.

How they had ever managed to stay in touch was something of a minor miracle. Stephanie was already on her third husband and had travelled several times around the globe. For a time she had been a top glamour model; this year's face; an '*it girl*'; at a time when being one of those was an open passport to fame and fortune without any great need to let it drastically interfere with your social life. If you drank instead of ate nobody appeared to be overly concerned and if the drugs made your eyes appear somewhat unfocussed they also helped to keep your weight in check, so that wasn't all bad either. Then she had been swept up by the racing driver who preferred being stoned to driving round in ever decreasing circles on the same piece of track; later followed by the investment banker who it transpired was a good deal better at handling other people's money than he was with his own. Now she had moved on to a management consultant, who seemed to spend most of his time consulting with bright young things in short skirts who had come into an inheritance and needed a bit of guidance in how to manage it; many of whom he was able to steer towards the bedroom door with an annoying lack of effort.

Stephanie had always been attracted to total shits but it was a habit she should have weaned herself away from a very long time ago. The trouble was total shits tended to be more interesting; well, in the early days, at least.

In consolation for her marital shortcomings, she now had the gallery. She had always had an eye even when she hadn't got two half pennies to rub together and over the years that small talent had stood her in good stead. Even now, while the market was being optimistically described as 'a shade apprehensive', she had managed to turn over a reasonable profit and along the way she had racked up more than her fair share of minor triumphs. Ziggy wasn't ungenerous either. Shagging nubile heiresses was extremely lucrative so it seemed. Added to which, she had of course come away from her first two trips up the aisle not exactly bereft of funds.

It was frequently pointed out by her girlfriends who had secured substantially better divorce settlements that she should have hired a top Lawyer and gone for the jugular; that the pay-outs she had accepted should in this day and age be regarded as totally inadequate. After all, hadn't she abandoned a top modelling career in the cause of true love?

Well, in all honesty, no she hadn't. She had entered into both relationships with her eyes wide open and it was probably more her fault than the ex-husbands' that the marriages hadn't worked out. She wasn't very good with men if they didn't do what she wanted and she was aware this constituted poor ingredients when it came to a recipe for happy coexistence. The depressing part was that despite two abject failures she had still managed to follow up with a third man cut from exactly the same cloth; and it was equally obvious that a woman with any degree of sense would have already let Ziggy go the same way as his predecessors.

But somehow she couldn't. In her own way she was strangely fond of Ziggy, even though she couldn't believe a word he said. He appreciated her for what she was and never attempted to smother her. They both needed their own space and the appreciation of this requirement was a rare commodity where men were concerned. Besides, if she ditched Ziggy she would undoubtedly end up with someone a good deal worse.

Mickey Smith had by comparison done very little with his life and travelled almost nowhere. His solitary obsession had always been to run a two bit pub in the way the great impresarios constructed a Broadway show that was intended to leave the audience crying out for more. Mickey was a person who knew his place in life; and in his case, Mickey was convinced that place was grinning out a false welcome from behind a well ordered bar.

In truth they had very little in common. They had only met because they had grown up as next door neighbours. Her family from a line of bankers, painfully decent and proud to be members of the upper middle class; Mickey's, shopkeepers, who had pulled themselves up by their bootstraps, delighted that the fruits of their labour had seen them climb a little higher in the social hierarchy than at the outset had seemed entirely possible. Both fathers had been members of the Rotary club and they rubbed along nicely together; the mothers took tea, baked and ran their two houses as something of a joint enterprise. Pies and cakes had passed back and forth over the back fence, though when they entered through the front door you could guarantee it was with neatly brushed hair and no evidence of a gravy stain on the front of an immaculately ironed blouse.

Stevie hadn't really noticed Mickey until he was twelve. Although there was only a bit more than two year's difference in their ages it was at that time an unbridgeable chasm. She would probably have gone on not noticing the little monster as well if she hadn't been forced into acting as his child minder. Mickey was a total nightmare; twelve going on sixteen with a premature interest in girls in general and her in particular. She still shuddered at the lunges he had made at her at every opportunity. Mickey had always maintained she broke his heart; but he said it with that big grin he always had firmly in place; the one that everybody but her found impossible to resist.

So they kept in touch; saw each other at Christmases and family gatherings; then later at the succession of funerals as their parents one by one shuffled off to seek admittance at St Peter's celestial gate. He had always been there for her she had to admit; though usually with a hand on her bottom and an indecent proposal not far from his lips. She had kept him in touch with the career that had briefly blossomed, the places she had seen and the things she had done; and latterly the succession of unsatisfactory husbands and lovers who came and went like confetti in the wind. He, in turn, told her every detail about his dratted pub!

They had only really hooked up again when she had snagged husband number three and returned to the city of her birth to oversee the purchase and renovation of the gallery. At the time her hometown had been a cheap place to buy which provided good access to other major cities; and there was the advantage that moving back to somewhere with which she was already familiar would mean that she wouldn't need to waste time familiarising herself with the locality. In the early days Ziggy had been quite the enthusiast about the project as well, but like most things with Ziggy, that had lasted all of five minutes. Mickey however was made of sterner stuff; he had been a frequent caller, usually with some word of encouragement, or, more usually, a lunatic suggestion that was bound to earn her a fortune, the details of which would often have her weeping tears of laughter.

However, the best bit was the stuff they got up to when they judged they were off duty and in need of a laugh. They had always got on socially, probably because they shared the same sense of humour; and as soon as Mickey could be tempted away from his God awful pub he went through something of a transition. Mr Serious disappeared straight out of the window to be quickly replaced with Mr Up-For-Anything-Going.

They had done a lot of stuff that was better forgotten. Stupid things which had proved a lot of fun. In one year alone they had convinced an anally retentive front bencher that in order to swing an O.B.E. all he needed was to make a five figure donation to a charity supporting dolphin conservation. They had shut down the local Town Hall for a complete day so they were able to conduct a full scale anti-terrorist sweep that was due to be observed and graded by an unseen surveillance team from Whitehall. They had also tempted a 'national treasure', who was broadly loathed by everybody with whom he came into contact, to agree to open a national festival that would be attended by members of the Royal Family. The fact the event was being held just outside Aberdeen and amounted to little more than a local bring and buy sale was not immediately noticed by the star of stage and screen who had paraded round for most of the afternoon enquiring as to the whereabouts of the missing royal party, to the total bemusement of the native highlanders.

She and Mickey had enjoyed such fun until one day Rachael Broadbent put in her first appearance, smiling shyly and clinging to Mickey's arm in a worryingly proprietary fashion; five foot three with flaming red hair, eyes as blue as the brightest ocean and freckles that could not have been better positioned if they had been drawn on by an artist. Stephanie knew immediately this one was trouble; a fact that was duly confirmed by the effortless ease with which she had succeeded in steeling Mickey's heart.

What made matters worse, was that Rachael was really nice. There was absolutely nothing you could say bad about the kid. If she had been a bloke Stevie would have been smitten with her as well. The unfortunate part about the new relationship was what it did to Mickey. Rachael made Mickey boring; almost as uninteresting as her first two husbands, though possibly that was stretching the point a little too far.

For Mickey's part, he seemed determined to turn into a good fiancé, and when would he ever have contemplated doing something like that? He even started to do all the things normal suitors did; but when had Mickey ever been anything that could be mistaken for normal? Rachael had somehow managed to civilise the man; broken the rearing bronco that nobody else could ride. It was totally unforgiveable and it was at that point she realised that much though she liked the woman she would simply have to go.

It needed to be done with subtlety, but Stephanie Armitage was a past master when it came to being subtle. Never a word was spoken when an inference would work in its place. Girl talk gently steered to suggest that you somehow never finished up fully formed unless you had at some stage tasted forbidden fruit. That a kitchen sink and nappy changes became far easier to endure if you could still remember the crazy Monte Carlo bet, the heat beating down on the scorched virgin sands and the expression of someone who had found it impossible to tear their eyes from your face. It hadn't been easy but she had worked at it diligently for months at a time. In the end it was made simpler because Rachael was intelligent. Pretty soon she began to ask questions of herself. Did she feel that settling down with Mickey would ultimately leave her feeling short changed? And if that was the case would she, by the same token, also be selling Mickey short? Once the poisonous weed of doubt had been planted and watered it began to flourish entirely of its own accord.

When Rachael had teetered near the brink of reaching the sensible conclusion Stephanie had done all in her power to be of help; right down to offering assistance with a bit of extra cash and something more than a guiding hand in searching out the most appropriate phrasing for the goodbye letter. It was painful because Stephanie genuinely liked Rachael. The reason she had to disappear was certainly nothing personal; just business, as the Mafioso chief had expounded with such chilling clarity in the film, the title of which she couldn't quite remember.

So eventually Rachael had been persuaded to wave farewell and never return; because once the bridge had been burned out of existence there was clearly no way you could ever retrace your steps. And now Mickey was what? At this precise moment Stephanie wasn't entirely sure of the answer to that one. But being a manipulator by nature she placed her money on the fact she would pretty soon be able to return Mickey to the way she wanted him to be. And after all, she was nothing if not an expert on the workings of Mickey Smith's agile little mind.

So now it was perhaps best to forget what had just happened and turn her attention towards the next steps. Would Mickey still be intent on pursuing the little scam they had so cleverly cooked up together? Would he still have the motivation to carry on now the outcome to their plan had been rendered largely meaningless? The whole point of the strategy had been to protect his queen but he had been forced to stand idly by and witness her being swept from the board by a cunning stratagem. So, in those circumstances, who could blame Mickey if he now stopped to ask himself the question, was there any real point in continuing the quest?

She suspected that when that decision was reached the answer would be yes. Maybe not resounding or unequivocal, but yes all the same. After all she was working with considerable inside knowledge on this one as Mickey Smith was her specialist subject. And quite naturally she would be able to help him to reach the appropriate decision by whispering the right words into his ear.

Stevie stared at herself in the mirror and finger combed her luxuriant hair back into position. Best to proceed as if the outcome was already a formality and there was no uncertainty fizzing around in her mind. She applied an extra dab of perfume to her wrists and a bright red lipstick to the parts that she would be relying upon to sell her cause in the coming encounter. She surveyed the results and was pleasantly surprised. She turned sideways and admired her breasts, still firm like ripe summer oranges; removed her bra so her nipples would be clearly visible through the sheer material of her thin silken top. She would need to give the odious toad with whom she would soon be dealing every encouragement to play along with the ruse she was about to suggest.

So now the game was once more in play and straight away she could feel the tingle of excitement. The anticipatory shudder that swept through her body, made her cheeks burn red and brought beads of perspiration to her upper lip. She had never fully understood why it affected her like that. The thrill; the anticipation. It was better than sex.

The expectation that there would now be infinite opportunities in the coming years for the pair of them to cause total mayhem; that things would return to the way she required; the way they had always existed before the tiresome interruption had knocked their relationship off course. And that, most importantly, very soon she would have no cause to fear being bored.

It wasn't until Mickey got annoyingly side-tracked that she realised how much she needed him. It was something of a shock when it became horribly apparent there was no fun in playing games if you were doing it all alone; that winning or losing has to be shared in order to be truly appreciated or there was really no point. That the fix she needed to keep her up spirits up was her old pal Mickey Smith; Mickey with the big grin and endless appetite for mischief of the most inappropriate kind; Mickey, to whom she had no idea she was in anyway addicted until he had been unexpectedly ripped from her grasp. Mickey, who needed to return to her control because no other outcome was vaguely acceptable.

CHAPTER TWENTY

MONDAY 13th FEBRUARY 2017

Charlie Brinsworth's attention was caught by Mickey Smith gesticulating wildly as he strode purposefully towards the rear door of the pub. Charlie needed to get on. He had a planned appointment and was tight on time. His day was already in need of a sharp kick in the pants to get it moving along in the right direction. Another delay was the last thing he needed.

'Charlie, this time it's kicking off for real. I got a call from Billy Bean at the Stump. Two of his bouncers took a pasting last night and he said the Crown and Anchor got turned over and there was a mass brawl at the Marquis.'

'Well, I suppose it was on the cards. Eastgate have an interest in all three of those places. It will just be an opening salvo from the Tysons to show that they don't intend taking any prisoners.'

'Do you reckon I should get Trevor on the door full time for a few days as a safety measure? He's generally short of cash and will probably jump at the extra hours.'

'Might be a smart move. We should be alright over here because we have no Eastgate connections but you never know which way the thinking might go on that one. Being on Eastgate's patch might be enough grounds to make the Tysons think it's worth taking a pop, particularly if they are trying to make a point. Order me a dinner Mickey; don't care what it is. I'll be back in plenty of time to do it justice.'

Mickey looked a bit odd this morning, Charlie thought; nothing he could put his finger on, just a bit downcast which wasn't at all like Mickey Smith. Charlie had been awake since the early hours turning over the possibilities and had decided to lay off any further investigation into Anthony Noone's past. He now had a name and an address for the lanky git that the mysterious Mr Noone had no idea was in his possession. That was plenty to have up his sleeve for the time being.

It had also occurred to Charlie, that if Noone wasn't intending to reveal the combination of the safe or any details of what they would be looking for once they had busted their way in to the building, then he must be intending to be a member of the raiding party. The more Charlie considered the implications of that the less he liked it; but every time he thought about telling Noone where he could stick his bloody job, he saw visions of one hundred thousand pounds being washed down a giant plug hole; and instantly that picture caused him to think again.

Anyway, that was a problem for another day; Charlie's current mission was to recruit a breaker, and preferably one he could just about trust. He jumped in the car and headed for one of the less salubrious estates to the west of the city; remembering on the way the chef had mentioned last night it would be steak and kidney pudding for lunch. This thought lifted Charlie's spirits and his thoughts moved on to his new found girlfriend. It was Valentine's Day tomorrow and he had better get Sharon a card or he was likely to be very much out of favour. He hadn't seen a lot of her for the last couple of days what with one thing and another. Maybe tomorrow would offer a better chance. Perhaps he could even talk her into popping round and warming his bed. Suitably cheered by the prospect he took a roundabout much too fast and only just managed to keep the car on the right side of the road. Concentrate you old git! You're too long in the tooth to get overexcited by the thought of a woman. Stick with thinking about the steak pudding; you'll handle that a lot better if past experience is anything to go by.

Seamus MacGregor was often referred to as 'Paddy-Mac' by his friends; but as Charlie wasn't one of them he had always stuck with just plain Seamus. MacGregor was a slight man and by his own admission a fusion of Scottish and Irish blood; this went some way towards accounting for his strange temperament but failed to explain why his skin was as black as that of a West Indian fast bowler.

MacGregor had many virtues though it was fair to say they weren't universally recognised; and foremost by a considerable margin was his ability to break into virtually anywhere undetected. Amazingly, he still had the agility to shin up a drainpipe faster than a rat on speedballs despite the fact he was only about ten years short of getting a bus pass. He could also silence ringing alarm bells, disable motion detector sensors and redirect infrared beams safely out of harm's way without breaking into a sweat. In consequence, despite having no direct gangland affiliations, his talents were on occasions subcontracted in a variety of directions; to Eastgate or whoever was at the time in control of other sectors of the city.

Seamus lived on an estate made up primarily of high rise flats surrounded by two storey council houses, all of which had been constructed out of the cheap brick so beloved by the 1960's town planner. It was a development that, Charlie considered, gave the impression that it was trying a little too hard. There were vast swathes of grass, but this appeared to have been designated only to accumulate a selection of rusted drinks cans, discarded pizza boxes and empty cigarette packets. The areas of green were all bordered by prominent signs stating that ball games were not allowed which did little to make them appear better loved by the younger generation.

The clique of feral youths dressed in dark hoodies was usually in evidence on the estate as one would expect, but their presence tended to be restricted to a small concrete area used for parking and they appeared content to shun the vast open spaces that seemed to cry out for some form of occupation. The whole development gave Charlie the feeling that it had been put together by people who were convinced they knew exactly what the area's residents would require without feeling there was anything to be gained by soliciting their opinion.

Depressed by the vista, Charlie selected the block of flats furthest from the potholed roadway and attempted to gain entry, but found admittance was determined by knowing a keypad code. After declining an offer from a small boy to sell him the number while also offering to keep an eye on his car Charlie leaned on a series of buttons and was eventually buzzed in. The lift wasn't working so he climbed three flights in a spritely and determined fashion, before wheezing his way slowly up a further half dozen.

Seamus MacGregor looked indifferent to see him. In Charlie's opinion Seamus was predominantly of Scottish blood because he rarely expressed enthusiasm in any recognisable form and appeared to totally lack the spontaneity associated with his Irish, and presumably, West Indian forbearers.

'Charlie,' he said, neither as a question nor a statement; something just left floating in the tepid air of the sparsely furnished flat.

Unsmiling, Seamus made his way back to the chair he had just vacated and pushed a button on a remote control that served to kill the sound of the racing commentary on the large television attached to the wall; though, sadly not the picture, which he discreetly kept track of from the corner of his eye.

'Got a job if you're interested, Seamus.' Charlie moved some newspapers and an empty plate with ketchup stains and took a seat on the bright orange sofa that provided the only other seating that appeared immediately accessible. He glanced sideways out of the window. The view was spectacular but probably not greatly appreciated by his host.

'Don't know a definite date at the moment but it will be very soon; a matter of a few days at most,' Charlie continued.

'Right.'

A hard one to interpret; was that 'right' a positive or a negative or maybe just a request for more information. If it was the latter it would make things a bit difficult because Charlie shouldn't really give out a lot more detail until Seamus had indicated whether he was up for it or not.

'Nice little job for you Seamus. Probably just a security door and an alarm. Straight in and out and home in time for tea.'

'Right.'

'A big municipal building that used to be a factory. Heavy duty front access I would bet but probably not a lot of sophistication from the alarm system.'

'Right.'

'Seamus, will you stop saying fucking 'right'. Do you want a slice of the cake or don't you?'

'Depends, Charlie. Whose turf is it on and who am I working for? There's a lot of stuff going on out there at the moment and in the next couple of days there is likely to be a lot more stuff going on out there......and I wouldn't want to be part of any of it if it's likely to get up the wrong set of nostrils, if you take my meaning.'

'Look mate, I'll give it to you straight. It's a private job for some weirdo that I don't know from Adam. As far as you're concerned you are working for me. It's on the Tyson side of town but those boys probably don't even know this place exists. It's got absolutely nothing to do with any of the stuff that's kicking off at the moment. If I thought it had I would have steered well clear of it myself.'

'Right.'

'Is that an, I'm in 'right' or an I don't want to know 'right'?' Make your mind up Seamus; I've got a meat pudding with my name on twenty minutes down the road.

'It's an I'm thinking about it 'right'. Listen, if I do say *yes,* when do we do the recce?'

'Tomorrow.'

'Alright, Charlie, I'm in; but I'm not putting a price on it until I've taken a look and if I get a feeling anything you've told me ain't kosher the deals off. Oh, and if world war three breaks out between Eastgate and the Tysons anytime soon don't even waste your time ringing my number.'

CHAPTER TWENTY ONE

MONDAY 13th FEBRUARY 2017

Mickey Smith was collecting glasses when the door went back on its hinges with a resounding thump and straight away the signs were it was trouble. There were five of them; big lads dressed for action but not tooled up as far as Mickey could tell from first glance. Big Trevor got trampled by the initial onslaught but grabbed the figure last through the door and hung on tight; once Trevor grabbed you it wasn't likely you were going anywhere in a hurry and a lot more probable it would be curtains for the night; so that was one less to worry about.

Mickey deliberately smashed a glass on the floor and pushed a couple of the pubs regulars to one side to make a space; this would give the remaining four something to focus on which would stop them spinning on their heels and belting hell out of Trevor while he had his hands full.

The lead figure of the remaining four puffed his chest out a bit, acting like he fancied his chances or was looking to make a name. He put his head down and launched a charge in an attempt to knock Mickey off his feet so his mates could follow in with their size tens. It was a dumb idea. Mickey moved to one side and lashed out with his foot redirecting his assailant's momentum into a drinks table that he met head on. His wound immediately started to bleed all over the floor but to his credit the injured man tried his best to get back in the action and made it halfway to his feet. Mickey kicked him again, a good deal harder, and this time he hit the floor and didn't move.

That was better. Mickey figured if his luck held and they hadn't opted to send in anyone a bit tasty he might just be able to handle the three that were left; or at worst stop them from causing any great degree of damage.

Charlie, who had been reclining in his usual seat

making phone calls and looking very smug because he had remembered Valentine Day, chose this moment to put in an appearance. Moving quietly behind a tall bloke who seemed to be having trouble getting a clear line of vision between the top of his peaked hoodie and a headscarf he had tied over his nose and mouth, Charlie cracked him in the side of the head with his elbow. The man bellowed loudly and disappeared like a turtle inside his array of clothing before falling dramatically to his knees. Charlie lashed out with his boot at the general area of where he judged his face would have been located had it been visible to the paying public and was rewarded with a satisfying squelch.

Big Trevor had by now pretty much finished squeezing the life out of the man he had been grappling with and completed his performance by lifting the assailant high into the air and slamming him onto the floorboards.

There followed an embarrassing silence with nobody quite knowing what to do next. The away team were suddenly drastically short on numbers. Everyone looked at everybody else to see who was going to make the next move. A number of the pub's customers who had so far missed out on the action picked up bottles or glasses and edged forward looking keen to get involved; but as soon as the two attackers still on their feet got twitchy the majority took a couple of steps back again.

'Are you fucking off quietly or what?' Mickey shouted.

Both men made faces that appeared to indicate there wasn't anything they would like better but under current circumstances that was hardly going to be a viable option. This was the sort of thing they did for a living and they had reputations to think about. If word got back they had been taken out in one minute flat without at least putting up some sort of struggle they would be a laughing stock. Worse than that, they could very soon end up being directed towards alternative areas of employment. They adopted the faces of men who were aware that they were in for a kicking but didn't see they had a lot of choice other than to try to put on a bit of a show.

If it was their hope that the current state of play might lead to any forthcoming beating being inflicted in as merciful a fashion as circumstances permitted, then they were doomed to disappointment. People in this part of the world took badly against an attack launched in a place where they had gone to relax and forget the stresses of everyday life. In retrospect, the assailants would probably have understood that reasoning, even if they didn't necessarily buy into it at the time.

Rather than call the Police and spend half the night making statements, the party from the pub rounded up the walking wounded and dumped them on a street corner a couple of hundred yards away; even phoning for an ambulance that would transport the more severely injured to Accident and Emergency.

Granted, a few harsh words were exchanged in the course of this undertaking and there was even the odd threat of retribution; but on the whole matters were conducted in a reasonably civilised fashion.

Sadly, Charlie did have cause to stamp on assailant No.3's hand when he failed to grasp the way these things naturally came to a conclusion; but having produced a blade from an inside pocket the man was somewhat the author of his own misfortune. The crunch of his knuckles as they were crushed into splinters between boot leather and a paving slab made it probable that the ill-judged decision would provide a salutary lesson that would stay with him for some time to come; one that would doubtless be regularly reflected upon over the many months it would take him to regain the use of his hand.

In little more than fifteen minutes the tables and chairs at the pub had been righted, dress wear readjusted and the floor mopped free of blood. In fact, the air of conviviality in the Bear, combined with little evidence of an altercation, was a major factor in convincing the uniformed policemen who arrived only a few minutes after the clean-up operation had been completed that reports of a mass brawl at the Black Bear resulting in a number of severe injuries was completely erroneous.

'Tysons?' Mickey's question, softly into Charlie's ear as they closed up for the night.

'Odds on; but definitely not their first team from the way they handled themselves. You would have thought they had enough to keep them amused at the moment without turning over a scabby old boozer like this one.'

Mickey was about to take issue with the Bear being categorised as a 'scabby old boozer' when it struck him he might be wiser to bite his lip bearing in mind the visit he had lined up for the morning. Bugger Charlie Brinsworth and his lack of appreciation for a well-run hostelry specialising in the sale of quality ales and gourmet quality food. The Black Bear couldn't be so bloody bad; he noticed the ungrateful old bastard never missed a chance to get a meal here these days.

CHAPTER TWENTY TWO

TUESDAY 14th FEBRUARY 2017

Charlie set off early leaving a Valentine card for Sharon on the top of the bar. The words inside were painfully sloppy but in his experience women could never get enough of that sort of thing.

Earlier on, while he was shaving, Simon Bartol had interrupted his ablutions with some interesting news. According to Mr Bartol, who was widely renowned for always knowing which way the wind was blowing several hours before the man at the metrological office had figured out which set of stairs led up onto the roof, had phoned to report that the confrontation between Eastgate and the Tysons had gone up through the gears in the last twenty four hours; with Eastgate, the prime aggressor, coming out heavily on top.

During the hours of darkness the Tysons' most lucrative betting office had been torched and two of their premier gambling joints taken apart, with the result that they would be out of commission for the foreseeable future. This, coupled with numerous hits on Tyson controlled pubs and clubs, made it a sorry night for the east coast outfit. And to make matters worse, Leroy Brown's Rasta troops had completed the sorry picture by rampaging through vast swathes of Tyson controlled territory kicking the shit out of anybody who hadn't had the good sense to get out of their way fast enough.

Simon said, to the best of his knowledge there had never been any sort of alliance between Eastgate and the Rastas so how this sudden joining of the clans had come into being he had no idea, unless some serious money had changed hands.

Charlie was quietly pleased with that news. So far Eastgate had not interfered unduly with his business dealing since he had returned to the realms of society where you were permitted to have possession of your own front door key; while the Tysons had taken it upon themselves to send a hit squad over to the Bear without the slightest provocation. Alright, the bunch of Nancy boys who had been appointed to the task should have been signed up for a comedy special, but that wasn't the point. The Tysons' intention had been made pretty damn clear and it wasn't a friendly gesture whichever way you chose to look at it.

The other good point was that Simon Bartol appeared to have got over any ill will he might have harboured after Charlie doubted his word before the excursion to the Egret. This was good news as he needed an experienced distributor to handle the dope from the Vietnamese kids and if Simon turned arsey he would have to rethink his whole strategy. A good start to the day all in all, and Charlie hoped this was a portent of things to come.

When Charlie came downstairs there was no sign of Mickey who had probably nipped round to his girlfriends or taken a walk to the gallery owned by that crazy eyed, posh bitch with the legs who Charlie just couldn't bring himself to trust. He glanced at his watch and realised he would need to very quickly get his arse in gear or he would be late for his appointment.

He immediately headed across town and collected Seamus MacGregor at the bottom of a steep hill near the tram terminus. Seamus had chosen the meeting place because he said these days he was better at walking down a hill rather than up one. However, Charlie suspected there was every chance Mr MacGregor would be faster at both than a lot of people half his age; most particularly if there was a blue night flashing somewhere in the vicinity.

The traffic was bad as they made their way slowly across town and he could tell venturing this far into Tyson territory without a monogrammed invitation was making Seamus a shade nervous. Charlie wasn't the slightest bit bothered. From his way of thinking the Tyson family would currently have a lot more important things to occupy their thoughts than a minor boundary transgression after the events of the previous night.

They followed Anthony Noone's directions explicitly and duly arrived at the new library without incident; parking Charlie's car on the waste ground opposite the building that everybody seemed to use for the purpose. They crossing the road and pushing their way through a set of massive wooden doors that would have been in service for a century or more before Charlie was born.

It would be wrong to say the new library was chaotic but it was certainly enjoying a lively trade. Most of the custom appeared to be provided by men and women who had called in to access the internet on the bank of computers that had been provided for the purpose; though some could clearly be seen flicking idly through newspapers and periodicals as they sheltered from the lousy weather that seemed to have been the one feature of climate change that had existed for all of Charlie's lifetime. Babies and toddlers apart, kids were not very much in evidence, but it was probable the majority of the little swine would still be in school as the half term holidays weren't scheduled to get underway until the following week.

Nobody questioned their right of entry so the pair wandered up and down the aisles as if they owned the place and Charlie was forced to admit he very much enjoyed the tour. It was plain the building had once been a vast factory but it looked to have been thoroughly steam cleaned and then totally renovated at the taxpayer's expense with whitewashed walls and mustard yellow floor paint. The shelving on which the books were neatly racked looked robustly built out of solid timber and had presumably been rescued from the original downtown library building, before it was gutted for the conversion. The desks were of a decent size and topped in some sort of hard rubber compound or new generation plastic, and the computers looked as if they could quite possibly have been taken straight out of the box that very morning. The best part was everybody seemed happy. It probably wasn't as quiet as sticklers for protocol might have liked but the general atmosphere was good. Charlie was even considering joining until he remembered that he wasn't actually meant to be there; and he was still surveying the scene with genuine interest when Seamus tugged at his arm and pointed to a long wrought iron staircase that curved from the ground floor in a gentle spiral to the level above.

They ascended as quietly as possible though nobody was paying them the least bit of attention. Being a library it seemed only polite not to disturb the regular patrons' attention by clanking their feet on the metal treads. Upon arrival on the first floor they were greeted by a similarly extensive layout of racking, every inch packed full with books expertly divided by subject classification. The joists supporting the upper storey appeared to have been cut back for about a third of the upstairs area so the floor space was smaller, if none the less crowded. This arrangement gave the library something of the feel of a great church as it allowed a view all the way up to the roof timbers from the ground floor far below. The building also provided a spectacular indoor panorama, down across the library floor to the reception area and main entrance, from what was in effect an enormous balcony, guarded only by a sturdy set of banisters constructed from cast iron.

Seamus quickly disappeared towards a door marked *Staff only* while Charlie busied himself learning more than he had ever wished to know about the fauna of Patagonia. When Seamus returned after ten minutes they retraced their steps down the metal staircase and out into the bitter cold. Nothing was said, but Charlie sensed that his colleague wasn't happy.

'What's the matter, old son; access likely to prove a bit of a problem?'

'You sure this isn't some sort of wind up, Charlie? A kid of six could break into that place in his sleep. There's no security at all worthy of the name. The main doors are solid but will open with a key that I could cut in ten minutes flat and there's not even a bolt running down into the concrete floor to stop them flapping open. A strong wind could blow those bloody doors back on their hinges if it wasn't for the fact they weight a ton; I'm a bit surprised that hasn't already happened. To be honest mate, it's an insult to be involved in this sort of job. I've got a reputation to think about, you know.'

'What about upstairs? Did you get a look at the safe?'

'Second door along on the right. Bloody great big thing sunk deep into the floor; old fashioned and solid as hell. Might be German by the look of it but it's hard to tell because the nameplate's missing. If you want me to blow it there'll be a hell of a noise. It always makes me laugh when I see those old films where they put a blanket over the top to help muffle the sound. You try to blow that big old bastard and no way is it going to be quiet.'

'Door locks?'

'Not a single one. What's the matter with these people? Haven't they ever heard of security?'

'They probably aren't bothered, Seamus. There's no money to be made out of nicking a load of musty old books.'

'Can't disagree with that; come on then, what's the score? I've got a girlfriend with a drink problem and a Turf Accountant who reckons I owe him money both eager to see me.'

'Look, I'll cut you a deal Seamus. You break into the building any way you see fit, just as long as you don't make a mess; then plonk yourself down somewhere comfortable and file down a key that will open the front doors. After that you can bugger off home with a monkey in your hip pocket and no questions asked. You'll need to leave the key with me so I can lock up on my way out but that's not a problem; you can pass it over when I pay you the cash. What do you say......deal?'

'I say you're a bloody fool, Charlie Brinsworth,

because whatever you're looking for, it ain't going to be in here with a security set up like they've got. It's your money and I'll willingly take it but don't be surprised when you come out empty handed. Now let's get out of here before we trip over one of the Tyson firm and have some explaining to do......can you do a ton up front and drop me at the bookie at the bottom of my road?'

CHAPTER TWENTY THREE

TUESDAY 14th FEBRUARY 2017

Stephanie Armitage was stuck in the gallery with no constructive role to play as the drama began to unfold. She felt uneasy because Mickey Smith had been away a lot longer than expected and there was no obvious explanation for this unless things had gone horribly wrong. From bitter experience, she knew to trust the odious Oliver Dearlove about as far as she could throw him. The lecherous old toad would always try to work himself some sort of angle on any deal he cut. He wouldn't be able to help himself; the temptation would be too great. The difficulty lay in the fact the charmless Oliver was a talented reptile even at his advanced years; and to make matters worse he was fully aware that he still possessed a good degree of bargaining power. The worse kind of partner you could ask for; one who fully appreciated the full extent of their worth and would be prepared to play on the fact.

She was aware that Mickey was street wise but sometimes that counted for very little when dealing with the Oliver Dearloves of this world. Oliver would have the advantage because the deal was taking place in an area in which he was an acknowledged expert; the same area about which Mickey Smith knew virtually nothing at all.

Stephanie had done her bit in setting the whole thing up but the deal had only been approved in principle because the aged Dearlove had insisted on finalising any agreement with the client on a personal basis. She had been alright for sketching out details of the requirement but Oliver wanted direct negotiations with the man who was paying the bills before he finally contracted to take on the project. Well, at least she hadn't had her chest gently massaged by his bony talons for nothing at all. At least the bold colours had been firmly painted into place and it was now only down to

Mickey to cover the areas requiring a small degree of fine shading.

She had made Mickey aware that five to six grand was a fair enough price to pay for the work involved and certainly not to go beyond seven and a half. She had told him to set a firm date; ideally something totally unrealistic that would have the odious toad working day and night in order to meet the deadline.....and to make it entirely clear that final payment would only be forthcoming if the finished article was passed by her as perfect in every respect. Also Mickey was to be certain not to part with more than a thousand up front so the incentive to finish the work and collect the balance would be in no way compromised. It was simple enough as long as Mickey stuck rigidly to the script but that was something of a forlorn hope.

She had been around this particular block a few times in the past and could appreciate Oliver's desire to see what would effectively be the template from which he would be obliged to work. She could also understand why he would want to study the picture up close; to stand quietly and drink in every detail of the original while the opportunity was available. But even making allowances for that the pair of them had been gone for one hell of a long time.

Eventually, more than an hour later than expected, Mickey had put in an appearance; broad grin in place, Valentine card in hand accompanied by a single rose. You had to love the guy; even when he was off his game he still had a smattering of class. Rachael had been a mug to let him slip through her fingers; it was a decision she would come to regret. Big hug; twirl around the room; indecent proposal whispered in her ear. Mickey Smith should have been given an award for representing resilience on the hoof after being dumped by the love of his life barely twenty four hours previously. Only someone who knew him as well as she did would see the sadness in his eye.

'Put me down and tell me why you are so late?'

Stephanie Armitage had been the architect of the scheme and resolutely refused to allow her interest to get side-tracked away from the business in hand.

'Far too much to tell. Lunch, my Valentine. Luigi's, one hundred yards only in your stiletto heeled shoes. Sorry, the weather's still rubbish; would you like me to carry you in my arms?' Mickey Smith, with his usual abundance of confidence and charm.

A table by the window so they could watch the pedestrians with umbrellas and rain hats scamper by; a bottle of very cold prosecco accompanied by a small selection of mixed starters to nibble. Mickey, finally prepared to divulge.

'Strange bloke, Dearlove, don't you think? Can't say I took to him much. Don't think he liked me a lot either. Stared, took photographs on his poncy little telephone camera, then stared some more. For some reason he seemed to find the whole exercise ridiculously funny. At one stage I'm sure there were tears of laughter running down his cheeks. Wouldn't share the joke though and eventually we got down to business. We spent thirty minutes talking about the price alone. Ping pong with bloody pound notes. He stood up twice to leave then changed his mind; said if it weren't for the fact the Cheltenham Festival started in exactly a month and he had a couple of sure things lined up he would have told me what I could do with my commission.'

'Bottom line, how much?' Mickey was taking too long to get to the point for Stephanie's limited patience.

'We agreed on five providing he got every penny up front.'

'Mickey, I specifically told you not to.......'

'Wait for the punch line. You're not giving me the opportunity to explain. Mr Dearlove said he would sign an agreement stating that if his work was not delivered in one week and deemed precisely to specification, then he would be liable to return the entire fee.'

'Mickey, you can't trust a word that old man says. Give

it......'

'Hold fire, woman. I'm not entirely stupid. I dragged the old git up to the High Road and into the solicitors that handle the pub's account. I got him to put what he had said in writing and I got the contract witnessed by one of the partners as well as a secretary. If he doesn't come up with the goods exactly to specification then he's working for nothing because he will be obligated to repay the five big ones.....and if he's spent up we can take goods to the value out of that mangy mausoleum that passes for a home.'

It made some degree of sense but Stephanie still wasn't comfortable with the arrangement. Dearlove would have some sort of angle because it was having angles that got the old groper out of bed in the morning.

'Let me read the agreement.'

'Our copy's in a safe at the solicitors. I'm not stupid enough to be walking the streets with it tucked under my arm.'

'Listen Mickey, I think............'

'Well don't; no more work. Do something useful, MS Armitage or whatever fancy name that philandering swindler of a husband has got you using these days. Pick a decent bottle of red.'

'Mickey, has it occurred to you that.......'

'No, probably not. Now shut up about Oliver Dearlove. I've had more than enough of the old bastard for one day. What do you fancy? I'm going for the prawns.'

CHAPTER TWENTY FOUR

TUESDAY 14th FEBRUARY 2017

It was an evening when Charlie Brinsworth just wanted to sit quietly, nursing a pint of beer, while he tried to figure out how he could be so deeply immersed in Anthony 'Garfield' Noone's bloody project without knowing more about the man in question.

From time to time Sharon smiled across from behind the bar so Charlie reckoned the Valentine card had hit the right spot. However, she had already made it clear she wouldn't be signing up for any nocturnal shenanigans that evening as she had to get back to look after her kid, which was something of a disappointment.

Mickey was beginning to become something of a worry. One minute he was walking about with his chin on the ground and the next he was grinning like a bloody Cheshire cat. He looked like a bloke with a split personality who was on the verge of a nervous breakdown. This was just what you needed from the man who was supposed to be in charge of running your pub.

Sharon said the word amongst the staff was he'd just been dumped by the cute little red head he had been so careful to keep well under wraps. Probably trying to put a brave face on it and making a lousy job, had been Charlie's initial thoughts on the matter; but it didn't appear he had been right from what he was now observing at the other side of the bar. He had seen that look on men's faces before and in his book it usually came down to only one thing.

Mr Smith looking in anyway pleased with himself was even less explicable because Mickey had broken it to him Big Trevor the Bouncer had put in his notice. Apparently Trevor had only been working the doors to supplement his student grant and now, with his final examinations approaching, he needed to hit the books twenty four seven to make certain he secured a decent degree. Who ever heard of a Bouncer sitting for a law degree, anyway? Charlie hadn't even known he was a student. A natural talent being tragically misdirected, in Charlie's opinion. Trevor had proved very decent at damping down a ruckus before it got out of hand.

On a more positive note, work had been progressing nicely on the building conversion and it looked like the pizza parlour could be up and running in a matter of weeks. He hadn't been in touch with the Vietnamese dope growers but they knew what they were doing and he didn't want to give the impression he was breathing down their necks. It had occurred to Charlie that delivering pizzas would serve as an excellent front for pushing out dope. Kids whizzing about on mopeds with big cardboard boxes strapped over their shoulders was now the sort of commonplace sight that blended seamlessly into the background. It wasn't a side of the business in which he wanted to be immediately involved but as a distribution facility it appeared to have a good deal of merit. He made a mental note to talk to Simon Bartol on the subject the next time circumstances permitted.

So a lot of positives and only Anthony Noone's project that required a good deal more thought. The situation could be an awful lot worse; and as if that thought had acted as a trigger, suddenly it was.

The next time Charlie looked up the large frame of Spanner Hopkins was in evidence at the bar. He was accompanied by two smaller men, one of whom Charlie vaguely recognised as a long serving Eastgate regular called Jimmy something or other who specialised in driving jobs and was reputed to be a bit tasty behind the wheel of a car. The other character Charlie didn't know though he had the impression he might have seen him around. Charlie studied the body language of the three while pretending to be absorbed in a newspaper article about tree felling, which of late seemed the sole preoccupation of the middle classes in the locality; from the way the heads were nodding the bloke he didn't know appeared to be the one who was calling the shots.

Mickey was never slow off the mark in this sort of situation. He soon spotted Spanner and eased his way along the bar. Give Mickey Smith his due he was never one to take a backward step. There was a brief exchange of conversation and a lot of friendly smiles but Charlie could see there wasn't a lot of warmth in the one that was playing on Mickey's lips. He also knew that the daft bugger wouldn't hesitate to come over the bar if he thought he sensed anything resembling a threat from the unwelcome visitors. This was the first night they had stood Big Trevor down as well; bloody terrible timing by the look of things. Time to do something......any bloody thing before Mickey got overexcited and matters escalated out of hand.

'Spanner, you not talking to me these days? Introduce me to your mates you ignorant sod. Pull up a couple more chairs and take the weight off.'

The party exchanged glances and slowly crossed the bar. They seated themselves around Charlie's table as Spanner handled the introductions.

'Charlie Brinsworth, who used to run with that bunch of wankers from Bridgeland before he got banged up and took early retirement. Terry Brean, who has taken over the reins at Eastgate. My colleague, Jimmy Jones, I think you already know.' All said in a voice that sounded much too posh for Spanner Hopkins, like he'd been practising it while he had been brushing his teeth.

'It's always a pleasure to see you Spanner because whenever you are in the bar receipts go up. Nice to meet your friends as well; to what do we owe the honour?' Charlie, making sure he sounded light and relaxed while definitely not feeling either.

Terry Brean took charge of proceedings, anxious to push Hopkins and Jones sharply into the background. There was a degree of absolute finality about the way they were obliged to take no further part. Terry was the man and the other two were only here to provide hired muscle. It wasn't so much that it was a fact; it was the way the new boss-man needed everybody to recognise it as such. Words had been exchanged on the way over and Mr Brean had laid down the way the discussion was going to go and who was going to handle the talking. Charlie sat back and waited to see what it was the pompous little git had to say for himself.

'I thought it would be only polite to introduce myself around since I'm new in the top job. It's important that I can put a face to everybody with business interests on my patch. A little bird told me you had some unwelcome visitors last night. I would just like you to know that I take a very dim view of that sort of behaviour and the Tysons will be made fully aware that any recurrence will be very much frowned upon.'

'Very kind, Terry, but no need to concern yourself. It was nothing more than handbags at dawn. I heard you had a busy night yourself. Everything resolved to your satisfaction?' Charlie anxious to change the direction of the conversation before it veered into an Eastgate offer of protection which one way or the other would inevitably finish up with money changing hands or more likely Mickey taking a pop at the person who first broached the question.

'Let me just put it this way. It is highly unlikely old man Tyson or either of his sons will consider it is in their best interests to visit this part of town anytime soon. In fact if there was anything worth having on the other side of the city my boys could be over there tomorrow and clean the place out.'

'Nobody likes a war, Terry. It's bad for business; everybody's business.'

'Matter of interest, Charlie. How does it stand between you and that leery barman who keeps scowling in my direction?'

'He's my partner, Terry. Don't worry about his face.

He was born looking like that.'

'Oh, I wasn't worried, Charlie. I'm not frightened of the dark and I brought Spanner along just to make sure I get home safely. It was just I was wondering who I would need to talk to if a business proposition was to arise in respect of this lovely old pub of yours. Which one of you is the organ grinder and which one is the monkey, is the question I was asking myself?'

'Well, neither of us is very business minded, Terry. Just after a quiet life, if the truth were known.'

'Good to hear, Charlie. We all like a nice quiet life if we can get one. But you know how it works; you sometimes have to earn what you want in this life. Oh, while I think of it, your partner, Mr Smith, has some very strange family connections as I'm sure you are already aware. Just make sure he knows which side his bread is buttered, won't you? I wouldn't want there to be any confusion on his part as to who is running the show round here. Right, must be on my way; lots more calls to make; no rest for the wicked.'

'What the hell was all that about?' Charlie mumbled under his breath as he watched the Eastgate platoon disappear smartly out of the door. Christ almighty! If it wasn't one thing it was the next. If this was what being retired was like he was going to think seriously about applying for a regular job.

CHAPTER TWENTY FIVE

WEDNESDAY 15th FEBRUARY 2017

Stephanie Armitage opened half an eye and stole a glimpse at the digital alarm. Jesus, it was twenty past seven! Her head felt fuzzy and she was sure the noise that had awakened her was the front door downstairs being pushed firmly into place. She silently prayed it had been made by Mickey making his exit and not husband Ziggy arriving home unexpectedly. She looked around the room. Please God it was Mickey on the way out because there's no way she would be able to explain this lot. The bedroom was currently in a state nobody would believe.

Still naked, Stephanie pushed herself to her feet and set about stripping the bed and hunting down new sheets and a replacement duvet cover. She caught a glimpse of herself in the mirror. Mascara all down one cheek, a bite mark on her neck and lipstick everywhere except where it was meant to be.

'Nothing to smile about you silly cow,' Stephanie whispered at her ravaged reflection. 'Why the hell did you ever let that happen?'

What on earth had she been thinking? It was the wine; she blamed it on, the bloody stupid wine. Three bottles between the pair of them over lunch and they had just picked at bits of food instead of eating anything that might have helped to absorb some of the alcohol.

What they had done mainly during their extended lunch date was talk. Mickey Smith was always such great company and some of the stories he told were truly unbelievable; that, and doubtless completely untrue. That was what she adored about Mickey. He was priceless entertainment value; always had been.........well, up to recently anyway....... and now he belonged to her again without the need to even fork out a deposit to ensure he was returned to the world in pristine condition.

Men who made her laugh had proved so hard to come by. When she thought of some of the dinner dates she had endured over the years. For reasons she had never been able to determine, men always found themselves so terribly interesting. She had always struggled to imagine how they could be so utterly deluded. You should probably lay the blame with their mothers. God, those women had an awful lot to answer for.

At lunch everything had been lovely in the way meetings with Mickey were always lovely. Things only started to go wrong at the point when they had decided to skip coffee in favour of a quick blast from her espresso machine; just a quick five minutes so they could dust themselves down before getting back to work.

Alright, she had probably been a bit too affectionate as they walked the short distance back to the gallery; but she had always been affectionate towards Mickey without it ever getting out of hand. He was her mate and they had often held hands and cuddled without it ending up resulting in anything like this.

It struck her she had better change the pillow cases as well. She could distinctly remember having one shoved underneath her bottom in a moment of ultimate indiscretion. She had a horrible feeling she might even have positioned it there herself.

How did it ever get started? All she could clearly recollect was closing the front door to the shop and then finding herself in a passionate embrace up against the Regency chaise longue she has sold to that lovely old lady from Berkshire on the internet. It was only in the passageway because it was awaiting collection by a courier. Just as well it was there, if she was remembering correctly, or she might now be trying to extract splinters from a delicate area with the aid of a mirror and a pair of tweezers.

Bloody hell, how could she possibly have been so stupidly indiscrete; and to make matters worse the glass in that main door wasn't nearly as opaque as it had appeared when she'd checked it out in the double glazing catalogue.

Stephanie pulled on a dressing gown and started retrieving her clothes from the various unlikely places where they had come to rest. Where her knickers had got to remained a mystery that would require further investigation when her head was a good deal clearer. It wasn't as if there was a chandelier they could be hanging from; which in the circumstances should probably be regarded as something of a minor blessing.

The hallway was where it should all have come to an abrupt halt. Two dear old friends could have just about been excused for a few fleeting moments of mild passion; particularly after that overly robust Chianti which Luigi magicked up for special customers who settled their bills with banknotes of a high denomination. Stephanie remembered clearly, she had been right on the verge of giving Mickey a sharp prod in the chest and reminding him that she was a happily married woman, even if he would immediately have known the last bit was a complete lie. She had quite certainly taken some small steps in the right direction by managing to pull her skirt back down over her bottom and returning at least one breast to its lace trimmed holder; but that was the stage at which everything had completely fallen apart.

Mickey had stepped back like a gentleman, she remembered; given her his best smile and kissed her so gently yet sadly on the lips it could have been a beat from the wings of a passing butterfly. It was at that point Stephanie had realised she couldn't bear Mickey to stop seducing her or she would probably die. She wanted him to feel happy again; to go back to being the Mickey Smith who could always make her laugh. She wanted to feel him inside her so she could take away the pain; and she had ceased to give a damn about the repercussions that would almost certainly be a consequence of this feeling of utter madness. She had calmly beckoned with her index finger and then wiggled her bottom extravagantly as he followed her up the stairs. There was no excuse she could hide behind. She was as guilty as hell however good her intentions.

Her conscience might even have allowed her a bit of latitude if it had just been a quickie and Mickey had been halfway out of the door while she was still refastening the hook on her bra strap; sadly that had been far from the case. They had devoted a complete afternoon to gay abandon, luxuriating in each other's bodies, seemingly without a thought for anyone else in the great wide world. Mickey had held her so tight, buried himself so deep inside her it was as if he was trying to merge their two separate entities into one single unit. How many times? She didn't want to remember. What excuses? Absolutely none.

It wasn't meant to have been like that. Mickey's role in her life was already clearly defined. Friends should be held dear forever; friends who made you laugh needed to be treasured like nuggets of the purest gold. Sadly, in her experience, the lifespan of lovers had invariably been of a considerably shorter duration.

They might have even got away with it if the whole thing had been a disaster. Something neatly swept under the carpet as they welcomed back a happy return to the status quo. The last thing their relationship needed was for it to have been so bloody epic. Jesus bloody Christ, where on earth could they go to from here?

Perhaps she was reading it wrong. Probably it was just Mickey's way of getting Rachael out of his system. No doubt he was just treating her as a surrogate to work out all his accumulated angst over their split. That was better. She could cope with being used. Let's face it, having been the cause of their break-up she deserved nothing better.

Payment in kind, you deceitful bitch. It's quite probable you just got exactly what you deserved. Now take a shower, get some clothes on and sort this place out before somebody calls and you have a lot of explaining to do; explaining for which you are currently woefully ill equipped. You can sit and figure this whole thing out later when your brain starts working again.

While you're at it, you might also spare a thought as to how the toad will set about stitching Mickey up over the current deal; because the fact that he will is beyond any reasonable doubt. Then you might be wise to consider long and hard how you have probably managed to ruin the most treasured friendship you have ever enjoyed by the wanton acts of a single afternoon. Because no matter how much you try to kid yourself, friendship isn't going to survive an afternoon like that one; and God alone knows what might be coming to follow.

CHAPTER TWENTY SIX

WEDNESDAY 15th FEBRUARY 2017

Detective Inspector Daniel Loach exited the converted utility room he used as a private office, walked through the main administrative hub in what he hoped was an authorative manner, and beckoned D.S. Geoff Strickland to join him in the kitchen which doubled as a meeting room. There was one major difficulty with having Eden Place as a Divisional Headquarters for the Serious Crime Squad. It was far too cramped. However, D.I. Loach was reluctant to mention the fact to anyone who might have the power to do anything about the situation as it was far more likely they would choose to resolve the problem by cutting back on his staff numbers rather than offering more commodious accommodation.

Strickland entered the room three paces behind the Inspector, threw a dish cloth that had been lying on the table top in the general direction of the sink and propped a chair underneath the door handle. He reached out towards the draining board, slid across a saucer to use as an ashtray and lit a cigarette.

Loach frowned.

'Careful Geoff, there's a smoke detector directly over your head.'

'No problem, Boss; someone's removed the battery.'

Loach looked mildly displeased, confident in the knowledge of who that someone would have been. He waved a sheet of paper in Strickland's direction and lifted his eyebrows to make a questioning face.

'Still no signs of life?' he said nodding vaguely in the direction of the dirt encrusted back window.

'Never been quieter. The Tysons will presumably still be licking their wounds after Monday night's fracas. The Rastas have returned to their home turf to get stoned and drink the bottles of rum they pillaged while they were running wild; and Eastgate will now be sitting in the Pheasant patting themselves on the back and telling each other how clever they've been; after which, it's a safe bet the upper echelons will withdraw to a back room and settle down with a bottle of whiskey to figure out how they can best take advantage of the situation. The word on the wire is, an official peace negotiation will take place in the next forty eight hours; but it will only be a face saver. The Tysons will do well to get out of it with their shirts still on their backs.'

'Well, broadly speaking, I suppose that should probably be regarded as good news.'

'It certainly would be if you backed Eastgate to come out on top. Last night the new bloke in charge down there did a tour of pubs and clubs in the area just to emphasise that the old order was not just up and running but had got a full can of unleaded in the boot to cover emergencies. That would be just in case anyone was entertaining any silly ideas that things might now be in anyway different. I had them tailed and I've got a list of the places they visited if you're interested.'

Loache seemed to have other things on his mind and brought the conversation back on course.

'Read that email. The Commissioner is of the impression we should now devote all our resources to wiping Eastgate off the map.'

'And don't tell me.....the Chief Constable completely agreed with everything he said.'

'Got it in one. What I can't seem to make them understand is the way things happen in the real world. We have as much chance of crushing Eastgate as flying. They've got more troops than we have, they are better financed, drive faster cars, command ten times more authority, and, dare I say it, most of the time they're a good deal better organised.'

Strickland nodded and sucked on his cigarette. When DI Loache was off on one the best thing to do was to keep your mouth shut, sit quietly and wait for the forest fire to burn itself out.

'What they can't seem to grasp is that we don't run this city anymore; Eastgate do......and to be perfectly honest it's probably better that way when you consider the alternatives. If we had a load of small gangs engaging in minor turf wars all over the place it would be ten times more difficult to police the streets than it is now. The way it currently works, Eastgate do a lot of our job for us by keeping a lid on the volcano. Anyone starts acting silly they get a visit and if that doesn't work out they get dumped on the first stagecoach out of town or find themselves with two broken kneecaps. When Nat Dawson did his disappearing act, quite frankly I was shitting myself. Now this Terry Brean has taken over the reins and has proved his worth I'm sleeping a hell of a lot better. It makes no bloody sense but in the circumstances it's the best of a series of lousy options.'

Strickland made himself comfortable in his seat. He could tell from the D.I.'s face there was more to come.

'Do you know whose fault this is? Roy bloody Jenkins. When he was Home Secretary he did away with Bobbies on the beat and ever since that day we have been playing catch up. Crime prevention; forget it. We prevent bugger all crime. All we do is react to illegal acts once they have already been committed; and because we have no feet on the ground we never have the vaguest idea what to expect until it's actually happened. The whole system is a bloody shambles. I'll be glad when I've retired.'

That would be it then, thought Strickland. Once Daniel Loache finished a sentence referencing retirement, it was time to stop daydreaming and start paying close attention.

Loach regathered himself and veered back onto a previous tangent.

'That list you were telling me about; was the Black Bear one of the pub's that Brean chose to visit?'

'Yes,' said the Detective Sergeant without needing to run an eye over the written word.

'A bit after nine and Terry Brean was inside for ten to fifteen minutes before they moved on to the White Lion. Why do you ask?'

'Nothing really. It's just I stopped in the other night for a quick half. A relative of the wife's runs the place; her cousin I think. Miriam used to look out for him a bit when he was a kid. She hasn't seen him in years but I think she used to have a soft spot for the lad; said as a child he had a lovely smile. You know what women are like.'

'Yes, I get in The Bear occasionally myself. It always seems to be pretty well run and you don't get a lot of trouble. It's just been redecorated as well; bloody terrible choice of colours if you ask me. Right, what's the plan of action, Guvnor? Want me to pop down to the Golden Pheasant and ask Terry Brean if Eastgate fancy joining us in a partnership?'

Geoff Strickland turned the key in the lock, wandered out of the back door and lit a second cigarette. A lot of what Loache said was true but he knew in his heart it would be better for all concerned if Eastgate suffered a setback sometime in the immediate future. It needed to happen or the new man would be off to too much of a flyer. It was one thing coming out on top in a turf war but this represented too great an alteration in the balance of power for anyone to feel comfortable. Besides, Terry Brean had always been a cocky little sod and wouldn't waste an opportunity to rub it in. It wasn't something he could explain to the Inspector but none the less he knew it to be true. Eastgate were in need of a cow prod up the arse in order to get them back into line. Bugger this job; something else for him to think about.

And that was on top of the other little surprise. He had always been a collector of scraps of information and whilst this particular piece was of no immediate use he would tuck it away with all the other odds and sods he had accumulated over the years. Adding this to what he knew about Mrs Loaches' brother Gabriel it seemed the Smith family had more tentacles than a bloody octopus. How the hell a decent bloke like Daniel Loache had ever chose to get mixed up with that lot he would never understand.

CHAPTER TWENTY SEVEN

WEDNESDAY 15th FEBRUARY 2017

Having dedicated the best years of his life in the services of organised crime, Charlie Brinsworth could read undercurrents like the morning papers; and two things had happened already that day that had set his antennae quivering in the stiff winter's breeze.

Spanner Hopkins was a decent bloke in Charlie's estimation. Alright, Spanner would kick your head in as soon as look at you if the situation demanded because that was what he did to earn his pay cheque. It was, however, not inconceivable that he would steer you in the right direction if he thought you were half way straight. Allowing, of course, that he didn't judge you to be the sort of person who would disappear into the Gents when their round at the bar was coming close; or, worse still, claim to have left their wallet in their other coat. Spanner was principled, but understanding his personal code of ethics would have given a team of psychiatrist's apoplexy. However, if you knocked on alright with Spanner and he gave you a word of warning it was only an idiot who didn't pay heed to his advice.

That morning Charlie had sent Spanner a text to enquire if he fancied a pint; fully realising that in this particular case it was probable Mr Hopkins would freely interpret that as anything up to nine or ten. Charlie's offer had not been altogether altruistic. After the visit from Terry Brean the previous night he thought it would be wise to get a bit of an idea which way the wind was blowing down at Eastgate; particularly in respect of the gang leader's attitudes towards market development in relation to retail outlets possessing a liquor licence. Now the turf war with the Tysons had been resolved to Eastgate's satisfaction it was odds-on that the new man in charge would be looking to impose himself and lay out the direction in which he intended the Eastgate brand to develop. It was exactly the same as when a new Chief Executive took office in a legitimate company. The new man would always want to stamp his mark.

The reply he had received back from Spanner was troubling in the extreme.

Sorry, Charlie, you are currently bad news. Mr Brean didn't like the reception he received at the Bear, especially from your mate Mickey Smith. My advice would be to keep a low profile and hope it all blows over. You might be lucky as Breany will have a lot of other things to keep him busy. Keep your head down and cross everything you've got. Have a word in Mickey's ear as well. Terry Brean can be a nasty bugger given half the chance.

Well, Charlie had of course taken that warning very seriously. Just the thought of the effort it would have taken Spanner to type a message of that sort into a mobile using fingers the size of Walls' pork sausages fittingly emphasised the seriousness of the matter.

Taking on board the full brunt of Spanner's warning he had duly given Mickey a bit of an earful; enquiring why, if he smiled at every other misbegotten son of a bitch who ever set foot inside the pub, did he consider it a smart move to scowl threateningly at a person who could make it their business to do him a serious mischief.

Mickey, however, failed to be in anyway chastened by the wise counselling aimed in his direction, and made it crystal clear he had no intention of bowing and scraping to 'a jumped up little twat like Terry Brean'. He further stated that if Mr Brean thought it in his best interests to take the matter further, he would be more than pleased to accommodate his request.

Now, there was no denying Mickey knew how to look after himself. He had done a lot of that oriental self-defence shit you saw in the low budget films and under normal circumstances Charlie would have backed Mickey against pretty much anybody. The trouble was, the heavies attached to Eastgate were not 'pretty much anybody'; the other difficulty was there were dozens of the bastards and they tended to hunt in packs. Even a good bloke like Spanner Hopkins would have little alternative other than to do what he was told if the main man ordered him to dance a highland reel on Mickey's head and it was open to debate if even Big Trevor the ex-bouncer would have found it possible to restrain Spanner for any period of time after he had knocked back a couple of pints.

So that was problem number one. The other worry was of an entirely different nature, but all in all no less troubling.

Charlie had ventured out to visit Simon Bartol. No specific reason for the call, but as the conversion on the pizza parlour was proceeding according to plan and he didn't want to keep hassling the Vietnamese kids who were hopefully busy growing heaps of dope, he was at something of a loose end; and whatever you thought of his chosen vocation, Charlie took pride in the fact nobody could ever have questioned his work ethic.

He duly arrived, caught Simon in the office, which on balance was probably against the odds, and settled to a cup of tea and a general natter on a number of broad ranging subjects, a lot of which had bugger all to do with work. Some way into the conversation, which had been entirely convivial, Simon had suddenly blown him out of the water.

'You remember telling me to take a look at that bastard Woody? Well, I owe you a pint for that word of warning. I ran a check and he came out as

Ex-Eastgate.......and I'm not even very convinced about the ex.'

Charlie suddenly felt nervous. That possibility hadn't crossed his mind.

'I had no idea. I just remembered his face from somewhere in the dim and distant and somehow it wasn't a happy memory. What are you going to do?'

'Already done, Charlie; I got rid of the prick right on

141

the spot. You know as well as I do, a lot of the time Eastgate expand their sphere of operations by getting one of their boys working close in on a business until they have picked up on all the wrinkles. Then once they are clued up on the way things work they come in for a takeover.'

'What did you tell him?'

'Didn't need to tell the slag anything. Just said he had been fingered and to get his arse off of my lot before I put a boot up it. I'm far enough out of Eastgate territory that they won't push things too far without having a very good reason; and sussing out their inside man on a ferret job isn't likely to qualify in that direction. I also exchange Christmas cards and a few used tenners with officers at the local nick, so our friends in blue would be batting for the home side if Eastgate did decide to try their luck down this way.'

'The trouble is, Simon, Woods might have good reason to reckon the bloke who dropped him in it was yours truly; and the Bear is pretty much on their bloody doorstep. I've got a bad feeling they might think they owe me one for dropping you the word, especially as their new boss man seems to be a shade on the touchy side.'

'Sorry about that Charlie but in the circumstances there wasn't much else I could do.'

Well, that was fine for Simon Bartol to say being stuck out in the arse end of nowhere but the Bear being situated within spitting distance of Eastgate's back yard made it a tricky situation. If Mr Woods was still in Eastgate's employ and explained his dismissal as having been caused by being fingered by Charlie Brinsworth then it was highly likely Terry Brean was going to be none too happy about the situation. It was even possible he might consider it was in his best interests to seek some form of retribution so he could demonstrate how inadvisable it was for people to open their mouths when they would have done better to keep them buttoned.

Charlie returned to the Bear a troubled man, consoled

only partly by the fact it was Sharon's night off and he had already placed an advanced order for hotpot for lunch.

CHAPTER TWENTY EIGHT

THURSDAY 16th FEBRUARY 2017

Detective Sergeant Geoff Strickland had long been aware that to do his job to the best of his ability he must be prepared to confront untold horrors on a daily basis; yet, despite a couple of decades on the force, he still found himself ill equipped for the sight of Albert Dunn lying on top of a hospital bed dressed in off-white bed socks and a pair of red and green striped pyjamas.

Fair to say, the fact that on closer examination the colour of the stripes on the top and bottom of the patient's inelegant night garments failed to match did little to promote a picture of sartorial elegance; but seeing that Geoff Strickland was not a man noted for personal smartness, or indeed any degree of dress-code sophistication, it was highly unlikely offence to the eye would have been vigorously prosecuted on that count. The true horror of the apparition only became entirely apparent when you noticed the specific parts of Mr Dunn's anatomy that had escaped the confines of his disagreeable clothing; and the fact that large areas of his face were either obscured by rectangles of elasticated dressings or highlighted in shades of vivid yellow, purple and blue.

Albert had made it clear any number of occasions that he had been a victim of '*woad wage*'; a circumstance that had straightway provoked rapt indifference from the Detective Sergeant. Geoff Strickland didn't like Albert Dunn and cared nothing for the man's physical wellbeing. In point of fact, Strickland would cheerfully have battered Mr Dunn to death himself if it had meant he didn't have to listen to the ailing patient relate his sorry tale ever again.

Strickland, not readily noted for either his patience or bedside manner, had finally managed to interrupt a further rendition of the harrowing saga for long enough to make his lack of interest patently clear. The fact that a mad witch dressed in a purple sack and driving a stretch limousine had perpetrated an attack on the luckless Albert was purely his own concern. And further, if Mr Dunn persisted in repeating his tale one more time there was an excellent chance that a senior Detective Sergeant with a good number of years' service under his belt would be very likely to commit a similar assault; except that on this occasion Mr Dunn could rest assured it would most definitely prove fatal. On which note the policeman had bid the assault victim a less than fond farewell having in the interim consumed all the white grapes from his bedside bowl that he considered to be reasonably fresh.

There are doubtless a wide variety of attitudes to police work held by those who have taken the bold decision to follow in the hallowed footsteps of Robert Peel. Some officers of the constabulary inevitably took the view that it is something of a higher calling; some that it is primarily a cause for survival; a labour to be endured while taking as few chances as possible. The latter viewpoint being doubtless based on the indisputable fact that unless you were totally stupid it is unlikely you would ever be forced from a secure and respected position of trust in the community, which would in the fullness of time furnish the joint rewards of early retirement and an extremely lucrative pension.

Geoff Strickland, having with difficulty wriggled himself free from the lower orders, and now entering the autumn of his career, had over a period of time formulated his own personal perspective on the matter; and that, it is fair to say, was one that was shared by comparatively few of his colleagues.

To Strickland's way of thinking crime was not something that should be viewed as existing in a totally separate field. It was, in fact, little different from any other specialised branch of corporate industry, except for the fact it had two distinct divisions which operated as

145

opposing sides. In effect, which side of the line you worked was of little importance because criminality was a vast global network that by its very nature would always be fully integrated. It should be viewed in much the same way as an international corporation but one where two factions worked against themselves rather than having a single cohesive objective. The size of the industry was admittedly considerable; and its importance magnified still further by the intense media scrutiny to which it was constantly subjected. But putting that to one side the basics were still exactly the same as in any normal business; be it that the attention it received did sometimes give the misguided impression that the whole was infinitely greater than the sum of its constituent parts.

The way Strickland saw it, his function was to catch villains and where absolutely necessary make some effort towards upholding the letter of the law. His adversary's employment contract, if indeed one ever came into existence, would stipulate the direct opposite. They should break the law and go to all possible lengths to avoid apprehension, because incarceration would stop them from fulfilling their purpose in the grand scheme of things and thereby disturb the delicate balance that had existed for more than two centuries.

Despite fully embracing this extremely jaundiced viewpoint, Strickland very much admired his superior, Detective Inspector Daniel Loache, who was somehow capable of viewing things of this sort from an altogether loftier plain. Loache believed fervently in good and evil and set his stall out to defend one from the other to the best of his considerable abilities. He strove to be a good man and didn't see why everybody else should not follow a similar example.

In the Detective Sergeant's somewhat cynical opinion, totally failing to address the all-important factor; if that were indeed the case, they would both very soon be obliged to seek alternative avenues of employment.

What Geoff Strickland admired most about Loache was

the man's infinite capacity for understanding. Loache had pursued and captured the heart of Miriam Smith, who had come from a family of total miscreants; he had made her his own because he had looked at her and seen the good that lurked somewhere deep beneath a rock hard exterior. Miriam had once been trouble on two legs but now she was Loache's wife, a proud mother of two daughters and a much admired pillar of respectability in the local community. Loache had loved her into being a better person than she had at one time seemed capable; and bearing in mind where Miriam Smith had originally come from, that in itself was no mean achievement.

Strickland was similarly aware that without Loache's regular interventions his own gainful employment would have been terminated a very long time ago.

He was entirely conscious of his own shortcomings which were on the upside of considerable, and the manner in which the Inspector tolerated his deficiencies and tried to encourage him towards becoming a better person. He knew that in his personal case Loache was wasting his time and effort but none the less he still deeply appreciated his superior's regular interventions on his behalf and in consequence remained fiercely loyal even in situations when his personal views were totally at odds with those of his senior colleague.

Taking into account Geoff Strickland's mind-set it was not altogether surprising that his attitudes to twenty first century policing were considerably at odds with those stipulated in the latest official guidelines. Strickland would not hesitate to beat up suspects and threaten witnesses if he thought it appropriate; would accept bribes if he could see no reason not to do so and would steal from almost anybody without the slightest qualm. He also had no compunction about planting or withholding evidence if in his opinion it helped a tricky investigation come to the correct conclusion. None of these things were done with malice, though doubtless many of the criminals who found their way behind bars due to his actions would have taken issue with that statement. They were done because in Geoff Strickland's book they were an integral part of the broad rules of engagement; part of a policeman's functionality in the twenty first century corporate climate; a matter that the law breakers he encountered seemed sometimes to better understand than the judicial authorities and even the members of the public he was contracted to protect.

Geoff Strickland had known Anthony Garfield for years. His father had worked for Garfield senior for an eternity and deeply respected the man. However, the next generation down proved to have precious little in common and there had been no need to continue any sort of relationship once their respective parents had been consigned to the grave.

In consequence, it had come as something of a surprise when Garfield had approached him for advice on how 'a friend of his' could best gain access to an industrial building to retrieve some property which he would be unable to access by merely walking through the front door and issuing a formal request.

Strickland had initially made it clear he would not be able to solve Garfield's predicament.

Anthony, I'm a copper; I arrest people for doing that sort of thing. I certainly couldn't be seen to be offering you any sort of help even if we do go back a long way.

However, as the true facts of the matter gradually emerged and Garfield made it clear his proposal was to purchase specialist knowledge rather than solicit any form of direct participation, Geoff Strickland had gradually warmed to the proposition and eventually agreed to give the matter some serious thought; allowing that Garfield understood very clearly that his name was never to be mentioned in connection with the project in question.

Initially he had considered it might be enough just to put Garfield in touch with an accomplished burglar. However, without his personal involvement, it was unlikely the proposition would be readily accepted by any man sufficiently adept with a jemmy to have received trade accreditation. Added to which, he wasn't completely convinced Anthony Garfield had sufficient street smarts not to finish up on the wrong end of the deal.

What he needed was someone who was trustworthy, had the ability to organise, and at the same time was not adverse to getting his hands dirty; and after considerable thought he had eventually settled on the name of Charlie Brinsworth.

Charlie was a career criminal; but for one of that villainous breed he carried a reputation for being surprisingly honest. Indeed, he had over a period of years acquired the sort of standing in the trade it was impossible to buy. If he gave his word he invariably kept it. His hand shake was as good as money in the bank. He knew everybody who was worth knowing and had been involved in the business for all of his adult life with few members of the criminal classes having a bad word to say against him.

Being fresh out of prison, Charlie was now rumoured to be putting his feet up whilst living off the proceeds of the public house he had inherited from his father; doubtless supplementing his income with any ill-gotten gains he had been successful in hiding from the eyes of the judiciary. There was of course no possibility that way of life would be destined to continue. He had seen it a thousand times. Pretty soon Charlie would miss the buzz; he was an adrenalin junkie like the rest of them and would find it impossible to stay on the side-lines for more than a few months before he found himself needing the thrill of personal involvement. In these circumstances, it occurred to Strickland, he might do a good deal worse than point Anthony Garfield in Charlie Brinsworth's direction.

Before proceeding further, Geoff Strickland had mapped out a plan, then reconfiguring it, then starting all over again. He explained to Anthony Garfield the need for an alias and that a cut-out between him and Charlie Brinsworth was essential if he didn't want the risk of having the man on his back for the rest of his days. He suggested meetings were held at a remote location; mooted the car swap; even pointed Garfield in the direction of the lugubrious Albert Dunn to play a part in ensuring he escaped from the second rendezvous without picking up a tail. The most important advice he gave was how much information to let slip at each meeting; enough to whet Charlie's appetite without revealing too much of the important detail. Enough to get the fish interested in taking a nibble without any fear of it making off with the bait.

He also decided he had better keep a close eye on Charlie Brinsworth if he was persuaded into going for the deal. The advantage with co-opting an old lag like this one into the scheme was also its main drawback. All the while Charlie's shrewd little mind would be ticking over trying to feel out a bit more about the operation; and say what you liked about Charlie Brinsworth, nobody had ever accused him of being thick.

Geoff Strickland was confident he had done everything in his powers to bring about a happy outcome. He had already collected a wad of notes from Anthony Garfield to cover his own involvement so now if anything did go wrong it wasn't really his concern. Things had progressed quite rapidly and soon it would all be over one way or the other; and strangely, only now was he beginning to feel a little uneasy.

It was the last minute stuff that always got you going. Anthony Garfield's late request that Strickland put him in touch with someone who would supply him with a gun.

Under the counter for cash, Geoff; no bullets, naturally. Just something to keep in my pocket to help settle me down. As you will appreciate, I'm not really used to this sort of thing.

Strickland didn't like it. If Garfield was playing it straight there was no need for firearms; and if he wasn't, things had the potential to get very messy. Anthony Garfield, he noticed, was beginning to get a strange shine in his eye; and when push came to shove Charlie

Brinsworth wasn't anybody's idea of a pussy cat. His first inclination was to tell friend Anthony to get stuffed; but in that scenario any goodwill that existed between them would instantly disappear and if Garfield did get hauled in by the law how long would his name be likely to stay out of the investigation? The other point was, if he chose to back off Garfield was quite possibly enough of an idiot to attempt to make his own arrangements......and that would very probably be even worse.

In order to protect his own interests he needed to keep some degree of control, so he reluctantly decided to pass on the name of a contact. He then quickly made a phone call to smooth the path for the transaction; whilst taking the opportunity to also dictate the exact terms of its enactment.

CHAPTER TWENTY NINE

THURSDAY 16th FEBRUARY 2017

Mickey Smith wasn't given to deep analytical ponderings but was aware his current situation was totally ludicrous. Rachael Broadbent had meant everything to him and he desperately needed to come up with a plan for getting her back. The trouble was, he had been having difficulty thinking straight lately and he blamed that on all the stuff that was going on around him. These days, his head seemed to be permanently buzzing with static electricity. He wanted some sort of mental detox that would scour the inside of his brain and make all the bad stuff go away. As an interim measure he was making do with pints of extra strong lager with whiskey chasers but somehow that wasn't proving nearly enough.

The only constant in his life seemed to be the stupid scheme to defraud the person who was one of his closest friends; the man who had set him up in business when he was still wet behind the ears and had been supportive at all the right times, regardless of what was involved. True, Charlie was a villain, but he was the most honest villain Mickey had ever come across.

Then again, looking at the situation another way round, there was no denying Charlie had proved a pain in the arse by bringing all those lowlifes into the pub after he had worked his bollocks off to keep the Bear off limits to that sort of delinquent scum. Of course, it was Charlie who really owned the pub and there was no good reason why he shouldn't allow anyone across the threshold who took his fancy. He didn't owe Mickey any sort of explanation, even if it would have been nice to have his feelings on the matter taken into consideration once in a while.

The difficulty was, Mickey had set the rules for an awfully long time and was now finding it hard to accept any degree of shared responsibility. Not that Charlie ever interfered in the way he ran the place; just the opposite, actually. Charlie avoided any degree of involvement in the day to day running of the pub the way an alley cat avoids a puddle of rainwater. The situation was complicated and Mickey was useless at dealing with this sort of stuff.

Balanced against that was the fact that thanks to Charlie there was now an excellent chance he would very soon get his head kicked in by members of the Eastgate squad. While Charlie had been in prison he had done very nicely, thank you very much, at staying under Eastgate's radar; but as soon as Charlie had put in an appearance the invisibility cloak had immediately slipped away and in a matter of days Mickey's pride and joy had become a focus of unwanted attention. Not that Charlie had seemed particularly bothered by a succession of reprobates wandering in and out of the door as if they owned the place; Charlie had spent most of his life in the company of miscreants of that sort and looked completely relaxed in their company.

Mind you, being fair to both parties, nobody had forced him antagonise Terry Brean and his scumbag entourage. That had been entirely his own choice so there wasn't really that much of an excuse for him to hide behind on that one. He should have just smiled and taken no notice when the annoying little git had started to get uppity. It wasn't as if that would have been totally beyond his acting powers. Christ, he had done that sort of thing umpteen times before, though admittedly always through gritted teeth.

What had really made his blood boil on this occasion was the way he had seen Brean eying up the Bear like it was something he intended adding to his list of birthday presents. That little twat, who had probably never done an honest day's work in his entire life seemed to fancy he was just going to walk in to the pub that had been Mickey's whole life and start giving the orders. Well, dream on Terry fucking Brean; that was going to happen over his dead body. A very distinct possibility, now Mickey had found the time to give the matter in depth consideration.

Then there was the other stuff Charlie clearly had simmering away on the back burner. He admitted to that pizza parlour up the road but Mickey was pretty damn sure Charlie had a lot more going on besides that little number. He had seen the way Mr Brinsworth scuttled out of the door each morning with a look of concentration on his face. That had nothing to do with pizzas or Mickey was a poor judge. Charlie had other schemes brewing and he would lay a pound to pinch of shit they were some distance outside the law because that was the territory to which Charlie would naturally gravitate.

Added to which, the randy old goat was now shagging his top barmaid. He had seen the looks Charlie and Sharon exchanged when they thought nobody was watching and he hadn't missed the patter of footsteps on the stairs at all hours of the night. Charlie had bought her a Valentine card as well; and you can bet your savings he wouldn't have done that if Sharon had just been popping up to Charlie's room to help him with his stamp collection.

Christ, what did he sound like? They were both comfortably over twenty one and could do what the hell they liked. He would be sitting them down and offering advice on contraception next. It seemed like the wiring in his brain was starting to come loose. What on earth was the matter with him lately?

Well, perhaps when you thought about it, there were reasons why Charlie Brinsworth did deserve to get stitched up. It wasn't as if old Charlie would miss a few bob and Mickey had always been scrupulously straight when divvying up the takings. And that, despite the fact Charlie just shoved the wodge of notes straight into his back pocket without even bothering to give it a glance. Clearly, Charlie was doing alright; anyone with eyes in their head could see that for themselves. Yes, Charlie probably deserved everything he had coming after all the disruption he had caused over the last few weeks. It was only justice, wasn't it?

Mickey shuffled outside and lit a cigarette. The back yard was currently bathed in shafts of weak sunlight that heralded a premature outbreak of spring, which would doubtless be snatched back in double quick time as soon as the weather gods figured out they had stamped their foot down on the wrong pedal.

Who was he trying to kid. It was a lousy trick to play and Charlie Brinsworth deserved better. Added to which, now the necessity to provide his vanishing bride with a decent future had disappeared on the fast train south, he had even less excuse for his behaviour. Charlie was a stand up bloke and he needed to find some way to put the whole thing right. Yes, he knew it would cost him a lot of cash to straighten out the mess he had caused, but in the circumstances what else could he do? Money wasn't everything in this life; you had to be able to look yourself straight in the eye when you were shaving in the morning; and he had found that quite difficult for the last couple of weeks.

Mickey stubbed out his cigarette and immediately lit a replacement. He was only wearing a sports shirt and jeans but for some reason he didn't feel in the least bit cold. Even the bloody weather was now conspiring to make him feel completely unsettled.

Right; while he was tackling all the big issues, what did he do about his love life? It had seemed so simple when Rachael disappeared over the horizon. He knew he would miss her; of course he would miss her; he had loved her to bits. But facing facts, if he kept his head down for a few months and absorbed himself in his work then sooner or later he would emerge from the dark tunnel in which he currently felt trapped. There was no way he was going to appear on the market as a jilted lover even if that role did present opportunities. He had received quite a number of winks and nods and even the odd scribbled phone number while he had been playing the faithful fiancé but now the opportunity was open to him he felt no urge to chase down any of the interested parties.

The situation with Stevie should never have taken place. She had probably only allowed him to ravage her out of pure pity. *Poor old Mickey, a consolation shag to set you up and get you on your way. You'll be fine now. Just toddle off and throw yourself back into organising your grotty little pub.* Stevie was capable of that. She weighed up all the possibilities. She was a woman who could view things from that sort of perspective.

That wasn't anywhere near fair. He had always enjoyed a special relationship with Stephanie Armitage and he knew she was a person he would find impossible to replace in his life. They just got on; always had; she found him amusing; while he got a kick out of making her laugh. He was Stevie's clown; he couldn't deny it; no point in pretending it was any different. He performed, she clapped her hands and they both got out of the relationship what they needed. For her nothing was ever serious; even the current conspiracy was little more than two naughty schoolchildren acting out a devious little charade while teacher was looking in the other direction.

Now, what happened? He had always had feelings for Stevie; just not in that particular way. She had always been some way out of his reach so he had never seriously considered the possibility that they might end up writhing around on her pristine Egyptian cotton sheets; and now the situation had changed and he was at a loss to think how this would affect the way they had always reacted to one another.

He was fully aware he needed to sit down and talk to her but he didn't know how to start the conversation let alone what he was going to say. What did she feel? Probably embarrassed that she had let a grinning little irk like Mickey Smith anywhere near the royal bedchamber.

If he chose to face facts, the Stevie Armitages of this world were out of his league. They interbred with people with titles or money and knocked out litters of ill-mannered children with too many teeth who went on to provide work for the next generation of psychiatrists.

Besides, if he was being brutally honest, Stevie wasn't always that nice a person. She had another side to her; one that could on occasions be quite frightening if you didn't do exactly what she wanted. She was always good for a laugh but that didn't necessarily make her the sort of woman you would want to be entangled with in any other context. And anyway you looked at it Stevie Armitage was never going to be a person who you could rely upon to be at home frying up the spam fritters when you staggered home after a hard day at the coalface. She wasn't like Rachael in any respect and it was Rachael he wanted and Rachael he couldn't bloody well have. That was the long and short of it. All this other stuff was just an aberration brought about by her unexpected departure. Just something else to mess with his head; as if there wasn't already enough.

Things were further complicated because the scam in which they were currently involved had an awful lot riding on it. It represented a way to lever open a door to a completely different sort of future. The sort Stevie had always had mapped out before her; but one he had never come close to attaining. An opening that might change everything; one that could even cause Rachael to have second thoughts about what Mickey Smith had to offer as a life partner.

He needed to reach a decision; was he in or was he out? It was a problem; another problem he felt unable to solve while the buzzing in his head persisted. A further difficulty that he felt completely inadequate to deal with and wanted desperately to go away.

CHAPTER THIRTY

FRIDAY 17th FEBRUARY 2017

The first message had come through while he was still eating breakfast. They had then played text ping pong for fifteen minutes to make sure the detail was fully understood, before everything went quiet. When Charlie sent a speculative follow up thirty minutes later he might as well have saved his time. Antony 'Garfield' Noone's communications device was now without a sim card or possibly a battery; it could even be nestling comfortably at the bottom of a river bed for all he knew.

Charlie was running late. Sharon had obtained the services of an understanding babysitter the previous night and had stayed over at his place until the small hours. They currently had a nice relationship that seemed to suit them both but Charlie wasn't stupid enough to think that would last forever. Sharon was a good looking woman and would have no shortage of volunteers to hold her hand on a cold winter's night. She also had a kid to think about with no hope of any support from the little girl's waste of space father who had hit the road as soon as sperm donation had progressed into a requirement for parental responsibility. Charlie needed to get his head straight about where he and Sharon were going. He liked her a lot and didn't want to muck her about. In his experience, women like that didn't come along very often so he needed to make some big decisions pretty damn quick.

In a lot of ways the idea of settling down quite appealed to him but he wasn't sure if he was genetically equipped to cope with such a drastic change to his routine. Also, it had to be admitted, he didn't have much of a C.V. to present even if he was lucky enough to make it through to the final interview. This was all stuff that he needed to consider but now wasn't the right time. Get the job with Antony Noone sorted and then he would give the matter his undivided attention. The extra cash in his back pocket might also go some way towards making him look a more appealing prospect if he decided to put his past life behind him and make an attempt to go straight.

Charlie turned his mind to more pressing matters. Something was wrong with the way Anthony Noone was playing his cards. It wasn't that he was making mistakes. It was the fact that he wasn't making the mistakes that should have come about automatically.

Noone didn't claim to have any experience of this sort of situation but he was covering himself like a true professional. He wasn't getting lucky; he was getting his card marked by someone who knew what they were doing; and to Charlie's mind that only left two possibilities. Either it was a set up by the forces of law and order with the purpose of catching him with his hand in the till or Noone had a knowledgeable friend from the wrong side of the law who was guiding him along, step by step.

The former was unlikely. Whilst Charlie had enjoyed a fairly successful criminal career, he just wasn't a big enough fish to warrant that degree of attention. The smart money would be on the involvement of someone who worked outside the law and had the experience to know how to handle this sort of situation; and if that were the case Charlie wanted to know his name and boot size even if he had to break bones in order to get the information.

Charlie cleaned his teeth for the second time that day and lumbered slowly down the stairs. Mickey was hovering in the bar with a dishcloth in his hand looking industrious. This is what Mickey usually did when he didn't have anything specific to do with his time but was reluctant to admit it. Mickey was always happier when he considered himself to be busily engaged in achieving something that would be of great benefit to the pub, even if he hadn't yet managed to positively identify exactly what that might be. He specialised in a sort of proprietorial hover that said, *this is my place and isn't it sparkling clean; go on, try to find a ring mark from a pint pot on any of the surfaces.* Charlie always wanted to shout, *get a life Smithy; there'll be beer stains on that bar long after you are dead and buried*, but he never did because Mickey wouldn't have understood. Mickey approached every day the same way. He was a natural worker and didn't know how to be anything else. Instead, Charlie waved cheerily and headed to his usual table to text Seamus Macgregor, before having one final try at dredging up something on the internet about Anthony Garfield. However, before he got started with either of those tasks a random thought flashed across his mind.

'Mickey, I hope you don't mind me asking but is there something a bit queer about your family?'

Charlie immediately realised he hadn't put that as tactfully as he might have done but fortunately Mickey still had that slightly weird look in his eyes that he had been sporting since the bust up with the little red head and didn't seem ready to take offence.

'Why do you ask?'

'It was just something that git Terry Brean said when he made his courtesy call the other night; something about your family being a bit strange.'

'Well, my parents owned a shop and sold stuff for a living. Terry Brean would probably consider anyone who grafted in order to put bread on the table a bit peculiar, so perhaps that's it.'

'Yes, I take your point but I think we are probably looking for something a bit more unusual than that.'

'I've got loose connections on both sides of the law; does that help?'

'It sounds a lot more promising.'

Charlie sat back in his chair and waited for Mickey to explain. He didn't.

'How does that work, Mickey?'

'You are one nosey bastard, Charlie Brinsworth.'

'Yes, that being accepted, will you tell me or do I have to ask up and down the High Street? Someone will know;

round this way someone always does.'

Mickey wiped industriously at a large aluminium ashtray that he kept in the smoking area in the back yard. The fact you could already see your face in it didn't seem to bother him one bit.

'This is just the way I remember it so don't take it as gospel. My father's sister had a lot of problems. She had a regular bloke for a couple of years but they never married and he disappeared or died or something. The lady also had an ongoing problem with drink, drugs or maybe both. She died quite young and her two kids, Miriam and Gabriel virtually bought themselves up with a bit of overseeing from my old mum and a couple of other relatives. Gabriel was heavily involved with the Eastgate firm before he upped sticks and disappeared overseas; went by the street-name of Angel so I was told. For a time I think he was something of a big hitter, but that was a very long time ago and well before my time. Miriam, Gabriel's sister, also had her own set of troubles but it looks like she straightened herself out because she's now married to a copper called Loache. Quite a senior copper I thing; D.S. Strickland's immediate boss, if what he told me was true. I only know because Loache put his head in here a day or so back to say hello; seemed like a decent bloke on first viewing. Is that enough to stop you knocking on doors with a clipboard and a questionnaire?'

'Bloody hell! Why didn't you ever say anything?

'Because it's none of your bloody business, Charlie Brinsworth. Oh, and just for the record I haven't seen either Miriam or Gabriel since I was knee high to a duck and I wouldn't recognise either of them if they walked through that door in the next ten minutes.'

'What else do you know about your friend, Mr Loache?'

'You really are pushing it, aren't you? He isn't my friend and the only time I've met him is when he walked in here and introduced himself. We have no plans to meet again and I didn't invite him to pop in next week for a

161

family reunion or try out for the darts team.'

'I remember Angel Smith; he had a heavy reputation back in the day. Any idea where he disappeared to?'

'No....and the answer to your next question is, mind your own fucking business, so don't ask it.'

And with that Mickey picked up his cleaning rag and disappeared out of the door in a huff.

CHAPTER THIRTY ONE

FRIDAY 17th FEBRUARY 2017

Oliver Dearlove was in raptures. He had a full week to finish the painting for that horrible little barrow boy Mickey Smith and he knew for certain he could complete the task comfortably ahead of schedule. His original plan had been to deliver the finished work a matter of minutes before cut off time but he wasn't sure he would be able to contain himself for that long. Even now he could feel the excitement building up in his chest as he imagined the look of horror on Smith's face when he unveiled the finished work for his inspection. Not to mention, the unmistakable disappointment in the eyes of that rather tasty ex-clotheshorse who seemed to have an appointed role as his fancy piece, intermediary and personal advisor.

The curtain was nearly ready to go up on his masterful production; there was not too much longer to wait. First it would be necessary for him to suffer the slings and arrows of unjust recrimination. He would need to practise looking forlorn, crestfallen; possibly even a little tearful. He must try to make that last out for as long as possible so it would be possible to get maximum benefit from the point at which realisation would eventually dawn on the unhappy customer.

Later there might be suspicions of his true intent but at this stage it would be far too early for thoughts that would fit comfortably into that category. Now there could only be looks of abject horror which would slowly graduate into expressions of uncertainty as it slowly became clear that he had fulfilled his contract to the letter and there was no room for any comeback.

Perhaps this would be the point at which to offer an olive branch. *'I could of course try to rework the painting to your revised specification'*. A straw for Smith to briefly cling to, before it was unceremoniously wrenched from the man's feeble grasp. A scintilla of hope on the distant horizon that a rescue mission was possible, before it was kindly pointed out that it would probably be better to just start afresh, bearing in mind the difficulties that would be involved in attempting a convincing modification to the existing work.

Then, the bombshell; he would of course have no alternative but to charge the same again.......and take a little longer to come up with the finished canvas, as he was completely exhausted after working night and day to meet the strict terms of the original contract.

Dearlove rummaged in the pocket of his smock and located his copy of the written word. His eyes glinted as he reread the stiff sheet of paper for the umpteenth time.

I, Oliver Dearlove, contract to deliver to Mr Michael Smith, an exact copy of the original painting titled 'Charlotte Langthorpe', within a period of seven days; or shall forfeit the agreed fee of £5,000, payment of which has already been made in full.

Simple and succinct; signed, dated, witnessed; nobody would be able to lay a glove on him. Then, another couple of weeks of work, an additional five grand safely trousersed and off to Cheltenham races with a spring in his step to put that cash to good use. Oh the unbounded joy!

When Oliver Dearlove considered he hadn't felt this happy in a very long time. Taking all things into account his life had not been an entirely merry one. The early days of painting kippers on a plate, surrounded by a bevy of adoring girls dressed in large shapeless jumpers and skin tight jeans, had been all too short. His talent remaining largely unrecognised; his work consistently labelled interesting but highly derivative. His difficulty had always been that he could do too much rather than not enough. He grazed in many pastures rather than limiting himself to a single field; and thanks to the morons who passed judgement on such things, his versatility had been a hindrance rather than the great asset it should naturally have become.

It was unjust but still an undeniable fact. He had been held back by the very talent which should have served to propel him ever forward. When he looked at other artists of his age who had ground out lucrative careers by reproducing numerous spin-offs on the same hackneyed theme, he wanted to spit. Men and women who were not fit to clean his brushes had been lauded to the high heavens for coming up with one miniscule speck of dubious creativity; before settling back to churn out unending copies with the slightest of variation in content and theme but never a single one that hinted at any sort of advancement in thought or technique. The taste of the buying public and the critical buffoons who steered them towards their purchases was beyond reason. There was little wonder van Gogh had felt frustrated enough to lop off a chunk of his ear!

In some ways perhaps he had got the last laugh. How many of those jackanapes could claim to have had major works hanging in famous galleries throughout Europe and North America; some, even to this day, being viewed by appreciative audiences of literally millions year upon year. Granted, they didn't carry his signature but did that make them any less his work? Of course it didn't; it was his hand that had guided the brush, was it not?

The first time, quite naturally, had been a total accident; a bet if he remembered correctly, and he was sure that he did. A canvas that could pass for a Modigliani. It hadn't even tested him.

Because he had only been playing at the deception game at that time he had adopted the style but not bothered with any of the peripheral niceties. Yet, he could not deny that was the single act that had served to show the way forward; to focus the bright beam of his talent onto fertile pastures where money was waiting to be harvested by putting to use his unique array of talents. The beginning of a long learning curve for a man still young in years, now taking a totally new direction in his chosen profession.

He had needed a confederate to cover the aspects with which he wasn't conversant. Someone above reproach to handle the more practical side of affairs. It took a little time, but the right person was found and she performed the organisational role with aplomb. It helped that she was a woman, he felt, though he found it difficult to understand whyever that should have proved the case.

People had no idea of the level of difficulty that was involved in producing a first class forgery. You didn't just have to get under the skin of the artist you were imitating; you had also to appreciate his or her temperament, and even the particular mood they might have been experiencing when they bent to pick up the brush. This was not overlooking the fact your work would need to be discovered in a suitable frame and painted on the correct type of canvas using the right kind of brush; and don't even get him started on the paint itself, a subject upon which you could write for a lifetime without scratching the surface. The research alone was balls aching and you were always aware the tiniest mistake would lead to your ruin.

Then there was the need to leave little clues rather than a full-blown route map. You couldn't make it too easy for the ferrets who would pore over your work looking to enhance their dubious little reputations by highlighting any inconsistency they might stumble upon. It was always necessary that you left them something to justify their miserable existence, as well; even if it was one dried out bone to be shared amongst a whole pack of snarling fangs.

It became something of a battle of wits, which had suited his temperament admirably; served to guarantee that he could never get bored or complacent ....and when he proved successful, as had so frequently been the case, the feeling of exhilaration was utterly fulfilling.

His big advantage was his versatility. The very thing that had proved his biggest liability in his intended career had now become his greatest asset. He could range from Pollock to Gauguin, Dali to Vermeer. For a time he was totally untouchable; they didn't have the slightest clue where he was coming from next; right up until the Turner which was, upon consideration, perhaps half a step too far. And that one bad call was what had earned him several years' incarceration and a time in which to reflect upon his sins.

After his release matters had become considerably more difficult. He was now a marked man. About this time ageing techniques had also begun to improve. Scanning; bah! Even now the very sound of the word sent a cold shiver running down his spine. Plus the fact he knew he was regularly put under surveillance. There was a constant interest by the authorities in what Mr Dearlove might be up to at this moment in time.

His current life could of course have been far easier if only he had been able to part with the treasures that he had accumulated along the way; but how could that ever be possible? Everyone was a burning memory. The Georgian candle sticks with the profit from the Klimt; the beautifully engraved finger bowl from the Munch that they had debated over so long and hard before successfully coming down on the wrong side of the fence. His collection of treasures stood as evidence of his life's work; a testament to his achievements; how could he possibly bear to be separated from them? That could never be an acceptable form of justice.

So life had forced him into a second change of vocation. If you couldn't imitate a style then why not produce a direct copy? There was a market for that skill and he latched on to it like a new born baby to its mother's teat. It wasn't as lucrative but it was considerably less chancy and had served to enable him to indulge his various hobbies while others were left grubbing for crusts in the gutter. Kept the Bookies off his back, as well, when the nags proved disinclined to run in the way the form book indicated they might; and most importantly stopped him having to sell off all the things in life that he held most precious.

Life also had its moments of divine satire but few like

the one presently in prospect. He laughed out loud as he gorged on the sublime irony of the current situation; and this time his amusement came about for an entirely different reason.

If the world had only chosen to recognise his wondrous talent in the manner that good sense demanded, then his life would have been so much simpler. Mind you, there had been compensations along the way and the one currently in prospect would certainly be a moment to relish. The only question that concerned him was, who would he ever be able tell?

CHAPTER THIRTY TWO

FRIDAY 17th FEBRUARY 2017

In an uncaring world where fortunes can change in the blink of an eye it is good to have a pillar of faith to which it is possible to cling in moments of worrying uncertainty. An anchor point that can be immediately recognised and guaranteed not to alter with the passing of the days; somewhere that remains happily unaffected by the curses of political upheaval, climate change, Brexit, Scottish independence and would likely prove resistant to a nuclear bomb blast or even an invasion from outer space. For Brendan O'Sullivan and Spanner Hopkins, such a talisman was the Eagle public house, situated at the town end of the old London road.

It would be misleading to suggest the Eagle was in any way prepossessing, least of all in terms of architectural heritage. The building had been constructed in the mid nineteenth century using poor quality, over baked brick, sanded mortar and second hand slate. And if the pub had ever enjoyed a moment of glory, one could only think it would have been in those first heady days when it might have been perceived as a pointed to better times; a rarity indeed in that grubby area of town.

Despite any minor drawbacks, it quickly became apparent that the Eagle had a significant role to play in the great scheme of things. Within days of its doors first being thrown open to the paying public the pub had found a market niche which it fully embraced and was quick to exploit. A happy situation which guaranteed an income for its owner, while at the same time providing a valuable service to a largely undervalued strata of society. The Eagle became swiftly recognised as a place where people of limited means and humble origins would feel no pressure to appear in any way upwardly mobile. A venue where what you saw was most decidedly what you were going to get. Somewhere ideally created to cater to the needs and desires of the downtrodden and disenfranchised; a place where anyone who admired a marked lack of pretention would feel completely at home.

Brendan O'Sullivan had been mates with Spanner Hopkins since God needed help tying his shoelaces. The pair had first met at school before graduating to become fellow gang members working out of Eastgate headquarters at the Golden Pheasant public house. In 2005, O'Sullivan had mysteriously come into money and had gone under the wire to open an Undertaker's business. The means by which his friend had financed that venture had at the time been something of a mystery to Spanner Hopkins, and it was a subject about which he was little wiser even to the present day. And taking into account the fact O'Sullivan was as close mouthed as a Solicitor's Clerk when it suited him, Spanner considered it unlikely he would learn the full truth of the matter until Brendan was flat on his back receiving the Last Rights.

The divergence in their avenues of gainful employment might have been the breaking of lesser friendships. In the case of O'Sullivan and Hopkins it was of little consequence. They continued to meet regularly in the Eagle, which they had first blessed with their unwanted patronage as underage drinkers; they continued to retell the same stories they had been happily recycling for decades; they drank too much and laughed too loudly at their own private jokes; and still put the fear of God into anyone who was unwise enough to request that they keep the noise down, while they were engaged in the practise.

Also, strictly in accordance with convention, O'Sullivan continued to con Hopkins into buying three beers out of every four, while exclaiming loudly for anyone to hear that Spanner was a burden on his finances that he only endured due to a naturally charitable disposition.

It might have come as a surprise that Brendan

O'Sullivan had chosen this sort of work-life balance. Seeing O'Sullivan dressed in his best black Undertaker's suit he could quite easily have been taken for a pillar of the establishment; and, indeed, to all intents and purposes that was not so very far from the truth. His business was a hub of industry and a model of efficiency. His men were never ill disposed or badly dressed when they arrived to perform their duties, and they did so in a manner that testified to the fact they had been thoroughly drilled in every aspect of their job requirement. Their mentor believing that perfection was a minimum requirement for an O'Sullivan employee and that anything less than flawless precision was an insult to the person in the wooden box as well as the one who would ultimately be required to pick up the tab on the deceased's behalf.

That is not to say that over the course of the last twelve years the odd body had not found its way into an unmarked grave on Brendan O'Sullivan's watch; or indeed that every burial plot in the cemeteries he patrolled with the vigilance of a black suited wraith could claim to house no more than a single corpse. O'Sullivan was a pragmatist and realised that sometimes it was necessary to bend with the wind; and he had observed first-hand what an ill wind could do to the unsuspecting; and had seen mightier oaks than O'Sullivan Bespoke Undertakers levelled to the ground when their owners had not anticipated the direction from which the next winter's gale might be expected.

Nights out with Spanner Hopkins acted for O'Sullivan's like a release valve. There was never any need to tell Spanner too much about the traumas he had encountered in his working day because Spanner was not the type to be overly interested in that sort of thing. Equally, Spanner didn't harp on about what had been taking place down at the Golden Pheasant because O'Sullivan would have his ear close enough to the ground to know most of that for himself; and the bits that he didn't already know would probably be best left unsaid. Besides, they had a shared past of nearly five decades which took

171

up enough of their time without getting too heavily involved with the troubles of the present day. It was the way they liked it and the way it had been for more years than either man cared to remember.

Tonight the pair were sitting at their usual table, but that fact aside, everything else was contrary to normal proceedings. Voices were not raised and the only laughter emanating from their whispered discussion carried a hard and bitter edge. To illustrate the magnitude of the seismic shift which was currently influencing proceedings at the window table of the pub, an unprecedented occurrence had already been seen to occur; Brendan O'Sullivan had been witnessed to trudge across the beer soaked floorboards in the direction of the bar on more occasions than Spanner Hopkins!

The locals gave sideways glances in the direction of the two men, before hastily refocusing their attention elsewhere. Something was evidently not right but sure as hell nobody drinking in that particular bar was going to be the one foolhardy enough to enquire as to the cause.

It would be fair to say O'Sullivan had heard vague rumblings in the past few days and had chosen to dismiss them out of hand. It looked like this had been a mistake. He might have been able to do something, though God alone knew what that something would have been. Anyway, it was too late now. What was done was done and there could be no going back. He knew his friend far too well for that to be anything approaching a realistic possibility.

'So I told him to stick it where the sun doesn't shine.'

He would have done, as well; and made no effort to control the volume of his voice while he was doing so; Spanner was well known for not mincing his words on occasions when he judged plain speaking to be the order of the day.

'Leaning on shopkeepers; is that what this bloody business has come down to?'

That would indeed be something of a change of focus

172

for Eastgate and as O'Sullivan was one of the local businesses that were likely to be affected by the change of direction, that in itself was no small cause for concern. But new brooms were notorious for sweeping clean and new gangland bosses for trying to stamp their authority by implementing fresh initiatives, and sadly that was just the way of the world.

'He'd been talking to the kids and leaving the old hands like me completely in the dark; not that there's more than three or four of us left from Uncle Edgar's day. Now there was someone who really knew how to run a gang; God rest his soul. Breany reckons he's going for a complete change of strategy and said if we didn't like it then we knew what we could do.'

'And that was when you told him to stick it where.........'

'Yes, then I collected in what I was owed and walked straight out of the door. Didn't even stop for a last pint. Christ, I've worked for that mob since I left school, Brendan! It's a bloody strange feeling being unemployed when you get to my age; especially when it's for the very first time in your life.'

Brendan O'Sullivan considered his friend's predicament; and balanced that delicately against the fact that his glass was nearly empty.

'Strictly speaking Spanner you've never had a job in your life. Bet you've never heard of P.A.Y.E. have you?'

Much to O'Sullivan's relief, Hopkins gathered up the receptacles and disappeared in the direction of the bar. This gave him a little time to think, but not very much. The Tysons would of course welcome Spanner with open arms; but there was too much history between the firms and it would be unlikely to work out in the long term. He wasn't black enough to be a Rasta; though to be fair, Spanner would be able to handle the rum intake standing on his head. All the smaller gangs would treat him with suspicion in case he had been put in as a plant. Freelance? Spanner just wasn't a freelance sort of bloke; he needed a specific niche that catered to his strengths in an established organisation........ maybe something on the door at a big hotel or gambling joint? A loud scrunch of boot leather on unswept floorboards signalled Spanner's return.

'Look mate, there's no need to worry. I'll fix you up with a decent suit and you can pitch in at my place for a bit until things work themselves out. You never know, you might even take a liking to it the same way I did.'

He wouldn't; but in the circumstances what else could you say? Hang on, he's thought of something......and it looks like it might have gone some way towards putting the wind back in his sails.

'Brendan, I just remembered something; Eastgate are planning to turn over the Bear tomorrow night. Fancy a bit of fun to bring back memories of the old days?'

Brendan O'Sullivan leaned back in his chair and focussed on a large cobweb which was wafting in the breeze close to the central light fitting. Given the wide choice of words at Spanner's disposal, those were undoubtedly the ones he had least wanted to hear.

CHAPTER THIRTY THREE

SATURDAY 18th FEBRUARY 2017

It was horribly early when Mickey Smith arrived at Stevie Armitage's gallery and leant heavily on the doorbell. The weather was still pretty bleak but that didn't matter. He just wanted to get there and say the things that needed to be said. Mickey had been awake for half the night planning everything out and he now had a complete speech memorised to perfection. It was good as well, even if he did say so himself. It covered all the bases and was heartfelt while at the same time explaining his reasoning in a concise and logical manner.

Mickey rang the bell and straightway caught sight of her silhouette through the frosted glass as she stumbled down the stairs. Seconds later the bolt was drawn back allowing the door to open a small crack before slowly widening as she recognised the caller. Stephanie was wearing a dressing gown, mainly unbuttoned, and her hair was pointing in six different directions at the same time. She blinked, appearing vaguely bewildered; looking for all the world like a hamster that had just crawled out of a nest of shredded paper and found itself in an unexpected patch of sunlight. Stephanie Armitage looked totally dishevelled but still good enough to eat.

He tried to remember the opening line he had committed to memory but it was long gone. Instead, he stepped forward, took her in his arms slid his hands inside her bathrobe and squeezed her body to his as tightly as possible. It was meant to show her that everything was alright; that their relationship was completely back to normal. In retrospect, it was a mistake.

A disembodied voice floated down the stairs.

'Steph, I'm going in the shower. Is it the postman?'

'Ziggy', she mouthed without actually making a sound.

She yanked Mickey into the hall and pushed the door shut with her bare foot; then made a half-hearted effort to disentangle herself from his arms. They came to rest at the foot of the stairs with Mickey holding on for dear life. It seemed like the best thing to do because if he let her go he didn't know what would happen next. They stood there entwined but in total silence. Mickey wanted to explain himself but couldn't summon up the words. Stephanie wanted to replay the last minute of her life with her having chosen not to answer the door.

A ravaged figure came shuffling down the stairs, clad in red silk pyjamas and suede slippers with a black sleep mask pushed high onto his forehead. He pushed past in the direction of the downstairs kitchen muttering to himself in a preoccupied fashion.

'Stephanie, I can't find a bath towel anywhere. If that's the postman you are currently clutching to your bosom can you enquire if he's got my recorded delivery? I'm still waiting for the tickets for Barcelona and they assured me they would be here by yesterday at the very latest.'

Ziggy clattered about out of sight for a couple of seconds before returning in the opposite direction carrying a pot of yoghurt and a very small spoon.

'Morning, Mickey; sorry, didn't recognise you with your head buried in my wife's cleavage. Lovely the way you two always play so nicely together; I've always been a great admirer of social interaction. If you can just hang on for ten minutes while I grab a shower and call a taxi I'll be out of your way. You didn't notice my passport on the hall table yesterday evening, did you dear?'

'We had a long discussion about the state of our marriage last night,' whispered Stephanie caustically. 'It didn't go quite as I had expected,' she added, nodding her head in the direction of the brown suede slippers turning the corner and disappearing from sight at the top of the staircase.

'I can't get divorced again, Mickey. It's far too soon. I'm still getting over the wedding. Besides, I've got a strong feeling the divorce settlement would prove to be a massive disappointment. Ziggy seems to have anticipated what might happen next and has moved all his assets offshore. Besides that, he's the only husband I've ever had that I actually like. Oh Mickey, I'm terrible with men. What a horrible mess.'

Mickey disentangled himself and patted Stephanie gently on the back, then walked through into the small downstairs kitchenette. Stephanie buttoned her dressing gown in a belated effort at respectability and made a couple of half-hearted backward sweeps with her fingers as she tried to adjust her hair. Suddenly the mood changed and the business woman was in evidence. She glanced in horror at the wall-clock, grabbed the kettle and marched hurriedly in the direction of the sink.

'Right, I need to get organised. The gallery opens in forty minutes. I'll need to get a shower as soon as Ziggy's out of the way. Want a quick coffee? I'm having one.'

Mickey braced himself. It was now or never.

'Stevie, the thing with Oliver Dearlove. I've decided that I don't want to go down that road. I've thought it over for half the night and it just isn't something I feel comfortable with any more.'

Stephanie frowned, either at what Mickey had said or the way the back spray from the tap had dotted the front of her dressing gown with a shower of water droplets.

'Mickey, we discussed this twenty times already. From your point of view it's a win-win situation. There's no way your mate Charlie would ever need to know.'

Mickey located a crumpled packet of cigarettes in his jacket pocket, lit two, and passed one across.

'I'd know. You're right but I still can't do it. It's been playing on my mind and it's getting to the stage where I'm waking up thinking about it in the middle of the night. I could square it with my conscience before the split with Rachael but now I've got no excuse. I just didn't make allowances for the way it would mess with my head.'

'You are a complete idiot, Mickey Smith. It's all about

bloody Rachael woman, isn't it? Now she's packed her bags you've completely lost your motivation to get off your arse and make something of yourself. Don't you think it might be a good idea if you started thinking outside that particular box; what about considering your own situation for a minute? That fucking pub can't remain the entire focus of your attentions for the rest of your life. There's a big wide world out there in case you haven't noticed.'

'Listen Stevie, I'm not bloody doing it. Let's get that straight right now. We've had some good laughs along the way but I'm finding this one just a bit too close to home for it to be a comfortable fit. I don't care about the money anymore. I'll cover your slimy friend Oliver and then we'll draw a line in the sand. Sorry Stevie, I've made my mind up. It's just the way it's got to be.'

The door partially opened and Ziggy, with something that looked like a turban covering his hair, stuck his head through the crack.

'Congratulations Mickey, I think that's a new record. It usually takes me a lot longer than that to get her glaring daggers. Now I hope you are beginning to appreciate the agonies I have been forced to suffer in recent months. Stephanie is a very difficult woman to live with. Any chance you could see your way towards testifying as a character witness if we ever end up in court?'

Stephanie picked up a pan scourer and aimed it inaccurately at her husband's head. It hit the wall and fell to the floor without making a sound.

'Bugger off Ziggy; and for your information we have been married for just over two years and you failed to remember both anniversaries. And don't think I've forgotten that I caught you taking the telephone number of that little chambermaid while we were still on our honeymoon. My lawyer will rip you to shreds if we get near a courthouse. Did you interrupt running round in circles because there was something constructive you wanted to say or were you just passing through?'

'Just wanted to bid the pair of you a fond farewell, my love. I need to be in Barcelona by this evening. I just wanted to make sure you had everything you might need and would be able to manage without me for the next ten days.'

'Over there with Fishface, I presume?'

'Jilly Gurnard is my Secretary, Mickey. Lovely girl but for some reason Stephanie has never warmed to her. Her father's a mover and shaker with Deutsche Bank and her brother runs the United Nations pretty much single handed.'

'A lovely girl who has packed so much of her underwear into my husband's luggage over the last six months it's a wonder the poor woman has any left. If she's trying to send some sort of message can you tell her I got it the first time. Anyway, Ziggy, you obviously have things to do so don't let me keep you.'

Ziggy opened the door a little wider, fully crossed the threshold and smiled warmly.

'I was wondering. As the local taxi service appears to have ceased to function this morning, would one of you mind dropping me down at the train station?'

CHAPTER THIRTY FOUR

SATURDAY 18th FEBRUARY 2017

Anthony Garfield had needed to think very hard about how he should enact the role of Anthony Noone. He concluded, the character needed to be something of a mixed bag but should never come across as particularly clever. The story line he was selling would inevitably be difficult to put across in an understandable fashion; the more so, because in the main it was totally true. Anyway, Garfield now felt happy he had captured the essence of Noone the man. The new skin had finally ceased to chafe at the edges and was beginning to feel a remarkably comfortable fit.

The name itself had been settled upon only after careful deliberation; and, in his opinion, the choice reflected that he had the right disposition for the sort of operation in which he was now engaged. Anthony Noone; *A. NO ONE.*

Alright, it was clear the subtlety had sailed clean over the heads of everybody involved, but nevertheless it still made him feel a little bit superior. And regardless of his confederate's lack of imagination, it was still nice to have offered up some tantalising clue to the subterfuge he was perpetrating, even if everybody had proved too dim to pick up on the fact. Damn pity, he would never receive the plaudits he so richly deserved.

As far as he could determine, things were now running along relatively smoothly. No reason to expect otherwise; the ground work had been meticulously undertaken; and nobody could deny he was overdue a bit of decent luck. Long overdue if some form of equitable balance was ever to be struck that might serve to level the scales.

He had been left in a comfortable position when his dear mother had unexpectedly popped her clogs not six months after his father's body had been committed to the ground. He had been the sole beneficiary of the estate; not necessarily a situation he would have enjoyed if the death certificates had been dated the other way around. But there he went again, judging the old boy too harshly. Would he have been summoned to his father's bedside in his final hours if the man had still harboured a grudge? Was that occurrence alone not a clear demonstration that he had been weighed, measured and ultimately absolved of all past sins?

In all probability his father would have issued an outright apology if he hadn't been too proud to spit out the words; an acknowledgement that he had made a number of catastrophic mistakes and now accepted full responsibility for the sorry outcome that had come as a result; a declaration that he could now see that he had forced his only son into a situation where it had been possible for him to respond in just one way. Yes, that made a degree of sense. His father realising at the very last, that the troubles that had served to split the family asunder had been entirely of his own making. And with the grains of sand fast running out, taking the opportunity to mend fences while there was still a little time.

It had of course been a humiliating experience. Coming down from University to take his place at his father's side only to be castigated for underachieving in his scholastic studies; not to mention that bit of trouble with the bedder that was frequently referenced but never discussed. What did it really matter? A Third was still a degree wasn't it? Alright it wasn't as good as a First or a Second but was there any need to split hairs over what amounted to a triviality? Were the social aspects of a university education to be totally ignored in favour of a library stuffed with dry books fit to induce narcolepsy? And that irk who got glassed in the Refectory had brought it on himself, so why he had been held responsible for that one was difficult to understand.

It had been damn right vindictive of his father to exile him to the lower reaches of the Sales Office; oblige him to work cheek by jowl with ill-bred people who were clearly his social inferiors; and this with the stern parental message ringing loud in his ears. *'There's no easy ride for you here, son; if you want to make something of yourself you'll need to work your way up from the very bottom'.*

Well, he had certainly tried his best......for a time, at least.......but the situation had proved completely impossible. He was a fish out of water. He knew nothing of engineering tools and to this day their weird applications remained something of a closed book. He also had to admit the job bored him rigid; nobody but an imbecile could derive any degree of pleasure from this type of work; and to make matters worse his colleagues revelled in the depths of his ineptitude. What could be more entertaining than to deride the boss's son, who was so clearly out of his depth?

In those circumstances was it even a little surprising that he had become resentful; that very soon he had begun to harbour a grudge?

In planning for the future, the old boy had made one small error of judgement. Just a tiny thing but it is amazing how even the most minor miscalculation can come back to haunt you at a later date. He had inadvertently handed out a weapon that he had not recognised could prove potentially lethal. For my twenty first birthday, at a time when my star still shone bright in a cloudless sky, father had gifted a five percent stake in the company. Give the old boy his due; that particular time-bomb could only have been detonated in the most unusual of circumstances; and who might have guessed that such a strange situation would ever come to arise?

Things actually started in earnest with the demise of a certain Mr Herbert Varley; Varley was old money who owned a significant chunk of the company's shares but took no interest in its day to day running. A daughter inherited, an Oxford educated blue stocking if memory served, and she proved an entirely different proposition. She came to see my father to discuss what role she could play in the future development of the business and promptly departed with a flea in her ear. Big mistake on daddies part but he had always been an irascible old buzzard; and in this case the discourtesy was destined to come back to bite him on the bum.

Varley Junior.....Barbara, Brenda possibly; certainly something of the sort......took umbrage at the rebuttal and offloaded her shareholding to a couple of London sharks called Cragg and Watson. Over time, these gentlemen worked diligently to increase their holding in the company until it stood at something over forty five percent. Then one dark and fateful day I received a polite invitation to meet with them for a spot of dinner; and by chance the summons found me with my spirits at a very low ebb.

Well, quite naturally I said no. How could I stab my own father in the back even in the event that he was currently treating me like a dog that had thrown up in the middle of the boardroom carpet? But needless to say they didn't give up at my initial refusal and little by little the cash offer went steadily higher, while at the same time my fortunes at work got progressively worse.

It was something of small consequence that eventually tipped me over the edge. The old man summoned me to his office and instructed that, as I had proved totally useless in the Sales Office he was transferring me with immediate effect to the shop floor. '*Might do you good to get a bit of grease under your fingernails for once in your life*', was, I seem to remember, his final word on the subject. Well, a man can take only so much and within the week the deed was done and I sat back to await developments with an air of distinct trepidation.

Without much delay Armageddon was upon us. Cragg and Watson arrived at the works with legal representation and in a trice father was ousted from the padded chair at the top of the table and unceremoniously deposited in the gutter outside.

I was, as fully expected, immediately ousted from the family home and diplomatic relations became someway short of frosty. Mother professed her disappointment;

father bemoaned missing the opportunity to have a vasectomy. I took the hint, tied a spotted handkerchief to a stick and struck out for the highway. An invitation for Sunday lunch looked unlikely to be in the offing anytime soon.

As it transpired, the situation proved even more unfortunate than I had anticipated. The new owners of the company sold everything that wasn't nailed down and proceeded to run the business into the ground. I did receive a payment but it was a good deal less than I had been promised. A hand shake without witnesses clearly stood for nothing when dealing with men like Cragg and Watson, who clearly realised I was in no position to take the matter to court.

I seethed, but thought it expedient to bide my time. Revenge is a dish best served cold and I am not a man to forgive or forget. I took small consolation from adding two names to the list of people who would be hearing from me at some future date; thereby pushing a couple of university lecturers and a number of desk jockeys from the company's Sales Office a little lower down the priority list.

As you can well imagine my name was not being toasted in the alehouses of the local community, so I took the opportunity to seek my fortune further afield. And until I was summoned to my father's bedside, shortly before he breathed his last, I was a stranger to Thorton Chumley as I had been denied permission to ever darken the doors of the family home.

Sad to relate, in the intervening years my finances dwindled significantly. Atrocious luck with a couple of business ventures; the market crashing significantly when I had been most heavily invested. It wasn't until recently that I started replaying my father's last utterance; turning the numbers of the combination over in my head and hearing again his final words.

'When I got back from Italy I didn't need to invest everything to set up the company. What was left over is

184

behind a false plate in the back of the safe. If you are ever desperate for cash you might want to take a look. I swear to you there is hundreds of thousands in the secret compartment at the back'.

So now it looks like the tide is finally on the turn. Geoff Strickland, not a man with whom I would ordinarily have chosen to associate, had proved remarkably useful; but his part in the enterprise is over and now I am completely on my own. One thing for sure; the past years have taught me much and I have no intention of coming out of the current undertaking feeling short changed. I am not the same man who was turned over by that pair of asset stripping shysters all those years before. Fate has decreed that I now cloak my body in a far harder shell.

Today, I gritted my teeth and went to a nasty little house on a bleak council estate and purchased a firearm. I added to the order six small bullets that probably cost me a good deal more than they are actually worth. They are only to act as an insurance policy, but what is it they say about insurance? That you can never have enough.

I'm not quite sure whether I could actually shoot someone in cold blood but it would probably not prove too much of a problem. It's important not to lose sight of the fact that in today's world one hundred thousand pounds is still an awful lot of money........and when I considered the matter it became apparent, Charlie Brinsworth, hasn't really needed to do very much to earn such a significant sum. No need to reach a decision on what might need to happen at this point in time; the gun will just serve to provide an interesting option. One that can be taken up or ignored as circumstances dictate. Strangely, I have never used a gun to kill a fellow human being; but the sanctity of human life has never been a subject that interested me to any great degree, so I don't think my conscience will make any effort to deter me from doing what is required.

Once I have money in my pocket I intend to leave instructions for the disposal of the family house with a firm of Estate Agents and be on my merry way. I have several people I am looking forward to meeting up with again and it has been necessary to delay one particular reunion for far too long because of the great distance involved. I have been carefully watching the career of Sebastian Cragg who for some years has stationed himself in Toronto, Canada. I can't put into words how anxious I am to re-establish that acquaintanceship and encourage it to progress.

Arnold Watson is much closer to hand but his name is already scored with a line in my little black book. The unfortunate man was abducted from his family home some years ago and is now buried in a small copse, a hundred and fifty metres from the bottom of my garden. It's quite picturesque down there and I often admire the spot in question when I am out for a stroll. I'm confident my father would have heartily commended that particular outcome for Mr Watson. One down, daddy, but a few more still to go.

CHAPTER THIRTY FIVE

SATURDAY 18th FEBRUARY 2017

Mickey drove the car at a leisurely pace in the direction of the train station. Ziggy tapped impatiently on his knees to encourage the vehicle to go faster but Mickey remained unmoved. This was the nearest thing to fun he he'd experienced since he had rolled out of bed that morning.

Ziggy's car was a Mercedes soft top and Ziggy was the sort of man who suited a vehicle of that sort. In Mickey's opinion he would have been driving something similar if he had a three pounds fifty bank balance and a meeting with the debt collectors scheduled for the following day. Neither was likely to ever be the case but it served as testament to the man's attitude to life. Ziggy would always come out as one of life's winners even in the event that he ever happened to lose. Mickey's only surprise was that he hadn't been asked to wear a peaked cap and keep his eyes on the road while his passenger sat in the back puffing on a Cuban cigar.

'Mickey, tell me straight, are you and Steph........'

'No. Definitely not. We could never be anything other than friends.'

'It's just we had a long conversation last night and I got the impression there might be something that............'

'Well, it's nothing I know about.'

'It's hard to read you two. I know you've always been really close and I make allowances. You argue like husband and wife even when.....'

'It's her. The woman's always been unstable. I can't imagine why you ever married her. Most of the time she's completely off her head.'

'She says pretty much the same about you; but she usually smiles while she's saying it. Doesn't it ever annoy you being treated like her lapdog? I honestly think she considers you to be one of her personal possessions. Listen, the reason I asked the question.......any chance you could keep an eye on her while I'm away and let me know if.....'

'I've got no idea what you're talking about and *no* in that order.'

'Right. That's pretty much what I thought you'd say.'

Mickey deposited Ziggy and his pigskin valise at the train station, drove back, garaged the car and pushed the keys into his jacket pocket. That way Stevie might have to ring him if she wanted to use the vehicle.

He didn't want to see her just at the moment; at least it was probably best to steer clear of her while she was in one of her moods.......and anyway, he wanted it to be her who contacted him and not the other way around. If he was the one who made the first move it would look like he was in the wrong when it was pretty damned obvious who had started the argument. Bloody cheek she had, insinuating he had no life outside the pub. That was complete rubbish. Hadn't they got up to all sorts in the couple of years before Rachael had come on the scene? And even after, there had always been some sort of scam on the go to keep Stevie amused. The trouble with women was they never seemed to understand that men needed to earn a living and couldn't just be hanging around at their beck and call all of the time.

Mickey got fed up with wandering aimlessly. He located a park bench and plonked himself down. The little kids who were running round it waving sticks in the air and screaming loudly left in a hurry when he scowled menacingly in their direction.

The situation he now found himself in had come out of nothing. The fat Canadian with the wife who looked three parts Indian had stared intently at Charlotte Langthorpe's image on the wall before declaring it to be an undoubted masterpiece. He sounded confident as well; like he actually knew what he was talking about; though with

Canadians naturally liking the sound of their own voices it was always a bit hard to tell. *'Pre-Raphaelite for certain; Millais, he was pretty damn certain. Had Mickey had it authenticated and valued? What did he mean by hanging a work of art of that quality on the wall of a backstreet pub? Didn't he realise it could be worth a small fortune? In his opinion it put the artist's depiction of Lillie Langtry in the shade.'*

A week later, slightly less maybe, he had mentioned the incident to Stevie and in five minutes flat she had been on the phone to someone called 'Bernie' who was knowledgeable in the area and promised he would come over and give his opinion. There followed an in depth appraisal with much pursing of lips before it got marked down as a strong probable. It wasn't signed but apart from that seemed perfectly authentic. In Bernie's view it should be submitted for appraisal by a recognised expert.

This was where the problem really started to kick in. Mickey had begun to turn over in his mind what he could do with a sizeable windfall; discounting for the moment that the painting wasn't his to sell. Stevie was no help, repeatedly pointing out that an opportunity like this didn't come along every day and he would be a mug not to take full advantage of the situation.

It really came down to a matter of conscience. Mickey decided to ignore his; Stevie didn't have one. Suddenly, the decision became a lot simpler. The bitter irony that needled him was that if the discovery had been made a few weeks earlier Charlie would still have been in prison, so the disappearance of the artwork would very likely never have been commented upon one way or the other.

As it was, a problem immediately presented itself. Mr Brinsworth, a man of leisure since his release from prison, now chose to park his carcass underneath the bloody painting every day of the week. He had even been known to peek up at the lovely Charlotte with a strange look in his eye when he thought nobody was watching. In Mickey's view, it was just a pity the artist had chosen to depict a

189

good looking woman. If it had been a vase of flowers or a bowl of fruit it's doubtful if Charlie would have given it a second glance.

The idea to redecorate the bar had been Mickey's. Stevie had been all for taking it off the wall and blaming its disappearance on the cleaning lady or a passing tradesman with light fingers. It was a good plan and would, Mickey felt, be relatively simple to organise.

The bar had been in need of new coat of paint anyway. All Mickey needed to do was redecorate and then say the old paintings didn't fit in with the new colour scheme and he would dispose of them in the nearest skip. A really smart plan; pretty much fool proof; but it proved a total disaster thanks to Charlie's preoccupation with the lady on the wall.

There had been a second option but Mickey had never been keen on the idea. Stevie knew a back street bloke who had the ability to knock out copies of anything you cared to mention in the style of the original artist. He had a big reputation in the field, according to Stevie, but there was also a downside. He was an awkward old bugger with a police record and he charged a small fortune for his work.

Mickey had teetered on the edge before deciding he might as well jump. This was his big chance. This would give him the opportunity to look after Rachael in the way she deserved. And for a full five minutes everything in the garden had looked rosy. Then his fiancé had left him and shortly after, his conscience caught up with what it was meant to be doing for a living.

Now, Rachael was long gone, he was going to be five grand out of pocket, his relationship with Stevie was on a knife edge and there was a scabby looking dog urinating up the side of his bench on which he was sitting. Serves you right you daft bugger. This sort of caper isn't for you. Stick to pulling pints. You're out of your depth with something like this.

Mickey headed back to the Bear to catch the early bar.

He had wasted half a day thinking in ever decreasing circles and it hadn't done him the least bit of good. He pushed open the door and surveyed a scene of utter devastation. Broken chairs, upturned tables, smashed glasses and bottles; with God knows what dripping down the walls. At least there was something solid on which to focus his attention. Spanner Hopkins was sitting on a stool by the bar with a pint glass in his hand and at his side was a bloke dressed as an undertaker with a baseball bat in his hand. The perfect end to the perfect day, thought Mickey, before launching himself in their direction.

He remembered his first stride quite clearly and maybe the start of the second before things went dark and fuzzy. Sometimes it was best to just recognise when it wasn't going to be your day.

CHAPTER THIRTY SIX

SATURDAY 18th FEBRUARY 2017

After a long day in the gallery Stephanie Armitage was looking forward to a nice relaxing bath. She would fill the bathtub to overflowing with very hot water and put in a sprinkling of the stuff she had been given for Christmas but thought she would probably never use. She would light a scented candle, put on her pure silk eye mask and lay back and relax. She was forced to admit, today had proved a big disappointment and Stephanie didn't react well to any sort of setback.

On a positive note, at least Ziggy was out from under her feet. Against all the odds Stephanie found she had become oddly attached to her husband, even though they tended to argue if they were under the same roof for long periods of time. Ziggy might be annoying but for all his faults he was at least never predictable. Boring men were in her opinion the worst by far. Also, he was not the jealous type and gave her plenty of scope to get in and out of trouble as she saw fit. On the other hand he did have a tendency to be disruptive and sometimes Stephanie thought she liked him best of all when he was several hundred miles away tending to his own affairs.

Even though she constantly berated it, Ziggy's liaison with Fishface was just about ideal. It meant Stephanie only tended to see him for short periods of time, and when she did he was relatively undemanding. Ziggy and she rubbed along nicely together because they both knew exactly what they were getting for their money and made allowances for the other's idiosyncrasies. Quite naturally she sometimes bemoaned her fate but in reality their marriage was an equitable arrangement that suited both parties perfectly because neither had the sort of personality that made them suited to living in each other's pockets. They both had their eccentricities. She with her paranoia about being bogged down with the mundane. He, with the need to be chasing the next deal, the next woman, something, anything; and probably secretly realising that when he was eventually successful in running his quarry to ground, the result would always prove slightly disappointing and the pursuit would need to be restarted all over again. They were a couple, she felt, who would be ideally suited to each other a little further down the line; and for the present it was just necessary that they endured each other's quirks and foibles until the passing of the years bought about the happy realisation that their hour had finally arrived.

In order to keep Stephanie's world merrily rotating on its axis, Mickey Smith had a totally different function to fulfil. Mickey was there to provide amusement and joy; to keep her spirits light and avoid her ever being bored. And, sad to say, of late Mickey had proved delinquent in fulfilling these duties; a fact that Stephanie found extremely perplexing. She had just about been able to excuse his adoration of Rachael, who had temporarily proved something of a fly in the ointment; an annoying fly that she had quite enjoyed swatting when the need had come about. But that little episode had in itself proved surprisingly engrossing and, if she were being really honest, quite good fun in a macabre sort of way. So now, with that small blip having been satisfactorily taken care of Mickey should logically have returned to heel; but annoyingly that was not proving to be the case.

She was fully aware Mickey had always secretly adored her; but that was only right and proper; the way things were meant to be; the way nature had clearly intended. It was quite nice to be sought after because both parties had seemed to realise the rules of the game demanded that she was never actually attained. Mickey was there for the laughs not the romantic stuff. Lovers were ten a penny but how many men were in any way fun to spend time with? Very few in her experience; on the whole they were a pretty glum lot; especially when they were trying to convince you that it was in your best interest to share their bed for the night.

This was clearly where it had all started to go wrong. A couple of glasses of wine too many and they had been at it like rabbits. Not that she hadn't enjoyed herself; but that was very much beside the point. Becoming her lover was not Mickey's role in the big scheme of things and she felt it had served to affect the natural balance of their relationship. Worse than that, he was no longer doing what she suggested. Mickey had always possessed a moral code which she totally lacked and it was becoming frighteningly evident he was prepared to let it affect his decision making process. This wasn't at all the way it was meant to work. Mickey did entertainment; she controlled decision making. A strict rule he now seemed prepared to ignore.

As if that wasn't bad enough, Mickey continued to be obsessed by that ridiculous little pub. It wasn't even as if he owned the place. All he really did was polish glasses and smile nicely at the customers while his gangster mate, Charlie Brinsworth, sat in the background pulling the strings. The plan to pinch Charlie's bloody painting had been a hoot until Mickey had suddenly got cold feet. Just recently the man seemed to have completely lost all sense of proportion. This did not bode well for their future relationship and quite obviously drastic action needed to be taken.

She had not had too much difficulty in disposing of Miss 'butter wouldn't melt in her mouth' Rachael Broadbent. Now, it seemed bigger issues were demanding her attention. It would of course be extremely convenient if an accident could be arranged to befall Mickey's buddy, Charlie Brinsworth, because he was also starting to become something of an issue; but it was quite probable mobsters like Charlie took special care not to make themselves available to be pushed down a flight of stairs. You would think there would be somebody you could hire who would take care of this sort of thing, and presumably there was. It was a great pity she had never moved in the sort of circles where girls passed on references covering that particular skill set because at this point in time it could have come in very useful indeed.

So what else was there? The pub; well now, that place really was the proverbial sitting duck.

She had once set light to a motor boat in Cannes; well, either Cannes or Nice; it was difficult to remember all of the details because it had happened so long ago. To the best of her recollection that little project had gone off like a dream. The owner had been a horrible little Armenian who had scammed her first husband, Glenn, on a dope deal. It was always drugs with Glenn; a lovely man but one with victim stamped in capital letters across the centre of his forehead. For reasons she had never fully understood that night had marked the first step on the road to their divorce. From that day on Glenn had never seemed to look at her in quite the same way. Ungrateful in the extreme, she considered, taking into account the fact it was she who had been obliged to make the problem go away. How was any of it her fault? There was no way she could have known that the bloody Armenian would have picked that particular night to sleep out on his boat.

The more she thought about it the better sense it made. That pub had been a millstone round Mickey's neck for far too long. If it disappeared from the face of the earth it would be doing everyone a favour. It would free Mickey up to be his old self, cut his ties with Charlie Brinsworth, and enable life to get back to the way nature intended.

Thinking along those lines she might even persuade Mickey to take a job in the gallery. He had always had a way with the public and he was ace at spouting unadulterated bullshit. The punters who drifted in off the street could hardly be described as discerning, so the fact Mickey had no idea what he was talking about would be unlikely to prove any great handicap. Besides, it wouldn't take her long to teach him enough to get by on; and Mickey was nothing if not a quick learner.

The more she considered the idea the better she liked

the idea. If Ziggy was away and trade fell flat they might even sometimes put up the closed sign and sneak upstairs for a kiss and a cuddle. That sort of stuff would be permissible providing it was never allowed to slip out of context. Much though she would like to pretend differently she had quite enjoyed being ravaged on that rainy winter's afternoon. She could offer herself as a special bonus if Mickey did all the right things and made a good job of keeping her properly amused. But only if he behaved himself; only if he did exactly as she told him without allowing his stupid conscience get in the way.

CHAPTER THIRTY SEVEN

SATURDAY 18th FEBRUARY / SUNDAY 19th FEBRUARY 2017

Everybody in the bar had enjoyed a good laugh when Mickey Smith's head was eventually released from the confines of Charlie Brinsworth's sports jacket. Everybody, that was, except Mickey, who looked anything but happy with the situation.

The mob from Eastgate had put in an appearance sharp on 6pm and according to eye witness reports it had taken only a matter of seconds for the main bar room to be completely trashed. For some reason that Mickey failed to fully understand, Spanner Hopkins and his mate, Brendan O'Sullivan, had been drinking in the pub at the time and had chosen to pitch in on the side of the locals. That had tipped the balance in favour of the Bear's defence force and bought about an undignified withdrawal from the Eastgate battalion. Not that the retreat had made an awful lot of difference to the overall outcome. The raiding party had already achieved their objective. The bar area was now transformed into a scene of total devastation.

The crowd that had been involved in the fracas had quickly settled down for a victory session with Charlie offering drinks on the house; but Mickey failed to see there was anything worth celebrating. After stamping up and down for a bit surveying the wreckage, he had briefly occupied himself by righting a few pieces of damaged furniture and clearing up the odd broken bottle. Pretty soon however, he gave up the fight; disappearing off to his room with a bag of crisps and the remains of a bottle of brandy. Somehow Mickey hadn't felt in a celebratory mood.

It was now ten o'clock on Sunday morning and Mickey

Smith had been up and about since the crack of dawn. It wasn't easy cleaning up this sort of mess but somebody had to do it and there was no way he could have left things like they were for his aged cleaning lady to sort out.

Another hour of hard work and the bar would look as good as it was possible to get it in the time available; one more spin of the hour hand and it would be incumbent upon him to once again draw back the bolts and throw open the doors to the waiting public. Mickey would be opening those doors right on time come hell or high water. Nothing on God's earth was going to stop him. It was a matter of pride. There was no way he was going to see his pub closed down by a bunch of Neanderthal scumbags.

The service bins in the back yard were already filled to bursting. Even with the regular collection being due the day after next he still reckoned it would take at least one trip to the Recycling Centre to get things properly sorted; not that any of the stuff he had dragged from the pub looked like it would be in any danger of being recycled.

Mickey took time out to survey the scene. The walls of the pub had come out of it alright once he had sponged them down with several gallons of soapy water. The new coat of paint had done a decent job at protection, even if it had played havoc with his eyesight during the cleaning process. The floor was also fine. The blood stains could hardly be noticed now he had subjected them to a good scrubbing with hot water infused with a dose of vinegar and disinfectant. He had lost three chairs, one table, probably twenty odd glasses, quite a few full bottles of miscellaneous liquids, mainly beer and lager; and one of the spirit optics had taken a direct hit from something heavy; thankfully, without allowing the gin bottle held in its neck to topple free and smash on the floor below.

All in all Mickey thought the Bear had got off pretty lightly; well pretty lightly if you didn't have a fair idea that one of the paintings that had been mashed in the skirmish was worth an awful lot of money.

None of the wall pictures had survived. They had been

far too easy a target for anyone with a stray bottle in their fist. Charlotte Langthorpe had fared no better or worse than her contemporaries but that didn't say an awful lot. Sharon, who had come in early to help out with the cleaning operation, told him Charlie had personally taken the painting's shattered remains to a rusty brazier at the back of the yard and downed a large scotch in her honour; before stepping forward to apply a ceremonial Swan Vesta to the funeral pyre. To an innocent bystander the lady would have been seen to depart to the afterlife with as much pomp and ceremony as a Viking warrior on his journey to Valhalla.

As Charlie appeared to have no idea of the painting's worth, and was anything but an art lover, Mickey was at a loss to understand why that particular portrait had always been so special to him. Mickey had started to detest the very sight of Charlotte Langthorpe from the precise moment he first became aware she was going to set him back a cool five thousand pounds.

Mickey stopped what he was doing as his mind caught up with the implications of current events. At least the activities of the previous evening would finally put one matter to rest. Stevie would now have to concede that their ill-judged foray into substituting the portrait was now dead in the water. Even she wouldn't be able to come up with some sort of diabolical scheme to replace a painting that everybody knew to no longer exist.

A creak of the floorboards and a muffled groan announced that Charlie had belatedly decided to put in an appearance. In the course of the hostilities it looked like he had taken a couple of direct hits as he was now sporting a magnificent black eye, nicely offset by a length of frayed Elastoplast which had clearly been applied to his cheek by someone with no expertise.

'Feeling better this morning, Smithy? I can always ring up the Pheasant and invite Eastgate back down for a rematch if you are still feeling touchy about missing out on the action.'

'It's all a bloody joke to you, Charlie Brinsworth, isn't it? In case you're interested I've been cleaning this lot up since half an hour after you eventually staggered off to bed. What do you reckon will happen if we aren't ready to open up those doors at twelve sharp? I'll tell you; the crowd that drink in here would waltz straight down the road to the Cottage or the Bridge and we'll end up losing their trade to the competition.'

'Living under the same roof as you, Mickey Smith, is like having a wife with all the disadvantages and none of the benefits. You are fast turning into a right old woman. Would it have been so terrible if we stayed closed for an extra couple of hours while we cleared this place up properly? Missing the midday opening would just have served to ratchet up the tension. You watch; they will be streaming through those doors this evening like we are giving out free beer. The story about what happened last night will have circulated round the neighbourhood during the day and the world and its wife will be in here tonight to see if they can spot where the blood stains seeped into the floorboards. You've cleaned it all up haven't you? Bloody idiot. We could have doubled our takings if you had left a big pool of the red stuff on the floor in front of the bar for people to admire. They love a bit of gore round here, always have. Hang on a minute; shout over that cook of yours and see if he can lay his hands on a bottle of ketchup. Nobody's going to taste it to see if it's the real thing, are they?'

'Not a chance. I've been mopping those bloody floorboards all morning as it is. I notice you've only chosen to put in an appearance with your bright ideas now all the work's been done. What's the matter; were you frightened of being asked to get involved?'

'I had bigger fish to fry, Mickey Smith. While you were skulking in your boudoir last night with your head in your hands I was addressing our major staffing shortage. Were you aware that Spanner Hopkins is now gainfully unemployed and that for a reasonable hourly wage and the odd pint of best bitter our vacancy for an experienced bouncer could be made a thing of the past? No, don't thank me. It's not unusual for my intentions to be cruelly misunderstood.'

'If we make free beer part of the deal with Hopkins we'll be out of business by the summer.'

'Typical of the hurtful ingratitude I've come to expect from you, Smithy. Listen, I told the big bastard to get himself round here tonight for a chat. You'll have to sort out the detail of his terms of employment. I've got some important business that requires my urgent attention. Don't cock it up, Mickey; Spanner's the right man for that vacancy. Nobody from Eastgate is going to fancy putting a foot inside the Black Bear if word gets out Spanner Hopkins is working the door.'

CHAPTER THIRTY EIGHT

SUNDAY 19th FEBRUARY 2017

The thumping at the door of the funeral parlour reverberated along the quiet street disturbing the tranquillity of the cold winter's morning. It was loud enough to act as a clarion call for a late riser still snuggled beneath a warm duvet cover, and would have been similarly unwelcomed by any young mother attempting to catch up on her beauty sleep after a troubled night nursing a hyperactive, insomniac infant. It might even have inclined a couple considering the acquisition of quality soundproofed double glazing to glance once more at the advertising leaflet stuffed behind the clock on the living room mantelpiece; or acted as a confirmation that they were definitely doing the right thing for a couple of retirees in the process of abandoning city life in favour of an isolated rural retreat.

These were not subjects foremost in the thoughts of Brendan O'Sullivan who didn't give a flying fart about the interests of any of his neighbours. He merely recognised the noise as a manifestation the sort of distraction he had been at pains to avoid. Brendan had struggled out of bed at an early hour and gone to his funeral parlour specifically so he would have the peace and quiet that he required in order to complete some subtle but imaginative adjustments to his tax return. The matter was of some urgency as he had a busy period in front of him and the form needed to be submitted in a matter of weeks.

In order to avoid being bothered by the outside world while he was immersed in the process of creative thinking, he had turned off his phone and told absolutely nobody where he could be found. Yet despite his best efforts, it appeared that some annoying bugger had still been successful in tracking him down.

O'Sullivan cursed under his breath before making his way warily to investigate the unwarranted intrusion. He reasoned that anyone guessing where he might be found at this delicate time would be precisely the sort of person he would be most anxious to avoid. A supposition manifestly reinforced when he slid the door open a couple inches and came face to face with Detective Sergeant Geoff Strickland of the Organised Crime Unit.

'It's Sunday. We're closed,' said O'Sullivan, holding little hope that Strickland might take the hint and leave him in peace.

'Kind of you to offer, Brendan; a strong white coffee with just half a teaspoon of sugar,' said Strickland. 'Let me in while this door is still on its hinges; it's fucking freezing out here.'

O'Sullivan let out an audible sigh; yanked open the door and stuck his head round the corner to ascertain who might have witnessed the arrival of his unwelcome visitor. The answer was nobody and Brendan O'Sullivan duly tucked himself back inside the door, uncertain whether the lack of an eyewitness to the intrusion was necessarily positive news.

Strickland pushed his way through the reception rooms and into the private quarters, before taking a seat at a kitchen table in order to allow O'Sullivan free access to the tap and kettle. O'Sullivan ignored the invitation, shuffled his papers out of Strickland's sight and stood with his arms crossed, awaiting developments.

'What do you want this time? I'm not getting rid of another body for you so don't ask the question. We're square after the last time and I don't fancy you being in my debt. People who you owe a favour must spend half their lives listening for footsteps on the street.'

'Put the bloody kettle on and stop whinging, O'Sullivan. Do you think I'd be paying you a call if I had any choice in the matter? All I want to know is what went off at the Black Bear last night? Personally, I don't give a shit but my D.I. is related to the cheeky little git who runs the place and I've been designated to keep an eye out in case he grazes his knee. Don't give me any bullshit, Brendan. I'm not in the mood. You and your gorilla mate Hopkins were spotted going in last night and rumours are already on the street that there's another turf war about to kick off. Well trust me my friend; that isn't going to happen. So just tell me in simple words what the hell happened.'

'I didn't leave the house last night. Your informant needs to pay a visit to Specsavers.'

'Brendan O'Sullivan, I am arresting you for the murder of Nathanial Dawson. You are not obliged to say anything but anything you do say will be written down and may be used in evidence..........'

'Alright, alright, don't bother going through the full charade because you'll be wasting your time. Do you think I was born yesterday? Let me guess; you've had a witness come forward who can positively identify me as the person he saw standing over Dawson's corpse with a smoking gun in my hand.'

'Brendan, I've got someone lined up who will swear on his mother's life to anything I want him to. It might perhaps be in your best interest to consider signing a full confession right now and save the court a lot of unnecessary time in finding you guilty.'

'You really should have a go at becoming a full time comedian, Strickland. There's worse than you on the telly and you can bet they get paid a small fortune despite being as funny as piles. Listen, we both know who topped Nat Dawson and don't think for one minute I'll be frightened to use it if I'm pushed into a corner. I looked in the body-bag before it went in the incinerator so I know exactly what I'm talking about; and if the truth ever comes out you've got a hell of a lot more to lose than I have. You committed the murder; I just got blackmailed into disposing of the body by a bent copper. I wonder who will be likely to come out worse if that little lot ever becomes common knowledge.'

'Look Brendan, why don't we stop threatening each other and just do this the easy way. You tell me what happened down at the pub last night. I drink my coffee and bugger off. I'll forget it was you who provided me with the information. Christ, it's not like we've never had this sort of conversation before.'

'Do I detect a change of heart, Detective Sergeant Strickland? Two minutes back it was threats; now it's just a question of a little bit of help so you can report back to your governor what's going on round here and look like you've got your finger on the pulse.'

'Let's help each other, Brendan. You wouldn't want anyone knowing about the little bits of assistance you've given me over the years. That would be bad for your image anyway it played out; nobody likes a grass. And let's be honest; if anything ever surfaces on Nat Dawson it won't be doing either of us a lot of favours.'

'Alright. Now we understand each other I'll give you a quick run through but that's as far as I'm going. Fifty quid will cover it, so let me see your hand in your pocket before I get started. Oh, and just in case you were thinking that it might suit your purpose if I accidentally tripped over a kerbstone and broke my neck, then just be aware I have gone to some lengths to cover that eventuality, so you had better hope I live to a ripe old age or you will be up to your neck in it, Detective Sergeant. Right, now we understand each other, I'll put the kettle on. I've only got tea mind you and it's the one the monkey's drink, so don't go getting over excited.'

CHAPTER THIRTY NINE

SUNDAY 19th FEBRUARY / MONDAY 20th FEBRUARY 2017

Bleak summed up the outlook; and when combined with desolate and uninviting that just about covered all aspects of the view out of the side window of Charlie Brinsworth's battered Toyota. He had chosen to park his car on the wasteland diagonally opposite the new library half an hour in advance of schedule in the hope of avoiding any last minute surprises. This had proved a bad decision. Since his arrival the area in front of the building had remained totally deserted, the weather was bloody freezing and as the clock hands worked slowly towards the midnight hour he had begun to get a distinct feeling of foreboding.

Despite keeping the engine ticking over with the heater on full Charlie felt anything but warm. The side windows had long ago fogged up which didn't trouble him greatly because there was little to see on either side except a wilderness of scrubland dotted with half demolished buildings and small mounds of aging brick and concrete. The surrounding land appeared to have become something of a fly-tipper's paradise. A quick recognisance had revealed an aluminium kitchen sink, a smashed wardrobe and what could conceivably have been the remains of a sizeable plastic bath coloured in a delicate shade of blue that could possibly have been aquamarine. The ground underfoot was currently topped with a crust of hard frozen clay mixed with a sprinkling of gravel; but Charlie would have been prepared to wager that come the first downpour it would turn into a treacherous bog that would be capable of swallowing anything short of a double-decker bus.

In the time he had been parked there only three cars had driven past, none of which had been going slow enough to have noticed a ten foot sign offering a night out with a page three model and a bacon sandwich for two pounds fifty. The area looked uninviting enough that if the waterway flowing fifty yards to the rear of the library building had been the river Styx, it was unlikely the ferryman would have taken it upon himself to walk over and enquire whether the advertised serving came with brown sauce and if they had any ethical dilemma with cutting off the rind.

Charlie had been careful to keep his trusty crook-lock in easy reach. The steering lock hadn't had a key that would turn in the recess for as long as he could remember but the length of steel was pretty much ideal as a weapon. If you had a pick axe handle, a baseball bat or a length of lead piping in your car then there was always a chance that your motives for being in possession of such items could be held in question. Everyone knew why you had a crook-lock shoved into the gap under your front passenger seat, so nobody asked the question; but if push came to shove it was just as lethal as anything else to use as a club.

Twenty years before this area had been wall to wall factories and steel plants but looking at it now it was difficult to see any great hope of an imminent return to its former glories. The new library only blended in with its current surroundings because from the outside it still looked like an engineering works that was somehow managing to hang on in there, despite the downturn currently being experienced by the manufacturing sector. If you looked closely a silhouette of *Marsh Lane Works* could still be seen engraved into the stonework over the main door though the actual lettering had clearly been missing for some considerable time. It seemed plain barmy to have relocated a library here even if it was currently doing a great job at keeping regiments of senior citizens off the streets once their Winter Fuel Allowance had been spent in the pub. There must have been a better location somewhere in the city but this would doubtless have been the cheapest option available and it was a safe bet money would have ended up being the deciding factor.

A sharp tap on the window made Charlie jump. Seamus Macgregor's lugubrious countenance, shrouded in a hoodie and black woollen bobble hat, could just about be identified through the misty gloom. Charlie leaned across and released the door lock.

'Nice weather for the time of year, Charlie.'

'Only if you are related to a polar bear. Get your arse in here Seamus and shut the bloody door.'

'Nice weather if you are breaking in somewhere, I mean. No bugger's going to put his head out of doors on a night like this unless he is getting paid for the privilege and I don't know anybody from over this way who ever had a job even when they were still in fashion.'

'Very philosophical that, Seamus. They should arrange to get you down to Brighton to address the Trade Union Congress. I'll keep those words in mind for when I get round to writing my memoirs. What do you know?'

'Only that you're wasting your time looking for anything worth pinching in that place over the road. I can't understand what's come over you Charlie Brinsworth. I thought you were one of the few people on our side of the law who had his head screwed on but it turns out you're just as crazy as the rest of the silly beggars. Here's the key. I didn't bother to lock up because I could see your car from the doorway. Nobody's about anyhow. Got a little brown envelope for me? I'd better be making tracks.'

'You tried the key in the lock?'

'No, I just took a guess at what I thought would be about right and left it as that. Of course I tried the key in the bloody lock, you pillock. I've been sitting in that doorway filing the bloody thing down for the last half an hour.'

'How did you get in?'

'Back window over the door. Just popped the catch and closed it after me. It took precisely twenty seconds balancing on the guardrail before I was on the inside. Easiest five centuries I've earned in a long while. You must have money to burn.'

'O.K. Seamus that's you done. Get on your way and I'll see you when I see you. Keep yourself out of mischief.'

'A little bonus from your Uncle Seamus, Mr Brinsworth. When you get round to hauling your arse up the stairs you'll find the door to the safe is hanging open on its hinges. There's nothing in the building of any value so the library staff use it as a store cupboard; and because they don't want to be fiddling about with a combination lock that serves no purpose, they don't bother to set it up. I did have a quick look at what was inside just on the off chance but there was nothing I could see except a load of old papers. Best of luck, Charlie; I did warn you before you started that you'd be wasting your time.'

Charlie sank back in his seat to contemplate the next phase of the operation. There was still half a chance Anthony Noone would choose not to put in an appearance. Up to now it had cost him nothing but petrol to run Charlie all over the place but if he showed up now a hundred thousand smackers would be on the line.

No sooner had the thought entered his head than a blue/grey Rover hove into view. Anthony Noone, like the pillock he was, parked the car right outside the front doors of the library building, positioned himself on the steps and lit a cigarette. Charlie closed his eyes in horror. Why didn't Noone just put up a sign advertising they were intending to rob the place? Charlie leapt from the car and shot across the road as fast as his cramped legs would allow.

'Move the car over to the other side of the road, Anthony. It sticks out like a sore thumb.'

Noone looked a shade put out by the suggestion but chose to comply without argument; returning moments later with a small canvas bag over his shoulder and a good deal less shine on his shoes.

Charlie led the way up the front steps to the main entrance. He beckoned Noone across the threshold and slammed the heavy door firmly into position. Was there any purpose in applying the lock? Probably not. He still had a haunting memory of a situation years ago when a key had snapped as soon as it had started to turn. That had very nearly caused a major disaster. The team he was working with had ended up exiting a high building from an upstairs toilet window, climbing across a decidedly iffy asbestos roof and down to ground level by means of a drainpipe that had finished up by coming away from the wall. Charlie liked to think he had learned from that experience. Working on the principle that anything that could possibly go wrong probably would, he now endeavoured to keep things as simple as possible. It was good sense to give bad luck as few chances of affecting any outcome as was humanly possible. He checked the doors at least gave the impression of being securely closed and hurried off in pursuit of his lanky accomplice who, now they were safely inside the building, had suddenly developed a surprising turn of foot.

He caught up with Anthony Noone who had positioned himself halfway up the metal staircase and was busily surveying the layout.

'God it's changed out of all recognition. I can hardly believe what they've done to the old place. 'That,' he said, indicating somewhere off in a distant pool of gloom, 'used to be the wages office; and over there was,' a casually waved hand in the direction of another patch of impenetrable darkness, 'the bay that took care of final inspection.'

Noone dropped to his knees, fished in his bag and withdrew a heavy duty torch covered in hard rubber that could easily have found service as a searchlight at a prison of war camp.

'Down there,' he continued, shining several hundred units of candlepower into the bowels of what had hitherto been little more than a black abyss, 'was the entrance that led through to the heat treatment plant; and over there......'

'Anthony, turn that fucking torch off before we get a jumbo jet landing on the roof,' shouted a voice that had intended to be delivering a hissed whisper; the sound echoed round the empty building like the roar from a cannon. 'If you must keep that bleeding thing turned on put a handkerchief over the face and point it at the floor. Jesus Christ, I hope nobody was passing. They'll think we've got a celebrity in here getting in some practise for opening the Blackpool lights.'

Charlie edged up the stairway past Noone and as soon as they had reached the first floor quickly led the way across the floor, past the book shelves and through the exit door leading to the row of administrative offices. The last thing he wanted was his associate examining the view downstairs from the balcony area. Chances were he would suddenly whip out a camera with a telephoto lens and start taking snaps for his scrap album.

Charlie was starting to get edgy. Noone had appeared to have no experience in the field of breaking and entering and should have been a bag of nerves. This wasn't proving the case. The posh bastard was handling himself like he was enjoying a night out at the cinema. Either the man was a total idiot or the lanky bastard had been around the block a few times and wasn't fazed by the first hint of danger. It was difficult to know which of the two possibilities was likely to prove the more dangerous.

They followed the path of the small corridor for a few steps until Charlie eased open the second door on the right as Seamus had indicated. The housebreaker had been as good as his word. The door to the safe was wide open to the outside world.

Surprisingly this didn't seem to please Anthony Noone. Charlie surmised this was because he would now have little opportunity to impress with his mastery of the safe's mechanism. He decided to take a small risk since they were now at the back of the building and flick on a table lamp. It gave some sort of outline of the dusty room, even if it wasn't offering any competition for Anthony Noone's mobile searchlight.

'Just for the record, Anthony, what was the override combination for the safe that your old man set up?' he enquired out of curiosity.

'1923, the year the old man was born.' Noone replied, eyeing the huge metal box with a look of total concentration. 'If I'm honest I would have preferred to find the thing still locked. You have to understand, that for me this is more than just laying claim to my inheritance; it's also something of a rite of passage. My father's legacy being handed down to me as a bequest from one generation to the next. You understand how I'm feeling, I'm sure. Now, stand back over there, Charlie. I want to tackle the next part entirely on my own.'

Charlie thought this was bullshit but settled himself on a hard-backed chair near the door. Noone heaved the safe door back as far as it would go and proceeded to pull out each of the metal shelves complete with whatever paperwork was resting upon them. He laid each tray on the floor in a haphazard sort of way until Charlie pointed out they would need to be returned to exactly the same position they had formerly occupied if they wanted to give the impression that nothing had been disturbed. Noone looked unimpressed but thereafter condescended to take a little more care with the extraction process.

When the safe was completely empty he produced from his bag two screwdrivers, an adjustable wrench, a set of allen keys and a pair of flat nose pliers; along with the large torch which he shone into the safe's deepest recesses. He then positioned himself half inside the metal box and clattered about for what seemed like an eternity. Charlie, stayed seated, listening to the sounds of industry as Noone prodded, scraped and banged; his endeavours punctuated only by odd sigh of exasperation and the occasional oath.

After several minutes Noone emerged red faced and sweating. He immediately turned off his torch and moved to the centre of the room looking slightly agitated.

'Found what I was looking for but I can't shift a screw at the very bottom; it's right at the back on the left; can you give it a try?'

Charlie rose from his seat and edged forward, before

dropping to his knees. He advanced as far as possible and half turned to enquire where exactly he was meant to be looking. Then all he saw was stars before everything went completely black.

CHAPTER FORTY

MONDAY 20th FEBRUARY 2017

Despite the plunging temperature outside the car, Anthony Noone was bathed in a film of sweat. The bitter cold weather was finding it impossible to displace the heat from the adrenalin rush he was still experiencing as his heart continued to pound against his ribcage. It was taking a considerable effort for him not to exceed the speed limit and he was fully aware of the need to avoid being picked up on a traffic camera. He had taken an unconventional route when crossing town with the express purpose of minimising the chances of being spotted on C.C.T.V. but the way those accursed cameras were popping up all over the place, he was aware this action offered no guarantee of success.

Noone was in little doubt a police investigation would soon be underway and that every piece of recorded data from the area surrounding the new library would be subjected to minute scrutiny. In consequence he had taken the precaution of covering both front and rear number plates in a thick coating of mud before he had set out from the car park. This at least gave him a small degree of deniability, even if it had been a thankless task getting the frozen muck to adhere in the required manner. He had also rehearsed a story to explain his presence in that part of town in the middle of the night; just in case luck was against him and he got picked up in a random trawl. A search for a 24 hour chemist to seek treatment for a persistent migraine sounded a good deal more plausible than many of the ideas he had briefly entertained.

Despite those considerations he remained confident he had little to worry about. He had planned each step of the way as carefully as possible and whilst there was always a small element of risk he felt pretty sure he was worrying unnecessarily.

This night, Noone sensed, could prove a major turning point in his life; he was overdue a change of fortune and every sign indicated that it was at last starting to take hold. Things would go better for him from this day forward; he could feel it in his bones.

On the seat beside him was the cardboard container. It was a bit shorter than the size of a shoe box and a good deal thinner and was sealed with an excessive quantity of thick brown adhesive tape. The compartment in which it had been hidden had been covered by a metal disc that had been attached to the dummy wall at the back of the safe. The thin metal oval that covered the hole had proved to be an ornate badge displaying the manufacturer's logo. This had been bolted to the wall of the safe the wrong way round so the maker's identity was masked from view. Wonderful stuff! Dear old daddy; paranoid to the very last! The metal disc had been fixed in place by two solid bolts, but, with a little pressure, it had been persuaded to swivel to one side once he had dislodged the first of the fastenings. The cardboard box had needed some manoeuvring to drag through the rectangular aperture hidden beneath, but had eventually succumbed to a combination of brute force and dexterity.

He hadn't yet unsealed the package. He had decided to hold off on that until he had completed his journey so he could savour the moment in the comfort of his home. He had every confidence the experience would be well worth the wait.

The business with Charlie had been unfortunate; but given the circumstances his alternatives had been somewhat limited. There was no way he could justify paying out one hundred thousand pounds for the minimal contribution his partner had made to the project. It was an obscene amount of money when you took into account the degree of effort Charlie had been required to make. The outlay was totally unwarranted; it had merely been made to sucker Charlie in; he would never have suggested it in the first place if he had intended to honour his side of the deal.

He had already found it necessary to suffer the expense of Geoff Strickland which had proved a drain on his limited resources. You would have thought the amount of years the pair of them went back Strickland might have offered his services for free.......but sadly, that had never looked like being the case. It was all about money with some people; never a case of performing a small favour for an old friend or just acting in a comradely manner for old time's sake and doing the decent thing. When he thought about it, he had never liked any of the Stricklands. The whole family had always seemed to him as common as muck. Why his father had ever chosen to befriend Strickland senior in the first place remained something of a mystery. No surprise the son had gone bad and finished up working as a policeman; he probably wasn't fit to do anything else.

All things being equal, he had actually preferred the company of Charlie Brinsworth to that of Geoff Strickland. Charlie had at least proved an honest criminal whereas the Detective Sergeant was quite clearly corrupt to the core. On balance he thought that made Charlie the better man. At least he had never made any pretence of being something that he wasn't.

And taking that into account he was sorry the way things had worked out for old Charlie. He hadn't seemed an inherently bad man; more a victim of circumstance one might suspect. He had always known Charlie would need to be incapacitated once the package was located and he had taken that into account when laying out his plan. It was obvious he would require some sort of club. It might have been difficult to explain away a cosh if it had been spotted in his bag but the torch had just as much heft and provided the perfect solution. A weapon with a dual purpose capability; what more could you ask?

He wasn't entirely sure why he had chosen to take things a little bit further than he had originally intended;

partly as extra insurance against ever being tracked down and put on the spot; partly because it was annoying to have suffered the inconvenience of acquiring the gun without actually putting it to some form of use. Maybe a bit of it was just pure irritation at having the lump of metal digging into his spine while he was heaving away at the back of the safe.

He had, for a brief moment considered locking Charlie's unconscious body in the empty metal box but the outcome of that course of action would have been entirely unpredictable. Probably, being the career criminal he was, Charlie would have elected to keep his mouth shut; but how could you ever be certain that would prove the case? He might have been so desperate for revenge that he would say almost anything. There was no way you could predict the depths to which the lower classes might sink in that sort of situation; how could you ever second guess the reasoning of a cornered rat? All things considered, it was perhaps better to just take away the uncertainty and leave nothing to chance.

So, what should he do? Just shoot Charlie and draw a neat line under their collaboration? Bring their partnership to a final conclusion in the most irrevocable manner possible? The more he thought about it the more it seemed like the most sensible solution. So he had taken careful aim and fired two shots into Charlie Brinsworth's head from point blank range. There was no point in getting involved in an argument with your conscience when it was so clearly the right thing to do.

CHAPTER FORTY ONE

SUNDAY 19th FEBRUARY 2017

Mickey was forced to admit Charlie had been one hundred percent correct in his evaluation. It was only eight o'clock in the evening and already the Black Bear was full to bursting point. There were at least four times as many people in the main bar as there had been for the previous night's altercation with Eastgate, but seemingly every one of them had performed some understated act of heroism that they were too modest to discuss in detail. Mickey's main concern was that after a few more ales a deputation might decide to march down to the Golden Pheasant in a bid to take matters further. Not a smart move any way you looked at it, but taking into account the way the evening was progressing it was impossible to rule it out.

Spanner Hopkins was now gainfully ensconced on a bar stool, just to the left of the main doors. Pint in one hand, a half a chewed pork pie in the other, he looked like he had been in that position since time immemorial and not just since Mickey had set him on an hour and a half earlier. The newly appointed bouncer looked for all the world like a Mafia Don, dressed in a well cut black suit that appeared to be fresh out of a tailor's window. Nearly everybody who passed Hopkins stopped to say a word or shake his hand and a succession of pints had found their way onto the windowsill just behind Spanner's head from patrons wishing to convey a mark of respect.

Mickey also noticed a gaggle of old Eastgate stalwarts had settled themselves in at the far end of the bar. Doubtless this lot had also received their redundancy notices with the coming of the new order and had resolved to move their patronage up the road from the Pheasant to the Black Bear. It was possible that this relocation had been prompted as a show of solidarity with Spanner

Hopkins but it was much more likely it was because they were no longer being made to feel welcome in their old stomping ground. Either way it provided Mickey with extra trade; albeit not from a source he would ever have chosen, had he had been given the option.

Mickey sighed; casting an eye around the pub, he was forced to conclude this place now bore very little resemblance to the pub he had been running for the last twelve years. Everything had now changed; the decor, large swathes of the clientele......and most significantly of all, the atmosphere. He had always taken some pride in managing a hostelry that appealed to those whose tastes veered towards the conservative. The mob now propping up the bar were anything but reserved; raucous would have been a better description. He could see the way things were going; it would be only a matter of time before Charlie would be pushing to get giant television sets mounted on the walls and a line of one armed bandits installed in the hallway leading to the ladies' toilets. He didn't like the direction things were taking. This had ceased to be the type of pub he wanted to manage. It was like a much loved child who had suddenly morphed into a rebellious teenager with acne, angst and a severe attitude problem.

Mickey was still deep in thought as Simon Bartol appeared out of nowhere and positioned himself at the bar; not surprisingly he was in search of Charlie. No, Mickey didn't know where he had gone. No, Charlie wouldn't have left that sort of information with anyone else. No, he wasn't sure if he would be back shortly or even if he would be back at all. Yes, he would pass on a message that Bartol wanted a word about their mutual interest. No, he didn't know when he would be able to deliver the message and no, he wasn't in any way privy to Mr Brinsworth's business dealings. Having seemingly received no satisfactory reply to any one of his questions, Bartol screwed up his nose, downed the dregs of his pint and was gone.

There followed a half an hour of industrious pint pulling before his next visitors arrived; D.I. Daniel Loache and D.S. Geoff Strickland, both looking a shade furtive.

'Hello Mickey, I see the little dust up you had in here last night hasn't kept the crowds away. Is that Spanner Hopkins I see propping up the door frame. Please tell me Eastgate haven't got you paying protection already?' enquired Strickland with feigned concern.

How did it come about that Strickland already knew what had happened the previous evening when Charlie had gone to great lengths to make certain nobody called it in? Strickland had a bloody good source of information somewhere close at hand and Mickey would have very much liked to know exactly who that was. Everybody claimed they wouldn't have spat on the Detective Sergeant if he was on fire but somebody out there must clearly be passing the word.

'Mr Hopkins is only on the books as of tonight, Mr Strickland. My previous bouncer was obliged to jack in the job at short notice so he could return to his studies and Mr Hopkins found himself between jobs so I set him on. Can I get you gentlemen a refreshment?'

'No thanks, Mickey. D.I. Loache and I were only passing by. No time for rest in our game you know; not even on a cold winter's night when the God fearing are already at evensong. I don't suppose you get a lot of that sort in here, do you Mickey? Talking of which, where's Charlie Brinsworth got to? Not occupying his usual seat, if my eyes don't deceive me.'

'I'm told he's enrolled at a yoga class, Mr Strickland.'

'Charlie? Surely not. The only time I ever saw Charlie sit on his arse and make his mind go blank was during an interrogation when he was nervous he might start telling the truth. Anyway, pass on my regards when you see him.'

The officers of the law exchanged a look and gathered themselves for an immediate departure. As Strickland pushed his way through the crowd Loache leaned back.

'Don't let yourself get drawn into anything that's not in

your best interests, Mickey. Oh, and the wife told me to pass on her regards.'

Strange bedfellows you ended up with in the police force, thought Mickey. If those two weren't working together they wouldn't have given each other the time of day; but, as things stood, the job served to give them a common interest that bonded them tighter than glue. It would be interesting to know if Loache was aware Strickland was on the take. Maybe he knew and was past caring.

'A large rum,' said a cultured voice from a time gone by that floated across the bar in a manner that seemed entirely out of keeping with the present surroundings. Sharon gave her regulation smile and quickly retreated to the back of the bar and fiddled with the optic; turning sideways to shout out the price.

'I think you might find this one is on the house, my dear,' said Oliver Dearlove with a saccharine smile.

'I think Mr Dearlove might find it isn't,' said Mickey, speaking to Sharon without looking up; giving the impression he was absorbed in matters of far greater importance.

Dearlove did a wonderful impression of looking both aghast and demeaned at the same time, which made little impression on the barmaid who kept her hand held to the optic.

'If that's the case make it a single,' Dearlove said, retrieving a purse with a leather drawstring from his jacket pocket.

Mickey kept his head down, deeply engrossed in a piece of paper giving details of the carol service which had taken place at a local church the Christmas of last year. He could play this game forever. There was a wad of leaflets covering every aspect of human life stacked neatly beneath the bar which he used to rest pitchers on when he was filling them with ice. The depth of the stack testified to the infrequency of the demands he received for chilled wine. The Bear wasn't that sort of pub and the few bottles of fizz he did hold in the cellar had never been within a hundred miles of France, let alone the vineyards of Champagne country.

'I just popped in to let you know your commission will be ready for collection at midday tomorrow, Mr Smith,' said Oliver Dearlove running out of patience with Mickey's disinterest in his unexplained appearance. 'I do hope it satisfies your requirements. I worked on it night and day and I regard it as some of my finest work......even if I do say so myself.'

'If it's finished you should have brought it with you,' said Mickey, pushing his pile of papers to one side and finally looking up. 'I would have been happy to stand you a drink for your trouble.'

'The paint hasn't dried,' hissed Dearlove angrily. 'This is a crafted work of art we are discussing; painted in oil, not emulsion!'

'That's fine. I'll be over tomorrow then, allowing that I can get hold of Ms Armitage. I'll be sure to give you a bell if there's any sort of problem.'

CHAPTER FORTY TWO

MONDAY 20th FEBRUARY 2017

Charlie Brinsworth regained consciousness and immediately wished he was already dead. His head throbbed, his body ached, one side of his face burned like it had been scalded with the steam from a kettle and he was totally deaf in his right ear. He staggered to his feet, out of the door and stumbled his way along the short corridor, managing to keep upright only by extending his arms outright and wavering from side to side between the confines of the supporting walls. He located a door with a sign he couldn't read and hoped it would prove to be a toilet. With his prayer having been answered he still failed to reach a cubical; instead sticking his head in the nearest wash-handbasin and being violently sick. This accomplished he sank to the floor and lay there panting for breath before once again blacking out.

How much time passed he had no idea. Instead of feeling better he felt considerably worse. He levered himself up onto his feet using the front of the sink as a support and turned on the tap to wash away the contents of his stomach. He now had a splitting headache and electric sparks had started to appear on the periphery of his field of vision. He wanted to die because that was the sensible thing to do; anything else was going to involve him in a good deal of pain and he wasn't sure if he could face any more than he had already experienced. He spooned water from the tap into his mouth, gargled and spat. This did little to improve his condition so he stumbled his way to the nearest cubicle, pushed open the door and took a seat.

He needed to work out what had happened and then make a plan of what he intended to do next; but with impaired vision, damaged hearing and a splitting headache this was likely to prove anything but easy. He sat back far enough to lean on the cistern and closed his eyes. This didn't help a lot either but now he was no longer moving about his head throbbed a little less. Although he was still fully clothed he now started to shiver.

Despite this state of discomfort his memory began to slowly reengage. That bastard Noone had been behind him. The lanky twat had clubbed him with something or other while he was bent down in front of the safe. He reached up, felt the egg like swelling on the back of his head, and received the required confirmation that his befuddled assumption was seemingly correct.

Right then, lousy though he felt, he needed to pull himself together and get out of this place; but first he had to go back along the corridor and check out the room containing Noone's massive safe. He winced at the thought but within seconds had forced himself up onto his feet. He then proceeded to slowly retrace his journey one torturous step at a time.

The electric sparks dotting his vision were now a little less bright and he noted the toilet door was marked with a prominent sign saying *Ladies*. Charlie would have liked to laugh out loud but the thought of what that might do to his head was enough to deter him.

The room housing the safe was still shrouded in gloom. His impaired vision meant he was currently unable to read his wristwatch but he was aware that the sun didn't come up until around seven o'clock at this time of the year. If he was lucky, then maybe there was still time. He took a couple of hesitant paces forward, fumbled around and eventually located the switch operating the table lamp.

Nothing seemed to have changed very much since his head had received the battering except that objects which had previously been reasonably distinct had now acquired a fuzzy edge. He dropped to his knees, took a deep breath and slowly edged his body across the floor in the direction of the huge metal cabinet.

It took him several minutes industrious groping before he encountered the sliding plate and slipped his hand into the cavity it had covered. The space was now empty but it wasn't hard to figure out its purpose. Charlie withdrew his hand and slid the metal disc back into what he imagined to be its original position. Presumably it had once been secured by some sort of fastening pin but he had enough problems without trying to figure out where that might have ended up. Working on the principle nobody was likely to notice the omission he gritted his teeth and pressed on.

Now came the hard bit. If he wasn't going to leave clear evidence there had been a break in he would need to clean the place up. Charlie eased himself on to his hands and knees and one by one dragged the shelves across the floor and fixed them into what, he hoped, was their correct position. That completed, he lay on his back on the floor with his arms spread wide and thought how wonderful it would be if the ceiling would collapse and crush him to death. That way at least, the agony would immediately be over.

When that didn't happen, he heaved himself to his feet, pushed a couple of things into more likely positions and stood back to survey the results of his work. The sparks of light when he moved his head from side to side were no longer so much of a distraction. Whether they had actually become less severe or he had just got used to them it was difficult to say. He took one final look then headed for the staircase, taking due care to close the door tightly behind him. The key to the front entrance was still in his pocket which was a major blessing. He hoped that anything that was found to be out of position would be attributed to an oversight by staff departing hastily to enjoy a weekend of leisure.

Now if he could just drag his weary body across the road without getting mashed by a container lorry there would only be just the steady drive across town to negotiate before he would be able to sink into his bed and sleep off the horrors of the night. But even now his mind was racing ahead. Noone, Garfield, whatever the snotty nosed git was now calling himself should start counting the hours because he was now living on borrowed time. Charlie did not consider himself a vindictive man but he set some store by just retribution when it was well merited. Anthony Noone had chosen to cross a line and there was only one way the debt could now be settled. Charlie vowed he would put Noone in the ground or die in the attempt. If he had been able to see straight enough to accomplish the feat, it was a promise he would have been prepared to carve out in stone.

CHAPTER FORTY THREE

MONDAY 20th FEBRUARY 2017

Anthony Noone had no further part to play in proceedings. Noone was now dead to the world and he made the ideal corpse as no headstone was needed to mark his place of rest and no tear required to trickle down a careworn cheek as witness to the sorrow at his passing.

It was instead Anthony Garfield, feeling somewhat chipper after the events of the night, who arrived in the village of Thorton Chumley in the small hours of Monday morning; and that same man, now clear eyed and confident of what the future held in store, who took the necessary care as he approached the top of Mount Drive, exhibiting a degree of stealth and caution that would have done credit to a prowling fox.

Garfield was well aware his neighbours on the quiet cul-de-sac missed very little and he had no wish to advertise his recent excursion. In consequence, he cut the engine of his car at the top of the road and allowed the vehicle to coast the last fifty yards while out of gear. He then edged soundlessly onto the paved driveway, exited the vehicle like a fleeting shadow and closed the car door with nothing more that the faintest of clicks.

The front door made a small squeak as it slid back on its hinges but nothing that would have attracted the attention of anything but the most vigilant guard dog. He cocked an ear just to be on the safe side but the house was in complete silence. All was well; why would he expect any different?

Moving forward at pace he placed his coat on its usual peg on the hat-stand in the hall and strode through into the sitting room; dropping the well wrapped parcel he had been clutching in his free hand onto an aged sofa as he hurriedly brushed past. From the sideboard he extracted a

227

tumbler and a bottle of whiskey that was three parts full and headed for his favourite armchair, positioned by the fireside. He then froze in alarm as it became apparent this seat was already occupied.

'Evening, Anthony. Successful night's work I trust. I'll join you in one of those if you don't mind.'

'What the fuck are you doing here? You scared the shit out of me. How the hell did you get in anyway?' said Garfield, frantically trying to recover his composure.

Geoff Strickland uncrossed his legs and eased himself forward in the chair.

'Tricks of the trade, Anthony. You don't get to be a copper for as long as I have without knowing how to get a kitchen door open in the middle of the night without waking the neighbours. When you have a bit less on your plate allow me to give you some advice on security systems. A kid fresh out of borstal could have cracked your back door in two minutes flat without breaking sweat.'

Garfield fetched another glass, blew on it; then flicked it with a handkerchief to remove a film of dust. He passed it to Strickland, without comment, along with the bottle.

'Well, don't keep me in suspense. I've been sitting here freezing my arse off since midnight,' said Strickland, in a tone that suggested he had been kept from his bed at Garfield's insistence.

'Nothing to tell. Everything went like clockwork. Listen it's been a long night for both of us; why don't you knock back that drink and we can get together tomorrow after we've had a chance to catch up on a bit of sleep? If you want we can meet up, have a couple of drinks and a bite to ....'

'Better to do it now, Anthony. While it's all still fresh in your mind,' said Strickland, settling back in the chair in a manner that made it abundantly clear he was going nowhere in a hurry.

Anthony Garfield began to feel anxious and attempted to settle his nerves by slipping his hand into his pocket and rubbing his index finger along the short barrel of his concealed gun. The feel of the cold metal was strangely reassuring and immediately had the desired effect.

'Charlie Brinsworth's housebreaker fixed the door and we walked straight in. I opened the safe and sorted out what I was looking for and we breezed out again. Like I said, it all went completely to plan.'

'Then you paid Charlie off and drove straight back here?'

'Yes. That's precisely what happened.'

'Something isn't quite right there, Anthony. Presuming that package you chucked on the sofa over there is what you were looking for in the safe, then what did you use to pay our friend Charlie? Last time we spoke you gave me the impression you were virtually skint.'

Anthony Garfield was starting to feel a little angry. What business was any of this of Strickland's? The man had done a relatively undemanding job and been very well paid for his services. That should have been an end to the matter. What right had he to be sitting here demanding answers, like he was talking to some ruffian he had just dragged in off the street. Didn't the man understand his involvement was over? Whatever had gone on that night was none of his bloody business.

Garfield sank his hand deeper into his pocket and gripped the barrel of the gun a little tighter. He adjusted his grip so his palm made contact with the butt and allowed his finger to edge down towards the trigger.

'I had Charlie's money already put by,' answered Garfield curtly, endeavouring to keep all emotion from his voice.

Strickland picked up the whiskey bottle and poured himself a generous shot. He waggled it in Garfield's direction like he was acting as host but his offer was completely ignored.

'I don't think that's altogether right, Anthony. In our initial conversation you mentioned you were running short of cash and had already found it necessary to remortgage this house. And when you paid me out you didn't part with the money like you were a man with a hundred grand stashed away under the floorboards. You paid it like you might have a couple of hundred put to one side for emergencies but that would be about it. Want to try answering the question again? Truthfully this time.'

'What I did or didn't do to settle up with Charlie Brinsworth is my concern, not yours. Charlie was well taken care of; that's all you need to know. Now will you finish your drink and get out. It's been a long day and I'm going to bed.'

Strickland placed his glass on the table and appeared ready to stand.

'Not until we've sorted this out, you aren't. Tell me what happened or I'll come over there and beat it out of you.'

Garfield got a proper grip on his gun and now was ready to use it. Then he stopped and reconsidered. What did it matter if Strickland knew the truth? He would find out as soon as he got into work, anyway. The policeman was as implicated as he was even if he hadn't been the one who actually pulled the trigger. Telling him what really happened might serve a purpose. It would demonstrate to Strickland the sort of man he was dealing with and encourage him to show a greater degree of respect.

'I shot him,' said Garfield.

'You shot Brinsworth? What the fuck did you do that for?'

'Because it was the logical thing to do. With Charlie Brinsworth out of the way there is no possible link to me and correspondingly none to you; no looking over our shoulder for either of us. A nice tidy end to Mr Brinsworth's involvement'

'You bloody idiot. Why do you think I had you operating under a false name? Why do you think I set it up so you drove half way round the world each time you met up with him?'

'It's alright for you, Strickland. It wasn't your face

230

Charlie could identify. I killed him because it left things neat and tidy. Surely even a dimwit like you can see the advantages of that,' spat Garfield indignantly.

Strickland took a long pull on his drink; then took an age to refill his glass. This time he made no effort to offer the bottle in the direction of his host.

'Just tell me exactly what happened.'

'I told you already. I shot him.......twice. Twice in the head. Charlie Brinsworth is now as dead as the meat in my fridge.'

'Let me get this straight. Charlie was standing in front of you and you swanned up to him and shot him twice in the head and then you stood and watched as he fell over onto the floor bleeding puddles of blood?'

'Yes, exactly that........well, actually no. I enticed Charlie to kneel down in front of the safe and I hit him over the head with a torch and knocked him senseless. Then I considered the situation and decided it would be a lot less complicated if he was dead so I shot him in the head. I fired twice just to be absolutely sure.'

'The gun you are carrying was firing blanks you bloody idiot. Do you honestly think I would have let an idiot like you loose with a firearm that would fire real bullets? The lump of metal in your pocket that you keep fiddling with is about as lethal as a starting pistol. The only way you could have done anyone any real damage with that thing is if you knocked them senseless.'

'But I.............'

'Just sit down and keep your mouth shut while I think. Alright, the way I see it there are three possibilities. Maybe you killed Charlie when you bashed him over the head; you had better hope that was the outcome as it's probably the best chance you've got of coming out of this alive. Then there's the possibility he might be still be lying on the floor of the library where he will be discovered in about,' Strickland turned his arm and studied his watch face, 'three or four hours. If that is the case you can bet he will be wheeled off to hospital, fixed up, and the police

231

will be called. That isn't good but because of what he does for a living he will probably keep his mouth shut. What he will also do, however, is devote every waking hour to finding you; and believe me, Charlie Brinsworth knows all the right people to get in touch with to make that happen. The third possibility is that he came round after you left, hosed himself down and is now pulling in every favour he has ever been owed to get a lead on you. If I was a betting man I'd go for option three. Charlie isn't a young man but he's got a very hard head. My suggestion to you would be to start looking at departure times for planes out of the country. Trust me when I say, Charlie Brinsworth is not going to take this well and don't labour under the illusion that you aren't going to talk to him when he tracks you down. You'll be begging for him to listen to you spewing your guts out after he's had hold of you for twenty minutes. Take that as guaranteed.'

'I'm not going anywhere,' said Garfield, struggling to regain his composure. 'This is your fault. If that gun had worked.......'

'Shut the fuck up. You've caused enough trouble for one night. What's in the parcel?'

'I don't know. I was just going to check it when......'

'Well don't just sit there. Open the bloody thing up and take a look......and Anthony, pray it's diamonds; because the way your arm was swinging when you came in through the door it certainly isn't bars of gold.'

Garfield went to the kitchen and returned with a steak knife. Strickland stood back a few feet. Garfield was just about stupid enough to give it a try. After several attempts he pierced the tape and tore back the stiff paper covering. He immediately let out a whoop of delight.

'Money, Geoff; it's full of banknotes.'

Garfield wrenched a wodge free and then tipped the parcel up, shook it, and let the rest fall into a heap on the table top. He selected one at random and viewed it quizzically.

'High denomination, look at all the zeros. What

currency is it?'

Strickland approached the table cautiously keeping an eye on the steak knife; he selected the nearest piece of paper and held it out for examination. After several seconds he selected another from a different part of the pile, and then a third. He then smiled sardonically to himself, and without a word turned about face and returned to the armchair; dropped into the seat and lifted his glass to his lips.

'Lire, Anthony. You have been royally buggered, my son; Lire went out of circulation in Italy when they joined the Euro......and I reckon that would have been somewhere around the millennium.'

Garfield reacted with disbelief. His face took on a crazed look and he started rooting around in the pile of notes looking for something to give him fresh hope; anything to offer an alternative explanation and avoid him facing the truth. After a full minute of fruitless searching he unearthed a small brown envelope which on closer examination proved to be an old fashioned wage packet. The paper sleeve had his name written neatly across the top and the figure ten scribbled in the money column. He eyed it with a look of desperation; then ripped open the top with trembling fingers, cupped his palm and turned it upside down. Out of the packet fell a number of coins and a small piece of paper that might have been ripped from a diary or notebook. The paper showed writing but it had faded with time and was now indistinct. Garfield screwed his eyes and held it up to the light.

The wages of sin, Anthony. Ten pieces of silver. This is what it feels like to be let down by someone you thought you could trust. The day you sold your shares to those thieving bastards, you effectively killed this company.......and by doing so, you also killed me. I hope you feel shame, son, because I feel shame for you.....you did something I can never forgive.

Garfield let the paper drop from his hand and walked zombie-like to his seat where he sat with his arms at his side and his face expressionless. After several minutes he mumbled.

'He must have planned it this way from the start. God, I had no idea how much he hated me.'

All this time Strickland had sat motionless in the armchair. He didn't even appear to have tipped the bottle to top up his glass. He stared straight ahead seeming totally lost in a deep pattern of thought.

At length he got to his feet and moved across the floor in the direction of the front door; and as he passed Garfield's chair he pivoted and raised a hand as if to pat the disconsolate house owner on the shoulder in a gesture of consolation.

Anthony Garfield knew nothing more. The shot fired from the pistol that had appeared like magic in Strickland's hand made little sound. The corpse did not even register a look of surprise as it was angled back into the chair by a sharp tug at a handful of overlong hair.

CHAPTER FORTY FOUR

MONDAY 20th FEBRUARY 2017

After a bit of prodding and poking Strickland was satisfied Garfield's body looked to be correctly positioned. He stepped back to survey his handiwork from a number of different angles just in case anything had been missed. Once satisfied he rubbed the gun clean with a handkerchief and clicked on the safety catch. He then touched the weapon against different parts of both of Garfield's hands, before manipulating it into the dead man's grasp, guiding his index figure to the trigger and allowing the gun to fall to the floor. Almost as an afterthought he produced a pencil stub from his jacket pocket and used the blunt end to click the safety lever back into the off position.

Still deep in concentration Strickland spoke for the final time to his erstwhile colleague; seemingly anxious to voice an apology that Anthony Garfield could take with him on the mystery journey for which he had just been allocated a one way ticket.

'Sorry about that, Anthony; nothing personal. You somehow managed to turn the whole thing into one bloody great charade and as you rightly figured out you were the only person who could connect me to any part of it. I'm sure you understand.'

Strickland crossed himself and took two paces back. His eyes flicked around the room as he assessed what still needed to be done; then he stopped and stood rigid as if a random thought had suddenly crossed his mind.

'And Anthony, just in case there is reincarnation, you don't need to fire a gun twice like they do on the television; not as long as you get close enough to make sure you hit what you are aiming at the first time around.'

Now seemingly satisfied, Geoff Strickland returned to business. In days, possibly hours, this room would become a crime scene while due consideration was given to whether Anthony Garfield had committed suicide or had been assisted in his passage to the other side. He needed to point the general direction for the investigating team without laying it on too thick; to leave things tidy but not too tidy; to maintain a small hint of mystery.

Strickland returned to his seat and took a long pull from his glass. What he really needed to know was what had happened to Charlie Brinsworth, because good old Charlie's current condition affected every other consideration. Weighing up the odds he was inclined to think Charlie would have found some way to make his escape from the library building; and possibly was even now reclining in a hospital bed claiming to be the victim of a mugging or a hit and run accident.

Had Anthony Garfield taken the trouble to fix the safe back together and tidy the room before he left? No idea; he would if he had any sense but maybe he thought leaving a dead body lying in the middle of the floor would serve as enough of a distraction to whoever was investigating that they would have interest in little else. Presumably Charlie had a key to lock up the front door on the way out but had he been in any condition to use it? The man was a wizened old pro; the answer to that one was quite probably yes.

If Garfield had tidied up after himself Charlie would only have needed to stagger out of the door and get as far away from the scene of the crime as was humanly possible. If he hadn't it was a different matter altogether. There was always something you missed in these situations and in this case it was a question he should have put to the dead man before he blew his brains out. What did the room look like when you walked out of the door, Anthony? Simple enough but he had missed the opportunity. Bloody idiot.

He crossed the room and removed Garfield's gun from his pocket and checked for spare ammunition without finding any. One mistake was enough; two in a single night would be totally unforgivable.

He paused to consider. So adding up the numbers, it was quite possible the library was clean.......or even if it was slightly less than pristine, there was a good chance that whatever was out of place would maybe be put down to something other than a break in. There would be no smashed windows or damage to the doors or windows to act as a clue. An old building like that could perhaps have been affected by a minor earth tremor caused by a passing lorry; maybe the scene had been visited by a poltergeist; there were plenty of crackpots with broad imaginations who would buy into that sort of crap. Just as long as Charlie had got out in one piece there was maybe not too much to worry about on that score.

Strickland shook off his concerns. He went upstairs and located an ancient, brown leather attaché case into which he stuffed the pile of Lire notes. He placed this under Garfield's bed where it was out of sight and yet bound to be located by even the most basic of searches of the premises. He took the glass from which he had been drinking and several more that he collected from the sideboard and gave them a thorough wash. One clean glass might have raised suspicions; half a dozen and nobody would pay any undue attention. It was the way these things worked.

That short message from Garfield's father was interesting. Just the sort of wording that a son might choose to ponder over for one last time when he was on the verge of blowing his brains out. Strickland gathered up the note and put it in plain view; then, secured the edge of the paper to the table top with Garfield's whiskey glass to ensure it couldn't get overlooked.

He hesitated, again surveying the scene. Something about it still wasn't quite right. The room had something of the wrong feel. Did it maybe look a bit too much like the elaborate set up he had gone to such trouble to construct? He thought for a minute. Perhaps there was a better way. Why not add a few touches that would maximise the potential of the scene he had already created? And while he was at it, point a finger in a new direction entirely.

Strickland slipped silently out of the front door, leaving it on the latch and hiked to the top of the road where he had left his car. He quietly opened the boot and rummaged amongst the pile of miscellaneous debris that filled every corner of the confined space. There were a couple of clear choices on offer but only one would best serve his purpose. He hesitated again, unsure, before coming to the conclusion it was definitely the right option. He delved into the car boot and retrieved a crumpled carrier bag from somewhere near the bottom of the vast heap of junk. He checked the contents were still intact and immediately retraced his steps.

Once back indoors he quickly removed from his parcel a polythene bag containing the contents of an ashtray and tipped it unceremoniously into a peddle bin under the sink. He next extracted a spirit glass and, with infinite care, filled it half full with whiskey before swilling it around and discarding the contents down the sink. He turned the tap on full to get rid of the smell.

He stopped for a moment and considered the situation carefully; then having reached a decision rolled the glass across the floor so it landed up against the front wall of the house. It was now partially obscured by a set of aged floral curtains that stretched all the way from ceiling to floor.

That felt better. The look of a constructed setup remained but the evidence would now lead the investigating team in the desired direction. A bit of initial confusion would do no harm either; offering conflicting avenues for the senior officers to consider and argue over before they were helped by the evidence to figure things out. There was a distinct possibility it might even end up back on his desk if everybody did their job properly. Now that really would be something he would thoroughly enjoy.

Perhaps an anonymous phone call from a worried neighbour to set the ball rolling or would that be pushing things a little bit too far? No need to decide on that now. There would be plenty of time to consider that possibility later in the day. Strickland completed a final check to be certain nothing had been forgotten, before once more making an exit through the front door and pulling it silently shut behind him.

It had been a bad night all round; there was no point in pretending any differently. Yet, at the same time, it was undeniable things could have worked out a hell of a lot worse. The fact he had been unable to achieve a further payment from Garfield, was, of course, a major disappointment; but if you put that to one side for a minute, any other appraisal of the evening's activities came up with a lot of positives. And Garfield himself? Not much of a loss to have one less idiot consuming the planet's resources.

Strickland pointed the car towards town, lit a cigarette and flicked on the radio in the hope of catching the remnants of one of the early morning news bulletins. 'You lucky bastard,' he muttered to himself as the hot air blower kicked into life with a mighty roar. 'If this pans out right it could be just what the doctor ordered.'

The Detective Sergeant now had a long day stretching out before him but there wasn't a lot he could do about that. He had a supply of Benzedrine tablets in his desk drawer which would help to keep him on his feet and somehow he would manage to soldier on with half an eye open. These days soldiering on was acknowledged a basic requirement of the job.

CHAPTER FORTY FIVE

MONDAY 20th FEBRUARY 2017

Oliver Dearlove pulled back the light linen cloth which was draped loosely over the front of the easel for one final peek, before reluctantly allowing it to drift back into place. The more he looked at it the more he was convinced he had produced a masterpiece. Undoubtedly one of the finest pieces of work he had turned out in the last thirty or forty years; and that in itself was something of an irony.

He had only set out to produce an inaccurate replica, God damn it, yet somehow Charlotte Langthorpe now contrived to look so much lovelier than in the original. Her cheeks glowed more radiantly; her eyes smouldered like hot coals, warm and inviting, as they bored deep into your very soul. The hair; there were not words in his vocabulary to adequately describe the sheen and lustre. The nose was bordering on perfection; slightly tilted to the sky as an indication you were unlikely to prove worthy of her attention. But then your eyes were drawn to the tight smile playing on her delicate lips, which indicated that none the less you were invited to do your best to alter that perception.

It was exactly the same in every tiny detail while at the same time being so very much better. He hadn't known he still had it in him after all these years and if he wasn't careful it was going to be all for nothing. He knew he had to do something but already it was far too late. Fucking hell, what a time to have an accident of this sort! Why did it all have to all come together at this precise moment? Life made no degree of sense.

Dearlove decided that he couldn't bear to part with it. Without intention the finished article had turned out just too damned good. Regardless of any other consideration, a work of this quality would be totally wasted on the uncouth barrow boy and his tarty bit of skirt. And thankfully, unless they were totally brain dead, they couldn't fail to notice it would be absolutely useless for their purposes. That part of the plan, at least, had been satisfactorily fulfilled; it was just the rest of it......why did it have to be at this precise moment in time that every brushstroke he applied had turned into utter perfection. Life could be so abominably cruel.

Much though he craved an extra five grand he would make another copy for four, or if pushed to the limit even three and a half, in order to have this version of Miss Langthorpe adorn the walls of his home. Admit it Oliver; anything they bloody well want just as long as they don't disappear out of the door with her image tucked underneath an arm. Regardless of the cost she must take her rightful place alongside his other treasures. Be carefully hung in the place where she could be best appreciated; appreciated by persons of discerning taste; appreciated by him.

Dearlove twitched slightly as another thought crossed his mind. There was of course a secondary danger which he must be certain to guard against. Smith's tart was nothing if not shrewd and couldn't fail to recognise the quality of his work. It was not inconceivable that as a second option she might fancy acquiring the portrait for her tasteless little gallery. This must not be allowed to happen. His need was much the greater. He must hold on to this work regardless of what it might cost him to do so. He had put too much of his very being into the finished article to let it fall into the hands of rampaging philistines. There were occasions when an artistic creation was more valuable than money itself.

Dearlove sensed their approach even before the overloud banging at the outside door. Put these thoughts of dread behind you Oliver. It is party time and you must rise to the occasion. Take just a moment to muster up a serious yet weary countenance. Give the next minutes your full attention; now's not the time for any kind of slip, no matter how trivial. Hit the mark and make ready to summon the required pathos for the performance that will bring down the house. The curtain is about to rise and already the audience hold their breath in anticipation of what you will bring to the stage; stay calm, Oliver; it is essential that you now give only of your very best.

'Come in Mr Smith, Miss Armitage. Push the papers onto the floor. Take a pew; make yourselves at home. I want you in prime position for the grand unveiling.'

Ideally, he had wanted to string this out for a bit longer but he couldn't offer any refreshment. He had polished off the dregs of the rum bottle the night before and the milkman had stopped delivering after the disagreement over the last bill so he couldn't even make do with a cup of tea. When did he ever order natural yoghurt? Did the graceless lackey take him for a complete fool?

His customers didn't look overly excited at the prospect of claiming their prize but maybe they were making a pathetic attempt to appear calm while in reality their palms were already damp with perspiration. A lover's tiff on the way over? Quite possibly. It was plain the atmosphere was running a little cool. Enjoy the moment you perfidious swine; you won't be so bloody calm in a minute! Dearlove feigned a cough to suppress a giggle of excitement and quickly covered his mouth with a handkerchief that was daubed with streaks of bright yellow paint.

Alright, calmly now, onto the introduction. Nothing that might detract from the moment of shock that was just around the corner. Just a throwaway line that would sound in keeping when they eventually got round to replaying the sequence of events that led up to the revelation of their tragic misfortune.

'I can't begin to explain the trouble I went to get an exact colour match. A copy of this sort has to be precise in every tiny detail or it would have been entirely without merit.'

A couple of disinterested nods. Come on, show some interest you pair of insipid bastards; surely you can summon up more enthusiasm than that. My God, the younger generation! Don't they get excited about anything these days?

Alright, my patience is at an end. We shall proceed forthwith and bugger the pair of you. Stand back and prepare for fireworks. Lights, cameras, action. Let the unfurling commence and the slings and arrows of outrageous fortune be loosed so that I can deftly parry them with my trusty shield before proceeding to lay claim to the day.

Dearlove pranced excitedly to the easel and swept back the covering cloth with a flourish that would have done credit to a matador intent on tormenting an enraged bull.

Total silence, but it was immediately obvious that Stephanie Armitage at least had engaged with the painting; in fact she appeared to be totally transfixed.

Oliver Dearlove took a step back and awaited the tide of condemnation that would soon flow in his direction. He coughed to clear his throat as he practised his watertight defence; *but you clearly stated that you required a copy of* ***the original work****; look I have it here in black and white on the contract signed by both parties.*

He wanted a mirror to hand. He had worked hard on the look of hurt and now had it down to absolute perfection.

This was exactly how the original painting looked I can assure you. Yes, the colours were most definitely that bright. I researched all aspects in the finest detail. I can even offer first hand testimony because in my younger days I viewed the work in its original form.

Come on you cretins, come on, cut to the chase. I haven't got all night to stand here waiting while you think up the best way to vilify my creative efforts and break my gentle heart. I have all my lines memorised; if anything I'm over rehearsed; let's be having you; why the bloody delay?

If you wanted a copy of the painting the way it looks now you should have been specific about that requirement. I'm not paid to be a mind-reader, you know. I can only work to the instructions I am given and I did that to the absolute letter. The painting on the wall of the pub hadn't been cleaned since the day it was first mounted. Little wonder the colours were muted after it had been hanging in a place like that for decades on end. Why do you think I spent so long studying it in situ?

Ah, signs of life. Mr Smith has raised his carcase from the seat, moved forward and is even now grasping the painting in both hands. God, I hope the Neanderthal doesn't intend to smash it over my head. I abhor violence; especially when I'm on the receiving end. Alright, hit me if you must, but I beg you, don't damage the portrait.

'Alright Oliver, I suppose this will do. Shove it in a bag and we'll be on our way. Any problems from your end, Stevie?'

It will do! It will fucking do! What is the imbecile saying? Doesn't he see it looks nothing like the work he wanted me to copy? Is the man totally fucking colour blind!

'I think you have surpassed yourself Oliver,' from Stephanie Armitage, giving him the benefit of a calculated smile. 'The blue is worthy of Caravaggio; the yellow would have made Van Gogh eat his heart out.'

But that isn't what you want, you daft cow. Can't you see it bears not the slightest resemblance to the work you wanted me to copy? Are the pair of you stoned out of your tiny minds?

Steady down now, Oliver; try to stay calm and think lucidly. There is a rational explanation for what is happening and in a moment your mind will clear and you will be able to identify what that is. Ah, the woman's moving closer. Please God, let her say something that makes some small degree of sense.

'I had no idea the colours in the painting were originally so vivid, Oliver. What a clever old thing you are. Let me in on your secret; how did you ever manage the research?'

My God. Whatever drugs the pair of them are taking I

hope I can get hold of some. What the hell is the answer to that?

'I'm afraid it's a secret I am not permitted to divulge, not even to a lady as lovely as you. Listen, Ms Armitage.....Stephanie, I sense something might be slightly amiss. If there is anything at all you find unsatisfactory with the painting.......if in any tiny respect it fails to meet with your needs then I would feel it my duty to produce another copy. I am only happy when my customer is totally satisfied. I'll drop everything else and start immediately if that is what is required. It will be my pleasure to do so.'

'Oliver, please don't concern yourself. The painting meets perfectly with Mr Smith's requirements. Come on Mickey, grab the frame. It's time we were out of here. Mr Dearlove will doubtless have a good deal of other important work that requires his expert attention.

CHAPTER FORTY SIX

MONDAY 20th FEBRUARY 2017

Charlie Brinsworth awoke from a deep sleep and checked his watch. Jesus, it was already well past twelve. He should have been up and about hours ago.

He pushed out of bed, padded across the room and examined his face in the mirror. There was no hiding the fact he looked like he had just clambered out from underneath a double decker bus. Two yellowish, purple bruises obtained in the confrontation with Eastgate and one side of his face appearing to have been sandblasted. Not to mention the egg sized lump on the back of his head, received courtesy of the lanky git he was now going to tear into small strips and feed down the nearest manhole cover.

Charlie carefully washed his face, cleaned his teeth and shaved the bits that were still somewhere approaching a normal colour; before quickly throwing on the first clothes that came to hand and gingerly making his way downstairs. He reached ground level and positioned himself in a nook at the back of the bannisters; stretched and waggled his limbs about to assess which bits were still in some sort of working order. Not too bad considering. It was pretty obvious he had been suffering from concussion when he got back from the library last night but a decent night's sleep seemed to have restored him to something approaching reasonable health.

No sign of Mickey behind the bar. Possibly that was a good thing. Sharon was busy serving a customer so she was only able to make a pursed expression with her lips and furrow her forehead as he shuffled by to make his escape. Alright, he looked like shit, but there wasn't a lot he could do about that situation. The fact Sharon was serving provided a lucky escape because he had been able to make it out of the door before she could start asking the sort of questions he really didn't feel equipped to answer.

Considering the condition he had been in the previous night his attempt at parking hadn't been altogether bad. He had got at least three quarters of his vehicle into its allocated parking spot and had failed to graze the nearest bollard by a clear half centimetre. Charlie settled in the driver's seat, turned the key, gunned the engine and slowly manoeuvred out onto the front road, his appetite for breakfast currently blunted by thoughts of revenge. Thorton Chumley would take about forty minutes at this time of day and he couldn't wait to get there. Anthony Smartarse was going to be very sorry indeed before this day was out. Charlie's adrenalin was now pumping. He was so keen to reach his destination he found it hard to resist putting his foot to the floor and taking his chances with any traffic cameras.

As it turned out the flow of vehicles on the potholed back roads was lighter than Charlie had anticipated and he completed the journey in less than half an hour. He slowed as he coasted through the village and this proved a lucky break because it enabled him to catch a glimpse of a police car out of the corner of his eye. He quickly cancelled the car's indicator and drove on round the corner and past the village pub until he hit a slightly wider section of the road which may have been intended to serve as a lay-by, or more likely had just been carved out of the surrounding farmland as a convenient passing point. He parked the car, eased his frame carefully out of the door and walked back in the direction from which he had come.

It was a tricky situation because he definitely didn't want to be seen by a member of the public and even less by anybody wearing a blue uniform. He had no legitimate reason for being in the village, short of claiming to be lost; and the state of his face wasn't going to convince anybody he had just popped down to volunteer his services to run the tombola stall at the next community fete. He turned up his jacket collar and sidled down the small lane trying to avoid drawing unwanted attention.

It certainly was a police car. The vehicle had its blue light flashing and was parked sideways across the entry to Mount Drive. He craned his neck in an effort to ascertain which house was the centre of the police activity but without moving closer that was damn near impossible. The easy answer would be to go into the pub, order a beer and engage whoever was serving in casual conversation. The person behind the bar counter would be bound to know what was going on; somehow they always did. However, he definitely didn't want to show his face in the village in case it was remembered after he proved successful in beating friend Anthony into a pulp, so sadly that line of enquiry would need to be shelved for the current time.

Thwarted, Charlie returned to his car, completed a seven point turn, and retraced his route. He tried to sneak a look as the road bent round to the left but with little success. Was it a coincidence or had Anthony Garfield somehow been successful in attracting the attention of her Majesty's finest? He had no answer to that question, but either way he wasn't going to make much progress with this mission while large numbers of the local constabulary were parked on the lanky twat's front doorstep. The sensible option was to abort the mission for today and try again tomorrow when hopefully the custodians of law and order would be gainfully occupied elsewhere.

Charlie drove back into town and took the opportunity to check out progress at the Pizza development. He then headed across town to the office that was the hub of Simon Bartol's taxi business and caught the main man lounging behind a paper strewn desk.

'Good to see you Charlie; called in last night; did Mickey tell you? What the hell happened to your face? Get the wrong side of the girlfriend, did you?'

'A small disagreement with deputation from Eastgate a couple of nights back, Simon. Nothing serious; gave them a bit of a spanking if you must know. Small amount of damage to the pub but we soon patched it up. I've recruited Spanner Hopkins to keep an eye on the door so maybe they'll decide to leave us alone.'

'No way that's going to happen, my friend. Terry Brean's new in the job and he can't afford to look weak while he's still finding his feet. If word gets around your lot gave a kicking to a deputation of his boys and there was no comeback then a few others might begin to fancy their chances of doing the same. Eastgate have got far too much tied up in the protection racket to just laugh it off. Take my advice, Charlie; get tooled up and watch your back.'

'How's business, Simon? Not often I find you sitting around scratching your arse.'

'Middling to crap. Listen, grab a coffee from the machine and pull up a chair. There's something I want to run by you. How do you fancy selling on the dope growing business your Vietnamese kids are setting up? A couple of major busts have gone down recently and I've run into a bit of a supply problem. I've given it some thought and come to the conclusion it will be in my best long term interest if I take the whole business in house.'

'Bloody hell, Simon. That came a bit out of the blue. I'm only just getting geared up for the first delivery.'

'Think it over and get back if you're interested. It's a long term strategy from my end and I'll give you a fair price.'

'Fair enough. I'll consider what you're saying. Got a figure in mind so I've got some ball park idea what we're talking?'

'Charlie my friend, if you're up for it we'll put our heads together and work something out. We're both reasonable men and reasonable men have better things to do than fall out over money......hey, have you been listening to local radio? Some bloke's been found dead over on the south side. Reading between the lines they don't know if he topped himself or was helped on his way. There's not much detail yet but you can bet it will be the headline in tonight's paper. Perhaps it will give the coppers something to occupy their time and stop them getting under our feet.'

CHAPTER FORTY SEVEN

MONDAY 20th FEBRUARY 2017

'He knew exactly what he was doing all along, the devious old bastard,' Stephanie Armitage said, spitting sparks of uncontrolled anger.

'Original colours, my arse,' she continued in much the same strident tone. 'He deliberately produced a painting that he knew would be useless to us because that's the way the conniving old toad gets his kicks.'

She paused briefly for breath, her eyes still flashing undiluted anger.

'Then the idiot falls head over heels in love with his own work. Did you see how much it pained him to see it disappearing out of the door? He was virtually in tears.'

'So in a way it's fortunate we have no use for the thing,' re-joined Mickey Smith, trying to figure out how being five grand out of pocket on a deal he had never fancied in the first place was in any way lucky.

'Don't you try to weasel your way out of this one, Mickey Smith,' said Stephanie Armitage, launching into a fresh assault. 'He pulled the wool right over your eyes, didn't he? I thought you were meant to be streetwise? Dumb-arsed more like it.'

'It was you who introduced me to him. Best copyist in the country were your exact words, if I remember. Didn't choose to mention at the time he was a con-artist on the make, did you?'

'A man who makes his living out of copying other peoples' work and who has gone to prison for forgery was hardly likely to be Jesus Christ reincarnate. All it needed was for you to keep your wits about you and follow what I told you to do and you made a pretty poor attempt at doing both. I'm disappointed in you, Mickey. I expected better. You haven't been the same man since that little red head dumped you. Why don't you make a bit of an effort to pull yourself together?'

'For Christ's sake woman, let it go. It's my five grand that's disappeared down the tubes. All you've lost is the chance to have a good laugh at us poor bastards who can't tell a van Gogh from a Gainsborough.'

'Well, at least that proves you've heard of two artists, which I suppose I should take as vaguely reassuring.'

'Stuck up tart!'

'Ignorant Neanderthal nincompoop!'

They walked on in silence for two blocks until Mickey caught his foot on a piece of uneven pavement.

'Careful! That painting can still earn us a great deal of money if I place it with the right buyer.'

Mickey shrugged his shoulders as if unconvinced.

'If you say so.'

'I do say so. If I can't get twenty times what you paid for it I'll eat my hat. Why do you think the toad was nearly in tears? Because we were swanning out of the door with what I would describe as a minor masterpiece and the old devil was well aware of the fact. Listen, to what I'm saying my artistically challenged friend; I've got an eye for these things. That painting is premium quality and once I've talked it up in all the right places it's going to attract a lot of interest from the sort of people who have money to burn.'

'Sorry Stevie, that isn't going to happen. I've made my mind up; I'm not going to sell it.

'Are you mad? What else can you do with the bloody thing? Don't you want to be rich?'

'Stevie, will you please get off my back! I've made up my mind what I'm going to do with the painting and it isn't being sold.'

'I don't know what's the matter with you, Mickey Smith. You used to be a good laugh to be around but lately your head is all over the place. And another thing; these days you always seem as miserable as buggery. Lighten up a bit for Christ's sake. We could make a killing on selling that portrait and have a few laughs at Oliver Dearlove's expense along the way. What have you got against having...........'

'It's the pub.'

'Please Mickey spare me the bloody pub. I've heard enough about your pub to last me........'

'I'm jacking it in.'

'Don't be so ridiculous. You live for that place. God alone knows why but you always have.'

'I've fallen out of love with it, Stevie. It's not the same as it used to be. It's become Charlie's place not mine anymore; full of crusty old ex-cons, bent coppers and Christ knows what else. I need a fresh challenge so I'm going to straighten up with Charlie and head off somewhere new and make a fresh start.'

'You sure that's a good idea?'

'Absolutely certain. I've thought of little else for the last couple of weeks and it's definitely what I want to do. The painting.......the painting is going to be a goodbye present to Charlie. He was always staring up at the old one before it got mashed in the punch up with Eastgate and if this thing I'm lugging around is half as good as you say it is then maybe he'll take to it in the same way.'

'You are seriously off your head. The very thought of leaving your mate Charlie with a painting like that. I hope you're joking. Anyway, I can't see you going anywhere. I've never known you take a holiday let alone contemplate anything a bit more drastic.'

Mickey hesitated, because she was right. Besides, he didn't want to think about it just now. Telling Stevie any sort of detail had too much of a ring of finality to be casually discussed while walking the street.

'I can't put a date on it but just take it I'm definitely going. Not right away because there's still trouble with Eastgate simmering and I'm not heading out until that's sorted, one way or the other.'

'You're just making excuses. Anyway, the troubles at the pub are your mate Charlie's concern; nothing to do with you.'

'We're partners, which means we share the bad stuff as well as the good; and, to be honest, a lot of the shit that is coming in our direction is strictly down to me.'

'Very noble you first class idiot. Exactly the sort of answer I would have expected from a meat head like you. Anyway, what about me? Are you intending to pack your bags and just leave me here?'

'You aren't my responsibility, Stevie. We're just friends, remember? Besides, these days we don't even seem to be able to walk up the street without getting into an argument. You've got the gallery to keep you amused and what about Ziggy. You are still married you know.......or have you been through so many divorces in the last few years that you're beginning to lose count? Anyway, I think I'd like to be by myself for a bit. My head's been all over the place lately and I need some space to sort myself out.'

'Well thanks for that, Mickey; at least I know where I stand. I'm pushing off now; a bit of a hectic afternoon lined up I'm afraid. Best of luck with whatever you decide to do. It's been nice knowing you. You used to be a lot of fun once upon a time.'

CHAPTER FORTY EIGHT

MONDAY 20th FEBRUARY 2017

It was early evening and Charlie Brinsworth was occupying his usual seat in the bar, cursing the fact he had forgotten to order a portion of the chef's steak and kidney pudding which had now run out. Sharon was on duty behind the pumps but had made it crystal clear she was not talking to him. This was presumably because he had hurried out that morning without telling her where he was going and had failed to offer any explanation about the further deterioration to the state of his face. That was the trouble with being in a relationship of this sort. You had to remember to do things that were a complete waste of time. He had tried to explain that he had been in a hurry to get to an appointment but she was having none of it. Now, when he ordered a replacement pint she banged it down on the bar and made him sign a chit of paper to confirm he had taken possession. Bloody women; they were all stark raving mad.

Mickey had arrived back from his travels about two thirty with a parcel under his arm and the look of a man who had taken anti-post odds of even money on a horse that had romped home at seven to two. Charlie had no idea what exactly was wrong with Mickey these days but he was certain it would be something to do with a woman; because where Mickey was concerned, women had always been his Achilles heel.

Charlie was hoping for a bit of peace because he wanted the opportunity to mull over Simon Bartol's offer to take over his cannabis farm. Simon was a decent bloke and Charlie had no doubt he would be sensible when discussing the proposed buyout; but at the end of the day Mr Bartol was also a shrewd businessman so Charlie wanted to be sure that if he did decide to accept Simon's proposition, it wouldn't be something he'd later regret.

There was also an urgent need to plan a further visit to Thorton Chumley for the following day; and a requirement to confirm whether or not the mystery body that had been discovered in the village had any connection to his erstwhile partner in crime.

However, the main reason Charlie wanted a few quiet hours was one that he was anxious to keep to himself. If the truth were known, now his blood pressure had returned to something approaching normal, he was beginning to feel the injuries he had sustained in the previous couple of night's activities. When he got knocked around these days it took a bit longer to shake off than it had when he was a few years younger. He now had aches and pains in places that a year or two back he wouldn't have known to exist. It was probably time he faced up to the fact his best years were behind him and started treating his body with a bit more respect. No shame in that; he wasn't a kid anymore. But as this was something he found difficult to clear with his ego, he pushed his discomfort to the back of his mind and took another pull on his drink.

Deciding he couldn't put it off any longer Charlie dragged himself to his feet, taking care to suppress a groan. He then wandered around the bar casting a look at recently vacated tables. Disappointed by the result of his search, he then made a detour into the back bar, returning with a newspaper neatly folded at the racing results. He flipped over the pages until he arrived at the front where he hoped to find items of up to date news. There was nothing in the headlines; nothing caught his eye on the inside pages either. Page seven had the article but there was precious little in it to get excited about.

The body of a middle aged man was discovered at a house in the picturesque village of Thorton Chumley. No further details will be released until relatives of the deceased have been traced and informed. At this time the police are not seeking any person or persons in connection with the death but a forensic search of the premises is underway and enquiries are ongoing.

Thanks for that. Absolutely bloody useless. The newspaper hadn't told Charlie a thing that he didn't already know. Call that news. No wonder today's kids got all their information off the internet.

He dropped the paper onto the table top and looked up to see a familiar figure veering in his direction carrying a very large whiskey.

'Evening Charlie, I left my wallet in the car so I put the drink on your tab. I hope you don't mind. The lady serving seemed to think you wouldn't object. She said as far as she was concerned I was welcome to put the whole bottle on your account as long as I signed for it.'

Detective Sergeant Geoff Strickland settled in the seat opposite and took a delicate sip of his drink.

'Your face looks terrible, Charlie. Were you making an effort to blend in with the new decorations? It might be worth your while to get someone with medical experience to take a squint. Looks very nasty from where I'm sitting. Reminds me a bit of one of those Picasso pictures but with far brighter colours. What happened this time? Did you fall down the stairs or walk into a door?'

Charlie ignored the remarks and looked pointedly at his watch.

'Still putting in the hours I see, Mr Strickland. I thought the latest statistics showed that crime was meant to be falling? What they should have said, was the recording of it was falling because these days nobody down at the station bothers to answer the bloody phone. Now I've gone legitimate I'm strongly considering forming a pressure group to complain about the way things are being handled in this city. It's a poor state of affairs when honest citizens don't feel able to sleep soundly in their beds.'

Strickland picked up the newspaper from the table, appearing oblivious to what had been said.

'Now we have developed this close friendship, how about we cut out the formality? Make it Geoff; anything else doesn't sound right when we are sitting here enjoying a quiet drink. After all, we're both off duty in a manner of speaking. It will only need to be Mr Strickland or Detective Sergeant the next time I come round to arrest you. Don't suppose the man in the street ever imagines the likes of you and me enjoying a moment of relaxation in each other's company. Don't suppose it ever occurs to them that we have more in common with each other than almost anybody else on the planet.'

'That's very philosophical, Geoff. Was there anything specific you wanted or were you just passing by and decided it might be a good opportunity to demonstrate that you had more strings to your bow than a GCSE pass in woodwork?'

'Nope. Purely a social call. I've had a very busy day and thought I'd just enjoy the odd glass with an old business acquaintance on my way home; an old business acquaintance to whom I might be able to offer a good piece of advice. Shall we have another? I've just about got time. Don't disturb yourself, Charlie. I'll fetch them. I told the lady serving the drinks to keep your tab within easy reach.'

Geoff Strickland sauntered to the bar, shared a joke and brief conversation with Sharon, and returned to his seat in jocular mood.

'Nice girl that; I was thinking I might ask for her phone number. She happened to mention her current boyfriend is proving to be unreliable and she might very soon be looking for an upgrade.'

'Piss off, Strickland. She's out of your league.'

'Well, until I found out she was hanging around with the likes of you I would have been the first to agree.'

'Do I get to hear this piece of advice or are you hanging on to it until you've got enough evidence to run me in? The last time you did me a favour, Detective Sergeant, I can't help but remember I ended up serving two and a half years.'

'Now, now, Charlie, no point in being bitter. I was only doing my duty as you are well aware. As it happens, I was talking to an old pal of mine just before I knocked off tonight. An old pal who is working on that case you were studying in your newspaper with such interest when I walked in the door. He said he thought he might be stuck out in that village in the middle of nowhere for quite a while because the enquiry wasn't proving as straightforward as had originally been anticipated. What the difficulties are I have no idea, but for some reason the investigating team are finding it hard to arrive at a satisfactory conclusion as to cause of death.'

'Who's the stiff?' asked Charlie, in a voice that he hoped sounded suitably casual.

'Sorry Charlie, I can't be seen to tell tales out of school. We have a strict moral code in the force on matters of this sort as I'm sure you are very well aware.'

Charlie looked up to the ceiling, seemingly lost for words. Strickland swallowed half his drink and produced from his pocket a large packet of peanuts.

'I hope you don't mind but I noticed these behind the bar while I was waiting to be served. I've been that busy today I've hardly had time to scratch my arse, let alone get anything to eat.'

Strickland ripped open the cellophane wrapper, swallowed a handful and masticated enthusiastically. Charlie looked away. He had spent a lot of his formative years living on peanuts, crisps and anything else that came to hand and the rustle of the packet still made him feel queasy.

'Anyway, the interesting thing my mate passed on was that they are now increasing the numbers on the investigating team because they want to examine a variety of different aspects. My pal's been given the job of quizzing the locals on any unusual sightings. People they have seen in the district that don't look like they belong in such genteel surrounding; that sort of thing. I've been landed with that detail on numerous occasions over the years. It's a ball aching job I can tell you.'

The policeman stopped to shovel in more nuts, grunting

his appreciation at the quality. Charlie retrieved the newspaper and smothered a grimace.

'A whole heap of people noticed a stretch limo carrying a Hen Party going through the village the weekend before last,' continued Strickland unabashed by the apparent loss of his target audience.

'Not really what my mate was interested in but it just shows you the sort of thing that people's memories can turn up when you start asking the right sort of questions. Also, a couple of locals reported seeing an old Toyota RAV drive into the village earlier today; then ten minutes later it drove out again without seeming to have had time to fulfil any useful purpose. One of the witnesses said it was red and covered in mud; the other thought it was the old, short wheelbase model they discontinued years back, and the colour was brown. As you can imagine, that was much more the type of information my mate was looking for.'

Strickland hesitated for a moment, then smiled and slowly brought his drink to his lips.

'No road cameras out there of course, Charlie, and needless to say nobody got a look at the car's number plate. As far as I know nobody saw the driver either but you can bet the investigating team will be asking around because you never know where this sort of thing might lead. Don't suppose you were out that way today, by any chance? Knowing that you drive a brown Toyota RAV that matches the description I thought it was beholden on me to at least put my head in here and ask the question. '

'Afraid not. Today, I was tied up in a business meeting for nearly all of the day. And to be honest, I'm not sure I could find Thorton Chumley on the map if you offered to pay me. I can produce witnesses to confirm my whereabouts if that would help put your mind at rest.'

'Of course you can, Charlie. I never for one moment doubted that would be the case. Just thought I'd do you a favour and let you know which way the wind was blowing. The last thing you want is to get drawn into a case which is nothing to do with you when there's no need; especially with an arrest sheet like yours to take into account.'

And with that Detective Sergeant Strickland finished his drink, pocketed what remained of his bag of nuts and without another word walked purposefully towards the door.

Charlie sat back in his seat and stared into space as he tried to figure out what he had been told, and more specifically the bits he was expected to work out for himself. After a few minutes Sharon walked across from the bar area and pushed in beside him. She ruffled his hair which proved extremely painful, but he managed to hide the discomfort. Sharon was smiling again so it looked like he might have been forgiven for his earlier transgressions.

'What did he want? I'm not one to complain but you do have some very peculiar friends.'

'Hard to argue; and I must admit, that one's probably the oddest of the lot. I was just sitting here trying to figure out what it was he was trying to tell me. With Strickland you can generally tell when he's lying because you see his lips move but today he decided to use some form of subliminal messaging I've not come across before. I'll have to give the matter some thought. It was worrying. The only time I could be certain he definitely wasn't telling the truth was when he talked about having a friend.'

CHAPTER FORTY NINE

TUESDAY 21st FEBRUARY 2017

Detective Inspector Alan Bateman took one last look around the sitting room of 14, Mount Drive. Nothing had changed. No new clues had sprung out of the woodwork to demand his urgent attention. Bugger. He would now have to reach a decision based on the information that was already in his possession, and in his opinion that wasn't enough.

He took a crumpled pack of cigarettes from his jacket pocket and located his cheap throwaway lighter. At least out here he could puff away to his heart's content without his shrewish wife demanding that he *take that filthy thing out into the garden*. He was the one who paid the bloody mortgage, wasn't he? He was the one who put in fourteen hour days while she luxuriated under a hairdryer reading lurid magazines and sipping cups of that foul, weak tea with the nettle infusion. Getting married had been the biggest mistake of his life. Well, that and choosing to support a football team that made it a policy to never win anything and sell all their best players. Thank God for the small mercy they had never had kids. At least his wife rapidly succumbing to a violent headache the minute he showed the slightest sign of amorous affection had some small mitigation. With her ability to permanently radiate a miasma of abject misery even when she had nothing to do but sit on her arse all day, children would have been the final straw.

There had been a brief moment, a lifetime ago, when his career had appeared to be going somewhere but that was now little more than a far distant memory. There was no point in trying to put in the brown nosing required to secure the next rung on the ladder with Margaret for a wife. She had a tongue like a honed razor blade. The memories of the summer barbeque at the Chief Constable's house still kept him awake at night. None of the other wives had let out a scream that could be heard in the next county when the Chief had patted them playfully on the bottom. From that moment he knew for certain that any hope of his ever attaining another promotion had disappeared down the khazi.

Bateman stubbed out his cigarette on the fire surround and threw the mangled stub into the hearth. Where the fuck was Gull? Out the front chatting up that little blonde with the big tits who was meant to be keeping the raptors from the press from marching up the front path to take photographs, if he knew the randy little sod. Bateman crossed the room and attempted to force open a front window without any degree of success. He gave up, went out of the room, along the hallway and threw open the front door.

Just as he thought. He had no idea what the women saw in the Detective Sergeant unless it was something vaguely primeval. It most certainly wasn't a spark of intelligence, that was for sure. Though now he came to consider it more carefully, Gull did look a bit like that sex crazed, Cornish Gypo with the tin mine who all the women appeared to be going crazy over since he took his shirt off on the telly. Load of bloody tripe that was as well. The storyline could have been written by a two year old. It didn't seem five minutes ago that the only thing to get your blood racing on a Sunday night was *Songs of Praise* and now it had come down to this. Bloody typical of the B.B.C. The whole corporation was stuffed full of lefty, tree huggers who didn't have a clue what constituted a decent night's television viewing.

'Detective Sergeant, when you have a moment,' Bateman yelled caustically. Had his utterance been pointed enough? Kevin Gull was as thick as two short planks so it was often necessary to qualify when you were being rude to him in case he hadn't picked up on it. Still, he couldn't very well shout, *get your arse in here, shithead*, with a gaggle of scumbag reporters lurking behind every section of privet. He would just have to wait his moment and give Gull a good going over when he filled out his next competency assessment. It wasn't far off if he remembered and that at least was cheering news; it provided him with something to look forward to.

Kevin Gull entered slightly out of puff and looking warmer than he should have on a midweek afternoon in late February. Those roses in his cheeks had nothing to do with an extra pair of thermals, thought Bateman. That hot flush is solely attributable to rampant lust.

For no apparent reason his mind flicked back to his wife, Margaret; the only woman he knew who wore more clothes in bed than she did when going out on a winter's morning to fetch a loaf of bread from the local shops. They had also had their moments, he reflected, though it now seemed a very long time ago. It was hard to believe they had once made love on the windowsill of the Chief Super's office, just for the hell of it. God, that must have been a few years back. If they tried that sort of thing these days it was more than probable they would overbalance and finish up as a mangled heap of skin and bone in the courtyard below. Margaret must have put on at least three stone in the intervening years. Besides which, he would never be able to bear that sort of weight since he'd fallen off the outhouse roof and needed to get the vertebrae in his lower back fused together.

Bateman shook his head to dispel the unpleasant image and forced himself to concentrate.

'Kevin, it's make your mind up time. Let's run through what we've got for one last time and then arrive at the most logical conclusion. There are only two choices, after all; either the bugger topped himself or some bastard helped him on his way.'

Kevin Gull slowly extracted his notebook and rested it on his knee. This did little to settle Bateman's nerves. As far as he had been able to ascertain Gull used pieces of paper exclusively for collecting women's phone numbers.

'Right, start from the very beginning. What have we got?'

'An unexplained cadaver, Inspector.'

'Good, good'; it wasn't in the least bit good but at least it had got the Detective Sergeant started. 'Now sum up for me the contradictory points of evidence that have been discovered.'

'Well, when we arrived we assumed it was a straightforward case of suicide because the body was resting in a chair with a glass of whiskey and an acrimonious note that we assume was written by the deceased's father on the table in front of him. And the murder weapon lying where it might naturally have fallen from a suicide's grip.'

'Excellent! But........'

'But when we looked more closely at the crime scene in a broader context we found a variety of things that failed to substantiate our original hypothesis. Namely; it was established by forensics that whilst the gun had been held close enough to the deceased man's head to produce powder burns, the muzzle of the firearm had not actually been touching the skin. This is unusual. In 99% of cases they stick the barrel up against the temple to make certain they aren't going to miss. Also, we found a second whiskey glass, which forensics confirmed had been recently used, on the floor near the front window which was partially concealed by the curtains. Thirdly, the tidy bin in the kitchen was full of cigarette ends. We know the dead man was a smoker but it represented a lot of cigarettes for one person to get through, allowing that it was a single day's consumption. Added to which, it was pretty obvious the cigarette tabs were from a number of different brands. Finally, when we searched the house we located a large amount of obsolete currency hidden in the master bedroom for which we are currently unable to provide a satisfactory explanation.'

'First class; and from this information what did you deduce?'

'That we cannot yet be clear whether the deceased committed suicide, was assisted in committing suicide, died as the result of manslaughter.....or was murdered.'

Well, it was about as much as Bateman had expected. Gull was fine with the fancy words and the stuff he could repeat parrot fashion but he was never going to come up with anything earth shattering. Right, better move on; time to try another tack.

'And what did we get from our enquiries in the village?'

'I put Connelly on the houses immediately surrounding the crime scene and Waller on the village, farms and smallholdings in the local vicinity.'

'And what startling revelations did we elicit from our bloodhounds in the field?'

'Nothing of significance.'

'Christ almighty, we must have got something. It is totally impossible that we interviewed the best part of a hundred people and got nothing at all.'

'They keep themselves to themselves round here, Inspector. A lot of them avoid mixing with one another because they don't get on.'

'That's as may be, Kevin, but they aren't bloody hermits. Somebody must have seen something.'

'Waller located two farm labourers who saw what they thought might be a suspicious character lurking at the top of the drive the Sunday before last. They had just come from the pub where they had been having a bit of a session and couldn't accurately describe the man other than to say he wasn't young. They did speak to him but neither of them was clear as to exactly what was said......except they thought it might have been something to do with religion.'

'Did Waller get the impression they were taking the piss! You notice this sort of thing never happens to detectives on the television. If it was Hercule bloody Poirot asking the questions one of the drunks would have noticed the man smoked Gauloises, had a thread missing from the lapel of his suit and spoke with a Liverpudlian accent. Alright, what else?'

'In relation to vehicles, an old Toyota RAV was seen to pull into the village then leave again a few minutes later. This was early yesterday afternoon. It didn't appear to have called in anywhere. Nobody got the number and there is a dispute over the colour. That apart, nothing of interest that caught the locals' attention since the discovery of the body.'

'And?'

'Oh, a stretch limousine containing a Hen Party turned round in front of the village pub a couple of Saturdays ago. Everybody in the village remembered that one. They talked about it like it might have been the highlight of their year.'

'Heaven preserve us. It's frightening. You do realise that the constitution gives these people the right to vote. Alright, anything on the deceased?'

'His father was apparently quite well liked. He was one of the few from the new builds who used the village pub and shopped locally and because of that he was accepted as part of the community. The son wasn't anywhere near as popular. Described as 'snotty' and 'high and mighty'. He didn't mix with the locals and most of them wouldn't have given him the time of day.'

'Alright, how did Connolly get on?'

'Even worse. Garfield didn't appear to have any visitors. He wasn't friendly with any of the neighbours and nobody had any clue what he did for a living.'

'Surely there was somebody round here who had some sort of connection with the man?'

'It would appear not; and neither could Connolly find anybody prepared to admit they made the phone call that drew the matter to our attention.'

Alan Bateman located his pack of cigarettes and was about to light up when a mobile telephone rang. He was about to tell Gull to turn the bloody thing off when he discovered it was his. He hesitantly announced himself and then listened without interruption for a full minute. Before, to Gull's great surprise, breaking into a beaming smile.

'Right, Detective Sergeant, get hold of a laptop and get that lot typed up; two copies, no spelling mistakes and let me have it sharpish. Then you can position yourself outside the front door and get back to chatting up that little blonde you've been working on for most of the day.'

Kevin Gull stood open mouthed wondering if he had fully understood the instruction. Bateman, cigarette in hand, was now striding the room with a face like a man who had just been reprieved from the gallows.

'They picked up a print on the whiskey glass that was under the curtain and it provided a positive match; and on that basis we are instructed to hand the case over to Organised Crime. Detective Inspector Daniel Loache will be taking over the enquiry personally and we can expect his arrival within the hour. Kevin, before you start typing nip over to the village shop and check they've got a printer you can plug into; they're a shade primitive out this way. Oh, and buy a candle for Inspector Loache; we'll light it for the poor bugger.'

CHAPTER FIFTY

WEDNESDAY 22nd FEBRUARY 2017

Stephanie Armitage fidgeted about with a couple of mundane jobs but accomplished remarkably little in the process. Everything that was important had already been taken care of and the stuff that was left outstanding seemed hardly worth the effort. She got a cappuccino from the machine in the kitchenette, seated herself in a comfortable chair and waited for fresh inspiration.

It didn't take much brainstorming for her to reach the conclusion she didn't want to do this anymore. It had been alright running the gallery when it was sandwiched between other things but now the counterbalance had been removed, the day job had turned into a wearisome chore. The blame for this, of course, lay squarely with a certain Mr Michael Smith. In the space of a few months Mickey had progressed from being an inspired and willing confederate into a copper bottomed bore.

It had always been necessary to accept that the bloody man was obsessed with his dreary little pub but when they had been together he had developed the ability to put that part of his life on the back burner and only turn the heat back up once she was safely out of the way. She had the gallery, he had the pub; neither of them had the slightest interest in what the other person did to put bread on the table so they stowed their work load like baggage that wouldn't be required on the voyage.....and for better or worse the arrangement had worked out to their mutual satisfaction.

Then bloody Rachael Broadbent had arrived on the scene and quickly altered the balance of their relationship. Rachael, with her hair brighter than a winter's fire and her perfectly distributed range of symmetrical freckles. God bless her, the girl didn't have a bad word to say about anybody. She genuinely didn't seem to have a single bad bone in her entire body. Boring cow! With that sort of attitude how did she ever expect to be anything approaching an entertaining companion?

That analysis was far from fair. It was just Rachael was a good girl at heart and since as early as she could remember good girls had always bored Stephanie Armitage to death. Being bad was so much more uplifting she failed to see how anyone could fail to appreciate the fact.

She wondered if Rachael had been different when she and Mickey were alone or if she insisted on making love with her nightdress pulled up no further than was strictly necessary, the curtains tightly closed and all lighting completely extinguished. Perhaps she had been a totally different person once the front door was locked and barred but somehow Stephanie found that hard to believe. Yet, there was no denying there must have been more to her than just a pretty face because Mickey Smith had been decidedly smitten. And there had been an awful lot of pretty faces interested in sharing Mickey's life over the years, so Rachael must have had something a little bit special; a special something that she kept completely invisible from everyone but the man she loved.

Rachael herself could quite easily have been tolerated. She did impinge a little on Mickey's availability but to give the girl her due, she seemed to intrinsically understand that he was a person who needed to be guided with a loose rein in order to feel completely comfortable. Rachael wasn't jealous either; she had appreciated that the relationship Mickey enjoyed with his oldest friend was based on needs other than love, and that sex had never been part of that particular equation.

The difficulty was that Rachael had somehow contrived to take away Mickey's spirit. His badness if you wanted to label it for what it was. She made Mickey more conventional; better house trained but at the same time far less interesting. It was almost like her goodness seeped out and bleached the character of the old Mickey Smith until he was no longer recognisable as the genuine article; and quite obviously the new model had failed to impress her one little bit.

Even after Rachael had been satisfactorily disposed of her poison still continued to spread through Mickey's veins. These days, Mickey Smith was little more than a shadow of his former self.

She also blamed the afternoon they had spent having alcohol fuelled sex. That had served to change the dynamics of the way they related to one another. Mickey had proved great entertainment on a dreary winter's afternoon after she had knocked back a couple of glasses too many, but that had never been his designated role in her life. That afternoon she had lost her aura of unattainability and in doing so surrendered her godlike status. In Mickey's eyes she had transformed into an accessible commodity rather than someone it was his job to amuse........and ultimately obey.

That had been a very big mistake but there was no point in crying over spilt milk. Her relationship with Mickey was now beyond salvation and she might as well accept the fact. She would get this place on the market at the first possible opportunity and move on to something new. She fancied somewhere warm this time around. Somewhere where men wearing designer sunglasses could admire her beautifully shaped legs, rather than surmise what they might look like, were they not cosseted in a pair of thick woollen tights.

Ziggy wouldn't give a hoot what she did. Ziggy took little interest in anything she got up to so long as she was suitably occupied and not throwing tantrums in the house or getting under his feet. She could head off on the next NASA space probe and Ziggy would happily wave her goodbye at the launch pad without any obvious sign of distress. She admired Ziggy for his lack of possessiveness. It was a rare virtue in a man. She would need to make sure bloody Fishface didn't get her hooks too deeply imbedded in his flesh. Ziggy was a bastard; but he was her bastard and for the time being at least she wanted it to stay that way.

Mickey had sent a text to say he would be calling around in the morning and she had initially thought it might be in her best interests to avoid him by pretending she was occupied elsewhere. She didn't like scenes and it was pretty obvious their relationship had now run its course. Such a pity; she and Mickey had enjoyed a very special rapport. He would be extremely difficult to replace.

However, it hadn't been long before it occurred to her that avoiding Mickey was not an option; he was the only gateway to getting her hands on that wonderful picture. Oliver Dearlove was many things including a creep and a rogue but my God the man was an outstanding talent. She could place that portrait of Charlotte Langthorpe for a hundred thousand, maybe more if she was given free rein and she knew at least two people who would be prepared to fight each other to the death in order to add it to their collections. Why Mickey wouldn't just pass it on to her made no sense. It was another clear demonstration that he could no longer be relied upon to listen to reason and do as she instructed. A few months ago a situation like this would never have happened but these days Mickey was a loose cannon. Stephanie needed him to return to his senses even if it was only for the next couple of days.

She decided the best bet was to dress appropriately and try to charm him into seeing a bit of sense. Men invariably proved a pushover if the question you asked was appropriately timed. Yes, that was undoubtedly the best solution. Mickey had always been a sucker for her when she had made it clear she wasn't available, so why shouldn't he be even more eager to do what she wanted if she indicated that was no longer the case?

She must also remember to set up an initial meeting with the Estate Agent and sort out the details of putting the gallery on the market. Possibly this was rushing things a little but now she had made her mind up that she wanted to leave she was anxious there should be no unnecessary delay.

CHAPTER FIFTY ONE

THURSDAY 23rd FEBRUARY 2017

Terry Brean was in the main interview room at the central police station, accompanied by his Solicitor, Ike Green. Terry and Ike were seated on plastic topped chairs supported by tubular metal struts that would have fitted in better at a junior school classroom. In front of them was a solid wooden table scarred by carvings, stains and blemishes. Ike was seated on Terry's left hand side and there were two vacant chairs on the opposite side of the room. Terry and his Brief were studiously ignoring one another. They had just concluded an initial discussion which had exhausted all they had to say on the subject and there would be nothing more to add until they were given more idea of why Terry was being detained. Inside, the Eastgate gang leader was quietly seething but he had experienced similar circumstances to this on numerous occasions in the past and knew not to give any indication that he was in any way rattled.

It was pretty obvious that the plonkers who had orchestrated his detention would leave him to stew for a short time in order to get his nerves jangling before they made a start on the interrogation. In the ordinary course of events this wouldn't have bothered Terry one little bit. He had been in this sort of situation many times before, but on previous occasions had always been aware precisely why he had been picked up and exactly what he would need to do in order to be back walking the streets in twenty four hours' time.

That was the way the law worked and it was better to let the legal system grind forward at its own stubborn pace and act as your friend and ally rather than try to fight against it. If they hadn't charged you within the specified time limit you would be free to walk out of the door, even if it was blatantly obvious you were as guilty as hell. No ifs or buts; that was the way the justice system worked. They knew it and they were fully aware that you knew it as well. It was a straight battle between the plod and the ticking hands of the clock. And the bastards wouldn't dare charge him with anything unless they had an extremely good chance of getting a result because they knew the Terry Breans of this world had access to lawyers who could rip a hole half a mile wide in any case that wasn't completely watertight.

Like almost everybody in his profession, Terry had experienced the odd occasion when things hadn't worked out entirely to plan. When that situation had occurred he had served his time and felt he was a better man for the experience. It would surprise nobody that you invariably came out of prison having gained a good deal of knowledge that you hadn't possessed when you went in the door.

Prison wasn't so bad as long as you didn't let it get on top of you. When you arrived in your cell word soon spread if you were from a big outfit like Eastgate and you would be accorded respect in line with your gangland status. It worked like a class system so people knew their exact position in the big scheme of things and the small timers didn't get above themselves; and it was not a system to be taken lightly if you knew what was good for you or your family members on the other side of the perimeter wall.

Another point that was relevant but often overlooked; the higher you climbed up the greasy pole the less hands-on you tended to be when it came to getting involved in the frontline action. You planned, you oversaw, you gave the orders; but it was invariably somebody from lower down the pecking order who got tasked with carrying out the actual crime. In consequence, there was less chance of you getting convicted even if things did go completely tits up, because your lofty status would ensure you had never gone anywhere near to the scene of the crime. And because of that, people of Terry's seniority tended to spend very little time in rooms similar to the one he was now occupying.

Taking the foregoing into account, there was of course the possibility that one of the junior employees, lower down the food chain, might get leaned-on and coaxed into telling tales out of school on the promise of being allocated a lighter sentence. Surprisingly, even in this day and age, transgressions of that sort remained something of a rarity. Inside or out, life could prove very tough once you had been fingered as a snitch.

There was, however, one big fear that those in positions of authority carried with them like a battle scar; something it was necessary that they learned to live with, because there was no possibility it would ever go away. If, due to adverse circumstances, bad planning, or any of a hundred other reasons, a situation did come to arise where you were unlucky enough to take a tumble from the ladder; then it would be a very long time before you made contact with the ground. The more rungs you had ascended in your criminal career the further you had to fall if a grand day of reckoning ever came about. And, in those unhappy circumstances it would be good to see a multitude of friends waiting with a safety net when you chose to view below; because who amongst us has not made enemies who might be welcoming a catastrophic outcome.

But, while those dark thoughts were quietly percolating away at the back of Terry's fevered brain he was doing his level best to appear totally relaxed. But his calm exterior served only to mask a frenetic attempt to assess what the hell was happening. And once he had weighed out the facts that were in his possession, and guessed at a few that might have passed him by while his concentration was focussed in other areas, he was forced to admit that he was starting to feel more than a little uneasy.

The way he saw it, his major concerns were twofold; and both were more than a little unsettling in their own right. Firstly, the police unit that had picked him up that morning had undoubtedly been from Organised Crime. The Officers conducting the actual pickup had been the usual team of big fuckers with their brains in their biceps and Terry had hardly bothered to give them more than a sideways glance. They were the foot soldiers, the errand runners, the carrier-outers; not the smart boys who were paid to do the thinking on an operation of this magnitude. However, while he was being dragged out to the car for the short drive down to the Police Headquarters, he had noticed, seated in a vehicle on the other side of the road, a copper called Loache. And unless there had been some sort of major reorganisation to the forces of law and order of which he was not aware, then Loache was the Detective Inspector who ran the Organised Crime Unit. And holding that position made Mr Loache a person of some seniority in the big scheme of things, and in consequence a person whom Terry had no desire to meet.

As it happened, Terry knew a thing or two about Loache. The man had a bit of history with Eastgate, as was to be expected bearing in mind what he did for a living. He had worked his way up from walking the beat rather than being one of those over educated twats who got parachute promotions as soon as their incompetence became impossible to ignore. Loache was one of those who had been there, done it and got the t-shirt; a fact that Terry found troubling in itself. Added to which the Inspector had gained a reputation for proceeding meticulously with investigations and by that token avoiding unnecessary mistakes. So if it was him pulling the strings on this particular enquiry then he must be confident that any resulting charges would have a decent chance of standing up in court.

As if that wasn't enough to worry about, there was the fact that the person driving the vehicle in which Loache was the passenger, half hidden by a sun visor that had been purposefully pulled down as low as it would go, was Detective Sergeant Geoff Strickland. Strickland was a total bastard and operated as Loache's rottweiler. The man was devious, manipulative, conniving and totally untrustworthy; he also carried a reputation for being exceptionally violent if given the slightest provocation. So much so, that word on the street suggested that Detective Strickland would have been out of a job a very long time ago if it wasn't for the fact that Loache regularly succeeded in covering his arse. From where Terry's stood it was a great pity Strickland hadn't been booted out of the door a long time ago, because he would have employed the conniving fucker without a moment's hesitation.

But, putting all of that to one side for a minute, the main reason that Terry Brean wasn't feeling half as confident as he was trying to appear was that for once he had absolutely no idea why he had been pulled in. No clue whatever. He couldn't even take an educated guess. Granted, he had a good deal of stuff on the drawing board and even some in the early stages of implementation, but there was absolutely nothing that he could think of that would account for him having been dragged in off the street by a unit from Organised Crime.

Being new in the job he had been especially wary. In fact, if there was any criticism to be levelled it was that he might have been too cautious. He hadn't even got round to settling the score with that pair of losers from the Black Bear; a matter which he must remember to move to the top of the agenda as soon as he was back in circulation.

Terry stood up, shoved his hands in his pockets and walked around the room a couple of times at a leisurely pace. That bunch of tossers peering through the one way double glazing weren't going to see him get twitchy. He was aware, there was an old saying bandied about by Lawyers which stated, it was never wise to ask a question in court to which you did not already know the answer. Terry could see the wisdom in that; he found it unbelievably irritating to find himself in a police interview room without knowing exactly what crime the bastards were going to try to pin on him.

If he had been aware of the answer to that question then

he would, quite naturally, have taken the appropriate action and arranged an alibi. That was nothing more than common sense. But being in this battle scarred shit hole with his backside parked on a plastic chair and no bloody idea why they had pulled him in, left him feeling strangely vulnerable. How the fuck did you prepare to answer a charge to which you were totally innocent? It was a question that, until this point, had never crossed his mind.

The door banged back on its hinges and Loache and Strickland shuffled in carrying mugs of coffee. A more innocuous commencement to proceedings would have been hard to imagine but Terry could already feel a trickle of cold sweat running down his back and he noticed that Ike the Brief looked like he would have paid big money to be somewhere else.

Well, here it comes, thought Terry. At least now the waiting was finally over; at last he would soon get to learn how the stitch-up was intended to work.

CHAPTER FIFTY TWO

FRIDAY 24th FEBRUARY 2017

Mickey Smith was up and about bright and early. The weather was lousy but that didn't concern him. He hadn't slept well and hoped he would feel better if he was on his feet getting a bit of exercise.

The buzzing in his head was still there. The last couple of weeks he couldn't seem to shake it off. It had become a constant backing track to his working day; a backing track like the over orchestrated lift-music he had always despised.

Mickey took a quick shower, ran a comb through his hair, pulled on a shirt, a pair of jeans, walking boots and a newly purchased black anorak. He headed out of the pub by the back door being careful not to let it slam and disturb anybody who might be having better luck at getting some rest

It was a cold miserable day; not raining exactly; just misty, with enough water vapour in the air so it was difficult to tell the difference. Mickey didn't give a shit. Weather was weather; you just had to wear the right clothes and grit your teeth. He had been feeling very strange for a while now and he didn't think that a bit of water vapour was going to prove a greater inconvenience than the churning in his head.

There was a large white van parked directly opposite the pub with steamed up windows. No sign of anyone inside but it was a dumb arsed place to leave a vehicle of that size on the narrow roadway. A tradesman on an early morning call out, maybe? It probably belonged to some bloody plumber who was earning a day's wages in ten minutes flat by changing a tap washer.

Mickey turned left, then left again and headed up hill towards the park. It would be quiet up there in weather like this; nobody to disturb his concentration; no one to interfere with his pattern of thoughts.

He was scheduled to drop round at Stevie's later in the morning. He had sent her a text the previous day to tell her to expect him. There was nothing good likely to come from the visit but it needed to be made. No point in parting company with an old friend like Stevie without making an effort to mend a few fences. Particularly not an old friend he had been wrapped round in a warm and comfortable bed barely a week before.

He stopped for a moment to reflect on their current relationship, before letting his thoughts run on. It was like lifting the needle on a long playing record and replacing it after skipping a couple of tracks you didn't really want to hear. Regardless of their long history, there was no way he was letting her get her hands on that painting. And that applied regardless of what she decided to put on offer. Mickey was fully aware Stevie could be very persuasive when something she badly wanted was at stake.

Right now, the portrait was safely stashed in his room; propped up against the wall behind his bed with Charlie's name written in large letters on the brown wrapping paper that he had carefully taped in place. He would present it to Charlie when he got round to telling him he was heading off; saying goodbye to the Bear for the very last time before hitting the open road. It would be the right and proper conclusion to this whole fiasco. He owed Charlie for a lot of things and felt a fool that he had considered defrauding him out of what was rightfully his; this would serve to settle the score. Make things right with his troublesome conscience at the same time. Pass on something his partner would actually like; remember him by; possibly even treasure. A gift that would represent his final goodbye to a life he now intended to totally abandon. A clean cut that would sever the invisible knot that had bound the pair of them so tightly together for so many long years.

Suddenly there was shouting and something leapt into

Mickey's field of vision. Instinctively he dived to one side and raised his fists. What the hell. A figure wrapped in an overcoat and scarf had come out of nowhere and was blocking his path. The first thing he noticed was the eyes. Small rivets of steel, burning white hot with hatred and accusation.

'It's no good to you, so why don't you to let me have it back. I'll make it worth your while. I'm not an ungenerous man.'

It was Oliver Dearlove and he had obviously been drinking. In fact he seemed to be maintaining an upright position by willpower alone. He staggered forward to paw at the front of Mickey's coat. The stench of his breath nearly took Mickey off his feet.

'You churl; you have no understanding of the significance. That painting is the culmination of a life's work. It belongs to me, don't you see? It is the thing for which I wish to be remembered. It represents my finest hour.'

Mickey pulled free. Dearlove might be drunk but he was having no trouble articulating his thoughts; and loud enough so they could be clearly heard by half the people living on the road.

'Forget it, Oliver. The painting is spoken for; it's a present for a friend. The deal was, I paid you five grand and you knocked out the copy. The contract was met by both parties so it ends right there. Forget it and move on.'

'It's not a fucking copy, you Neanderthal moron. It's an original. My fucking original. The best work I've ever done.'

Dearlove stumbled two steps backwards and regained his balance with the help of a conveniently situated telegraph pole.

'I painted the first one you clot. Surely you realised that? Your bit of skirt did. I could see it in her eyes. She spotted it straight away.'

'Look Oliver, why don't you head off home and get a few hours sleep. This will all...........'

'Years back, more than thirty, the Landlord at the Black Bear commissioned me to paint this damned woman and dress her like she was of noble birth. It nearly killed me. She wasn't interested; no matter how much I implored wouldn't sit straight. Three hundred quid and I sweated blood for every penny.'

'What the fuck are you talking about?'

'The face and parts of the body, yes; though even those features were dutifully enhanced........everything else came from me, my talent, the product of my imagination. Even an idiot like you must surely have recognised the backdrop. It was painted in the saloon bar of that nasty little pub where you spend every day of your life.'

'Oliver I don't give a toss if you used the Queen as a model and painted her in the nude. The simple fact is, it isn't for sale. Now piss off and leave me alone.'

'A copy! How dare you reference it as a copy. It's no such thing. It's a reworking of an original theme. My original theme!

'Sorry mate, I'm not interested. Now please step out of the way and let me get past.'

'You cannot deny me. Don't think you've heard the last of this Mr Smith. I have access to a gun and I know how to use it. That painting means everything to me. I'll have it if it's the last thing I do.'

'Try sticking your head in a bucket of cold water, mate. It works for me every time.'

Mickey pushed past Dearlove and continued his climb towards the park. What the fuck was the old coot going on about? He quickly came to the conclusion he didn't want to know. He had plenty to think about just now without taking anything else on board.

Mickey turned right at the top of the hill and followed a line of battered railings that were overdue for a paint job. He entered the park through a set of heavy wrought-iron gates that had been wedged open to allow access with a length of rotting timber. Once inside, he made his way through the middle of a flower garden bereft of vegetation except for a couple of sad looking bushes that gave the impression they were on their last legs; then past two dilapidated tennis courts with no visible line markings. He assessed the possibilities and veered sharply to the right, choosing to follow a line of horse chestnut trees that ran adjacent to a long established footpath which ran parallel to the river.

Up here it was a different world. On the right, the river swirled gently past, seemingly in no particular hurry to get anywhere of importance. On the left grassland for as far as the eye could see with no sign of a goalpost let alone a Spartan dog walker hurling a stick for his trusty hound. The view served up a stark vision of what might one day become the planet's inheritance; spoke articulately of the bleak future that could await after some idiot had chosen to push the button that released the missiles into the air. With the mist still swirling the atmosphere was positively eerie.

Mickey shuddered, pulled the zip on his coat a little higher and quickly pushed on towards the bridge that would enable him to cross the river and loop back towards civilisation by using the towpath on the other side of the water. It was then he heard the tap of footsteps echoing from behind; and moments later the apparition hove into view.

CHAPTER FIFTY THREE

SATURDAY 25th FEBRUARY 2017

Charlie Brinsworth felt mildly affronted. Cod, Spanish style? What the fuck was Spanish style cod? It was common knowledge to anyone from these parts that cod came in batter with a plateful of chips and a dollop of mushy peas on the side.

Charlie would be the first to admit his experience of continental cuisine was fairly limited but on a rare visit abroad he had witnessed with horror chips being served in paper cones accompanied by some weird sort of salad cream. Taking this as an example it was frightening to contemplate what those barbarians from across the water might choose to do with a decent bit of fish. He was beginning to suspect it was time he had a strong word with the Chef. There was a fine line between experimental and pretentious when it came to acceptable cooking and to his mind the white suited twat in the kitchen was getting very near to crossing that particular border.

He ordered a portion for lunch anyway, but made certain to scowl while he was doing so. Hopefully after Brexit this sort of rubbish would be put behind the British nation and it would be possible to get back to eating normal food with names that could be articulated without some Dago waiter with a clipped moustache and too much hair gel laughing behind his hand at your pronunciation.

Sharon had stayed over at Charlie's place last night and they had tentatively discussed moving in together before deciding it wasn't practical. They got on like a house on fire but Charlie knew he was not genealogically suited to any greater level of domesticity than he was already experiencing. Besides, Sharon had a nipper and you couldn't mess around where kids were concerned. He had experienced a shitty upbringing and stood as testament to the fact it could have a bad effect on your outlook on life.

Surprisingly the decision had seemed to come as something of a relief to both parties and it hadn't served to ruin their night together. Sharon was clearly quite happy to continue their relationship without any change to the way things currently worked. Charlie hadn't known whether to feel happy or insulted. It was a blow to his ego. He was forced to concede that perhaps he wasn't the prime catch that every maiden dreamed about after all.

Regardless of Sharon's attitude to him as an ideal partner, he had already come to the conclusion that with a certain member of the Organised Crime Squad in and out of the Bear at all hours of the day and night it was probably a good time to clean up his act. Now he reconsidered the discussion of the previous evening he felt almost like he had been insulted. It was a poor state of affairs when a man with his standing in the criminal fraternity was not being pressured into making a trip up the aisle by a barmaid with responsibility for a small child.

Charlie wondered whether it was too early to partake of an alcoholic beverage. Just a pick me up to wet his whistle and help him think more clearly. After due consideration he deferred that decision; it seemed a little early to be gagging for a pint.

A more pressing concern was the fact that nobody had seen hide nor hair of Mickey Smith since the day before yesterday. He had headed out at the crack of dawn on the previous morning without leaving word where he intended going and had promptly disappeared in a puff of smoke. It was possible he was staying round with that posh bird with the two yards of leg whom Charlie had always found difficult to like. Nobody would blame him for that, least of all Charlie; the woman was certainly a looker even if she did have a strange look in her eye which had always made Charlie suspect she was slightly unhinged. But if that were the case it wouldn't have hurt Mickey to let somebody know what he had been planning.

The thing that made Charlie feel uneasy was that

Mickey's disappearing act was so completely out of character. Say what you like about Mickey Smith, he had never failed to put the running of the pub at the very top of his priority list. He lived and breathed the place; had done since the first day he started work. Charlie was getting a bad feeling about Mickey's disappearance and much though he had done his best to ignore it, it wasn't going away.

He pushed that thought out of his head, stomped out of the door, jumped in the car and headed over to Simon Bartol's car lot to discuss the Vietnamese dope growers. He had thought matters through this morning after Sharon had left and he had a proposition for Simon that would probably come as something of a surprise. He also had a figure in mind for what he intended to clear on the deal and he hoped Mr Bartol had deep pockets because if he went for the proposal it was going to set him back a good deal of cash.

Charlie returned in good time for lunch and as it turned out the Dago fish hadn't been all that bad. Not a patch on the stuff you could get from the chippy over the road, mind you. The only clear advantage in the source of supply being that he hadn't had to bandy words with that cheeky little git Lee who always seemed to be hanging around behind the counter when he went in for an order at weekends.

The meeting with Simon Bartol had gone on for two and a half hours but in the end they had agreed on mutually acceptable terms. Charlie had proposed he sold to Mr Bartol both the growing facility and his pizza outlet which was fast nearing completion. Charlie had gone off the idea of flogging pizza. Somehow the business didn't have any magic about it.....and he had come to be very wary of Italian cuisine after Sharon had talked him into trying sea food ravioli. Simon initially had been reluctant to expand his business in that direction but had come to see it would blend in ideally with his dope distribution network, and should pass under the eyes of the Eastgate contingent without attracting so much a second glance. Once he had convinced himself it was the way forward they had haggled on price for what seemed like an eternity before finally striking a deal.

It occurred to Charlie that he was now in the rare position of being comparatively wealthy and at the same time totally legitimate. He wondered how long that happy state of affairs would be likely to last.

The morning had gone too well for his luck to last. Five minutes after he had placed his plate quietly on the bar and before he had even got properly started on contemplating the possibility of sneaking upstairs for a short siesta, Detective Sergeant Strickland materialised at his elbow.

'Afternoon Charlie; missed lunch I see so perhaps you would care to invite me to join you for the brandy and cigars.'

'You just caught me on the way out of the door, Geoff. Would have been lovely to chat but I've got an important business appointment lined up. Must rush. The people I'm meeting can get very arsey if you turn up a bit late.'

'Pity that. I had a bit of news you might have found interesting, taking into account the fact that local crime appears to have now become your specialist subject. Never mind. We can always talk another time when you are less burdened by the weight of your business affairs.'

'Well, I can always find a couple of minutes for you, Detective Sergeant. Especially if it's something important.'

'No Charlie, I wouldn't dream of it. I couldn't bear to watch the news and see our balance of payment figures head into the red and know in my heart I was the man responsible. You get on your way. The interests of this great nation must come first. I'm only a humble copper after all.'

'Alright, cut the crap; what are you having?'

'A half of bitter and a large scotch. Shall be adjourn to your main office; second table along on the far wall I believe, unless you've decided to move premises.'

Charlie collected the drinks, added the cost to his ever increasing bar tab, and took his usual seat. He considered mentioning the disappearance of his partner to the policeman but decided against it. Old habits die hard, and where he came from you didn't talk to policemen of your own accord unless it was to tell them to get stuffed because you hadn't done it and they were arresting the wrong bloke. Besides, if anything had happened to Mickey then it was already too late to do much about it. And if that were the case it was pretty obvious who was responsible and he would settle the score without any help from Detective Strickland's side of the law.

'That article you were reading last time I was in,' Strickland began in a conversational manner. 'Did you hear we had pulled in Terry Brean?'

'No. How could I?' A blatant lie. The word had been on the street five minutes after the Eastgate leader had been lifted and Simon Bartol had given him a full update on the fact Brean was still being detained that very morning.

'We've charged him with murder and it looks like it will stick. The idiot left fingerprints all over the scene.'

'Fingerprints? Surely his Brief will find a way round that one.'

'It gets better. He swore blind he had never been at the house and voluntarily submitted a D.N.A. sample to prove the fact.'

'And.......'

'He must have been off his head. Terry's D.N.A. was found all over the victim's living room and on a glass he had been drinking from. Then when we checked the waste bin in the kitchen it was full of cigarette ends, three of which proved to be Terry's brand and showed clear traces of his saliva. Game set and match; he'll be going down for a very long time even if we end up having to drop the charge down to manslaughter.'

'Well, from your point of view I suppose it looks pretty

good. From where I'm sitting, perhaps a shade too good. Any specific reason why you are telling me this?'

'I always like to be the bearer of glad tidings, Charlie. I thought it would be a weight off your mind. It's no secret you and your mate Mickey Smith have been rubbing Eastgate up the wrong way of late. Looks like they might have a few problems of their own to sort out before they give any thought to paying you another visit. Doesn't look like Terry Brean is going to be on the street anytime soon.'

'Well, your kindness is touching, Mr Strickland. I would offer to buy you a drink if I hadn't done that already. Any other news? A premium bond win?'

'Best not to be flippant, Charlie. This should act as a salutary lesson to you. Hide as you might, in the end your sins will always find you out.'

Charlie remained seated following the Detective Sergeant's departure. Terry Brean's arrest smelled too much like a fit-up. In order to make the top table down at Eastgate Terry would have needed to be in the game for a lot of years and there was no way anyone with that sort of experience would have been dumb enough to leave a trail of evidence that obvious for the law to pick up on.

It almost seemed like that was exactly what Strickland had been trying to get across to him. *It doesn't matter if you are guilty or innocent, Charlie; give me any cause for concern and I'll find some way to get you nailed to a cross.*

Charlie dispensed with alcohol and ordered a strong coffee. There had still been no word from Mickey and his disappearance was now turning into a major concern. Was it possible with their leader out of commission a few of the meatheads from Eastgate had decided to take matters into their own hands? Charlie had to admit it was distinctly possible even if it didn't smell right. He'd give it a couple more hours then take some action of his own. He knew the numbers to ring and he wasn't short of funds. If Mickey had been taken out of the game someone was going to suffer big time. If you lost a partner it was your responsibility to do what was necessary to even the score.

CHAPTER FIFTY FOUR

SUNDAY 26th FEBRUARY 2017

Terry Brean paced up and down his holding cell trying desperately to think of something that might provide an explanation. He was damned sure he had never had any form of dealings with the dead man, Anthony Garfield, and would have been prepared to stake his life on the fact he had never travelled to Thorton Chumley; a place he couldn't have located if you had offered him a get out of jail card for accomplishing the feat.

He had just completed another long and painful meeting with his Solicitor, Ike Green, and if good old Ike told him one more time that *anything he said was completely confidential, so he had nothing to lose by telling him exactly what had really happened so he could provide the best possible advice*, then there was an excellent chance that Terry would very soon have a genuine murder charge hanging over his head. The simple truth was he had never met this Garfield character and as far as he was concerned Thorton Chumley might just as well be the name of a crater on the dark side of the moon. That being the case, he had still found it totally impossible to get any fucker to believe a single word he said.

The whole thing was bloody ridiculous. His fingerprints and D.N.A. couldn't possibly have been found in that house because he had never been through the door. Either there was some fault with the test results or someone had set out to frame him; and by the looks of it made a bloody good job of achieving their objective. Did the law honestly think he would have been dumb enough to volunteer a D.N.A. sample if there was even the smallest chance that it would have registered positive? Did they think they were dealing with a bloody idiot?

His Brief was proving no help whatever. The more he

explained the simple facts to Green, the less the solicitor seemed to believe him. What was he paying this cretin for? If Ike couldn't think of a way to spring him when he was one hundred percent innocent, then what good was he likely to be when he was guilty as charged and looking for some sort of technicality to get him off the hook? The most helpful proposal Ike had managed to come up with was to suggest that Terry claim that this Anthony Garfield was an old friend who had confessed he was in a state of depression; and Terry, out of the goodness of his heart, had made a visit to try to convince him not to do anything stupid. And the most ridiculous thing about that feebly constructed scenario was that it was beginning to look like his best bet.

Christ almighty, did they actually think that if he had wanted this bloke Garfield dead be would have set about topping him personally? It was a ridiculous presumption. He had people who were paid good money to take care of that sort of shit. Were they forgetting he was the main man over at Eastgate, or confusing him with the bloke who cleaned the toilets? All he would have needed to do was whistle and Garfield would have been in the ground without him having any need to raise so much as his little finger.

Terry was forced to acknowledge that if he went down for any length of time it would mean the end of his career. He hadn't been top dog for long enough to establish himself as a legend and any attempt at running things from behind bars would never work out. Even now the more experienced hands would be lining up a replacement candidate in case the jury voted the wrong way. And it was an unwritten law that once you were out, you were out for good. It wasn't like you could complete your sentence and re-join the gang a couple of steps down the ladder. The new man in charge wouldn't want that to happen and why should he take the chance of being usurped at some later date when it wasn't necessary? Once you had fallen from the summit you were out on your own. You kept well away from gang headquarters, made no regular contact with existing gang members and ideally moved yourself and your family a long way out of town. And if you didn't abide by those rules then it was probable you would arrive home one night and find a man dressed in dark clothing waiting on your doorstep; and in his hand would be a powerful handgun with a silencer that would ensure that your last moments in life would not be witnessed by an unwanted audience.

It was a complete sickener but there was no point in pretending that wasn't the way things worked. Terry had spent the last twenty years, step by step, working his way to the top of the hill and after barely a month at running the show he could soon find himself right back at the bottom again, grovelling in the dirt.

There had to be some way out of this mess but Terry was buggered if he could think what it was. Maybe there was some sort of trade off he could think of but at present nothing came to mind. He recommenced pacing the floor before giving up the battle completely. He then sat, contemplating the injustices of life, propped up in the corner of his metal framed bed.

CHAPTER FIFTY FIVE

SUNDAY 26th FEBRUARY 2017

It was late afternoon at the Golden Pheasant and the main bar was still full to bursting. The late football game had only just finished and it had attracted a fair degree of interest as it featured two sides vying for places in next season's European competitions. As the crowd began to thin a mud splattered white van sporting a stylised nameplate and the caricature of an electrocuted cartoon figure, pulled up directly outside the main doors and two men in soiled navy blue boiler suits stepped out of the doors. They pushed their way through the departing throng, arrived at the bar and ordered two pints of lager from Kirsty the barmaid, before asking her to direct them to a Mr Terry Brean.

Jimmy Jones was close to the bar and within earshot of the request and, it would be fair to say, that in itself was an unusual occurrence. In the normal course of events Jimmy was the last person you would have been likely to find hanging around in full view on a busy Sunday afternoon.

Jimmy was employed as a driver by Eastgate and had been for more years than he cared to remember. He was a bloody good driver as well and took great pride in his road skills because, to Jimmy's way on thinking, that was what proved to anybody who might harbour any doubts about his advanced years that he was still very much up to the mark.

Although Jimmy was very much his own man when he was out on the road, on occasions when he was required to be in the Pheasant he made it his business to be as unobtrusive as possible. That was because if he was seen hanging around with his hands in his pockets, people were very quick to find him some sort of odd job to usefully occupy his time. If the work they settled upon involved driving, then Jimmy was the last man to object. Driving was what Jimmy was employed to do and you would hear no complaint from him if the work he got allocated resulted in him sitting behind a wheel. However, all too often the tasks that got pushed in his direction were in no way vehicle related; and Jimmy deeply resented the lack of demarcation that currently existed within the Eastgate setup which could easily result in a career specialist like him being forced into doing odd jobs that had absolutely no connection to his specialist job function; and this only because he had been the first face some arsehole from higher up the food chain had happened to clap eyes on when he squinted round the bar.

As a defence against the arbitrary misuse of his dedicated skill set, Jimmy had found it necessary to become something of a master of disguise. And so proficient had he become at blending seamlessly into the background that a number of his mates now referenced it as his number one talent and suggested that he should seriously consider teaching it to chameleons.

Today, however, was a completely different situation. Jimmy was one of the few of the old guard who had survived the recent purge that had taken care of some very big names from the previous era, including the likes of Spanner Hopkins and several more of the recognised faces he had worked with for a hell of a lot of years. In these circumstances, and taking into account that Terry Brean was currently a guest of the boys in blue, he felt it incumbent upon himself to make certain that at this all important juncture he was not only present and accounted for at group headquarters but, more importantly, was noticed to have been right there in the front line where his many years of experience could be put to the best possible use. In consequence he had made a point of spending most of the day within a six foot radius of the foot rail of the main bar and was dressed in a multi coloured Hawaiian shirt that would have done credit to an American tourist.

'He's otherwise engaged,' said Jimmy, authoritatively

taking charge of the situation so Kirsty could get back to serving the thirsty hordes. 'Who might I say was enquiring?'

'Don't bother,' said one of the boiler-suited tradesmen. 'We could do with knocking off early, anyway. Been at it since eight this morning and this is meant to be a day of rest. Some bloody chance! We only agreed to take a look as a favour, in any case. Let it ride. We'll drop back here some other time.'

Jimmy assessed the situation and came to the conclusion it was worthy of further investigation.

'I look after things when Mr Brean is tied up on business. How can I be of assistance?'

'You can't; it's us who are providing the help.' A pause then a shared smile between the boiler suits, who looked so uncannily similar to one another that they could have been knocked out on the same production line.

'This bloke Terry Brean booked us to take a look at the wiring in this place because he reckons it's been done by a bunch of cowboys. He wants a written quotation to cover anything that needs doing to bring it back up to spec'. Cash in hand, you understand. We'll be working on our own time on this one. He said he needed any necessary upgrade to take place outside pub opening hours so there was no disruption to trade and we were to account for that in the cost. '

Well, that made a degree of sense. The Pheasant had been completely refurbished in mock Elizabethan splendour about five years previously by friends of the previous gang boss; and since that day the place had looked like shit and the electrics had been popping bulbs like they were going out of fashion.

'Alright, take your drinks with you and get on with it,' Jimmy ordered, beginning to enjoy the feeling of power. 'Give the estimate to me personally when you've finished and I'll see to it that Mr Brean gets it in his hand.'

Jimmy soon regretted his decision. Without delay, several bags of gear were dragged in from the van and strewn haphazardly across the floor. And from them an array of tools were extracted and spread over every conceivable work surface. In no time, fixtures were disassembled, panels were jemmied from various parts of the wall and floorboards were cut and lifted in all the least convenient locations. After two hours of clattering, banging and yelling the electricians beckoned Jimmy over to join them for a chat.

'Between you and me pal, this place is a fucking death trap. If I had anything to say about it whoever put this wiring in would be dragged out into the road and strung up from the nearest lamppost. How long's it been like this? It's a wonder nobody's been electrocuted. There's not an earth wire in any of the sockets let alone any sleeving on the wires, the cabling is obsolete, the conduits.........listen, am I boring you or would you like me to go on? My suggestion would be for you to carry on as normal for tonight but tell the staff to try not to touch anything with a plug on it if they value their lives. We'll rearrange our schedule, come back first thing in the morning and complete the inspection and let you have a full estimate. I hope your gaffer isn't short of a few bob. To put this lot right is going to set him back a small fortune.'

Well, under present circumstances that would be just about all Terry Brean needed to complete a perfect week. If he managed to avoid a custodial sentence, which Jimmy had come to understand was starting to look increasingly unlikely, then he was going to walk back into the middle of this lot. Still, at least those two characters told it the way it was without beating about the bush. And, Jimmy supposed, if it needed to be done it was better to know about it rather than remain ignorant.

Jimmy ushered the electricians out of the door and passed instruction to the bar staff to be careful with the electrics until he gave them an all clear. He qualified the warning with a reassurance that as the place had survived for five years without any major electrical disaster bringing about a disruption to service there would doubtless be very little to worry about.

Jimmy attempted to give the warning in a manner which convinced everybody who was listening that there was no need to be overly concerned about their safety; and he must have proved highly successful on that count because as the night wore on there was no evidence of anyone suffering fits of paranoia, let alone entertaining fears that their employment might be in anyway affected.

And so it would have come as something of a surprise to all concerned when, at 3am precisely on Monday 27th February, the Golden Pheasant became the scene of a mighty explosion that rocked the street on which it stood and woke up half the neighbourhood; and that by first light the pub that had stood on the site for as long as anyone could remember was transformed into little more than a pile of smoking rubble; having, quite literally, burned to the ground.

CHAPTER FIFTY SIX

MONDAY 27th FEBRUARY 2017

Charlie lay flat on his back in the middle of the bedroom floor and looked up at the picture he had fixed to the wall only minutes earlier. He had a feeling it was probably pretty damn good, without actually knowing why. Better by some distance than the one that had been hanging over his favourite table in the Saloon bar for all those years to his untutored eye.

In some ways the portrait looked identical to the old one, while in others it was totally different. Being no art connoisseur it was something he found difficult to put into words. The current version sparkled with colour the way he remembered the original had all those years before, when he was a kid. But there the similarity came to an abrupt end. Alright, you could tell it was the same woman; but the new painting positively reached out and grabbed you by the throat where the old one had merely looked remote, solitary and, from his perspective, pretty damned intimidating.

He cast a thought back to those far off days and immediately felt strangely uncomfortable. There was no room for this woman in his world after what had happened, most particularly in her bright new set of clothes. It brought the past back far too vividly. This was stuff he wanted to forget. He removed the painting from the hook on the wall, rewrapped it in its original brown paper and pushed it up on top of the wardrobe where it would be out of sight. He couldn't face looking into her eyes when he hauled himself out of bed in the morning. It just wasn't on. If the callous cow had had any interest in his wellbeing she would have hung around instead of pissing off out of the door. How could she have done that? He had thought about it a thousand times over the years but had never understood.

His father must have been off his head if he was deluded enough to think commissioning a portrait of his wife dressed up like Lady Muck was going to make any difference to her intentions. Even at Charlie's tender age he had been able to sense that his mother was already half way out of the door before the artist had picked up his brush. The title said it all; her maiden name of Charlotte Langthorpe. Her family had always been low on money but big on pretentions. Brinsworth would have been too common by half to have come under serious consideration.

He could even remember the day when the sitting had taken place. That tart of an artist parading up and down the bar complaining about the distractions caused by people walking about the place while he was trying to concentrate and cursing the quality of the light. His mother, sullen, bored and extremely uncooperative, obviously wanting to get the whole thing over with as quickly as possible.

Christ, what a mess it had all turned out. She had been out of the door inside a week and he had never set eyes on her to this day. His father had given up caring after that. No wonder he had grown up feeling hated. He just served as a reminder of everything his father had wanted to bury deep in the past.

The chances were she'd be dead by now. Would they have taken the trouble to let him know about her funeral if he had been banged up at the time? What the fuck did it matter. By then it was decades too late to make any difference for either of them.

Charlie pushed his past life from his mind and turned his attention to the next mystery. How the new painting could have got down the back of Mickey Smith's bed he had no idea. He would never have found it in a million years if he hadn't been turning out Mickey's room, hoping to find some clue to his disappearance. He probably wouldn't even have bothered to unwrap the bloody thing if his name hadn't been written boldly on the outside. The portrait looked like it had been freshly painted as well, but what did he know about that sort of stuff? Paintings were a closed book to him and he was more than happy for it to remain that way. He had experienced enough trouble with the original version of the bloody thing staring down on him from the wall when he was a kid. The eyes never leaving him, like they were questioning everything he did and not liking a bit of what they saw.

He had never felt happier than the night he had burned the remnants of that picture out in the backyard. When he realised it was ruined beyond repair it had been like gaining a reprieve from a life sentence. Alright, he could never have done it himself but he would have paid money to the bloke who put the beer bottle through the frame. Instead he had finished up clubbing him over the head with a chair. Life wasn't short of little ironies.

He should have just have let Mickey chuck the picture in a skip when they had been redecorating. It had been the perfect excuse. Why the hell hadn't he? He had no bloody idea. Maybe if Mickey hadn't been trying to steam roller him he wouldn't have put in an objection. He had always had an inbuilt aversion to being manipulated. That was his excuse anyway and if the real answer was anything different he didn't want to think about it. Especially not now, with Mickey being dead.

Because of the painting turning up and becoming a distraction, Charlie hadn't taken his usual stroll down to the bar until mid-morning. He had not slept well but somehow had still managed to miss the sound of the Golden Pheasant being blown to high heaven. He hadn't even heard the sirens from the fire engines which would in previous years have hurried past within thirty metres of his bedroom window; though that could be explained by the fact that the old fire station up on the hill had been recently closed down, making it necessary for the appliances to make their way to call outs from their new downtown premises on the other side of the ring road.

He didn't need updating on the latest news of the tragedy as local radio had been pumping out little else since it came on the air. Three people were missing, presumed dead, and the Golden Pheasant had been levelled to the ground. Current speculation attributed the blast to an exploding gas main. How long would they run with that idea before somebody came up with something different? The boys he had employed were top class professionals; it would be a case of sitting back and waiting to see.

Interviewees had come on the air in a steady stream. Mostly giving graphic accounts of having their windows blown in by the force of the explosion. The timing of the detonation had meant most people had been in bed, so minor injuries attributable to the blast had been comparatively few. Charlie knew he should feel guilty about the mayhem he had instigated but for some reason that emotion refused take hold. The people who had been blown away in the pub were soldiers in an enemy's army and they wouldn't have thrown roses into his grave if the roles had been reversed. The neighbours who had suffered damage to their property would get sorted out by either their insurance companies or the Council. If they had any sense they could probably fiddle the estimates and come out with some sort of profit on the deal. He had few regrets. He had done what he had to do and that put an end to it. It had been his responsibility to settle that score.

The one thing that continued to niggle Charlie was that Terry Brean was still alive; and that only because he was currently in police custody. Bloody police force; what did they know about justice! If what Strickland said was true it seemed unlikely that Terry would see the light of day anytime soon but that didn't alter the fact the tosser was still drawing breath. It was a shame that the place where he was currently being held was pretty much water tight but that was only going to serve to postpone Terry's fate. It wouldn't be too long before he was sentenced and then it would be a different matter altogether. Charlie would monitor the trial developments with interest. Having just got out of prison he had plenty of contacts still on the inside who would know what to do when an opportunity arose. He still had money put by and was determined to get a tidy ending no matter what the cost. That was just the way it needed to be.

There was no pretending the bomb hadn't been a drastic solution but given the circumstances it felt like the right call. When you thought about it, there had been limited alternatives. In situations of this sort you kept it simple. Hit hard and fast. Hurt your enemy as badly as possible before they had the opportunity to do the same thing to you. Got your revenge in first in a manner of speaking. Somebody had to come out worst in this sort of circumstance and the only rule in the game was to make certain it wouldn't be you.

A large part of the carnage had been to serve as payback for Mickey; but he had to admit that a small chunk of it had been strictly for himself. He had no intention of living his life jumping for cover every time a car backfired. Sooner or later they would work out who was responsible. And with that knowledge understand, why it was in their best interests to leave him alone.

So now he found himself marooned in the place he had spent a large part of his life despising; and strangely that situation no longer seemed all that bad. He was now street legal, some way from destitute and all off a sudden the wooden sign depicting the chained bear swinging in the wind on the forecourt looked more welcoming than it had at any other stage in his life. Granted, he would have to accept some responsibility for running the pub now that Mickey was gone but that wasn't the end of the world. He was beginning to feel remarkably at home now that the eyes were no longer glaring down at him from the wall above his head.

Charlie brushed those thoughts aside and turned his attention to a more pressing problem. Something called pollo cacciatore had found its way onto the lunch menu; bloody Italian if he wasn't very much mistaken. First he would head off upstairs and complete the job of unpacking his suitcases; and then it would be time for a little chat with that chef.

CHAPTER FIFTY SEVEN

TUESDAY 28th FEBRUARY 2017

In many ways it felt like shrugging off an old life in preparation for starting a completely new one. A gateway opening into the great unknown. The feeling of euphoria you get when your plane lands half way across the world and you step out to find your nostrils assaulted by a diverse range of strange aromas; mitigated slightly perhaps, by the trickle of perspiration that tells you that this place is very different from the one you just left behind and in consequence the winter leggings were probably something of a mistake. Stephanie Armitage, glowing slightly from her exertions, bustling along the crowded platform, retrieved a fashion magazine from her shoulder bag and settled back into a reserved seat in the corner of a first class carriage.

The train journey to London would take a little more than two hours and once there she had a reservation for a week at the Ritz while she decided what it was she wanted to do next. In the short time available it hadn't been possible to accomplish very much in respect of selling the gallery. As her priority had been to get out of the city with the minimum delay she had taken the decision to bundle all her remaining stock into tea chests and lodge them with one of those places that offered storage facilities for people in just such a situation. Then, after settling on a suitable valuation, the gallery itself had been left in the hands of a reputable Estate Agent. The property was large and in relatively good condition so Stephanie had every hope that a buyer would be located without any undue delay.

Stephanie knew she should feel sad to be abandoning the City where she had spent most of her formative years, especially as it was quite possible that it would be the very last time she would set eyes on so much that was reassuringly familiar; but in truth she hadn't been able to get out of the place fast enough. Any affection she had once felt for her birthplace was now a thing of the past. Mickey Smith had been very successful in ruining all that.

It seemed surprising that the drama had taken place only four days previously. Already, it felt like a faint recollection from the far distant past. She was now a woman moving on with her life and her focus must be only on the future; she had no room to carry old regrets. That slate now needed to be wiped completely clean. As a concession she would relive the trauma one last time before she banished it from her mind.

On the morning in question Mickey had arrived in accordance with his text message and for once seemed in high spirits. Babbling on about having seen an apparition in the park that was quite clearly the ghost of his girlfriend, Rachael Broadbent. What did Stephanie think of that? Could it possibly have been an angel? Did she consider it was some sort of mystical sign?

Without stopping for breath, Mickey had then segued seamlessly into a garbled story about being waylaid by Oliver Dearlove. Was the obnoxious Oliver from the spirit world, as well? She wasn't entirely clear on that point and requests for clarification had gone largely unheeded. Stephanie was equally unclear whether Mickey saw the whole episode as hilariously funny or just plain spooky. She noticed he had started to get increasingly hysterical as he related the tale but there hadn't been very much she could do to distract him. She couldn't smell alcohol on his breath so he didn't seem to have been drinking. Why he was laughing at all didn't seem to make a lot of sense but that was Mickey for you. It looked suspiciously like his recent experiences might have started to tip him over the edge.

She had resolved to remain calm and concentrated her mind on her prime objective; the acquisition of the wonderful painting. She had popped the cork on a bottle of champagne and filled two glasses to the brim. Mickey was laughing again; in a slightly frenzied manner, admittedly. Possibly that could be interpreted as a positive sign? It was very hard to know whether that was the case.

Intermixed with the laughter he had continued to mutter in a strangely incoherent fashion. She wished he would stop. She wished he would stop repeating that same story about seeing Rachael in the park. It was starting to get a little bit tedious. Why he was hallucinating visions of Rachael at all made no sense. It had been weeks since she packed her bags and surely he must by now have come to the realisation he was better off without her. Didn't he understand that he would now be free to do exactly as he pleased?

The whole situation had started to make her feel quite angry. She decided the time had now arrived to get everything out in the open. Enlighten Mickey as to why it was an advantage that Rachael wasn't around anymore. Describe the steps she had taken to facilitate the bloody woman's disappearance. Explain how she had got rid of the accursed girl so that he could once again return to being his normal cheery self. Warn him to forget completely about Rachael in the flesh or in spirit form because thinking about her wasn't good for him.

The sooner he embraced the fact, the better it would be. Once he grasped that fact he would be a step nearer to a full recovery. Quite possibly he would display gratitude; maybe take her in his arms and spin her around the room in the manner of the old Mickey Smith. Thank her for the supreme effort she had put in on his behalf. Conceivably, even promise she could have that beautiful painting she so deeply desired.

Well, as it turned out, not a bit of it. The words had barely left her mouth when Mickey transformed from his state of high spirits into a snarling spitting animal that she had found quite difficult to recognise. His face wore the deepest of scowls and he proceeded to lash out in all directions. His language had to be heard to be believed. The transformation was frightening. It was almost like he was looking at the world through a different pair of eyes.

He now had the absolute effrontery to accuse her of ruining his life. Well, thanks a lot Mickey! Not a shred of appreciation for the time and effort she had expended to get him free from that miserable cow. Did he think she had done it for her own benefit? From his current attitude you might have assumed that he had actually enjoyed being an uninteresting person.

Mickey was now in such a foul mood she was frightened to even mention the painting of Charlotte Langthorpe. The gorgeous portrait she had been so sure it would be possible to acquire. Damn the man! It looked like the new underwear would go completely to waste.

Mickey had lit a cigarette and stomped sullenly away to position himself on the small balcony overlooking the river. He was muttering to himself but most of what he said was either incoherent or difficult to understand. She could almost believe she had noticed a tear running down the side of his cheek. A real one, indicating genuine sadness. She sincerely hoped she was mistaken. That would be a further slight to add to the ever increasing list.

Then, without even bothering to turn and face her, he had shouted back over his shoulder that he was convinced she was completely mad. That she was deluded, irrational, totally self-absorbed and quite probably completely insane. That he was getting as far away from this place as he could possibly go with no intention of ever returning. That, thanks to her, his life was in pieces and would never be the same again.

Well, there are limits to the degree of personal abuse a girl should be expected to suffer. She had to confess she had been truly stunned by Mickey's callous attitude. The ingratitude of the man she found totally breath-taking.......and he appeared to have given no thought to the way this decision was likely to impact on her life. After all she had done for him! In his eyes, it seemed as if she now failed to exist.

She had picked up the jang bong pole that Ziggy had

acquired on his last trip to Seoul. She felt good to at last have a practical use for the bloody thing which had always managed to fall to the floor with a resounding clatter every time she was showing an important client round the gallery. Without giving herself time to over think the situation she had let the frustrations of recent weeks hone in on a satisfying outlet. She lifted the stick as high as was possible without taking the risk of tearing her new silk blouse, and hit Mickey with perfect precision on the back of the head. Then, having taken a full step backwards to steady herself, she had watched with detached fascination as her closest friend and recent lover had toppled over the art deco railings and impaled himself, twenty feet below, on the spiked iron fencing that marked the perimeter of her section of the property.

Unsurprisingly, she had been totally shaken by this course of events and had been obliged to take an extremely large gulp from her glass. She had not anticipated Mickey's fall; how could she? The way things had developed so quickly had taken her completely by surprise. She was quite clearly the victim in this melodrama not an accessory to her friend's premature death. But due to the strange set of circumstances that were currently unfolding the scene below now told an altogether different tale.

While her actions had obviously been fully justified Stephanie was already beginning to feel a sense of misgiving. She wasn't totally heartless; nor would she have taken such punitive action if Mickey had not bought it on himself. The whole situation was totally preposterous; but explaining it, she felt, could prove something of a trial.

It had come as something of a relief, when a few moments later she witnessed the forces of nature intervene on her behalf. As she viewed from above, Mickey's body could be clearly observed to totter; then sway precariously from side to side in the stiff breeze as it prepared to evacuate its temporary perch. When the parting of the ways finally came about, the fall itself was both sudden and dramatic, with a horrific crunch preceding the body rolling into the middle of a large clump of nettles; a point at which it briefly dallied for a second or two, before slithering majestically down the sodden river bank in the manner of a ship that had been regally christened with an expensive bottle of fizzy wine.

The last sight of Mickey Smith Stephanie had been able to observe, saw his corpse slide smoothly into the churning waters, creating barely a ripple; before, in the click of a finger, he had been taken up by the current and mercifully transported completely from view.

At this point Stephanie had needed to take a deep breath before she reached once more for her drink. She gave thought to the fact the river disappeared underground a couple of hundred yards from the studio and deduced there was a very good chance Mickey would remain undetected for some time to come. Even if the body was located why would anyone connect her with his death? It would plainly be put down to an accident, which was only right and proper in the circumstances because it had been only by pure chance he had met up with Rachael bloody Broadbent who had stolen him away and turned her lovely Mickey into a crashing bore. And in those circumstances, an accident was entirely appropriate as an explanation for why the poor man was now languishing on the bottom of a river bed, instead of cradling her in his arms.

Recalling the events of that morning had been extremely harrowing and Stephanie was glad the ordeal was finally over. Now she could put the whole thing in the past and not think about Mickey Smith anymore, which was good because memories of Mickey would inevitably be depressing. More so because she had decided that going forward it was important that she now became the sort of person who only embraced the positive aspects of life.

And as she was now intent on having fun and determined to view things from a positive standpoint she couldn't fail to notice the attention she was being paid by the nice young men who had helped carry her baggage onto the train and muscle it into the overhead racks. Now, they looked exactly like the sort of light hearted chaps who would prove amusing company and lift a girl's spirits; and if they displayed similar good manners in helping her alight from the train at the London terminus she saw no good reason not to enquire if they would care to join her for a bite to eat and possibly even a little more. Goodness, they really did look so alike that they could quite possibly be twins. She had never slept with twins but it was an intriguing prospect and at worst it would take another item off the bucket list. She wiggled in her seat, allowing her skirt to ride up to her thigh and give them a better view of her very long legs. She flashed an inviting smile and received a similar response from across the carriage. There we go; things were looking up already. She had a premonition London might very well turn out to be a great deal of fun. Having some proper attention paid to her by some interesting men was quite long overdue.

CHAPTER FIFTY EIGHT

WEDNESDAY 1st MARCH 2017

Rachael Broadbent slipped out of the shower, pulled on her dressing gown and walked slowly across the floor of her new flat, while still in the process of drying her hair. She flipped open the small lacquered box with the oriental figures on its lid where she kept her collection of jewellery and considered which pieces she might wear that night. No rings obviously; that would be crass because all her best ones were from broken engagements and it was important not give Martin the wrong impression. Besides which, a naked finger might invite a further acquisition if she was very lucky and she was always keen to extend her collection of beautiful jewellery which she absolutely adored.

She had only really got together with Mr Shaffer about three months ago when she sensed it would soon be time to move on from her relationship with Mickey Smith. Martin was a step in the right direction as he owned the casino where she worked; but quite obviously the matter had needed handling delicately and discretion because he and Mickey were acquaintances that were bordering on friends. She knew that in the final analysis friendship didn't mean a lot to men where the opposite sex was involved. However, she had her image to consider. She was Rachael Broadbent, an innocent in a cruel and uncaring world. She was vulnerable not predatory; and that fact had needed to be firmly established right from the start.

In the end it had worked out quite nicely. Rachael was, after all, an expert in this sort of thing. She had known for some time that Martin fancied her something rotten. It had just been a case of waiting for the right circumstances to offer themselves, and in the end the ideal situation had presented itself as she had known that it would.

She looked around the new flat and found very little that wasn't to her liking. Martin was married so now she had essentially become a mistress; and one that was likely to be pampered and cosseted, already housed in this lovely location in the very best part of town. A bit too near to her old life if she was being picky but you couldn't have everything; or maybe you could and it was just necessary not to become impatient and try to get it too soon. Rachael could wait; she was a planner; not at all the impetuous type.

The property was registered in her name as well, though quite obviously Martin would pick up the bills. That would probably come in very useful at some future date when it again became the opportune time to move on to greener pastures. The best part about being with a married man was that most of the bargaining chips would be on her side of the table when this particular segment of her life had eventually run its course.

In some ways waving goodbye to Mickey had been difficult. He had been a very decent fiancé and she wouldn't have a word said against him. She had no illusions about being a commitment freak; maybe a gold digger was more accurate but she hated that expression and couldn't see that it strictly applied. She always gave excellent value for anything she received and was fully aware what was required from her role. She catered expertly to a gap in the market; filled it to the very best of her ability and took her rewards as having been very well earned.

Alright, she wouldn't pretend that there had been no broken hearts along the way but that was part of the price her men had always seemed prepared to pay. Besides, the heart that got broken had never belonged to her, which in the final analysis was probably the most important thing; and she enjoyed what she was doing far too much to give any serious consideration to giving it up. She was barely twenty five and saw no good reason to change the pattern

314

of her life for at least another ten years providing that her looks held out. She turned to view herself in the mirror. At present she still looked quite lovely. All her major assets remained firmly intact.

She loved the first months of a new relationship. The breathlessness of it all. The wonderful presents; the meals in darkened rooms; the quietly holding hands; the abandonment to steamy sex. She tried to work relationships on turn-rounds off roughly a year which gave the opportunity for a sparkling entry and a calm and dignified exit. She had to admit that already she had become something of an expert at achieving both.

The latest transition had worked seamlessly as well; right up until the unexpected sighting of Mickey Smith in the park on that miserable February morning. Even that, she thought, she had handled rather well. Disappearing like some red haired wraith into the mist; before hastily legging it for fifty yards and leaping behind a tree as soon as she was confident she was completely out of sight. Mickey's face had been a picture. Rachael was certain that by now he would have convinced himself he had imagined the whole episode.

It had obviously been necessary to keep a low profile for a time following the break up as she was meant to be travelling the byways of the continent in search of worldly enlightenment. She had, in consequence, arranged with Martin that she took a month's holiday from the casino and had in that time restricted herself to going out mainly at night and in the very early morning; and even then, for the most part, keeping her hair covered in a hood, so her most obvious feature would not attract unwanted attention, because you never knew who you might bump into unexpectedly. Mickey had caught her off guard in the recent encounter with her bright red hair free from its covering. That had been a stupid mistake but Rachael was a quick learner. She would make sure it didn't happen again.

After a month it would be alright to return to normal

life. Martin had even arranged a promotion to floor supervisor at work. She could handle the job quite easily and nobody would put in an objection. It had any amount of diverse advantages when people became aware you were the owner's bit on the side.

One day she knew she would run into Mickey; maybe old Henry from the flat downstairs as well. It was inevitable that it would happen but by then she would have a plausible story polished and ready for immediate use. She might even become friends with Mickey; platonic of course because she would still have her future destiny to take into account. That would be nice but the chances were fairly remote. Life wasn't like that, which when you considered was a terrible shame.

The bit that still amused her most of all was the role of Stephanie Armitage in the whole escapade. Stephanie, she had found unspeakably annoying right from the day they were first introduced. The woman really was a monster. She seemed to view Mickey Smith as some sort personal court jester put on this earth for the sole purpose of keeping her entertained. Amazingly self-absorbed, was Stephanie; and Mickey did very little to help pull her back down to earth as he sat up on his hind legs waiting for a pat on the head. Ultimately attentive in case his mistress would be gracious enough to throw him a bone. It had made her shudder. Their relationship was positively unhealthy. It had been a permanent struggle to control her features when Stephanie was around; to stop herself throwing up on the floor.

Stephanie also imagined she was so extremely clever. She thought she had supreme taste and an eye for art which was paying for her keep. Actually she spent shed loads more than she ever earned from dabbling in the market, with the bills for her gallery being readily settled by her philandering husband so she wouldn't get under his feet while he was conducting his latest clandestine affair.

And the way the dozy cow thought that Rachael was dumb enough not to see through her stupid plan to get her out of the picture. Hijacking that little scheme had been such tremendous fun and she had finished up several thousand pounds to the good on the deal thanks to Stephanie's self-gratifying generosity; and this with the woman still being completely oblivious to the fact she was pocketing the cash and moving half a mile up the road. Wonderful stuff. Poor Stephanie really wasn't the sharpest tool in the box.

If there was one thing she regretted it was that Mickey's pal Stevie would need to remain completely oblivious of the fact that she had been taken for a complete fool. Still that was the way of the world. The likes of Stephanie Armitage, with her chiselled cheekbones and never ending legs always escaped from the trial without serving a sentence. Duplicitous cow. She hoped the day would arise when darling Stephanie eventually got her comeuppance. Rachael knew that was never likely to happen but it didn't cost anything to hope.

CHAPTER FIFTY NINE

SATURDAY 4th MARCH 2017

Raquel Walsh sat on a well-worn, low slung settee, which had a split in one of the arms through which fluffy, white stuffing was beginning to escape. She had for some time been intending to seal the hole with a small length of gaffer tape but kept forgetting to go to the shop and buy a reel on her journey home from the hospital. Currently, she was comfortably reclined in front of the television with her feet resting on a glass topped coffee table as she tried to reach a decision on whether there was still time to paint her toenails and allow them to dry before she was obliged to head off to bed. She concluded it was a job that could be held over until the next day and instead decided to think about James, because that seemed the best thing to do on a night when she was feeling on top of the world.

James had definite possibilities, unlike most of the men Raquel had come into contact with in the last few years; the majority of whom she judged to be suitable for reaching up to get things off a high shelf or rewiring a plug, but with no potential for developing into what the women's magazines laughingly referenced as a 'life partner'. When Raquel considered the matter, she had come to the conclusion she would slash her wrists rather than be stuck with any one of them in a confined space like a flat or a small house unless there was a radio on full blast, so she could avoid having to pay serious attention to anything they had to say.

That was not to undervalue their worth as a dancing partner or somebody to have a quick chat with down the pub when you were feeling a bit fed up or there was nothing decent on the telly. And to be fair, most of them positively excelled when it came to changing a fuse and carrying bulky objects that made your arms ache.

However, they had severe limitations when you entertained any hope of them ever developing into civilised human beings. She had never met a single one who seemed to have the vaguest idea why a toilet brush was kept in the lavatory or that it was of limited interest to hear how their modification to the carburettor had drastically improved the petrol consumption on their latest car. The mere thought of trying to engage any one of them in a meaningful conversation while she was lying on a sun-kissed foreign beach made her positively shudder.

A major plus with her having gained a nice steady boyfriend was the fact it would put Caroline's nose right out of joint; because, despite being her closest friend, Caroline was always inferring that Raquel was far too picky with her choice of men. The plain fact of the matter was, Caroline would wrap herself round anything with a pulse providing she got a bunch of flowers and a free meal out of the deal. She couldn't say it to her face, quite obviously, because it would be bound to cause offence; but some of the men she had seen coming out of Caroline's flat in the early hours of the morning made her wonder if the poor girl was experiencing problems with her eyesight.

And if she was being honest, Raquel resented the implication she had been playing hard to get, because it just wasn't the case. It was just she had certain standards that, frankly, Caroline didn't care to recognise. Besides which, she had been experimenting with a cabbage soup diet for absolutely ages so she could regain her bikini figure before the weather got better; and in those circumstances high calorie meals with strange, unsavoury men had hardly been at the top of her agenda.

Up to press, Raquel had been out on a date with James on only two occasions but that was not to be sniffed at when you considered she had known him for barely a week. She had never been courted by a policeman before and he hadn't come across in quite the way she had expected from a man in that profession. He was good mannered, shy and reserved; qualities you would never be likely to attribute to any of the mob from the Slug and Fiddle who she sometimes met up with at the weekend if she was looking for some particularly undemanding company.

In fact, she already felt so confident about James that when she met up with him tomorrow night she was wondering whether to ask if he wanted to stay over or if etiquette demanded that they dated a few more times before that was permitted to happen. She concluded the best solution would be to invite him up for coffee after the pictures and just let nature take its course.

It had been exactly a week since she had met James for the first time, when he had come in to take a look at Clint Eastwood who had ended up on her ward in intensive care. She had to admit she hadn't noticed him at the time other than to just clock a passing blue uniform of which there was never any great shortage in hospital wards these days. However, he must have seen her and made his mind up on the spot because when he came back the next day he had cornered her straight away by the bottom of Clint Eastwood's bed and asked if she fancied going out for a drink and something to eat. Raquel had been pleased to see that he seemed very keen as well; where James was concerned the uniform and the black stockings obviously pressed all the right buttons. Well, she had delayed for a bit before replying while she pretended to carefully consider the proposition because she didn't want to look like a pushover; but in truth she hadn't been near a good looking man for absolutely ages and would have seriously considered accompanying a chimpanzee to a tea party as long as it didn't eat with its mouth open or have a comb over.

Clint Eastwood was a nickname the nurses were currently using for the poor bloke James was meant to take a statement from as soon as he had properly regained consciousness. They had settled on it because he had been carrying no identification when they brought him in and you had to call the poor beggar something or other. They had first tried 'The Man with No Name' but it had worn a bit thin after the first couple of days despite seeming totally appropriate the first time they gave it a try.

Raquel had got the full story out of James on their first date but he had told her not to broadcast it because this sort of thing was meant to be confidential. That was another good thing about dating a policeman. She would be bound to get lots of inside stories on the crime stuff you read about in the papers and she would be able to look smug, when it came up for discussion in the canteen, when they were taking their break.

It transpired that 'Clint' had been fished out of a river by an old lady walking her two Labradors. She said she had only noticed him because the dogs kept barking at what she hoped might turn out to be an otter or at worst a water vole or one of those minks that had escaped from a farm where they bred them to make into fur coats.

The poor man had been floating in the middle of a fast flowing river and had somehow got tangled up with a shopping trolley that some halfwit had pitched into the water from the footbridge, just above where the waterway disappeared underground. Amazing to think that a bloke's life could end up being saved by some idiot who was probably only showing off to his silly-boy mates, but for all the world that seemed to be the case. Anyway, this woman...... James had mentioned her name but Raquel had forgotten what it was because that must have been nearly a week ago.......said she knew exactly what to do because she had never missed a single episode of either 'Casualty' or 'Holby City'; and the ambulance driver who picked up the three nines call said he thought she was not only telling the truth but was probably old enough to add 'Emergency Ward Ten' on to the list as well. Whichever way you looked at it she had been very brave to haul him out of the water and James said they would definitely be recommending her for a community award, which in the circumstances sounded like the proper thing to do.

Barry the porter, who many believe had been working

321

at the hospital since the day it was opened by Prince Albert, said he would have given the patient one chance in ten of needing to get new soles for his boots; and Barry, miserable old sod that he is, has earned a reputation for being very good at calling the odds on that sort of thing.

James said the police suspected that 'Clint' had been mugged because he didn't have a penny piece in his pockets or any form of I.D. They must have been very big muggers because his body showed really good muscular development and he had what you might describe as a very athletic look about him.

'Clint' had been a right mess when they brought him in, mind you; barely breathing, no pulse to speak of, hypothermia from being in the water, four broken ribs and a massive gash on the back of his head where he had been battered with something pretty solid. The only reason he was still alive was because the sharp implements that had been used to jab him in the chest had failed to properly pierce the anorak he was wearing. The majority of the anoraks they sell to youngish men these days are stab-proof since the increase in knife crime. The one that 'Clint' was wearing was not very long out of the packet and appeared to have been responsible for saving his life.

The patient still hadn't properly come round, despite showing good signs of improvement in the last few days, so it hadn't been possible to assess him for brain damage just yet; but there was a general consensus among the doctors in charge of his case that so far the signs were good.

Anyway, the thing that happened today that got me in a tizzy is a bit weird if I'm being honest; it was like fulfilling a dream; right up there with world peace, winning the lottery or having a night on the town with Thomas Schafernaker or Daniel Craig.

I always wanted to be a nurse right from being a small girl. I had fantasies about it; the Florence Nightingale story; Edith Cavell saving the lives of all those brave soldiers. I know it all changes when you get hands on with full time working and find it really involves emptying bed pans and helping old men to aim it straight when they are having a wee; but there's always a bit of it stays with you whether you like it or not.

Today I was walking past 'Clint's' bed and suddenly his eyes popped wide open and he just lay there staring up at me. And then, before I knew it, he reached out for my hand, grabbed my arm and pulled me so I nearly landed on top of him; then looking deep into my eyes he gave me the most wonderful smile that made me go weak at the knees. Well, this in itself was surprising because the poor bloke had hardly been awake since we had him in through the doors and up to press he had yet to speak a single word. But he looked me right in the eye and gripped my arm so tight I thought he was going to stop the circulation and said 'Rachael.......you're my red haired angel from the park'.

It's the god's honest truth. The bloke in the next bed heard it and so did one of the orderlies who just happened to be walking past at the time.

That's the reason I'm feeling so good just now, though obviously I could never tell that to James in case he got jealous. It's because when I was a little girl I always saw myself as a sort of angel nurse saving people's lives and it was pretty wonderful to see that 'Clint' saw me in exactly the same way.

Alright, I know he got the name wrong but that's easy to do. Even when I say Raquel down the telephone the person on the other end usually says Rachael back at me as if I don't know what my own name is. And how 'Clint' got hold of the name in the first place I have no idea because he's hardly had his eyes open in the last seven days.

That bit bothered me so much I had a word with a consultant before I came home at the end of my shift and he said you couldn't discount anything with the subconscious because it had powers we were only just beginning to understand. The bit about being in the park I figured out straight away. The walls in the ward are all painted in green emulsion. A bit light in colour for grass some would say but quite close enough after a mugger has done his best to bash your head in with something heavy.

But, if I'm honest, the bit that pleased me the most was that 'Clint' picked up on my hair colour. It's auburn really but I've been using this colour enhancer that my sister recommended to put in some highlights and it looks like it must be doing the trick.

In fact I was so touched by the remark that I've been keeping a special eye on my new favourite patient from the time that happened; and if he makes a full recovery James will have some stiff completion coming his way because 'Clint' looks like the sort of bloke I could go for in a really big way.

Sometimes life seems a bit rubbish when your father saddles you with a stupid name, just because he prides himself on having a cutting edge sense of humour; and don't get me even started on unreliable boyfriends, staff shortages at work and the lousy pay scale; but sometimes I still think being a nurse is the most wonderful job in the world.........and today just happens to be one of those days.

Lightning Source UK Ltd.
Milton Keynes UK
UKOW01f0812110218
317683UK00002B/95/P